Playing Her Song

by

Kimberly Keyes

Playing Her Song

Cover Art by *Diana Carlile*

The Wild Rose Press, Inc.
PO Box 708
Adams Basin, NY 14410-0708
Visit us at www.thewildrosepress.com

Publishing History
First Edition, 2022
Trade Paperback ISBN 978-1-5092-4257-3
Digital ISBN 978-1-5092-4258-0

Published in the United States of America

For some reason, the idea of Jackson writing the song that had haunted her from the moment she heard it flummoxed her.

"Truth is stranger than fiction," Callie said.

She took a deep breath and told herself to get a grip. What did it matter who wrote "Falling"? "Well, color me surprised. But as to your other claim, Cal, my crush on Jackson was a childhood thing. Ancient history. It vaporized the moment I saw what a jerk he was."

She expected her friends to continue ribbing her. Instead they both wore frozen smiles and stared at something over Julia's shoulder.

God. Not again. Not twice in two days. "Guys?" she asked, her voice cracking.

"Hi, Jacks," Callie said in lieu of answering.

Sue waggled her fingers hello.

Julia's skin went clammy, and she had the sudden urge to bang her head against the counter. But she swiveled in her seat to face Jackson Tate, in the, of course, hotter-than-hell flesh. How much had he heard?

Praise for Kimberly Keyes

LOVER'S LEAP:
"The author's writing flows so well, there were times I forgot I was reading fiction. I felt like another character in the story… Her writing strength lies in the uncanny ability to weave a captivating story. I can't wait to read more from her… Highly recommend!"

~NN Light's Book Heaven

~*~

"Kimberly Keyes' contemporary romance release does not disappoint! Lovable characters, amazing location, and twists and surprises to keep you turning the pages. I give it five stars!"

~Kat Drennan, author

THE TROUBLE WITH TIGERS:
"Kudos to the author on a well-written, totally engaging book. I loved the mistaken identity, the slow-burn of the building relationship between Kitty and Zeke, and the despicable secondary characters that twist the plot."

~Katie O'Sullivan, author

Chapter One

Julia Hudson followed Mrs. Tate—Lisa—as she clipped down the sun-dappled trellis-covered walk. Her mother's oldest friend, currently wearing her realtor's cap for Julia's benefit, unlocked the front door to the rental cottage and disappeared inside.

Julia paused on the welcome mat, struck by the stained glass window centered in the door depicting a dragonfly in a sky streaked with bands of sunshine. Dragonflies symbolized new beginnings, didn't they? Anticipation bloomed inside her, as if the calamities of the last thirty-six hours might herald something good about to happen rather than merely punctuate the end of life as she knew it.

Or maybe she was delirious from too much caffeine and pulling an all-nighter on the road from New York to Honeyville.

She rubbed a hand over her forehead. She should have grabbed a shower and a bed instead of allowing Lisa to drag her from her mom's kitchen the moment she let slip this homecoming was less a surprise visit than a soft place to land.

Channeling fake-it-'til-you-make-it, she fixed a smile in place and stepped inside. Cool air blotted out the humidity and heat that was North Carolina in the summertime, instantly refreshing her senses.

"What do you think? First impression."

Julia took in the high-ceilinged, cozy cottage. Luxurious surfaces and nice furnishings spoke of someone putting a lot of love into this place. Thanks to a skylight and an oversized, single-paned french door leading out back, diffuse light filled the space. "It's like a magazine cover. How is it this place isn't already taken?"

Lisa leaned a slender hip onto a brushed leather couch. Behind her, an archway opened to, Julia assumed, a bedroom and bathroom. "The residents of the main house won't rent to just anyone. I have an in, though." She sent Julia a wink.

That made sense. What didn't was why they'd rent at all. Whoever lived in the main house—make that mansion—didn't appear to need the extra cash. They also seemed obsessed with privacy, going by the thickly clustered cypress trees surrounding the estate and numerous *no trespassing* signs she'd spotted on the drive up.

"Check this out." Lisa opened the back door to a magnificent cedar deck. "Shared with the main house residents, of course."

Julia slid her hands into the front pockets of her jeans and wandered outside. The majestic Blue Ridge Mountains rose up in the not-too-far distance, all green and dense with summertime foliage.

Strange to find herself contemplating moving back to the small town of her roots. As if she hadn't spent the better part of nine years in New York carving out a life only to toss it away quicker than she could say, "You're sleeping with my assistant?"

She needed to sort through the mess she'd made of her life. Renting a temporary, furnished place would give her the time and space to do just that.

She glanced over her shoulder at Lisa. "How much does this place go for?"

Lisa waved a hand. "Sweetie, would I steer you wrong? You'll stay here rent-free."

"Free? What's the catch? Who do I have to sleep with?"

The silver-haired woman erupted with uncharacteristic bawdy laughter. "It probably won't come to that, dear."

"Aunt Lisa?" a low, masculine voice sounded from the small foyer.

Julia's stomach nose-dived. Lisa's nephew, Jackson Tate, here? Of *course*. Since she looked so lovely, having driven all night.

She glanced down at herself, grimacing. Indigo jeans and a fitted, zippered yoga jacket worn over a plain tank, hair in a ponytail, and, as she recalled, not a stitch of makeup. At least she had her back to him. Maybe he'd leave without noticing her.

Jackson's voice grew louder as he wandered farther into the room. "You didn't tell me you were coming b—oh." And he spotted her.

"Hello, sweetheart. You remember Julia Hudson, don't you? Annie and Jim's daughter? Your high school tutor?"

Perspiration sprouted over her body like she'd stepped into a sauna. Maybe he'd forgotten her?

"Of course I remember Julia. How could I forget?"

Forcing a smile, she turned to face him—and got the wind knocked out of her.

Jackson, the boy, was long gone. But the man who'd taken his place still had those eyes. Thick, black lashes framed irises of swirling green and brown flecked with gold, like the mountainside near sunset. His face was harder, more chiseled than she remembered. It matched his body, which still bore the steely musculature of an athlete.

Hair the color of toasted wheat hit at his collar, just like in the paparazzi photos she'd glimpsed over the years. But now, was the light playing tricks, or was that a sprinkle of salt? Graying at thirty-one years old? Didn't matter. It looked good on him. As did his five-o'clock shadow at not quite two p.m.

His broad mouth curved into a welcoming smile. "Julia. My God, how many years has it been?"

Four years of college plus nine in the big city made thirteen. But who was counting?

"Hi, Jackson, it's good to see you."

He wore a short-sleeved, athletic T-shirt, baggy exercise shorts, and sneakers, very much a man on his way to doing something physical.

Scratching her head, she slanted Lisa a brief glance. "What are the odds, all of us winding up at the same remote place at the same time?"

He grinned good-naturedly and slid a considering look toward his aunt. "I live here."

"Oh." She kept her smile in place but turned narrowed eyes on Lisa. "You might have mentioned?"

"Didn't I?"

Movement out of the corner of her eye pulled her attention back to Jackson. He'd rounded the sitting area and now stood close enough she caught a hint of his aftershave. Something spicy and crisp.

"It's a beautiful property, Jackson. Ready, Lisa?"

"Please don't leave on my account," he said. "Aunt

Lees? You changed your mind about my offer?"

"Actually, no. Julia needs somewhere to stay for a few months. This place is perfect, and you can't beat the rent."

Julia could. Just. Die. And she would. Right after she murdered Lisa. Funny, thinking of her by her first name came easier now that she was a dead woman.

"Ho, now, I wouldn't dream of invading your privacy. I-I'm sure you have people, uh, friends coming who'll need to…a place to stay and…" Lord. She was babbling. She blew out a breath. "Anyhow, nice seeing you." She beelined for the door.

"Of course you can stay here, Julia. As long as you like. It's not as if it's being used. Besides, I owe you."

She froze, one toe on the welcome mat. Surely he wasn't going *there*. She did a slow pivot to face him— then another voice emerged directly behind her.

"Dad, you in here?"

Julia shifted to see a young boy approaching the door, and there was no doubt who his father was.

"Inside," Jackson called.

"Excuse me, ma'am." The boy shimmied past Julia.

Jackson's son was eleven if memory served. Tall for his age, surpassing her own height of five foot four. Okay, five foot three, but with the heels she usually wore, five four plus.

"Uncle Grady's here," the boy announced.

Grady Toller? Oh goody.

Jackson's brows furrowed, and his gaze shot to Julia.

She pressed fingertips to her temple. Today started out so promising. She'd arrived in Honeyville at

5

noon, no speeding tickets, no accidents, her pared-down hoard of favorite possessions safe in her rental. Her mother and Lisa had greeted her with welcoming hugs, two sets of ears, and fresh-brewed coffee. She'd even begun to think she'd found a place to stay that wasn't her old bedroom.

She'd known there had to be a catch.

"Chase, go out and tell Grady—"

"Tell him what?" came a man's voice from the doorway.

She stifled a groan.

"I'll be out in a sec," Jackson said. "Just finishing up here."

Julia wrapped her arms around herself and tried to turn invisible.

"Sure, sure. Hi, Aunt Lisa, bye, Aunt Lisa, hi, Lisa and Jackson's friend." Turning to leave, Grady caught Julia's eye briefly. In a blink, he jerked to face her. "Julia Hudson?"

"In the flesh." This was so not her day.

Grady, a darker blond now, still with the boyish dimples, and in decent shape by the look of him, wrapped her in a bear hug and lifted her off her feet. "I thought I recognized that thick mane of hair. How long are you in town? Where are you staying?"

"You can put her down now." Jackson's voice came from just over her shoulder. Jeez, the man could move, and he hadn't made a sound.

With a lighthearted chuckle, Grady lowered her to her feet.

"She's staying here," Jackson answered for her.

Wait, what? Her gaze shot to his. Their eyes met and held for a timeless moment.

She'd decided in an instant she couldn't stay here. But something in his stare, some kind of challenge, froze the denial on her tongue.

Evidently taking her silence as assent, Jackson steamrolled ahead. "Julia, Aunt Lisa will get you a key. Unfortunately I don't have time to give you the tour right now. How about you come over for a late dinner? I'll knock on your door after I get Chase settled." As he spoke, he and Chase sidled around her, effectively forcing Grady out the door.

Julia opened her mouth to tell him dinner wasn't necessary, but Grady leaned his head past Jackson to blurt, "I'll get your number from Jackson. Let's do lunch." He broke off, aiming a playful scowl at Jackson. "Okay, okay. Where's the fire?"

Turning his back on Grady, Jackson threw an arm over his son's shoulders, shifting him so they both faced her. "Chase, say hello to Mrs....?"

And so the questioning begins. "Miss," she filled in. "Hudson. You can call me Julia."

"You can call her *Miss* Julia," Jackson said with a crooked grin. "Julia, my son, Chase."

"Nice to meet you," she said with a wave.

"You, too, Miss Julia." Chase sent her an identical grin to his father's.

Now *that* was cute.

She put her hands on her hips and stared after them as they disappeared onto the adjoining path. She'd landed smack in the middle of Jackson Tate's world. Jackson, whom she'd once vowed never to cross paths with again.

****

Jackson scrubbed a hand over his jaw and slid a

7

sideways glance at Grady. While the radio sportscaster droned on about the upcoming football season, Grady thumped the steering wheel in time to a beat only he could hear.

Julia Hudson. The girl who'd simply disappeared thirteen years ago, never to be seen again. At least not by him.

Yep, that last bit stuck in his craw.

She'd practically run out of there when Jackson walked in today. Meanwhile, Grady, arguably the bigger ass the night of their senior prom, got the big, warm welcome, like a long-lost friend.

"Dad, who's Miss Julia?" Chase leaned forward to poke his sandy-brown head in between the front seats.

Grady answered for him. "She's a girl we knew in high school, buddy. A real smarty-pants. She tutored your dad. Math, wasn't it?" He flicked his gaze toward Jackson, brows arched.

"Dad's *math* tutor? Dad, you never told me you got help." Chase dropped back in his seat.

"It never came up." He stared out his window at the passing cars.

"Yep, so you come by your math handicap honestly, kid." Grady winked. "Who knows, maybe she'll tutor you, too."

"I wouldn't mind that," Chase murmured.

Jackson shot his son a look. They'd talked about this last week. He thought Chase understood he wouldn't ride him about a few low marks in math.

Chase returned his stare. "What? Dad, Miss Julia's *hot*."

Yeah, she was. That bothered him, too, his reaction to the sight of her standing in his cottage. She'd focused those big blue eyes on him, and a zing went through his body like a live-wire jolt when the power was supposedly off.

She'd always been pretty, with that intense stare that seemed to see right into a person's soul, and that angel's smile. He didn't recall the rocking body, though. Except hadn't she knocked his socks off gliding down her parents' stairs in that sky-blue prom dress that matched her eyes, what was it, oh yeah, thirteen years ago?

But she hadn't been his date. She'd been Grady's, precisely because she'd been his dad's boss's daughter, the girl who tutored him in math and proceeded to magically bring all those meaningless X, Y, and Zs to life.

He'd thanked her by pawning her off on his friend for prom. Little wonder she hadn't spoken to him since.

'Til today. He closed his eyes briefly and replayed the moment their eyes met. A shock of unexpected desire went through him, aiming straight for his groin. He couldn't remember the last time a woman had that kind of visceral effect on him. It felt good. Satisfying. Like... He pulled out his phone and tapped out the words *thought I'd lost you, you were long gone, and now I find you, here all along. I get this feeling, you might be the key, to unlock what's lost, inside of me...*

Whoa. Could his longest writing dry spell to date be coming to an end?

"She is a hottie," Grady said, agreeing with Chase. "Maybe I should take a refresher math course."

He speared his old friend with a look. "Because it went so well the first time around."

Grady gave a derisive snort and fixed his gaze on

the road.

He wondered at his own snarky comment. He didn't need to get sideways over an incident that happened more than a decade ago involving a woman who obviously wanted nothing to do with him.

Seeing Julia had given him a rush. No biggie. Probably just the novelty of coming face-to-face with a blast from the past.

****

"Good night, buddy. Don't stay up too late reading," Jackson told Chase, swinging the bedroom door closed.

He smiled to himself as he strode to the staircase. His kid loved to read. He'd liked reading at Chase's age, too, something his own father hadn't exactly encouraged. Then again, his father hadn't approved of anything he did. The best he'd had to offer was indifference.

When Jackson learned Hannah was pregnant, he'd vowed to be nothing like his father. Had he succeeded so far? He hoped so. At least his kid knew he loved him.

Trotting down the stairs, he dug his cell phone out of his pocket and speed dialed his aunt. He'd make this quick. The dinner hour had long since passed. He didn't want Julia thinking he'd forgotten their plans.

"Hi, Jacks," she answered on the first ring. "I figured you'd be with Julia right about now."

"Me, too. Unfortunately, Grady had an errand to run before he dropped off Chase and me. Some medication he needed from the pharmacy like it was life or death." He shook his head and headed for the back door.

"Maybe Grady should drive separately when he has an agenda," she said in exasperation.

He had said as much to Grady. He'd actually wrapped up Chase's practice early to get home. Then Grady went mulish over his medication crisis.

"Aunt Lisa, I have a question, and I only have a sec."

"I'm all ears."

"Julia." He stared out the bank of windows that comprised the back wall of his house. Full-on dark outside now.

"Yes?" His aunt's voice had a smile in it, confirming his suspicion she was up to something—like maybe a fix-up, which was absolutely not going to happen.

"What's her story?"

"I told you. She's relocating here, temporarily. She needs a furnished place to stay while she decides where she's going next—or if she's staying put. She actually mentioned an extended-stay hotel if you can believe that."

"What's wrong with her parents' place?"

"Would that be an option for you?"

Hell. No. "Point taken. But how about explaining to me the part where you offered her the place I meant for you."

She hesitated. "I decided I'm too young to move into my nephew's home."

He pinched the bridge of his nose. He didn't like his aunt staying in that old house. First off, she was alone, and contrary to her statement, she wasn't a young chick anymore. Then there was the location, smack on top of a steep hill. A good snowstorm could strand her.

Besides, Chase needed a woman's influence in his life. Hannah had been gone a long time now, and since Jackson's mom died four years ago, Aunt Lisa was it.

"You might've mentioned something before I set the place up for you."

She sniffed. "I tried. Sometimes you have selective hearing. Chase'll back me up on that."

"What's that supposed to mean?"

She sighed. "The point is I'm not ready to give up my freedom. There. I said it. And anyway, all's well that ends well I always say."

Perpetually positive. One of the things he loved about her. He checked his wristwatch. Quarter to eight. "You never said why Julia came back."

"As to that I think it's better if she tells you. Take a little time to get reacquainted since she's going to be living practically under your roof."

"Just give me a road map. Did she get fired? Recently divorced? I don't want to step into anything when I talk to her."

"I suppose I can share a few details. She arrived this morning after having packed up all her worldly belongings and moving out of her New York apartment over the weekend, and she's out of a job. She didn't elaborate, but I gather her leaving had something to do with breaking things off with her almost fiancé, who happened to be her boss. I suspect cheating."

He moved the phone receiver away from his mouth to snort. Good ole Aunt Lisa. "Thanks. I'll let Julia take it from there."

"That would be best. I don't want to intrude on her privacy."

Chapter Two

Julia sat on the sofa, hands folded in her lap. Going on eight o'clock. Maybe Jackson had gotten tied up. Or maybe she'd been stood up. Only the boy she remembered had always shown up when he said he would. She'd wait a bit longer. What else did she have to do?

She smoothed her hands over the skirt of her white knit dress. It was nothing fancy. Just a short-sleeved, above-the-knee wrap number. But the cut of it made her feel feminine and, *yes, Chris, sexy*, and wearing it meant she could sport the high-heeled, nude wedges she'd bought the dress to match.

She had imagined herself launching the ensemble in the Hamptons this weekend at Chris's friend's house party. He'd played her for such a fool. He and her assistant.

She smiled to herself. She'd barely thought of her cheating ex almost fiancé all day. Having Jackson on the brain had seen to that. Some things never changed.

All these years she'd dreaded the day they'd cross paths again. She'd imagined the mortification of seeing him see *her*, the poor pathetic girl who had such a crush on him in high school she went to his prom *as someone else's date* just to be near him. For thirteen years she'd managed to avoid him. 'Til today.

She'd come out of the meeting relatively

unscathed. Maybe her recent worse humiliation lessened the sting. Small favors.

Her cell phone buzzed on the ottoman in front of her. "Hi, Mom."

"You get settled in okay? Your dad wanted me to check."

In the background her father bellowed, "I told you to let her be for five minutes, Annie."

Julia laughed. "I haven't unpacked the rental car."

"Why not? And did you tell Jackson thanks from us?"

She still couldn't believe her mother hadn't put up a fight when Lisa announced Julia's move into the cottage. At a minimum she'd expected a minor guilt trip from the most maternal, albeit sweetest, woman who ever lived.

Instead her mom had sung Jackson's praises. *So generous. Such a gentleman. One of the good guys.*

"Not yet. I'm still waiting for him to—Mom, Jackson's at the door. Gotta go."

"Have fun tonight, honey. I declare, if a date with Jackson Tate doesn't take your mind off things, nothing will." Her mom hung up before Julia could remind her it wasn't a date.

She approached the small foyer. Scrubbing damp palms against her hips, she pasted what she hoped passed for a natural smile on her face before opening the door, and *ho-lee cow*. He practically stole the air from her lungs. "Hi," she said, trying for a relaxed tone and sounding more like an asthmatic.

In all fairness to herself, though, earlier, dressed in shorts and a tee, he'd looked damn good. But now, freshly shaven, hair still damp from a recent shower, wearing faded jeans and an untucked, button-down shirt with the sleeves rolled up, he made her mouth water.

Twenty-nine going on seventeen all over again. How mortifying.

He grinned at her, arching his brows slightly. "Hi, back. Mind if I come in?"

Face flushing with heat, she stepped back and gestured for him to enter. "Sorry. Please. It's your house, after all."

"As long as you're staying here, it's yours, and, *my God*, it smells good in here." He spun around slowly, one hand tucked loosely into the front pocket of his low-waisted jeans. "I don't know how you managed it, but the air in here…it's like breathing liquid honey." His teeth flashed white as he shook his head as if to clear it.

"I'm not sure what the smell could be." Had she spilled her body wash in the shower? Smashed a bottle of perfume in her bag? She sniffed the air. She didn't smell anything out of the ordinary.

He gave a husky laugh. "I'm pretty sure *it* is *you*. I haven't been near you in years, but now that you're here—" He closed his eyes briefly and breathed in through his nose. "—I recognize the scent that hung in the air around you like it was yesterday. I thought your mom had a supply of fresh-cut flowers hidden somewhere near the dining room where we studied, until the time the four of us rode together in the car and…." His words dwindled, maybe due to the look on her face.

Because he'd brought up the night from hell, as she'd fondly dubbed it years ago.

Jackson laughed again, this time sounding more

than a little self-conscious. "You're looking at me like I'm crazy."

She nibbled on her lower lip. So many things ran through her mind. The compliment—he had just complimented her, right? The fact he'd noticed something more about her than her brain way back when, and flashing in neon lights in her mind—*the night from hell.*

"I didn't expect to hear anything like that from you." *Ever.* "Thank you."

He nodded once, propped his hands on his hips, and inclined his head toward the bedroom. "You get moved in okay?"

She twisted her hands in front of her, stopping the moment his gaze tracked to her fidgeting. "Jackson, I can't possibly stay here without paying rent. And—"

"Hungry?" he asked, cutting her off. " 'Cause I'm starved." He rubbed a hand over his flat stomach.

Her gaze followed the movement of those long, tanned fingers. Her mouth started watering again. *Lack of food.* "Apparently I am."

He gave her a questioning look.

She'd said that aloud. "Didn't you hear my stomach growl?"

"Mm, no. But good. Let's table this discussion 'til dinner. I wasn't sure what you'd like, but I put some things together for us. Let's go out the back. We can start the tour there."

"Sure. Let me get the lights."

"Grab a sweater while you're at it."

****

Jackson waited for her on the deck.

It'd happened again. That strange blend of

possessiveness and electricity. Was it Julia herself or some throwback to his youth? He pondered the question, then decided it didn't matter. Knowing why wouldn't change the fact he wanted to grab her, skim his hands down the clingy knit dress she wore, and then kiss those plump lips she liked nibbling.

Meanwhile, she seemed totally unaffected by him. Which was good. Very good. Julia was a nice girl and an old friend. Not the sort of woman he got physical with. She was more the sort a man looking for a relationship would snap up. He was not that man.

She emerged with her sweater thrown over one arm and brought her sweet scent with her. Vanilla? Honeysuckle? Whatever it was, he wanted to move in close and either breathe her in or eat her for dessert. He snorted softly, amused and disconcerted at the same time.

"What is it?"

Of course she'd ask. Julia as a teen drifted across his memory. Shy, but oddly direct, and aware of things most kids missed. She paid attention, picking up on things, some of which he hadn't wanted noticed. She always seemed one step ahead. He could admit to himself now what he hadn't understood then. She'd intimidated the hell out of him.

"Just thinking you've been gone too long." He scooped her sweater off her arm and, stepping behind her, held open the cardigan for her to slip her arms in. "Maybe you remember it gets cold in the foothills at night, even in the sweetheart of summer." He drew in a greedy lungful of her enticing scent, then made himself step back.

What had him feeling his oats? Julia was an old

friend—not an old flame. Too bad his inner, horny teen hadn't got the memo. *Get it together, Tate.*

"I remember," she said in a breathy voice, which acted like a finger sliding down his spine.

She tied the belt around her waist, and he placed his hand at the small of her back to guide her across the wooden deck. Not because he wanted to touch her. It was the gentlemanly thing to do. *Right.*

Aside from some meager moonlight and the recessed lights illuminating the twisting walkway between the cottage and the main house, they navigated in pitch darkness. Then they rounded a corner, and the deck opened to the back of his house. Light spilled out from the windows, casting the surrounding acreage in a muted glow.

A meandering paved path wove from the deck, across the lawn, to a courtyard and stone fire pit he'd built with his own two hands. Jasmine ground cover and a myriad of flowers and shrubs wound around the bricks in controlled chaos. Tight rows of giant cypress trees enclosed the entire space, opening to announce the Blue Ridge Mountains rising in the distance.

"It's beautiful, Jackson," she said. "Looks straight out of a fairy tale."

"Thank you. The house was the construction company's design, but the backyard and deck is all me."

A small smile curved her lips. "I'm impressed but not surprised."

Her compliment pleased him more than it should and left him wanting to ask her to elaborate. Instead he said, "Thanks. Not that I was fishing. Much."

Soft laughter escaped her. "You are one man who

doesn't need to fish."

"Now I'm blushing," he said, making light of caring what she thought a lot too much. Must be a holdover from when they were young. In his eyes, she'd stood so far above the rest of the kids who made up his world, and him most of all.

Whatever set her apart then hadn't faded with time. He narrowed his eyes and took in her perfect posture and indefinable distinctness that said she didn't belong mixing with the common folk. Not that she acted haughty or aloof. If anything, her soft-spokenness marked her as shy—yet when they were teenagers, at least, she hadn't shied away from speaking her mind.

Time had wrought some changes. The Julia who tutored him had possessed a fine shape, thin and hinting at things to come. Now she had curves in all the right places.

Between that rocking body and those sky-blue eyes, she was lethally hot. He wondered if she knew, if she used her looks to her advantage. Aunt Lisa *had* said she'd been dating her boss.

"You might as well tell me. Dirt on my face? Spinach in my teeth? Or maybe a bug landed in my hair."

It took him a moment to realize she'd caught him full-on staring. *Fool*. He jammed a hand through his hair. "Absorbing the unbelievable sight of you standing on my deck, I guess."

Her smile flashed white in the dim light. "That makes two of us."

"Maybe because you've avoided me like the plague for the last decade plus," he heard himself say. He sounded paranoid. Probably was.

Except she lowered her eyes and uttered not one word of denial.

So she had purposely avoided him. He had no idea why it mattered, but it irked the hell out of him.

A gust of chilly wind blew in off the mountains, and she dragged the edges of her sweater together. "You're right about that breeze. It sinks right into your bones."

She wanted to let the subject drop? No problem. "Let's head inside."

****

Julia exhaled a long sigh of relief. He hadn't pressed her to explain. Maybe she should have. But she'd chickened out, and he'd permitted her to do so, and anyway it was ancient history. With luck, that'd be the end of it.

The view of the house from the deck provided a welcome distraction from her spinning thoughts.

Wood-framed, floor-to-ceiling glass panels flanking two pairs of oversized, double french doors comprised the back wall of his house. Inside, strategically placed ceiling lights and table lamps cast an amber glow over earth-toned decor. Jackson's home looked like a little bit of North Carolina heaven.

Sharp, unexpected longing pierced her heart. Not that the ache could have anything to do with the man standing beside her. She could pin that squarely on the fiasco of a life she'd left behind her in New York.

Seeing Jackson after all this time was the diversion she needed, she told herself. She sent him a bright smile. "Lead the way."

They entered a house that was a long way from the small A-frame Jackson had lived in as a child. The space he called home was open and airy and downright elegant without one hint of pomp.

High ceilings with exposed cedar beams and an upstairs loft created a mountain-lodge feel. Clay and sage paint colored the walls. Rich-looking carpets and comfy seating areas sat atop thick, distressed, dark-wood flooring.

A huge stone fireplace with a massive hearth, topped with a giant flat-screen TV, dominated the wall to the left. To the right, another wall showcased musical instruments and complicated entertainment equipment.

"So this is what a world-famous singer turned songwriter's home looks like. It's gorgeous, Jackson."

He smiled, ducking his head. "Let's get some food in you."

His large, warm hand found the small of her back—again—as he led her across the room. They climbed a short flight of stairs toward a gleaming kitchen, lit with recessed ceiling lights and over-the-counter pendulum lamps. Similar to that of her place—no, *Jackson's* cottage where she had all but decided she couldn't stay—a huge granite counter blended the living spaces. A person could sit and chat with the cook, taking in the mountains, a roaring fire, and a private concert, all at once.

A perfect setup for entertaining, which begged the question—who did he entertain? Neighbors? Couples? *A girlfriend?*

For all she knew, his live-in girlfriend would traipse down the gleaming wooden staircase any minute now.

"Is it just you and Chase here, or is there a…?" She bit her lower lip. She'd know if he'd remarried. That juicy of a detail would have made the cover of all the magazines. But how did you ask a man you hadn't seen in years if he had a girlfriend?

You didn't. Not unless you had a particular interest in his personal life. Which she didn't. Embarrassed heat bloomed over her entire body. But maybe he hadn't guessed where she'd been going?

Jackson arched his brows at her, all curiosity and innocence.

If not for the mischievous glint in his hazel eyes, she might have bought his act. She put on her best poker face. "A roommate? It's a lot of house for two people."

A slow smile spread over his face. "Nope, just Chase and me."

"Is it warm in here?" She peeled off her sweater.

"Feels fine to me."

She pretended not to hear his soft chuckle.

He moved into the kitchen, crooking a finger for her to follow. "I opened some wine. One red, one white. I wasn't sure which you'd like."

She took in the two open bottles and empty wine glasses he'd had the forethought to set out. "Whichever you prefer is fine."

He shrugged. "To tell you the truth, I rarely drink the stuff. But according to the guy at the wine store, these both go down smooth."

She laughed, relaxing despite her Jackson Tate jitters. His laid-back attitude made it almost impossible not to. "Okay, I'll choose based on what we're eating, which is?"

He gestured to a line of takeout boxes. "I got Mexican, Thai, Greek, and barbecue."

She blinked. If she didn't know better, she'd say the man wanted to impress her. Then she remembered good ole southern hospitality—a lot of it in this case, but still. "Are you expecting more people?"

He grinned. "Have you met my son? It'll all get eaten, trust me. I wanted to be sure you wouldn't go hungry."

"Rest assured, Jackson. I like it all."

His smiling hazel eyes locked with hers. "Do you, now? That's good to know."

The rich velvet of his voice floated over her skin like a caress. Was he flirting with her? The mere thought had her face throbbing with heat. She hoped like hell her cheeks weren't beet red. "The red wine?" she squeaked.

He splashed wine the color of deep plum into the glasses. He handed her one before raising the other in a silent toast.

They clinked glasses, and she took a careful sip. Complex, a hint of olive and oak, and smooth as silk. "The salesclerk didn't mislead you."

"Glad to hear it. Have a seat? I'll fix us some plates."

Julia rounded the bar and slid onto one of the swivel stools. "Is Chase here? Sleeping, I take it? I hope our talking won't wake him."

"Chase's room is upstairs at the far end of the hall, so there's no chance. Speaking of Chase, sorry our afternoon ran late. You probably wondered if I forgot about our dinner plans."

"Not really," she fudged.

"Glad to hear it. Grady had an errand to run when we left the park, and then after I got Chase fed, he needed help with his homework." He paused. "He struggles with math just like I did. Luckily I had a great tutor, so I still understand the stuff—thank you, by the way. Not sure if I ever said that."

She nodded slowly as his softly spoken thanks warmed her to her toes. "I'm sure you did, but you're welcome anyway."

He gave her a pained smile. "Getting what's in my head into Chase's—let's just say I can't communicate it the way you did." He shrugged. "We'll muddle through. No biggie."

As he spoke, he piled two dinner plates with food. Chicken nachos. Sticky rice and sautéed vegetables. Greek salad. Brisket.

"That's plenty," she said when it appeared he'd add more. He'd have to roll her back to the cottage if she ate half of what he'd already dished out. "It's nice you help your son with his homework."

"It's what any dad would do," he said, brushing off her comment. He turned to the sink and rinsed the serving spoons.

She wondered at his words—especially as his father had been neither helpful nor kind to Jackson. Not by any stretch of the imagination. Mrs. Tate, on the other hand, had adored her son. Lucky for Chase, Jackson evidently took after her. The poor kid had lost his own mother as a kindergartener. The press'd had a field day with that story. A tragic car accident soon after the family had relocated to Honeyville.

"Not any dad, Jackson. It must be hard, being a single parent, tackling all the responsibility usually shared by two."

He seemed suddenly intent on closing the takeout

packages and lining them up on the counter.

Crap. She'd opened her mouth and inserted her foot again. "I'm sorry. I didn't mean to—"

Eyes still averted, he cut her off. "Hey, Julia, it's fine. Chase and I've been going it alone a long time now. I just didn't realize you knew."

About his wife's accident? Yeah, she did. The whole world did. But real smooth of her to bring it up. "Can I help you with anything now that you've served everything and cleaned up?" She gave a nervous laugh.

The tense lines on his face eased, almost instantly replaced by a bone-melting smile she'd bet he had down to a science. Knowing didn't lessen the impact on her one iota.

"How about you grab the wine and follow me."

He led her through the kitchen and turned right into a wide corridor. They passed a massive staircase, then an unlit, formal dining room on the left. Finally the space opened into a dining cove, or in country speak, a nook.

But this space was too elegant to be called something so mundane. Giving the room a candlelit feel, a rustic iron chandelier glowed on a dim setting above a round, scarred, wooden table. Four comfy-looking chairs and one curved bench framed the table. The bench nestled into an oriel window reaching nearly to the cathedral ceiling.

Outside, recessed spotlights lit up a cascading stone fountain. Massive cypress trees enclosed the space. The man liked his privacy.

Jackson set the plates on side-by-side place mats, then pulled a chair out for her.

"Chef's table," she murmured as he slid in beside

her.

"Excuse me?" He flashed his glamorous smile.

"You know those tables located in five-star restaurant kitchens?"

He inclined his head. "I've heard of them. Can't say I've ever eaten at one."

"Never? Usually they're the most coveted table in the place."

His hazel eyes gleamed with mischief. "Are you saying you like my table?"

She grinned. How had she forgotten how easy he was to be around? "Yes. Except, instead of a restaurant, it feels like we're tucked away in a secret garden or something."

"First a fairy tale, now a secret garden," he said in a velvet-soft voice. "I never knew you had such a romantic streak."

Flustered, she waved his words away. "Nah. I'm a numbers girl."

He picked up his fork and gestured for her to do the same before starting on his mountain of food. "You're a CPA by trade, right?"

He knew what she did for a living? Had he asked his aunt today, or had he kept up with her over the years? Probably the former. "Yes." She stabbed up a forkful of brisket.

He took a moment to chew. "Aunt Lisa says you're in between jobs at the moment."

And that answered that.

She shoved a loaded nacho into her mouth and held up one finger to buy herself a minute. A big thank you to Lisa for blabbing her business. If she'd only shared that Julia had resigned, fine. But if she'd mentioned anything about her ex... No. Lisa wouldn't do that.

She went for a breezy tone. "I'm taking a break from the big city, indulging in a quarter-life crisis. I'll sort something out."

"I can relate to that." Draping one arm across his seatback, he fixed her with a cool stare. "It's partly why we left the LA scene."

We. Jackson, his wife, and child.

"That and I wanted Chase to know my mom. At least he got a few years with her."

Jackson's mom had been killed in an accident perpetrated by a drunk driver. She felt for him, losing his wife and his beloved mother, both well before their times.

Julia had come home for his mother's service. It had been the one time she expected to see Jackson face-to-face. But Jackson hadn't attended, either the service or the gathering afterward. According to his red-eyed, grief-stricken Aunt Lisa, his father and he had had words. She hadn't expanded on the whys and wherefores, and Julia hadn't asked.

She knew of the troubled relationship between father and son, gathered through things she'd witnessed with her own eyes and then things Jackson let slip during their teenage friendship. Later, she'd overheard snippets of conversations between her mother and Jackson's mother and aunt. Mr. Tate was a lousy dad, no doubt about it. But to deny his only son the comfort of mourning his mother surrounded by others who knew and loved her took the cake. Of course, that presupposed Jackson's father had barred him from attending.

"I remember how close you were with your mom. I

never got to tell you how sorry I was."

"I miss her. Sometimes something strikes me, and I pick up the phone to call her—then I remember she's gone, even after all this time."

"I can't imagine." She paused. "You've had a lot of losses since moving home. Your wife, your mom. It didn't surprise me when you quit the band after everything. I'm glad you kept up with your writing, though."

His brows knitted. "Let me get this straight. You know about when I quit the band to write full time."

Her and about a billion other people, she wanted to say. She bit her inside cheek and nodded.

"Sounds like you pretty well kept up with my entire life. And yet I haven't seen your face for thirteen years." As accusations went, it was a direct hit.

But he hadn't been blameless. Not at all.

"Why, Julia? Why hold a grudge against me and not Grady, for God's sake?" Bewilderment and, if she wasn't mistaken, hurt echoed in his words.

Thoughts and images raced through her mind. How enamored she'd been with Jackson. How scared she'd been when Grady got her alone in the woods. How grateful when Jackson, her hero, had come to her rescue.

How hurt she'd been when she discovered just how Jackson's friend had come to ask her to the prom.

She couldn't do this. Not after all these years, and not fresh on the heels of the New York fiasco. Her emotions were too raw. Locking eyes with him, she said, "I don't know what you're talking about." She drew a shaky breath, knowing he could read the lie on her. Anyone could. She was a terrible liar.

He lowered his eyes. A muscle ticked in his jaw. "Okay, Julia."

Oddly enough, she felt no relief.

She'd lied. He knew. She needed to leave. She pushed back from the table, then froze—save for her heart trying to beat out of her chest—when his warm hand covered one of hers.

"I know a couple things about you, too," he said, rubbing his thumb over her knuckles.

She shot him a look and dropped the hand not covered by his into her lap where it clenched into a fist. "Such as?"

"Such as you graduated college with honors, a year early. You got recruited by a big firm in New York before even taking your CPA licensing test, which you passed on the first try. You moved to the Big Apple and never left—until this weekend when you packed up your life and drove home to Honeyville, North Carolina."

"More than a couple things," she said, breathless. No way could he have covered all that information in a five-minute conversation with his aunt today.

He pulled his hand from hers to cross his arms over his chest and took all the heat in the room with him. "You never married or hadn't the last I asked. I'm guessing no, since you recently broke up with your fiancé. Your boss, right?"

Her mind went blank for a timeless moment, then filled with one blaring thought. She was so going to kill his aunt. She smiled sweetly. "Are you going to tell me what color underwear I'm wearing next? Oops. I forgot to tell my mother or your aunt."

A beat of silence passed, then he threw his head

back and bellowed with laughter.

She wasn't sure when she joined in, but soon she laughed so hard she couldn't breathe. The guffaws didn't wane 'til both their eyes leaked tears.

"Jesus, that felt good," he said, swiping a knuckle over his cheek.

"It did." She spoke through a giant smile. This was good. They could end the evening on a positive note. "About your cottage—"

"Your cottage, you mean?" His unblinking gaze fixed on hers as if he knew the direction she headed and meant to mesmerize her into submission.

She steeled herself. "Jackson, I can't stay here."

"Why not?"

"Because. It's your house. Your home. Anyone can see you value your privacy, and—"

"Why do you say that?" he cut in, frowning.

She spread her hands. "Oh, I don't know, the acres of pristine forest surrounding your house? The guard gate? The posted signs reading *keep out*? The huge cypress trees only the Jolly Green Giant could see over?"

His lips twitched. "You always did notice everything. Okay, so I like my privacy—from the public. Not from family and close friends."

She let her eyes say the obvious. She qualified as neither. "And then there's this no-rent thing. I can't possibly stay here without paying my way."

"Julia."

"I can't."

He steepled his fingers in front of his face. "I don't need the money."

"That's totally beside the point."

He snorted. "Says who?"

"This isn't funny."

He sobered, though a telltale gleam of amusement shone in his gold-flecked eyes. "Can we continue this conversation in the living room?"

Where her sweater was—and the way out. She nodded.

They retraced their steps to the kitchen. After depositing their dishes in the sink, he grabbed her half-full glass of wine—she noticed he left his—took her hand in his warm grip, and pulled her toward the massive sectional leather couch in the living room.

His elusive masculine scent drifted over her in his wake. Warm male skin, freshly laundered clothes, spicy aftershave. She drew in a lungful of the heady aroma, and her lower regions quivered to life. Not good. Not *appropriate*. Not in line with her plan to leave her sex drive in park while she sorted through the layers of Chris's betrayal.

"Sit," Jackson instructed, crowding into her so she sat or risked standing nose to neck with him. He placed her wine glass in her hand, wrapping her fingers around the crystal. "Drink."

Anything to slow her erratic pulse. She sipped.

He plopped down beside her, somehow making the move look both graceful and sexy as hell. Not that he had to work at either.

"Listen up, Julia. You are going to stay here, and you're not paying rent, because my family owes your family and, more importantly, because I owe you."

She opened her mouth to speak, and he silenced her, holding one hand palm out.

"Your father hired my father when no one else

would. Oh, I see you didn't know that."

She didn't. Had never heard one thing about it. But then she couldn't imagine a scenario where her father would spread news about another person's misfortune. She shook her head.

"My parents never told me exactly what happened, but I overheard some of their late-night talks, being a nosy kid and all. Evidently the owner of the lumber yard and my father had words one night concerning, I don't know, the way Dad thought things ought to be run versus the way the owner wanted. They argued. Dad socked him. Dad got fired. After that, Mr. Craven—I think that was his name—"

"Craven Lumber," she said with a nod. She stared at him and sipped more wine.

"Craven had pull around town, and he wanted Dad gone. He let it be known anyone who hired George Tate would be persona non grata. People were afraid to go against him. Or maybe they didn't like my dad. Who knows. I do know your dad took a chance on mine and saved us from going under."

"Jackson, I had no idea."

"I figured." He rubbed a spot above his brow where a tiny scar marred the skin.

She couldn't make it out in the muted light of the living room, but she remembered it from when they were kids. She'd asked him about it once. It was the only time he had ever snapped at her.

"But that was between our parents."

"Damn it, Julia. What about what you did for me? When my dad threatened to take away everything I knew and loved? My only means of escaping him and…" He drew a slow breath. "If you hadn't helped me, I'd have quit my music, because my dad would have made me. I'd also have failed math and likely never gotten into the community college that got me into NC State. I'd never have met Hannah, and without her, there'd be no Chase. So you see, without you, I wouldn't have the best thing that ever happened to me."

And who could resist an argument like that?

He glared at her as if he expected her to try.

She beamed at him, helpless to resist the urge. "Okay, Jackson."

He opened his mouth, shut it, then slanted her a suspicious look. "You're agreeing to stay?"

She spread her arms in a conciliatory gesture and huffed out a laugh. "Until I figure out what's next, I'd love to. Thank you."

He slapped his hands on his knees and sent her a brilliant smile that hit her like a sucker punch. "Great. You have a key, right?"

She nodded. "Lisa gave me one this morning."

"Let me write down the garage code for you. I'll hunt up an opener for you tomorrow."

"No." She slashed her hand through the air in emphasis. "And before you start arguing, allow me to tell you I also like my privacy. I'll park in the spot beside the cottage—once I have a car."

He took a moment to digest her words. "What's that car parked by your place now?"

"A rental. I have to return it tomorrow." She shrugged. "Having a car in New York is more trouble than it's worth."

"Of course. I can loan you a—"

"Forget it," she said with a bemused laugh, at the same time he said, "—car."

33

She held her palm out to stave off an argument. "My parents are loaning me one of theirs. Dad's retired and doesn't do a lot of driving. They offered me his sedan 'til I decide if I need a more permanent solution."

He frowned. "But I have a perfectly good extra car no one's using."

She laughed aloud. How many times had she laughed tonight? Too many to count. "Why *do* you have an extra car? That's a bit decadent, isn't it?"

He gave a one-shoulder shrug. "Any self-respecting Carolina man needs a truck. Plus I like driving fast, so I have a sports car. And a motorcycle. If you change your mind, the offer's always good."

A wry smile curved her lips, and oh damn. There went those thirteen-year-old ice chips she'd packed around her heart, safeguarding her against Jackson's charms. Vaporized in the course of a single conversation.

The man had always had that certain something no woman could resist. Every magazine cover featuring his shaped-by-the-gods face and drool-inspiring eyes had served to remind her. But tonight, he'd added thoughtful, generous, and heartbreakingly vulnerable to the mix. That combination could decimate a woman's good sense—assuming she had any. She needed to get out of here before she embarrassed herself by melting into a puddle at his feet.

Instead she sat, watching him, watching her. As the moment stretched, Julia's awareness of him—how close he sat, how good he smelled, how silky his hair promised to be—amplified to the point of deafening. Her skin crawled, her toes curled in her sandals, and her fingers itched to reach out and touch him. Calling on all her will, she rose and stuck out her hand. "I better get going. Thanks, Jackson."

He stared at her hand, then unfolded himself from the couch. One corner of his mouth crooked upward as he took her hand in his warm grip and dragged her in for a hug. His chest was solid muscle, and his cologne smelled even better now that her nose was pressed into his shirt.

Desire, hot and swift, curled through her like smoke.

"Thank *you*, Julia," he murmured in a husky voice. "For saying yes." His arms tightened in a long squeeze, bringing more of him into contact with more of her.

Did he know what he was doing to her? Wearing her heels brought them together just so, nearly aligning her hips with his. She wanted nothing more than to press into him and sink her fingers into the hair brushing the collar of his shirt.

A moment later, he released her and took a step back. "I'll be gone tomorrow most of the day. Not sure if the place has everything you need, so feel free to let yourself in the back door to rummage—"

She shook her head—mostly to clear it. "No. I draw the line at rummaging."

He laughed softly. "I'll walk you to your door."

"I think I can find my way." She retrieved her sweater from the bar stool, then crossed the livingroom, giving the couch, and Jackson, a wide berth as she headed for the back door.

He appeared at her heels. "I'll stop when I can see your door."

"Did anyone ever tell you you're one stubborn man?"

"Who me?"

She stepped onto the deck and gulped crisp mountain air while the saying *jumping from the frying pan to the fire* blinked neon inside her head.

Chapter Three

In spite of the summer heat, Julia drove the entire distance from Jackson's estate to downtown Honeyville with the car windows rolled down. She needed to hear the whisper of leaves in the trees lining the streets and breathe in the fragrant air. Damp earth, fresh grass, a faint hint of horse dung. Only in Honeyville could she feast on this particular explosion of sensory wonderfulness. Her heart squeezed. *Home.*

A large dollop of gratitude and, of all things, *hope* filled her. Her parents, with their unconditional love and belief in her, her two oldest friends who she knew would have her back if only she'd let them. And the biggest surprise of all? Jackson Tate stepping in to help her pick up the pieces and maybe heal an old wound she hadn't let into the light in over a decade.

Her eyes stung as a maelstrom of emotion beat at the veneer of calm she'd wrapped herself in since leaving New York.

She pulled into the graveled Main Street parking lot, scoring a shady space next to a gnarled old oak. Now for the hard part, a.k.a. opening up her emotional can of worms with her two best friends. Best friends whom she hadn't seen for a good six months, and in whom she hadn't confided, even by phone, when things started going bad.

In fairness, she'd only had a vague sense of her

world tilting off its axis. Not 'til everything blew up, and she found herself on the road home, did she know how badly she'd blown it.

Minutes later she pushed open the door to Frank's Fair-Trade Cafe, setting off a familiar jangle of bells overhead.

"Look who the cat's dragged in, Frank, our very own Jules." Callie placed herself in Julia's path, forcing her to stand in the open doorway with the sun beating down on her like a hot spotlight.

Callie cocked her fifties-glam blonde head and narrowed her eyes. "Oh dear, that bad?"

Julia laughed. How like Callie to have her on the rails before she'd had her first cup of coffee. She loved that about her friend. Julia leaned in to hug her. "Is Sue here yet?"

Callie's ruby-red lips curved in a cat's smile. "Due any minute. I blocked off the cafe section for us. Cleared it with the boss." She lowered her voice. "Between you and me, he can be a real hard-ass."

"Ah." She smiled down at Frank, Callie's fifty-pound rescue dog.

The black chow-lab mix sat on his haunches, appearing to grin.

"Yeah, I heard he can be impossible to work for." She squatted to scratch Frank behind his velvet-soft ears. "Hey, buddy. How's business?"

He gave her hand a snuff before trotting off, tail in the air.

"Best thing that ever happened to me," Callie said, gazing after him.

Somewhere inside Julia's oversized purse, her cell phone buzzed. She was pretty sure she knew who texted her. Again. She dug out the phone as Callie led her toward the back of the store.

"This is perfect. You're five minutes early for our nine a.m. coffee date, and Sue will be here on the nose, as always. That means I get a jump on her. Muah-ha-ha."

"Ha. Ha." Cell phone in hand, she thumbed the messages button and silently read the last incoming text—from Chris.

—*So much for the chat I wanted to have this morning at home. I get it. You're mad. I'll see you at the office.*—

Unbelievable. All her things were gone, and Chris still hadn't clued in. A clear case of willful ignorance.

"Have a seat at the bar while I fire up the machine."

Julia set her phone on the polished walnut counter and slid onto a swivel stool.

"What's your pleasure?" Callie asked from behind the counter.

"Ginormous latte?" She scanned the bright, abstract oil paintings lining the wall high above Callie's head. "I like the artwork you have displayed."

"Thanks. New artist in town. Big-time painter from Ireland."

As well as selling fair-trade coffees and teas, Callie's shop featured locally produced goods. Art for purchase covered the walls; handmade jewelry, scarves, oils, soaps, and dried herbs spilled from the shelves. The shop smelled like a day spa, and thanks to the large windows in the converted, old grocery store, sunlight flooded the entire space, making the ambiance warm, inviting, and eclectic, kind of like Callie herself.

Behind the counter, Callie activated a bean grinder, and rich coffee aroma filled the space. "Spill it."

The front doorbells jangled. "Hello?"

"Sue's early," Julia said and half sprang from her stool.

"She'll find us. Sit." Callie's gaze lowered to her task as she worked the milk frother. A moment later she set a ceramic mug in front of Julia. "Man trouble, eh?"

"I kinda wanted to ease into it, but—" She paused to scoop up the warm mug with both hands. "—let's call it everything trouble." She relished several swallows of creamy, hot latte. "How have I lived without this?"

Sue bounded into the back room, her auburn flip glinting in the sun's rays streaming into the room from various windows. "Ah-ha. I knew I should've gotten here early."

Sue worked as the principal at the private Catholic high school all three girls had attended from preschool to twelfth grade. She was as punctual as a stopwatch.

"Unfortunately, you didn't miss anything." Callie set an iced coffee drink on the counter in front of the empty stool beside Julia.

Sue kissed Julia's cheek. "Swear?"

"Yep. You're just in time to hear Julia explain what she's doing back in Honeyville with everything she owns."

Julia straightened and glanced between her friends. "How did you—"

Sue rolled her eyes, and Callie's face split in an amused smile.

"This is Honeyville, Jules. You didn't seriously think you could show up without word getting back to us? Your mother told my mother, who told me, and I called Cal—mostly to make sure she didn't know anything I didn't."

"The Honeyville grapevine," Julia muttered, thinking of the blabbing Jackson's aunt had done.

Her friends looked at her with compassion-filled eyes, and her calm exterior cracked.

Dammit. She forced words past the sudden lump in her throat. "Just *Reader's Digest* version for now, guys, okay?"

They nodded.

"I don't know where to start. It's all so embarrassing." And disappointing. She'd made horrendous errors in judgment. Plus she was closing in on thirty.

Her cell phone vibrated on the gleaming wooden counter. All three sets of eyes fixed on the screen. Callie's aqua-tipped pointer finger swiveled the phone in her direction. She read the message aloud. "It's nine-oh-five. Where are you?"

Callie raised her caramel-colored eyes to meet Julia's. "Chris. Isn't he your boyfriend?"

"And boss?" Sue tacked on.

"Ex-boyfriend, and never my boss," Julia clarified, pointing a finger at Sue for emphasis. "He's not even a partner yet. But he is the firm's closer, the guy they send in to schmooze important potential clients. *Not* my direct supervisor." She lifted her chin a notch.

"O-oh," Callie intoned. "I knew I didn't like that guy."

Julia's mouth fell open in surprise. Before she could respond, Sue spoke up.

"Start at the beginning, get to the part where you

moved in together and church bells were on the horizon, and then tell us how he became the ex."

Julia and Callie stared at Sue.

"I'm in education. I have a methodical brain."

"It does sound like a good plan," Callie admitted.

Julia gazed at the beamed ceiling and sorted through her jumbled thoughts. "Okay. At first I didn't see him as boyfriend material. Not for me, at any rate. He seemed somehow wrong."

"You thought he was too cool for school, right? The textbook smooth operator?" Callie asked.

"No. I…well, sort of. He blew in from California a year and a half ago and right away ran with a flashy set, and I'm anything but. Is that why you didn't like him, Cal? You could've said something."

Callie opened her arms wide. "You seemed happy."

Julia nodded her understanding. "He seemed…superficial? Insincere, maybe? But after spending time with him, I saw a different side, or so I thought." She dropped her chin in her hand. "I started noticing all we had in common, like our careers and neither of us having been married, and I wanted to have a baby before I turn fifty." She grimaced. "What a fool I was. I should have trusted my first impression."

Sue nodded. "Momma always said first impressions don't lie."

"That's not true," Callie snapped with such vehemence Julia and Sue both stared at her. "Sorry. Go on. Please." Callie laid a hand over Julia's. "What made you override your intuition?"

"Chris paid me a lot of attention from the moment he transferred to our office. Since he was new in town, I assumed he wanted to make friends."

"So what happened? You get drunk at an office party and go home with him?" Sue asked.

Callie snorted.

"It could have happened," Julia said, defensive about her good-girl stigma.

"Did it?" Callie challenged.

Julia slumped against the bar on her elbows. "Hardly. In fact I never even took his flirting seriously. I admit I was flattered, though. Everybody, male and female alike, raved about his looks and charm, and he singled me out."

"Well, duh," Callie said. "You're a total bombshell."

Julia rolled her eyes. "We're talking about me, here. I'm—"

"You're what?" Sue demanded. "You're seriously hot, Jules."

"You guys are crazy." She looked down at herself. She wore cute skinny jeans with a flirty hobo-chic tunic she'd picked up in the village, and she'd long since lost the glasses thanks to Lasik, but underneath it all, she was a dud. Missing that certain va-va-voom. *Just ask Chris.*

Still. Unconditional love from her besties was salve to her wounded soul. Julia smiled at them in turn. "Being here does my heart good, you know? Thanks for being my cheerleaders. But it's not necessary, really. I'm not trying to run myself down."

"Let me see a picture of Chris," Sue said.

"I think I still have one." Julia picked up her phone and scrolled through her photos.

Callie's brows shot up. "Must be bad if you deleted

his photos."

"Found one."

Her friends leaned in together to study her former almost fiancé.

"Wow," Sue said. "Very fine." At Callie's pointed stare, she added, "But looks aren't everything. He's a total jerk, right?"

"Right," Callie answered for Julia.

She could've told them both Sue hadn't said anything the rest of the universe wouldn't. The tall California blond turned heads everywhere he went.

Callie picked up Julia's phone, thumbs scrolling through pictures. She wouldn't find another one of Chris. Julia had only kept that one because it had the marquee from Ryan Moore's concert in the background. She'd have to crop him out of it.

Sue angled her head. "Okay. So his handsome mug didn't sweep you off your feet. What finally sparked your interest?"

Julia smiled. "He came into the copy room behind me, humming my song."

"Your song?" Sue prodded.

"My all-time favorite. 'Falling,' by Ryan Moore?" She cocked her head, remembering. "I said something like, 'What? Are you a Moore fan, too?' He answered by flashing two tickets for an upcoming Moore concert and inviting me to go." She scowled. "Later I found out my assistant gave him the inside scoop on how big a fan I am."

"I love Ryan Moore," Sue said. "I saw him last time he performed in Asheville. Speaking of 'Falling,' I think I fell in love with him that night."

Callie slapped a palm to her forehead. "Good God,

not him again, Jules?"

"What are you talking about? I never had a thing for Ryan Moore, hot though he is," Julia said.

"Not Moore. Your all-time crush, the one who broke your heart and you never got over."

Julia's face burned with instant guilty heat. Which was absurd. She was over Jackson Tate. Long over him. Just because he'd turned her knees to jelly last night was no reason to think otherwise.

More to the point, Jackson had not performed that song. "*You draw me in, you draw me out, whatever you got, has me spinning about?* That song? That's by Ryan Moore." She crossed her arms over her chest. "And Jackson Tate is not my all-time crush who I never got over."

Behind the bar, Callie mirrored Julia's cross-armed stance. "Performed by Moore, written by Tate." Her mouth curved in a smug grin. "And how did you know who I meant if Tate isn't the one?"

Sue happily chimed in. "She's right, Jules. At Moore's concert he credited Jackson with writing his first big hit. I think they were friends in college or something."

"I'm surprised you didn't learn all this from those entertainment magazines you devoured over the years—the ones with Jackson's mug on the cover."

Julia's face throbbed like the time she spent all day at the lake at sixteen and got a major sunburn. She cleared her throat. "I know in recent years Jackson made a career shift, quitting his band to focus on his song writing, but I had no idea about 'Falling.' I mean, when it came out, Jackson hadn't made it big yet. He was still the lead singer in his Indy rock band. None of us had graduated college, for Pete's sake." As if that made a difference. But for some reason, the idea of Jackson writing the song that had haunted her from the moment she heard it flummoxed her.

"Truth is stranger than fiction," Callie said.

She took a deep breath and told herself to get a grip. What did it matter who wrote "Falling"? "Well, color me surprised. But as to your other claim, Cal, my crush on Jackson was a childhood thing. Ancient history. It vaporized the moment I saw what a jerk he was."

She expected her friends to continue ribbing her. Instead they both wore frozen smiles and stared at something over Julia's shoulder.

God. Not again. Not twice in two days. "Guys?" she asked, her voice cracking.

"Hi, Jacks," Callie said in lieu of answering.

Sue waggled her fingers hello.

Julia's skin went clammy, and she had the sudden urge to bang her head against the counter. But she swiveled in her seat to face Jackson Tate, in the, of course, hotter-than-hell flesh. How much had he heard?

His dazzling hazel eyes locked with hers. One corner of his mouth quirked upward in that half-grin thing he did that drove her crazy when she was a kid and, evidently, still did.

On the bar, her phone buzzed.

Jackson leaned over her to study the screen, giving her a tantalizing whiff of male skin and spicy aftershave.

He read her text aloud. "Shawn just informed me you quit. Julia, you can't be serious." He straightened and gave Julia a quizzical look. "From a contact named

Pig Face?"

Julia's mouth fell open. She closed it with a snap and aimed an accusatory look at Callie.

"Do you think someone should tell him you've relocated? Or is Pig Face a Honeyville resident?" His eyes sparkled with obvious amusement.

Julia rubbed her forehead. "Wow. I didn't expect to see you here this morning."

"I guess not." He coughed into his fist.

He had heard. Great.

"I came into town to take care of some business and saw your rental car out back. Thought I'd pop in and see how you slept last night."

Julia's story hadn't progressed past New York. She definitely hadn't related her new, temporary digs to her friends, and with their claims about Jackson being her all-time crush still hanging in the air, their current silence was deafening.

Jackson didn't appear to notice. "How are you ladies doing this fine morning?" He gave Callie a lazy nod. "The usual, doll?"

Callie handed him a drink in a to-go cup. Apparently she'd already made it.

"Got a minute?" Jackson asked, touching Julia's elbow.

From behind her gleaming chrome coffee machine, Callie grinned at her like she'd just won a bet.

Oh. Maybe because Julia had been staring daggers at her since she handed Jackson his drink. Wiping her expression, she hopped up from her stool. "Sure."

"We'll save your seat." Sue patted the cushion and sent her a sunny smile.

Julia followed Jackson as he wove through the

store racks, beverage in hand. Today he wore a khaki-colored, long-sleeved henley that emphasized the breadth of his broad shoulders and trimness of his waist. He still had the V-shape thing going. Her gaze slid lower to his very firm-looking—

"*Oof.*" She plowed into Jackson's backside, then started a slow tumble into a shelving unit filled with organic, tie-dyed T-shirts.

"Whoa." Jackson's free arm encircled her waist. He snugged her up against his hard body—all without spilling a drop of his coffee—and flashed her a relaxed smile.

"You stopped very suddenly," she accused.

"Frank," he said in explanation as he straightened and gestured with his coffee cup toward the dog.

Yes. Frank. She glared accusingly at him for lying smack in the middle of the aisle. His pink and black tongue lolled out the side of his mouth in a thoroughly sarcastic grin. This time she had no doubt.

" 'Scuse us, buddy," Jackson said and angled around the dog while pulling Julia along with him.

The moment they skirted him, Frank rose onto all fours, glanced up at Julia, and—she could swear—winked.

"Sorry for tripping into you." She extricated herself from Jackson's encircling arm. His fingertips grazed the small of her back, leaving a trail of fire.

"It helps if you're looking where you're going," Jackson said in a neutral voice. She'd have bought the innocent act, too, if not for the amused glint in his eye.

He *knew* she'd been ogling him. Her face throbbed with heat, but somehow she met him stare for stare.

He looked away first.

Small victories.

Not that he looked the least chagrined, swaggering the rest of the way to the shop door to hold it open for her while sipping his coffee.

Outside the air had warmed up considerably. She rolled up her sleeves. "You wanted to talk to me?"

He gestured for her to walk beside him along the storefronts. "I wondered if you needed me to pick up anything."

"Pick up anything?"

"For the cottage. Cooking utensils. Paper towels. Sugar."

She scratched the side of her head. "You brought me out here to ask about kitchen stuff?"

A boyish grin flickered over his face. "I got the impression you hadn't told your friends about holing up at my place."

"I was about to." Why did she feel like she needed to apologize? How did he so effortlessly throw her off her game?

His grin widened to a blinding smile. "Too busy roasting the pig?"

Laughter bubbled out of her. "That was all Callie, I swear. I didn't even know she'd edited Chris's contact information until that text came in."

"Chris, huh? Good to hear it wasn't you. If you labeled one man like that, I hate to think what you'd call me." He shot his empty coffee cup in a trash bin with a snap of his wrist.

Her stomach lurched and not simply because he'd overheard. Something in his expression told her she'd hurt his feelings. "Jackson, what I said back there..." Well, damn. Talk about a loaded subject. Did she dare open that can of worms?

He reached for her arm and shifted to face her, hazel eyes expectant. A long moment passed, during which she could swear he wove some kind of spell over her, as if his eyes had the power to suck all her brain energy out of her head while heating up her insides.

"Jules?" he prodded softly.

She tore her gaze from his and shoved her hands into the front pockets of her jeans. She could take the easy way and evade the truth—again.

But she'd hurt his feelings. Time to man up. Before she could second guess herself, she blurted, "Jackson, you were right last night—about how we left it years ago. I was really mad at you, for a *really* long time. I thought you were a jerk, mostly because"—she softened her words with a tiny smile—"you *were* a jerk, and I swore I'd never speak to you again." She sighed. "But that was then. We were kids."

"Kids or no, I was a jerk. I'm sorry, Jules."

He spoke so earnestly an almost irresistible urge to touch him, anywhere, and tell him not to worry about the past burned through her.

Jackson beat her to it. His fingertips glided down her forearm 'til he reached her hand and twined their fingers together. "I'm really, *really* sorry." His palm was warm and slightly damp.

Her stomach quivered, whether in reaction to his touch or the depth of emotion in his words, she couldn't say.

"Forget it," she said, her voice husky.

"No," he said gruffly. "You never let me apologize, never returned my calls. I even came over once, but your dad said you weren't home."

She remembered. She'd been upstairs in her room. She'd had to beg her dad to lie for her. Not one of her finer moments.

"I could tell your dad was covering for you. He turns red like you do."

"I do not," she erupted, and to her horror, her cheeks pulsed with instant heat.

Jackson's eyes crinkled at the corners, and his lips twitched, but he didn't outright gloat. "The next thing I knew, you were gone. For years, when I thought of you, of that night, I regretted never having said I was sorry face-to-face. Julia, I never should have let you go to prom with Grady. What he did, the way he treated you—"

The way *Grady* treated her? That was what he thought? That she'd held a grudge against him over Grady manhandling her that night?

"There was no *letting me go with Grady*," she interrupted and attempted to tug her hand free of his. Whether or not he noticed, he did not release her. Lifting her chin a notch, she went on. "As I recall, you made some kind of bet with Grady. He lost, and I got a date to the prom."

He rolled his neck 'til it made an audible crack. "Okay. Full confession. I wanted to thank you for tutoring me by taking you to prom, especially since your private school didn't have one, but I was too lame to take you myself because I…" He huffed out a breath. "God, this is embarrassing."

She smiled.

He grinned back at her. "You enjoying this?"

"Who, me?"

He chuckled briefly, then his face sobered. "I had

something going with Sheila. God, *Sheila*. I should have stayed out of her life, too." He jammed his free hand through silky brown hair that fell right back into place.

Since their hands were still linked, she squeezed. "Hey, Jacks, that wasn't your fault." *That* being Sheila's suicide dive off a hotel balcony later that year.

"Sure," he said. "No matter what you say, I know I shouldn't have left you alone with Grady at the bonfire."

"You didn't leave us alone. I went off in search of..." She cleared her throat. "The facilities. Grady followed me. That was not your fault, and I never blamed you. In fact, if you hadn't come when you did—" She broke off. She'd been shaken at the time. But in retrospect, she'd likely overdramatized the situation. "Actually? Nothing would have happened. Grady was drunk. Acting out. He apologized to me the next day and..."

Jackson glared at her.

"What now?"

"You let Grady apologize and not me? He's the one who ripped your pretty dress."

And you were the one who broke my heart. "I wouldn't say I *let* him apologize, Jackson. If I recall, he cornered me when I was checking the mailbox or something."

"Uh-huh." He sounded doubtful. "As long as you can forgive me now, Jules."

"Done," she said, somewhat awed to realize she spoke the truth.

He swung her hand in his, pulling her slightly closer, almost as if he meant to seal her words with a kiss. "Thanks." His gaze brushed her lips, and her heart tripped over itself.

But the moment passed, and he didn't kiss her.

She rushed to speak as if doing so would conceal any telltale signs of the insta-disappointment swamping her. "Hey, what are old friends for? I even showed up on your doorstep, delivering myself up on a silver platter."

Heat flared in Jackson's eyes. "That's something I'd like to see."

Whoa. Julia's already skittering pulse revved into high gear.

Abruptly Jackson released her hand and began sauntering backward, toward Frank's Cafe. "So like I was saying. Did you notice if the cottage needs a coffee maker or can opener or trash bags?"

Julia blinked at the quick subject change. "I haven't had a chance to do an inventory, but please don't trouble yourself. Anything I need, I can pick up."

He shook his head, an emphatic no. "It needs to be stocked for whoever uses the place. That's on me."

She stifled a groan of frustration. Jackson was downright stubborn in his generosity. In less than twenty-four hours, he'd given her a place to stay, offered her a car, and now intended to provide her with sundries.

"Jackson." Julia spoke in her sternest voice—the one she reserved for clients who wanted to skirt tax laws or claim bogus expenses sure to draw an audit.

He made a show of checking his watch. The shiny silver band glinted in the sunlight. "Gotta run. I told Bill I'd come by in five minutes, like ten minutes ago."

She glanced across Main Street toward Bill's Steak

House and Cantina. The local favorite had been around so long it was practically a landmark.

"I'll stop by tonight if that's all right with you?" he called from the middle of the street.

She frowned. She couldn't very well tell him no. He lived there, for goodness' sake. But saying yes felt like acquiescing again.

Evidently he didn't need an answer. He winked and jogged the rest of the way across the street. *Huh.* Another run-in with Jackson Tate ending with her asking herself what just happened.

Hadn't it always been like this? Hadn't he always knocked her off kilter? When she was a teen, she'd been putty in his hands, though she'd done her best to conceal how much she worshipped him. Not that she'd succeeded, which was how she ended up going to the prom with Grady, Jackson's BFF.

Well, damn. As her friends had so kindly pointed out, some things hadn't changed. Thirteen years later and Jackson had the same cataclysmic effect on her senses. Good thing she moved into his house.

Let's reflect, Jules. Fresh from a broken almost engagement, sporting a major crushed ego and a pretty well wrecked career, why not throw a stroll across quicksand into the mix?

Laughing out loud, she pulled open the door to Callie's shop.

Her friends pounced the second the doorbell tinkled, almost as if they'd been watching for her out the shop's window.

"What did he say? What's going on between you two?" Sue asked, grabbing her upper arm.

"Sue," Callie complained, taking Julia's other arm.

"Julia has to finish telling us about Pig Face. Afterward she can fill us in on Jackson."

Julia glanced between the two of them, then nodded. "That works."

Chuckling, Callie flipped the hanging sign on the door to *closed.* "Frank gave me the green light. We won't be disturbed again." She dragged Julia, and by default Sue, toward the coffee bar. "Resume the story with the Ryan Moore concert."

Julia took her time settling in. She still felt a little discombobulated from her conversation with Jackson.

"Chris was a perfect gentleman. He picked me up at my apartment and, after the concert, left me at my door with a kiss on the cheek and a request to see me again. He was so sweet and looked so puppy-dog hopeful I said yes. But I didn't think it would go anywhere."

"Explain," Sue demanded.

"I thought my lifestyle—early to bed, quiet nights, book signings, coffee shops, and yoga on the weekends—would be too slow-paced for him. I also thought his lifestyle wouldn't interest me. He races motorcycles in his spare time, for goodness' sake." She shrugged. "Turned out he didn't mind quiet nights, and I enjoyed riding on the back of his bike."

"That does sound fun," Callie admitted.

"So your instinct to avoid him was all wrong?" Sue asked, brows scrunched in evident confusion.

"Not exactly. In retrospect, I think he saw me as a challenge. He did say I gave that off-limits vibe. So he put in a lot of effort to woo me. I started to believe I wanted a future with him—enough that when certain issues cropped up, I ignored them."

Sue's eyes narrowed. "Such as?"

"He claimed he loved me, but…he never really listened when I talked, unless it was shop talk. He didn't ask about me. And then—" She broke off, unable to say the words *he rarely wanted sex* aloud.

She decided to jump to the point everyone could get behind. She twined her fingers on the cool, polished bar top. "I discovered him cheating on me."

"Oh, honey," Sue crooned, "why didn't you lead with that?"

Callie studied Julia with unblinking eyes. "What do you mean, discovered?"

"I walked in on him, naked with my assistant."

"Wait. Your assistant? Nicole? The anorexic?" Sue demanded, a look of horror on her face.

"Don't tell me they were in the loft where you lived together." Callie grimaced, hand to her throat.

"Yes to the anorexic part." Nicole resembled a malnourished child, and Chris had preferred *her* to Julia. That had to mean something. "No to the loft apartment. I arrived early to a friend's house in the Hamptons where we planned to meet for a weekend party. I wanted to surprise him. They'd just showered. She was wearing my robe."

"Nooo," Sue moaned.

"I hightailed it back to his—our place." The apartment had been more his than theirs, since she'd only just moved in. "I loaded the car I'd already rented and took off for Honeyville."

Callie rubbed Julia's back. "Poor you. No wonder you split. Who would want to go into the office every day to face a disloyal she-devil and a lying, cheating, scum-bum boss?"

Julia sniffed. "He wasn't my boss."

Callie gave her a sober look. "Boss or no, never, ever date a man named Pig Face."

All three fell out laughing, Julia 'til her eyes leaked tears. When she finally stopped, a huge weight had lifted off her shoulders, no matter that she hadn't told them exactly *everything*.

"I can't imagine him going from you to her," Sue muttered, then brightened. "Maybe he'll fatten her up and dump her. Or vice versa."

"Chris losing his GQ edge? That would be sweet revenge," Julia said.

"Hmm," Callie said, a speculative gleam in her eye.

"Hmm what?" Sue asked.

"Just wondering how a certain local distraction might factor in Julia's romance drama."

"I've been weighing the pluses and minuses regarding that very thing," Sue said.

"What distraction? What are you two talking about?"

Her friends turned their stares in her direction. Callie elbowed Sue.

After aiming a brief scowl at Cal, Sue faced Julia. "Tell us about crossing paths with Jackson."

Julia rolled her eyes. "Nothing to tell. His aunt Lisa—my mom's best friend?—offered me the use of his cottage."

"Did she?" Callie's eyes twinkled. "And where is this cottage?"

Julia bit the inside of her cheek to staunch a nervous smile. "On his estate."

"As in beside his mansion in the foothills?" Sue

practically vibrated with excitement.

"Yep," Julia answered, going for casual. Just another day at the office. No big deal.

"Jealous," Sue whined. "I've always wanted a look at the place. I've only glimpsed pictures in magazines." Her eyes narrowed with suspicion. "You've been inside."

Why did she feel like she got caught with her hand in the cookie jar? "Just for a few minutes. Last night."

Callie was grinning. "Last night? Dinner by candlelight?"

"No. No candlelight. What?" she demanded when her friends burst out laughing. "He got takeout for us, no big deal."

Callie covered her mouth, but a snort escaped. "I can't decide if I'm excited for you or scared."

Sue nodded. "I hear you, Cal. No better way to get over an ex than get under a new *future* ex. But you know what they say about out of the frying pan and into the fire."

"It's not like that," Julia insisted as if she hadn't had the very same thought. She glanced around in case Jackson showed up again to overhear things at the worst possible moment. "I need a place to stay while I sort out my life. He has a furnished place sitting empty. It all just kind of happened."

Callie smirked. "I'd so love Chris to find out you're staying with *thee* Jackson Tate."

"Talk about sweet revenge," Sue agreed.

"No doubt about it—but that would require me communicating with him again."

Callie's countenance went from playful to deadly serious. "You've told us what happened. But you didn't say how you are or whether you're home to stay."

"To tell the truth, I'm holding my own, taking it one day at a time. I don't know what's next. A job I suppose. But I need to be home right now, and CPA positions in our little town are slim to none."

Sue's eyes went bright. "I've got the perfect solution. How about a temporary job working for me?"

Chapter Four

The sun slanted low in the sky when Julia stepped out her back door onto the shared deck. She craned her neck to assure herself no one from what she'd privately dubbed *the big house* lurked about, then unfurled her yoga mat.

Barefoot, she stepped onto the soft rubber and drew her hands to prayer position. Eyes closed, she inhaled. Caught the timeless scents of pine, dirt, and sweet herbs. Exhaling, she hinged forward and hung like a rag doll.

No more Chris. *Deep inhale*. No more New York. *Deep exhale*.

She flowed upward, finishing with her hands in prayer position. *Set your intention*.

Normally she went for something simple to meditate on during practice. Stress relief. World peace. But today, she had a more specific aim. Clarity.

She moved through her postures. Point one. For years she'd waited for an unmistakable, forever love to burst out of her when the right guy came along. Only he never did. So despite having misgivings, she'd gone for it with the eminently eligible Chris. *And look how well that turned out*.

She'd confessed most but not all to Callie and Sue. Not the crux of the matter.

Chris's parting accusation echoed in her mind like

a broken record. *You should ask* yourself *why, Julia. What does Nicole offer me you don't?*

And there it was.

She had clung to fairy tales, only to quit cold turkey and find out she couldn't even settle right. Her best efforts had left Chris wanting. She had the looks, he'd said, but lacked the soul.

When she asked what that even meant, he threw his hands in the air and said the fact she had to ask said it all.

She *must* be broken.

She flopped onto her back and settled into her final pose. Staring up at the dusk sky, she watched as stars winked into view. Out of nowhere, words to her favorite song, "Falling," drifted across her mind. *In my secret heart, you're all I see, I'm falling hard, baby, catch me.*

The end of life as she knew it had started with "Falling." Stupid Chris humming her stupid, all-time-favorite, wonderful song. The one that spoke to her heart, assuring her all her dreams would one day come true.

She'd imagined the man of her dreams singing "Falling" to her. Her soul mate. At least she hadn't been fool enough to consider Chris that. She remembered one morning, hopped up on too much coffee probably, she'd announced to Nicole she'd marry Ryan Moore in a heartbeat if he asked, based solely on the masterpiece of that one song. Big mistake.

She huffed out a laugh. The beautiful weave of music and lyrics that drilled down to her very core had come from Jackson. Could she pick 'em or what? As far as first crushes went, she got a gold star.

61

They'd finally talked about prom night, and she hadn't even died of mortification. Actually, the moment had been pretty nice. Those magnificent hazel eyes, holding her captive. His warm palm against hers. The depth of emotion in his softly spoken words. And the surprise realization she no longer harbored anger toward him.

Her eyes drifted closed, and memories washed over her.

Post prom, a crowd of high schoolers had surrounded the bonfire on Grady's family's property. Jackson, his date Sheila, Julia and Grady, and other couples she couldn't begin to name.

She wandered off, and Grady snuck up on her in the darkness, startling her. She might've stalked back to the fire then and there—but he hooked her, saying he had a secret about Jackson.

Even he'd known her weakness where Jackson was concerned.

He gestured her closer, hand cupped over his mouth to whisper. The moment she leaned in, he grabbed her, smashing his lips against hers.

She lurched back, but he held tight with both hands—one lodged in her hair, the other fisted in her dress. Bobby pins scattered, loosing clumps of hair, and the delicate fabric of her bodice tore to gape open.

Then Jackson appeared from nowhere, breathing hard, as if he'd come at a dead run. She'd never been so glad to see someone in her whole life.

"I've been looking everywhere for you two." Jackson's rasping breaths made his tone that much more accusing.

"What're you doing here?" Grady countered.

"We're heading to the car. It's time for Julia to go home. I'll come back for you and Sheila."

Ignoring Grady, Jackson studied her, hands splayed on his hips. He took one step toward her, and she reacted without thinking, skittering back.

"Whoa," he said softly, easing forward. When he reached her, his fingertips brushed her cheek. "You're crying."

She started to deny it, then noted the cold breeze on her wet skin.

He rounded on Grady. "What did you do? I warned you to back off her, Grady."

Bitterness hardened Grady's laugh. "And I told you to mind your damn business." He dug in his tuxedo pocket and pulled out a jangling set of keys. He hurled them at Jackson who caught them with one graceful swipe, mid-air. "You take her home."

Grady set off at a jog toward the glow of the bonfire. He hadn't gone five feet before jerking around to face them. "When I lost that bet, I drew the shit end of the stick. That's the last time you best me, Tate." With that, he pivoted on his heel and disappeared into the trees.

Julia stood in stunned speechlessness, first because of Grady's ugliness.

Then because what she'd longed for had finally come true. Alone with Jackson, under the stars. But not like this. Not with tears staining her cheeks, a ruined dress, and hair sticking out in all directions. Reality had nothing on her fantasy.

"You okay?" Jackson asked in a voice that caused gooseflesh to spread over her arms.

"Yes." Lie of the century. Shivers wracked her

body. Whether from the chill night air or utter humiliation, she couldn't say.

Without a word, Jackson stripped off his suit jacket. He draped it over her shoulders, then pulled the lapels together. The heat from his body enveloped her, warming her to her curling toes.

"Julia?" He tugged on the lapels.

She resisted looking him in the eye and instead fixed her gaze on the front of his white shirt where it parted at the hollow of his neck.

"Julia?" he prodded again, and that soft tone had her tilting her head back to gaze up at him.

"I'm sorry, Jackson. I didn't mean for him to follow me," she choked. "And now my hair's a mess, and my dress..." She covered her face with her hands as she tried to swallow the immense lump in her throat.

"Ah, no, darlin', don't cry." He pulled her into his arms.

Pressing her cheek into his solid chest and resting her hands on his broad shoulders felt like the most natural thing in the world. Being held by him was everything she ever dreamt it would be and more. She snuggled closer.

"Okay, now?" he asked all too soon.

She nodded against him, and when his arms dropped from around her, she took a small step back, though she didn't really want to.

In the moonlight, his teeth flashed white. Then his hands were smoothing and tucking the loose strands of her hair. "A little mussed, but you still look really pretty, Julia."

A swarm of butterflies erupted in her belly. Hugging his compliment to her chest, she fought the urge to giggle. "You don't have to say that, Jackson."

He crooked a warm finger under her chin. "Hey," he whispered. "It's true."

They stared at each other, and the seconds stretched into the most deliciously intense moment of Julia's young life. She was afraid to move, afraid to breathe. He was so close. A kiss away.

A mad idea took hold of her. She could lean in and plant her lips on his. Now. This moment would never come again. Her heart pounded in her chest. Rushing blood thundered in her ears. She rocked forward.

Then Jackson shook his head as if to clear it and shifted to stand beside her, shattering the moment.

She gulped in air as spots danced before her eyes. She had been holding her breath? Next she'd make an even bigger fool of herself and faint, and all for nothing. She'd missed her chance.

"You okay? You look a little wobbly."

"Fine."

"That's my girl. Come on. I'll take you home." He put a hand on the small of her back and led her toward the road.

Leaves crunched underfoot as they tromped through the woods. The ground cover thinned nearer the road where glaring streetlights lit up a line of cars. Julia dreaded stepping into that light.

Jackson must have shared her reluctance, because his steps slowed. "Did Grady...did he hurt you?"

"No."

"I worried when I didn't see you for a while. I wish I'd come sooner. Heck. I wish I'd been wrong."

She stopped at the edge of the woods where the last of the shadows hid her. "You knew Grady would do something like this, but you fixed me up with him?"

He stood ahead of her, and his face looked stark in the artificial light. He shoved a hand through his shiny hair. "Of course not, Julia. Grady's normally a great guy. It's just when he drinks, he can act up. When I realized he brought a flask to the bonfire, I tried to keep an eye on you, but you disappeared."

"You sure kept a sharp eye on someone all right," she muttered. She shouldn't have said that, but now that she was out of his arms, something niggled at the back of her mind. Something Grady had said as he stormed off?

"What's that supposed to mean?"

"It seemed like one person had your undivided attention. Sheila."

Jackson laughed under his breath. "That's funny."

"What's funny about it?" she snapped.

"Sheila said the same thing about you."

She had? About her?

"Boy, is she gonna be mad when Grady tells her I'm taking you home." He grabbed her hand and helped her off the curb, ready or not.

Her heart plummeted. She hated ruining Jackson's senior prom, and by him having to take her home, she had done just that. "I'm sorry. You shouldn't have to—" It hit her. What Grady had said.

"It's okay." He opened her door. "She'll get over it."

Julia could barely hear him through the steam coming out of her ears. She waited in mounting anger while Jackson rounded the car and slid into the driver's seat. He started the car. Eased it out of its parking space.

"Jackson?" she said between clenched teeth.

"Yeah?"

"How was it Grady decided to ask me to prom?"

He hesitated, casting a furtive glance in her direction. "What do you mean? I already told you. He saw you at—"

Her heart squeezed like an elephant had a foot pressed to her chest. Worse, a huge lump in her throat made it painful to speak and garbled her voice so Jackson couldn't possibly mistake her misery. Still she wrenched the words out. "What happened? Did your parents insist you ask me? But that would've ruined your night with Sheila. So you came up with an alternate plan. Have someone else take me."

A muscle ticked in Jackson's jaw, and his hands gripped the wheel of Grady's fancy sports car so tight his knuckles went white. He kept his eyes glued to the road.

It all made perfect, horrible sense. Why Jackson's buddy, whom she'd never met, had developed a sudden interest in her. "Grady said he'd lost a bet. What was it? Rock, paper, scissors? No, you'd have a sports competition. Something that would give you the edge. Something you couldn't lose." She laughed bitterly. "You wound up stuck with me anyway."

Her seventeen-year-old self had been crushed. Her adult self finally understood Jackson not inviting her to the prom didn't make him the devil. Not even close. So why did the stars now look more like blurry fireflies in the sky?

The sound of her own soft laugh surprised her and loosened the worst of the knots choking off her heart. Tears leaked down her cheeks, and she let them fall.

Releasing the death grip she'd held on the past felt good, right—almost like grabbing onto freedom that had been there all along.

****

Jackson's tires squealed, hugging the curving road, as he pressed the accelerator. Another night he'd show up late at Julia's door. Not that he'd specified a time, and not that she made any promises about being there.

But he'd imagined heading over for a casual inspection of the cottage, late afternoon. She'd offer him a coffee, they'd talk as the sun slanted over the hills and maybe share dinner.

Instead he'd found himself backtracking into town to help Mr. Toller, Grady's dad, change two flat tires. Somehow he'd picked up enough roofer's nails to wind up riding on two rims on a little-traveled country road. With Grady in Asheville this afternoon on business, that left Jackson, or a tow truck, which would have stranded Mr. Toller for hours, according to Grady. So here he was, late again, and dirty to boot.

Once in his garage, he slammed his truck into park and hustled into the house. Since the cottage driveway came after his, and his house obstructed the view of the smaller dwelling, he had no idea whether or not a car filled the parking space. No idea if any lights burned inside. No indication one way or the other if Julia was home and, hopefully, expecting him.

He took the stairs two at a time, then jogged down the hallway to his bedroom, pulling off his clothes and kicking out of his shoes as he went in preparation for taking the fastest shower in human history.

She'd clearly tried to dissuade him from his so-called aim of checking out her household supplies.

With a self-derisive snort, he stepped into the steaming shower and soaped up. What exactly *had* compelled him to press seeing her? Because it wasn't thoughts of a coffee maker or paper towel holder keeping him revved all day.

He closed his eyes and let the water sluice over him. Since the moment he laid eyes on her in his cottage, he'd craved her, seeking out any excuse to be in her presence. Was it nostalgia over reconnecting with an old friend? Or the relief of finally unloading his years-old apology? *Isn't it that she always smells so damn good and her lower lip keeps demanding to be sucked?*

"Hell." He should not be thinking about her lips.

He toweled off and hurriedly dressed in jeans and a casual button down, reminding himself Julia and he were friends, period. She'd just ended things with one loser—and the Lord knew the guy was always at fault when a relationship went sour. The last thing she needed was Jackson screwing up her world more.

Besides, Julia didn't fit his easy-breezy, no-promises dating requirements.

He trotted down the stairs, jerking to a halt in the living room. He stared out the windows at the Blue Ridge Mountains rising up in the distance. Their majestic beauty at dusk always filled him with awe. Tonight, he felt something different. More like a yearning so fierce his insides ached. For what?

Something more came the quiet but sure answer.

He closed his eyes, covered his lower face with his hands, and called up a vision of his late wife to remind him what happened when he afforded himself the luxury of thinking he could have it all. *Help me,*

Hannah. Help me stick to the plan.

But he couldn't hold on to her image. Instead, he saw a smiling Julia outside Callie's shop, awash in sunlight.

With a groan of equal parts self-derision and frustration, he headed out and crossed the deck. No light emanated from the cottage, yet the back door stood wide open and—his breath froze in his lungs. Julia lay flat on her back on the wooden slats, not moving.

He charged toward her, sliding the last few inches on his knees. "Julia, are you all—"

She vaulted up to a sitting position, hair springing forward, hand pressed over her heart.

He jerked back, avoiding having his skull cracked by hers by a split second.

"Oh-my-God-don't-sneak-up-on-me-like-that," she rapid-fire gasped.

Jackson blinked once, then threw his head back and roared with laughter.

Her palm thumped into his chest, and a moment later he sprawled, spread-eagle, thankfully landing on his solid ass. He grinned at her. "What'd you do that for?"

She scrambled to her feet. "Someone was having a little too much fun at my expense."

"C'mon, darlin,' don't begrudge a man a good laugh." He held up his hand in a silent request for help.

After a brief hesitation, she wrapped her warm palm around his and tugged him upward.

He liked where he ended up—toe to toe with her. His gaze traveled down her body outfitted in a sleeveless tank, black exercise capris, and no shoes.

"Why were you laid out on the deck? You scared the hell out of me, right before nearly braining me."

Her mass of gold and dark-blonde hair, half in and half out of a ponytail, stuck out at a crazy angle. He tucked a loose clump of the silky stuff behind one ear, his fingers unable to resist lingering at her jaw-line.

She shivered and crossed her arms over her chest as a grudging grin tugged at the corners of her mouth.

Something inside him shifted and settled, like a puzzle piece slipping into place.

"For your information, I was practicing yoga."

He chuckled and pointed to what he could now see was an exercise mat styled with a lotus flower. "If that's yoga, I've been sadly misinformed. I pictured someone balancing on one foot, not napping."

Laughter bubbled out of her. "That was Shavasana."

He opened his hands in a throw-me-a-bone gesture.

"Dead man's pose."

"I…see?"

"There was a lot more vigorous activity going on before you got here, Jacks."

He rocked back on his heels. "Prove it."

She narrowed her eyes at him, stepped onto her mat, bent forward, and, before he could say ho-lee crap, swung her legs straight up in the air while balancing on the crown of her head.

Jackson gave a slow clap as his gaze roamed, starting with her nicely arched feet, skimming over slim ankles, shapely legs, and an enticingly rounded ass. Her tank was loose enough the bottom half tumbled toward the earth, providing him an intriguing glimpse of flat belly.

And then she was back on her feet, smoothing her top into place and rolling up her mat.

"That explains the hair," he said, his voice gruff. He wanted to grab a fistful of that wild mane and drag her in for a close-up body check. And what the hell was wrong with him? It wasn't like he was hurting for female companionship. Although, come to think of it, he hadn't accepted any recent invitations.

She snorted and disappeared through the open door. A moment later she stuck her head out. "I was going to uncork some wine to celebrate. You want to join me? Unless…maybe you have to get back to Chase."

"Chase is with his aunt."

"Great." She disappeared inside again.

She'd adjusted her ponytail.

He grinned and crossed the threshold.

****

"What are we celebrating?" Jackson's rich velvet voice acted like a proverbial caress over Julia's heightened senses. She should not have invited him in after taking that trip down memory lane.

She flipped on the counter lights and continued to the bedroom. She slipped on a long-sleeved yoga jacket, zipping it to her chin. The clinging clothing left little to the imagination, but at least it covered her neck to shin.

She eyed herself in the dresser mirror, removing the ponytail holder, which she'd already adjusted once thanks to Jackson's observation, and ruffled her hair. She shouldn't concern herself with how he thought she looked. She'd have to work on that.

Seeing him in the kitchen, hip resting against the

sink, gave her a little jolt. Why'd he always have to look so mouthwateringly good? "Hi."

"Hiya." He pulled two wine glasses from a kitchen cabinet. "What are we celebrating?"

"I got a job today. A temporary one anyway. I see you found the wine."

A corner of his mouth crooked upward, but he kept his eyes on his task of pouring. He handed her a glass. "Since it was the only wine here, not to mention next to the only thing in the fridge, I assumed this was what you wanted uncorked." He winked at her. "It was a screw top, by the way."

"Only the finest for you," she said, grinning.

"Congratulations, Jules." He clinked his glass to hers, and they both sipped.

Jackson's hazel eyes locked on hers over the rim of his glass, and her pulse spiked so sharply she thanked her lucky stars she didn't choke.

His eyes narrowed, and he set his glass on the counter with a decisive clink. "What's wrong?"

"Wrong? I just told you, I got a job—"

"I know, and I want to hear about it. But first, explain the tears."

Her free hand flew to her cheek. Those brief tears had dried to salty tracks by now. He truly did not miss a darned thing. Maybe she ought to have taken more time in front of the mirror.

Jackson gripped her shoulders with gentle, warm fingers. He stared down at her, and an echo of that night so long ago rippled through her. Jackson and her, all alone, standing toe to toe.

A decadent idea took hold of her.

"Jules?"

She could fudge, tell him she'd been crying about losing Chris, or tell him to mind his business. But, damn, she'd waited a long time for a redo. She hadn't even realized she'd been waiting. She inched closer 'til her bare toes touched the edges of his canvas shoes. His eyes widened slightly, but he did not retreat.

"If you must know…" She reached both hands to smooth over the neckline of his snug henley, and her legs went a little wobbly. Was she really doing this? "I was thinking about that night."

"That night?" He sounded dazed and breathless, exactly like she felt. "You mean—prom, the bonfire, and all that?"

She bit her lower lip to halt the nervous smile threatening to emerge and nodded. "Today it seemed like you thought I was upset with you about Grady manhandling me. But that was never it." Under her palms his chest felt as solid as granite.

"I'm listening." He swallowed audibly.

She licked her lips and watched his gaze track to her mouth.

"All this time, I thought that stupid bet you used to pawn me off on your friend was so awful. But tonight it finally dawned on me. You not wanting to take me to prom really should have been okay. You didn't owe me a date just because I tutored you." Her voice was as soft as a whisper now because she could barely push air through her lungs.

"That's, uh…not exactly…" His words drifted off, like he'd lost his train of thought. Maybe because she was sliding her palms down the wall of his chest.

Blame it on the night. Blame it on this man. Blame it on unfinished business. Blame it on Chris and the awful things he'd said.

"Do you remember that moment after Grady left? Before we started for the car?"

Jackson stared at her lips. He nodded, then shook his head.

"We were all alone, under the stars, and I'd liked you for so long. And you gave me your coat."

"I gave you…" He drew a shaky breath. Somehow his hands had found their way to her hips. He gave a gentle squeeze, then snorted softly. "Julia? I have no idea what you're talking about."

"Shut up, Jackson," she said with a husky laugh. And kissed him.

Chapter Five

Desire, swift and hot, scorched Jackson's senses before her mouth ever brushed his. Her lips, every bit as soft as his imagination had conjured, slanted over his, first haltingly, as if she took cautious sips, then in an increasing demand for more. Her elusive scent floated in and out of reach, at once maddening and intoxicating. Tiny tremors vibrated through her, making his skin prickle with awareness, though their bodies barely touched. He couldn't take it all in. Sweet Julia Hudson blew away every notion of erotic woman he'd ever had.

Needing more of her against more of him, he wrapped one arm around her waist, hauling her closer. He pressed forward, sandwiching her between his body and the wall.

Time to take control. He grazed her jaw with the knuckles of his free hand, urging her head back, deepening the kiss.

Her lips parted on a soft mew of pleasure, and his tongue slipped into her wet heat. She tasted like sweet wine and heaven.

Something between a growl and a groan sounded low in his throat as carnal hunger gnawed at his insides.

As if in response, Julia twined her arms around his neck and wove her fingers through his hair. Her nails scored his nape and scalp like a kneading kitten, and his entire body went hard.

He tore his mouth from hers to gasp. "Julia, sweetheart, what are you doing to me?" Then he was feasting on her mouth again.

Or vice versa.

She fisted one hand in his hair and tugged, nipping his lower lip. Hooking one sinewy leg around his thigh to anchor herself, she pulled herself up and into him. Her body was warm, soft, and inviting as hell.

Too much clothing separated them. He wanted to feel her skin beneath his fingers. He reached for the hem of her jacket. In the same instant, she broke off their kiss and slithered out of his arms.

He spun around, reaching for her. "Huh? Wh—"

"Wow. As do-overs go, that was…wow."

Jackson rubbed a hand over his face and shook his head. He was hard as a rock, horny as hell, and she was making. No. Sense. "Do-over?"

While he stared at her, his brain ground to mush, she scooped up her wine and floated out of the kitchen.

"Hold up. You can't just kiss me like that and…" He didn't know how to finish his sentence. Frustration, confusion, and hurt male pride warred within him. If he didn't know better, he'd think she was giving him the brush off. He followed her to the living room.

Only the pendulum lights over the counter and sink burned in the cottage, leaving the rest of the place in shadows. Naturally, she made her way there.

He crossed his arms over his chest. "You want to tell me what's going on here? I mean, I feel kind of cheap." He only half kidded.

"You do?" A small giggle escaped her, and she covered her mouth with her free hand. "Sorry. I laugh when I'm nervous sometimes."

He inched closer to take in her expression. Dazed eyes told him their kiss had blown her away as much as it had him. It helped soothe his wounded ego, but more importantly, it begged the question—why stop now?

"There's nothing to be nervous about, Jules." He reached to tuck a wayward strand of hair behind her ear, and she skittered backward 'til her rump contacted the arm of the recliner.

He jammed a hand through his hair and dropped onto the couch. "I'm not planning to attack you."

She ducked her head. "I know. I didn't want you thinking I'd pounce again."

He hooted with laughter. "Pounce. I suppose you did kiss me first."

She set her wine on a side table and covered her face with both hands. "I did, didn't I? I don't know what came over me." She dropped her hands and sent him a little smile. "Or maybe I do."

She started to pace. "Dad always says the best way to deal with an uncomfortable situation is straight-on." She stopped marching when she stood across from him. "I guess our conversation this morning stirred up a lot of memories, had me tapping into the girl I used to be. One minute I'm on my mat, and the next I'm back in time, standing with you in the moonlight, wanting to kiss you so bad it hurts. In my mind, you understand?"

"Oh, I understand." She'd painted an all-too-vivid picture. If she was trying to kill the mood, it was not working.

"I should probably apologize."

Adding insult to injury now? He wasn't some helpless man, and if he hadn't wanted the kiss to happen, it wouldn't have. He held up a hand, palm out. "No, you should not."

She gave him a grateful smile. "That's sweet, Jacks. I just…I don't want you worrying I'm still carrying a torch."

"Trust me. I don't. No one carrying a torch disappears on purpose for thirteen years." He cocked his head to study her. "Then again, that was quite a kiss." He leaned forward, caught her hand in his. Lightly tugged.

"It was." She slipped her hand from his grasp and took a step backward. "And it won't happen again, promise." She crossed her heart with a finger.

He'd just had the breath knocked out of him by the most rocking kiss of his adult life, with the most unlikely of women, and she thought he wanted her promise to never let it happen again? He opened his mouth to argue, then closed it with a snap. He rubbed his temple. What was he thinking? This was for the best.

Julia hadn't been the only one who'd wanted a taste. Now they'd given themselves one. A delicious, mouthwatering taste. But to let anything further develop between them was impossible. He didn't do relationships, with good reason, and Julia deserved nothing less. Even if he did want to drag her into his arms to take up where they'd left off.

He aimed his pointer finger at her. "Okay. I'm gonna hold you to that." He unfolded himself from the couch.

"You're leaving?"

By her tone, she wanted him to believe she didn't care one way or another, but she hadn't quite masked her disappointment. Good. She'd knocked him off his game. Fair was fair.

"Just grabbing my wine." And some much-needed distance. "Tell me about this job."

She followed him toward the kitchen and slid a hip onto one of the counter stools. He tried and failed not to notice her cheeks, still flushed from their heated kiss.

"It turns out Our Lady of the Blue Ridge's bookkeeper goes out next week on maternity, and Sue hasn't found a temp to take her place."

"Enter CPA Julia Hudson."

She nodded. "It's a perfect situation. It gives me a modicum of income while I decide on something more permanent."

"Sounds like a win-win. How's it going to be, revisiting your old stomping grounds?"

She laughed. "There was nothing there to stomp when Callie, Sue, and I attended. The school's grown, I understand. Sue says it's on the shy side of normal."

"The expansion took place several years back." Actually, he'd helped fund it. "It's what swayed me to send Chase to Our Lady of the Blue. I did my research and found Our Lady head and shoulders above the other local schools, scholastically speaking. But I also wanted him to have a more…" He shrugged.

She sipped her wine. "You wanted him to have a regular childhood, which includes sports programs, dances, etc. I get it. Especially considering your background."

Whoa. Which background item, specifically? The fact he came from no money, or the equally true fact that he and his dad had no relationship to speak of? "Not sure how my *background* plays into it."

If she caught the bite in his tone, she gave no indication. She swirled the last bit of wine in her glass. "You were a big sports guy with quite the following. Everybody wanted to know Jackson Tate."

He laughed aloud—at himself. He'd read her all wrong. "Everybody, including you, Julia?"

One corner of her mouth hitched up.

God, he wanted to kiss her again.

"I think we already established I was maybe your biggest fan."

He couldn't drag his gaze from her mouth.

"You're staring."

"Oops."

She wagged a finger at him.

He flashed her one of his supposed lethal smiles. "I have an idea. How about you kiss me one more time, and I'll—"

She got up in the middle of him talking and started for the back door. She swung the door open wide. "I have an early morning tomorrow. I'm returning my rental car before grabbing a ride with Sue to the school."

He laughed softly. "In other words, good night, Jackson?"

She smiled sweetly. "Good night, Jackson."

He jammed his hands in his pockets and strolled past her with a murmured, "Night, neighbor."

Outside, crisp evening air enveloped him. The sun had vanished, leaving behind a clear sky sparkling with a plethora of stars. The scents of eucalyptus and pine and jasmine mingled on the breeze. A night made for lovers.

He took his time crossing the deck. He could

almost feel Julia's eyes watching him, but that was probably wishful thinking.

Wishful thinking is you wanting her to call you back and drag you into her bed.

Truer words. So much for one kiss satisfying his appetite for her. He'd have to keep his distance until he got his inappropriate craving for her under control.

Which reminded him. He still hadn't checked out the cottage for things she might need. One more visit, he told himself, then he'd do the stand-up thing for both of them.

****

"It's a far cry from what you're used to in New York," Sue said, pointing Julia to a small but bright office situated within the administrative wing of Our Lady.

"Are you kidding? This is double the space I'm used to." Julia passed through the open doorway to find all the usual tools—nondescript desk, humming computer beneath said desk, standard monitor and keyboard, and a plethora of supplies. "I'll take it," she said with a sunny smile. "I like the paint."

Buttercup yellow covered the concrete block walls, which appeared all the sunnier thanks to light pouring in from a large window centered in one wall.

"Jules, I can't tell you how thrilled I am. You're an answer to prayers."

"Likewise."

"And here's Jane. Jane, meet Julia, the angel who's agreed to fill in while you're on maternity."

Jane's wide smile lit up her whole face. "Julia, nice to meet you. I was afraid Sue wouldn't find anyone, and me here about to pop."

Julia eyed her massive belly. Was she carrying triplets in there?

"I'll leave you to it. See you lunchtime, Jules?"

****

The morning flew by with Jane giving Julia a basic rundown of the school's tuition billing software, plus a list of vendors and utility companies she'd be responsible for paying. All in all, she felt she could hold down the fort.

Late morning, Sue stuck her head in the door. "I get one emergency handled, and doesn't another one rear its head."

Jane leaned back in her chair and rubbed her belly. "If it makes you feel any better, Julia's a natural."

"It does." Sue strode in and propped her hip on the desk.

"What's your emergency?" Julia asked.

"My summer enrichment math class is supposed to start in half an hour. Guess who just called to say she got rear-ended and is in the hospital getting checked for whiplash?"

"Your summer enrichment math teacher?" Julia guessed.

"And this isn't public school. I don't have a cache of substitute teachers I can call. By the time I round up a sub, it'll be too late. So unfair to the kids who sacrificed a large chunk of their summer break for the betterment of their young minds."

Jane gawked at Sue, then turned to Julia. "Is she serious right now? We are talking about math, aren't we? Can you say class dismissed?"

Sue shook her head. " 'Fraid not, sister. A few of these kids need these lessons to get off on the right foot come fall, Miss Poo-Pooer. Guess they'll have to make do with me."

"But you're lousy in math," Julia blurted, then covered her mouth with both hands. "Is that supposed to be a secret?"

Sue snorted. "You have a better idea?"

"I could maybe fill in this once if you have the curriculum. I did work at the math lab tutoring students all through my undergrad."

Sue straightened practically before Julia finished speaking. "You don't mind, do you, Jane?" Not waiting for an answer, she bolted for the door. "As for the curriculum, Jules. Kerri has her lesson plans all laid out for the entire course. Follow me."

Julia did, though the fact she'd just been had wasn't lost on her.

Twenty minutes later, Julia stood at the classroom door, greeting kids as they trailed into the room and took their seats. She'd skimmed the roster. One name in particular stood out. Chase Tate. And here he came now in his T-shirt, jeans, and high-top sneakers, whisking his hair out of his eyes in a move reminiscent of his dad.

His dad. *Whoa.* Last night. That kiss *she'd* initiated. She should not be thinking about that right now. Or ever again.

Fat chance.

Pushing the memory from her mind, she gave Chase a warm smile. "Good morning, Chase Tate."

His eyes lit with instant recognition. "Miss Julia? *Sweet.*" A heartbeat later, his expression darkened. "Um, are you our new teacher?" He looked less than thrilled at the prospect.

She didn't know whether to laugh or take offense. "No, just subbing today."

Chase nodded, still looking dour.

Several kids squeezed past him.

"Are you worried about Miss Jenkins?" Julia asked. "She had a little fender bender. Nothing serious."

He studied the tips of his sneakers. "Miss Jenkins? No. It's my dad…"

Julia glanced at the clock on the wall. Class was about to begin. "Your dad?" she prompted in a soft voice.

"Could you not mention this class to him? About you seeing me, I mean? Er…I'm kind of hoping to surprise him."

Chase wanted to surprise his dad with his class? Did that mean Jackson didn't know Chase was enrolled?

"Okay." She drew out the word. "I don't have to say anything about seeing you today." In truth she had no idea when she'd see Jackson next.

"Great." The smile he aimed at her glowed with palpable relief. He strutted to his seat, his boyhood confidence back in full measure, and threw over his shoulder, "You're the best, Miss Julia."

He sprawled in a desk in the front row and slid a glance at a pretty girl occupying the seat beside his.

She notched her chin up while rolling her eyes. "Suck up."

He flashed the girl a smile so similar to his dad's Julia could swear Jackson had cloned himself.

The prim little girl blushed and smiled with evident pleasure as she set about unnecessarily straightening her notebook and pencil on her desk.

The clock struck top of the hour. Julia strode to the whiteboard in the front of the room. "Good morning, everyone. I'm Miss Hudson, filling in for Miss Jenkins today. How about we go over what you've been studying up to now, and go from there?"

****

Julia had scarfed an apple on her way out the door at six a.m. Now, well past her lunchtime, she navigated the empty halls toward Sue's office, mouth watering with visions of a charbroiled cheeseburger dancing in her head.

"Thank God you're here," she told Sue when she spotted her behind her desk.

Sue's chocolate brown eyes went round with dread. "Why? What happened now?"

Julia pointed into her open mouth. "Feed me."

Sue snorted and rolled back her chair to rise. "What do you feel like? Lunch is on Our Lady for being my employee of the day."

"I accept. Does Beau's Barbecue still serve up the best burger in town?"

"Is the Pope Catholic?"

Julia slanted a look at her friend and pushed open the glass door leading to the parking lot. "Is that an appropriate joke for a Catholic school principal to make?"

"I thought it was better than the one about the bear in the woods."

Sue drove since Julia had no vehicle. Following lunch, she'd also volunteered to shuttle Julia back to her cottage. No doubt catching a glimpse of Jackson's estate sweetened the deal for her.

Julia's parents planned to deliver their car tonight along with dinner. She had offered to grab the car herself after work today, but they wouldn't hear of it. Julia understood. She smiled to herself as Sue parallel parked on Main Street, three blocks from the restaurant. Everyone wanted a peek at Jackson's mountain hideaway.

Hunger hastened their steps. "Sorry I had to starve you, but thanks again for covering."

"I'm kind of glad it's past the lunch rush hour. I want to ask you about something, and I'd rather talk in privacy."

"Is this about Jackson? Did you see him again last night?"

Julia stopped in her tracks. "No. I… It's not about him. Why would you think that?" She sounded guilty to her own ears. She hadn't admitted to planting one on Jackson. Why bother? It was a one-time deal. Hardly worth mentioning.

Sue strode on, tossing over her shoulder, "For one thing, you're practically living with him. For another, he is Jackson Tate."

"Living with him?" Julia squeaked, rushing to catch up. "I'm renting his empty cottage." So to speak.

Sue arched a brow. "Uh-huh. The one on his private property, adjacent to his residence."

They reached the entrance to Beau's. The barbecue restaurant had been around as long as Julia could remember. Even standing outside, she caught the mingled scents of smoked meat, fries, and garlic bread. Her mouth watered in greedy anticipation.

She grasped the sun-warmed brass handle, pulled open the oversized weathered door, and made a stab at changing the subject. "Has Beau had the place updated?"

Sue's warm brown eyes twinkled knowingly. "Nope."

Julia ignored the twinkle. "Good."

In contrast to the sunny day, the restaurant's interior felt like a cave. Wood panels covered the walls, and tiny fogged windows up near the ceiling let in meager light. Dark vinyl booths, glossy scarred high tops, and one cherrywood bar ran the length of the place. A faint scent of barbecue smoke permeated the air.

"Sit wherever you like," a voice called from a swinging kitchen door.

A few patrons sat at the bar, eating and watching sports on wall-mounted screens, and more still occupied tables in the rear of the establishment. In unspoken agreement Sue and Julia slid into a booth toward the front.

Barb, a career waitress who also happened to be the proprietress and Beau's better half, approached.

"Hi, Barb. How's business?" Sue asked.

"Can't complain." She pulled an order pad and pen from her apron pocket. "Hey there, Julia. An admirer told me you were back in town."

A rush of heat climbed up her neck. An image of Jackson, eyes heavy-lidded with passion, mouth hot on hers, sprang to mind. A nervous giggle escaped her despite her best effort to staunch it. She refused to look at Sue. "Not sure who that could be."

"See for yourself." Barb gestured toward the back of the restaurant.

Heavy footsteps echoed on the wood-planked floor

behind her. Her pulse went wild. Jackson? Here?

Across from her, Sue smiled at the approaching man. "Hi, Grady."

Disappointment and mortification collided inside her. *Delusional idiot.* Why on earth had she imagined Jackson would talk about her? Just because she jumped his bones last night, then tossed and turned reliving the memory, didn't mean he'd given it, or her, a second thought.

"Hi, Sue." Grady slid in beside Julia.

His liberally applied cologne filled the space, reminding her of high school when the boys doused themselves in it. "Hey there."

Grady flashed a braces-perfect smile. "This must be my lucky day. I was just telling Barb how I ran into you at Jackson's. Now here you are."

"In the flesh," she quipped, composure regained.

"Late lunch?" he asked.

Sue piped up. "It's my fault. Julia not only started her temporary bookkeeper position at Our Lady of the Blue Ridge today, but she also subbed for my math teacher."

He put his arm over the back of the bench seat and angled his body toward Julia. "A regular lifesaver. What in the world would Honeyville do without you?"

Julia chuckled. "It's getting deep in here."

Grady's blue eyes crinkled at the corners. "I wanted to give you a call to see about grabbing lunch or a coffee. I tried to get your number out of Jacks, but he said something about needing to ask your permission first." He rolled his eyes.

"I think that's nice," Sue said. "It's the gentlemanly thing to do."

Grady burst out laughing. "Right, Jacks the gentleman, when he's not—"

Barb's voice cut him off. "Are you going to let these ladies order?"

Julia blinked. If she hadn't read it wrong, Barb had shut him up. What exactly had she kept him from saying? Surely nothing derogatory about Jackson. Grady and Jackson were best friends, always had been.

They ordered two ice teas, two cheeseburgers with the works, and a basket of fries to split.

"She's a hoot," Grady said after Barb walked out of earshot. "Where was I?"

"About to bad-mouth Jackson?" Sue asked dryly.

"Hell naw. Jackson's the best. Best friend, best dad, best son." He laughed under his breath. "Just ask my dad."

"That's nice that your dad and Jackson are close," Julia said, silently adding *especially since Jackson's relationship with his own father is nonexistent.* Grady would be privy to the information, but it wasn't something for group discussion, no matter who knew or didn't know about Jackson's past.

"I'm just saying Jacks is more of a *ladies'* man than a gentleman, if you know what I mean?" Grady closed one eye and pointed a finger at Sue. "Common knowledge around here, ever since Hannah—and it'd be a good thing to keep your friend abreast of the facts."

Julia stared across the table at Sue.

Sue appeared engrossed in digging something out of her purse. "I think my cell phone's ringing."

Julia didn't hear a thing.

Grady tapped a quick staccato on the table. "Time

for me to get back to work. I'll leave you ladies to your lunch." He slanted a look at Julia and pulled his lower lip.

She laughed, shaking her head. "Why don't you give me your number?"

He grinned like a kid and reached in the back pocket of his khakis to pull out a slim leather wallet. He extracted an embossed business card and held it toward her between two fingers. "Office and cell, available twenty-four seven. And I make house-calls." He waggled his brows.

"Thanks, doc," Julia said, playing along, though she had no intention of actually calling the man. She didn't have anything against him, per se. But they'd never been close friends, and she wasn't interested in starting anything romantically. *With anyone but Jackson.*

Would that irritating inner voice shut up, already?

She and Sue exchanged looks when Grady exited the building—the sort only friends who've known each other forever can share.

"Poor guy. He's always had a thing for you, hasn't he?"

Julia looked down at the card she still held in her hand proclaiming Grady Executive VP at Toller Insurance. She dropped it in a zippered pocket in her purse. "Not at all. Granted, he took me to his prom our senior year, but that was more a pity date he got suckered into by Jackson. Other than that, our interaction was nonexistent." Except for him sneaking up on her at her parents' mailbox and scaring the crap out of her before offering her a heartfelt apology.

"There you go again, acting like any guy in town

wouldn't have jumped at the chance to go out with you. My older brothers all had mad crushes on you."

She laughed. "Come on. They all drooled over Callie, and you know it."

Sue rolled her eyes. "Callie *and* you. I don't know why I bother. You won't believe me if I tell you a thousand times. I suppose Grady's not hitting on you?"

"I'm not saying that. For whatever reason, he's interested."

Sue arched her brows. "Why not go out with him, Jules? He's cute. Rich. Clearly likes you."

Exactly what everyone said about Chris. "Why don't you go out with him?" she countered.

"Number one, he didn't ask me." Sue flashed a mischievous grin. "Now if Jackson asked…"

Julia blinked and told herself she didn't care if one of her best friends had her sights set on Jackson.

Sue burst out laughing. "You so do not have a poker face. I'm kidding, by the way. I know Jackson's off-limits."

Barb arrived with their burgers before she could tell Sue how ridiculous she sounded. She settled for aiming a glare in her direction.

As soon as Barb walked away, Sue said, "You wanted to talk to me about something?" She popped a ketchup-covered fry in her mouth.

Julia's mock anger vanished. "I do." She lowered her voice and leaned in close. "It's about Jackson's son, Chase. He's taking the summer math enhancement class."

Sue nodded and gestured with another fry for Julia to continue.

"Don't kids' parents have to sign off on

enrollment?"

"Sure do."

Julia picked up her burger and took a giant bite. She moaned, chewing, and considered how to phrase her question without betraying Chase's confidence.

"Hello? What about it?"

She held up a finger and finished chewing. "Chase is a great kid. Very motivated to succeed and smart, though clearly math is not his strong suit. I think I could help him there, by the way. I recognize his learning style. It's the same as his dad's." She grinned. "There's a girl in class who I think might be his girlfriend. Do you know Alana King?"

Sue arched her brows. Her face expression screamed *out with it.*

"Okay," she said with a grimace. "Chase might have asked me not to tell his dad he was taking the class in maybe the most cryptic way possible."

"Cryptic how?"

"He asked me not to mention seeing him or anything to do with the math class, claiming he wanted to surprise his dad."

Sue fell back against the bench. "Huh."

Julia dabbed her mouth with a napkin. "I guess I can understand wanting to surprise his dad by acing his math course, but wouldn't Jackson already know Chase's curriculum?"

"Damn straight."

"I thought as much. But if you saw his eyes. One minute he was grinning, saying something about seeing me at home later and—" She broke off to fix Sue with a stern look.

Her friend's eyes sparkled with devilry as they had

from the moment the word *home* left Julia's lips.

"This is serious."

Sue nodded. Crossed her heart with another fry.

"What are we going to do? We can't rat him out."

Sue frowned. "I'm not sure I'll be able to avoid it, in good conscience. I tell you what, I'll check the paperwork first. As I recall, Chase signed up for two summer classes. The math enhancement class you subbed in today and an extreme-fitness boot camp several boys are taking to get in shape for football in the fall."

Julia heaved a sigh. "That buys me a day, at least. Do me a favor? If you have to get Jackson involved, you'll let me give Chase a heads-up? I'll feel like the worst kind of jerk, otherwise."

"I'll try, Julia."

"Fair enough." Relieved to have Chase's strange request off her chest, Julia dove in to the second half of her burger. Two bites in, another thought struck. She slogged a mouthful of tea, then asked, "What was all that about Jackson being a ladies' man?"

She expected Sue to scoff at Grady's assessment. Instead, she gave Julia a frank look. "I know Callie and I tease you about Jackson. But if you're really not planning on starting anything with him after all this time, it's probably for the best."

Would she consider Julia kissing him last night starting something? She shook her head and, just for clarity, added an emphatic, "Nope. Not planning to start anything."

"I hate to say so, but Grady's right. After Hannah's death, Jackson became a kind of—" She broke off and blew air out of her cheeks. "Man whore."

Chapter Six

"Hey, buddy. Hoped I'd find you still here. Hey there, Dave."

Jackson broke off his conversation with Dave Briggs, owner and manager of Dave's Steakhouse and Cantina. He watched Grady approach wearing what he'd silently dubbed his insurance agent uniform. Khakis, a pastel polo, gelled hair, and a salesman's smile.

"What's up, G-man? Dave and I were just wrapping things up. Don't you ever work?"

Grady opened his arms wide. "What can I say? When you're a genius, you name your hours. You get all the deets worked out on your show?"

Jackson glanced a question at Dave who gave two thumbs up.

"As long as you show up the day of with your equipment, we're good." The equipment he referred to being a sound board, his guitar, and a mic.

In little more than two weeks' time, Dave's would serve as the venue for the annual fundraiser benefiting Honeyville's hometown charity, Helping Hands. Jackson was this year's entertainment.

He wouldn't collect a fee for his performance, of course. The money Helping Hands raised funded everything from supplying diapers for Honeyville's families in need, to treatments for locals with cancer, to providing folks necessary mental health counseling.

Besides, he hadn't played for an audience in a while, and he was getting rusty.

Grady's mouth split in a Cheshire Cat's grin. "I'm heading back to the office from lunch. I ate across the street at Beau's—sorry, Dave."

Dave waved him off. "I eat there all the time." He turned to Jackson. "See you two weeks from Saturday." He waved goodbye to Grady and headed for the kitchen.

"Sorry to interrupt, man," Grady said, hands on hips. "But I am glad I caught you."

Jackson spun his keys on his pointer finger. "Not a problem. Was there something you needed, or did you just miss me?"

"Ha ha," Grady said, rolling his eyes. "Actually, I wanted to brag, and I didn't think Dad would appreciate hearing me crow."

Jackson figured Grady was right on that front. Grady's dad, a man Jackson still referred to as Mr. Toller even in the privacy of his own thoughts, had a thing against anyone "tooting his own horn," as he put it. A great guy, just not the warm fuzzy type. If Grady wanted to boast about scoring a new client, he'd get no pat on the back from his dad.

"Lay it on me."

Grady rubbed his hands together. "Guess who I ran into at Beau's?"

The hair on Jackson's nape stirred as an image of Julia in her yoga outfit, hair tousled and looking inviting as hell, flashed across his mind. He smoothed the hairs down with a quick swipe of his hand. "The Easter Bunny? I give."

"Sue Lightbody and Julia Hudson. And guess who exchanged digits with me?" Grady bit his lower lip and extended a fist for a knuckle bump.

Jackson had a strong urge to extend his fist—right into Grady's shit-eating grin.

Something of what he felt must've shown on his face because Grady took a hasty step back and raised both hands in a conciliatory gesture. "Hey, man, I didn't know it was like that. I mean, I knew she was staying at your place, but I didn't think she was *staying* at your place."

He clenched his jaw at the insinuation. "Julia's a house guest and a friend, nothing more."

Grady laughed. "Right. Look, it's only coffee. Nothing to get your panties in a wad over."

He meant to tell Grady to go for it, but somehow the words wouldn't push past his lips. He moved to the exit and stepped onto the sidewalk, eyes on Grady—and got body slammed by a perfumed, curvy blonde.

"Jackson, oh my gosh, it *is* you."

Monica Fisher.

Monica's arms twined around his neck in a death grip. Jackson resigned himself to patting her shoulder in greeting. "Hiya, Monica. Good to see you."

Grady slithered out the door behind him and hastened down the sidewalk in the direction of his office. "Catch you lovebirds later."

Jackson ignored him. His focus was on getting Monica to release him without insulting her. "What brings you here?"

"You remember I work on Main, right? At Stella's?"

Stella's was a high-end lingerie boutique a few

blocks down the street. He'd had no idea Monica worked there. "Oh, right."

"Jacks, it's been way too long," Monica said, pressing herself closer.

She wasn't going let him go of her own volition. With an inner sigh, he pried the woman's arms from around his neck and put some distance between them. "Let me get the door for you." He stepped to the side and held open the door.

Monica frowned, her feet rooted to the sidewalk. "I didn't come for lunch. I came because Grady told me if I hurried, I might find you here. You haven't returned any of my calls."

"Oh." He was going to kill Grady.

He'd met her a few months back while hanging with the guys at the Sport's Shack watching a game. She'd come on to him hard. He'd been horny, having not been intimate with a woman for a good while—his choice. He hadn't meant to make a grand statement of celibacy or anything, but the truth was his never-ending string of one-night stands was wearing thin.

But it *had* been a while.

She asked him to drive her home, and he agreed. Once there, she invited him in, and he accepted the invitation, *after* he made sure she knew how things stood. She was more than okay with his no-ties policy.

When she called a few days later, she caught him off guard. They'd had *the talk,* not to mention he hadn't given her his number.

Unfortunately, Monica had selective listening. He hadn't returned subsequent calls. He felt bad ignoring her, but this wasn't his first rodeo. Far better to discourage unwanted advances from the get-go.

"What can I do for you, Monica?" He glanced at his watch, silently communicating he had somewhere to be. Not that he did. Chase was at summer school and afterward was heading to a friend's.

"Well"—Monica flashed a megawatt smile—"the Helping Hands fundraiser is coming up."

Movement out of the corner of his eye had him shifting his gaze across the street. Julia and Sue chatted on the sidewalk outside Beau's, hands shielding their eyes from the afternoon sun. Had they caught the spectacle of Monica plastered onto him? With any luck, no.

Damn, but Julia was a sight for sore eyes. Her hair gleamed in the sunlight. Last night, indoors, it'd been a sun-kissed tassel of dark blonde. Now it shone like polished gold.

"You're smiling. That's a good sign."

With reluctance, his attention reverted to the woman before him. "Excuse me?"

"The party. I said we should go together, and now you're smiling."

He was? He was. He wiped it from his face. "You know I'm playing that night, right?"

"Of *course* I know. You're the big draw." She had inched closer again and now gazed up at him with doe eyes. "So? How 'bout it?"

"The thing is, Monica, I already have a date."

She blinked. "With who?"

This should teach him to keep his liaisons to a minimum. "I have to run. Maybe I'll see you at the fundraiser?" He did a quick traffic check and trotted across the street.

Jules and Sue had moved a block. He caught them

after a short jog, and he didn't mind the view one bit. Julia wore a fitted, cream-colored jacket with a matching pencil skirt that came to just above her knees. The clothes hugged her curves, not so much they screamed *look at me*, but enough to capture Jackson's full attention. The toned calves and high-wedged sandals with the straps around her slender ankles didn't hurt.

"Ladies, hold up."

****

Julia stopped walking but chose not to glance back at Jackson.

Last night she'd felt empowered by her decision to seize the moment—partially due to Jackson's ardent response to her overture.

As of five minutes ago, all her inner kudos had spiraled the drain, thanks to learning Jackson's predilection to bang anything in sight. Granted, Sue had issued a small retraction. Something to the effect his wild carousing seemed to have died off over the last year.

Her words might have mollified Julia had Jackson not provided an illustration of his very active womanizing the moment they exited Beau's. She could only pray the image of Jackson glued to a blonde bombshell with curves for days hadn't permanently imprinted itself onto her brain.

She didn't think she was a moron for instigating last night's kiss. She *knew* she was.

"What's up, Jacks?" Sue asked. "Who knew Main Street was this happening at three thirty on a Monday in the heart of summer? We ran into your sidekick a few minutes ago."

"So I heard." The edge to Jackson's tone drew Julia's gaze despite her intention to ignore him.

Their eyes met and held.

"Hi," Jackson said in a soft voice that had her stomach quivering, damn him.

She waggled her fingers, afraid to test her speaking abilities.

His gaze did a sleepy yet thorough sweep, starting with her head and working downward. By the time his eyes locked on her butter-colored espadrilles, Julia's pulse skittered like pop rocks.

How was it possible? She *knew* what kind of man he was. Another player. Evidently her body hadn't gotten the message.

"Grady says you exchanged numbers," Jackson said.

Pretty much the last thing she'd expected him to say. Julia frowned and aimed a *what-the-heck* look at Sue.

Sue threw her hands in the air. "Good grief, it's high school all over again. Don't you boys ever grow out of that locker-room stuff?"

Jackson shoved his hands in the front pockets of his worn blue jeans and grinned. "Nope."

Sue rolled her eyes but smiled with indulgent affection. "Admission is half the battle."

"That's not what he…" *Damn.* How to refute Sue's none-too-subtle inference that Jacks and Grady competed for her without putting Jackson on the spot? Best to change the subject. "Er, nice to see you, Jacks, but we were just leaving. Was there something you needed?"

"I wanted to offer you a ride home. You returned

your rental today, right? No reason for Sue to drive all the way out to our place. I mean your place and my place." He coughed into his hand, and his face turned a dull shade of red. "Same address, different houses."

"We get it," Sue said, her lips twitching with obvious amusement.

Accepting a ride with Jackson the playboy was the last thing Julia wanted to do, but telling him no would seem weird, like she'd rather put Sue out than ride with him. Which she would.

Sue would rescue her from this quagmire. Sue, her loyal friend. Sue, who knew she should keep her distance from Jackson.

"You are done for the day?" he asked, sounding unsure for once. He turned to Sue. "She's finished, right, boss lady?"

"Yep."

So much for help. No problem. She could handle this. She searched her brain for a quick excuse, like needing to swing by Sue's for—

"No reason he can't ride you home."

A pregnant silence ensued.

"I mean, you can *drive* her home, not ride her."

Julia couldn't breathe.

Shrugging, she sent Julia an apologetic smile slash grimace.

Jackson didn't outright laugh, but his eyes gleamed with mirth. "Great. Is your car far? We can walk you to it."

"No need. Jules, see you in the morning? Bye, you two." She was halfway to her parked car, keys at the ready, before Julia could open her mouth to say goodbye.

"My truck's parked around the corner." Jackson had moved to her side, and his low voice curled into her ear. His hand at the small of her back sent a shiver of awareness dancing up her spine.

She hadn't recovered from last night, clearly. That magnificent kiss had been a really, really bad idea.

They fell into step beside each other, and she expected Jackson to remove his hand. He didn't. His lingering touch made her want to do foolish things, like nuzzle the underside of his jaw and lick the salt from his neck.

A balmy breeze made the leaves on the surrounding trees sing and caught Jackson's aftershave, teasing Julia's already heightened senses. She breathed in cedar and spice and something utterly masculine that sent a thrum of heat swirling low in her belly.

She drew herself up to her full height and squared her shoulders. She could do this.

Chapter Seven

Jackson held the passenger door open as she climbed up into his gleaming black truck. The interior smelled of leather and Jackson, fresh from the shower.

Without a word, he leaned across her, clicking her seatbelt in place. She breathed in deep through her nose. *Yep.* A conflagration of soap, shampoo, and aftershave. Her toes curled in her shoes.

"I would've done that," she said when he straightened.

He flashed her a chagrined smile. "Kind of a habit I guess."

She told herself not to get her nose out of joint just because he made a practice of seeing all his women safely strapped in. "I see."

"It's easier than reminding Chase to do it. Aunt Lisa says I ought to quit babying him."

He closed her door and trotted around to the driver's side.

Her face went hot. She hoped he hadn't read her wrong assumption on her face. Or maybe he had and was covering. Or maybe she was overthinking. She closed her eyes and imagined banging her forehead against the dashboard. *Get it together, Julia. It's a ride home, not an indecent proposal.*

He turned the key in the ignition, and blessed cool air blasted out of the vents. He slanted her a glance.

"You look flushed. Tough day at work?"

"Believe it or not, I find digging into the school's books a welcome distraction."

"I can understand that." Glancing in his rearview mirror, he maneuvered out of the parking space.

"Thank you for the ride. Sue volunteered to chauffeur me back today, but you don't exactly live on a main drag, so it would've made for a really long day for her."

He nodded. "Sue's a good friend."

She sank into the comfortable leather seat. Tall trees, lush with leaves, framed the road and blocked the direct rays of the sun. In the muted light, Jackson's lightly tanned skin radiated vitality. Something inside her twisted just looking at him, exactly as it had when they were teenagers. And the more she looked, the more she wanted to, as if she could drink him in. He intoxicated and terrified her all at once.

She dragged her thoughts back to the conversation and her eyes to the road. "Sue, Callie, and I were inseparable as kids, all the way through high school. I imagine it was the same for you and Grady."

He barked out a laugh, and her gaze drifted helplessly back toward him.

"Not exactly. I kind of hated Grady when we were young. He was a pest, always showing up, getting pissy when I wouldn't let him run the show. Maybe it was me. Dad always said I had a will of iron no one could bend." The corners of his mouth turned down.

"So what happened? How'd you and Grady end up bosom buddies?"

Jackson sent her an amused look. "I wouldn't go that far." Returning his gaze to the road, he cocked his head in thought. "Grady's…different. He was a pain in my butt growing up. But later, when life threw some curve balls my way, Grady was always there when I needed him." His hands flexed on the steering wheel, as if he relived some of those curve balls.

She fisted her hands, staunching the urge to soothe him with her touch. "I'm glad he was there for you."

"About Grady. Are you planning to see him?"

"See him how? When?"

"You know exactly what I mean, sweetheart," came his hushed reply.

Maybe. But she needed a minute to think about her response, something made more difficult by his casual use of the endearment *sweetheart*. She had zero interest in Grady, not that it was any business of Jackson's. "My curiosity about your friendship stemmed more from my interest in you."

Her words echoed in the silence, and she mentally cursed herself. So much for thinking her answer through. She cleared her throat. "That came out wrong."

His lips twitched. Great. He was laughing at her.

Only he wasn't.

In a velvet-soft voice, he said, "Seemed all right to me. I'm curious about you, too, Jules. So many questions running through my mind."

Her heart jumped to her throat, and she willed herself to calm the hell down. This was Jackson, the town playboy. Hadn't she learned her lesson with smooth-talking Chris?

Chris never turned your brain to mush with a single look, an inner voice said, as if that made any difference at all.

"Anyhow, I'm glad to know you and Grady aren't an item because I have a favor to ask."

She breathed a sigh of relief. The conversation had veered back into safe territory. "Sure. Anything."

His fingers drummed the steering wheel. "I need you to be my date to the Helping Hands charity event in a few weeks."

She stared at him, unable to manage a single word in response. She suddenly felt like she hung at the top of a roller coaster, all dizzy and breathless and slightly nauseated.

He flicked an uncertain glance her way. "It's not a full-on dinner, but there'll be heavy hors d'oeuvres, cocktails, a silent auction, and live entertainment." He cleared his throat. "A.k.a. me. The board asked me to play this year, and I agreed. All for a good cause." He blew air out of his cheeks.

If she didn't know better, she'd say he was nervous.

"What else? Oh yeah. Dress code. Every lady wants to know that." He flashed her a smile. His face bore a distinct ruddy tinge. "Cocktail attire. I'll buy you something if you don't have anything with you."

What was it with him and paying for everything? She found her voice. "Jackson, you don't have to buy me a dress."

"Great, you have one. It's all set, then? I have to be there a little early. I hope that's not a problem."

"Wait." She drew a breath. Examined her nails. Found a tiny chip in her red polish. "Exactly why do you need me to be your date, Jackson?" She placed extra emphasis on the word *need.*

He navigated a hard curve. They'd reach his estate

soon. "Does that matter?"

She pressed her lips together. "Depends."

"I'm listening."

"Is this an attempt to atone for not taking me to prom?"

A beat of silence passed, then he threw back his head and hooted with laughter. "What in the world? No. Why would you think that?"

She lifted her chin a notch and refused to dignify his question with an answer.

He reached across the console to cover her hands, still clenched in her lap. His palm was warm, the pads of his fingers slightly calloused. He cleared his throat in an obvious attempt to rein in his humor.

"No," he repeated, then swiped his thumb across her knuckles before withdrawing his hand. "I have an admirer who won't take a hint. She asked me to go with her. I told her I already have a date."

"Why not ask the blonde you were draped all over on Main Street?"

Should she bite out her tongue now or wait 'til she was safely alone in the cottage?

"Monica? Who *I* was—" He broke off and started again. "She's the—" He swiped a hand across his jaw. "—a friend. Nothing more."

She let the ridiculousness of his statement sit a few seconds. "In point of fact, *I'm* a friend." She wanted to add *and she clearly isn't,* but for once she held her tongue. She didn't want to appear jealous. Because she wasn't.

"I know." He jammed a hand through his hair. Because he was Jackson Tate, the silky locks refused to muss and instead fell back into perfect place. "But I didn't ask her, I asked you."

But why? she wanted to scream. Especially since they were, by his own eager admission, *friends.* And who could forget the pact they'd made last night—after that damned kiss she'd initiated—to keep things between them on a strictly friendship basis?

"Okay, I get it. You don't want to go with me. Sorry I put you on the spot. I'll—"

"Jackson?"

"Yes?"

"I'll go with you."

A muscle in his jaw ticked. "You don't want to, though."

She stifled a laugh. "I do. I want to go with you."

He slid her a sullen glance. After a moment his features turned hopeful. "You're sure?"

"Yes. I'm sure."

The corners of his mouth curved upward. "Okay. Thank you."

Summoning her willpower, she forged ahead. "Just friends, though, right? Sorry to state the obvious, but I want to keep things from getting complicated." *For me,* she added silently.

"Oh." He made a gesture with his head and shoulders that said *duh.* "Of course. Friends." He reached over and patted her thigh, then drew his hand back to the wheel.

He pulled up to the guard house at the entrance of his estate and nodded to the uniformed man inside. A moment later, the gate opened, and Jackson motored onto the private road.

****

Jackson waited with growing impatience for his

garage door to open. Out of the corner of his eye, he saw Julia sit up, gather her purse into her lap, unbuckle her belt. No doubt about it, she planned to bolt. Trouble was he didn't want to let her. Not yet.

He'd barely cleared the garage door before pressing the button on his rear view to close it. Behind them the door slid soundlessly down, enclosing them in the large, dimly lit space. Visions of high school, of making out in a parked car and steaming up the windows, flooded his mind. He wondered what she'd do if he pulled her across the cab into his lap.

Probably slap him and never get into a vehicle with him again.

"If you wait a minute, I'll give you a hand down."

Before his feet hit the concrete, she had her door open to jump.

He smiled to himself. He could've predicted she'd refuse his help. "City girls," he said under his breath.

"What was that?"

"City shoes," he said louder. He met her at the mudroom door and eyed her high-heeled sandals. The woman had fine taste in footwear. "Glad you didn't twist an ankle."

She cocked her head and angled one shapely calf to inspect her ankle-strapped, three-inch wedge. "Ha. These are nothing. I could jog the length of an entire shopping mall in them if need be."

He laughed and opened the door.

She marched through the unlit room straight to the connecting door leading to the hall, opened it, and stopped. "Left or right?"

A simple word would have sufficed. But instead, his hands found their way to either side of her hips to urge her left. Her body was firm yet supple, like perfectly ripe fruit. In those heels the top of her head came to just beneath his chin. Thoughts of pulling her into his chest swamped his mind. He released her, fisting his hands at his sides before he got himself into trouble.

The hallway was dark and silent except for their footsteps. He wanted to say something, anything, to make her stay. But why convince her to spend even five minutes with him? It couldn't lead anywhere good. For that matter, what on earth had prompted him to ask her on a date? Not that he regretted the impulse, since she'd said yes.

The archway at end of the hall led to a high-ceilinged crossroads. The left opened to a large formal dining room. Straight ahead was a partial dividing wall, behind which was the kitchen nook where they'd eaten two nights ago. A corridor off it wound around to the kitchen. And to the right was the direct route to the living area—and the way out.

Julia stepped right.

"This way," he said, then grazed her left elbow with his fingertips.

After the briefest hesitation, she veered toward the kitchen. The gaze she shot over her shoulder seemed wary, as if she felt the charged sexual energy zinging through him.

In the kitchen he flicked on under-cabinet LEDs. "I'm sure you're ready to get to your place and unwind after your first day at work, but do you mind if I slog some water first?" he asked, already taking a glass from the cabinet.

"Jackson, I can find my way from—"

"No. I'll walk you," he said and turned on the filtered tap to fill his glass. He kept his gaze on the water stream, not meeting her eyes. He sounded like an overbearing ass, like he thought she needed an escort to cross the deck. He couldn't make himself care. It was this or let her walk out without him. He slammed the entire glass of tepid water like he hadn't had a drink in a week, then set the glass in the sink.

When he looked up, he found her sky-blue stare locked on him. Something flickered in her eyes. Heat tempered with resolve. Like she wanted something very badly yet didn't want to want it. Like she struggled against the same desire he did.

Her gaze, riveted on his mouth, batted at his crumbling willpower.

Her hand darted out as if she meant to touch his face. She drew it back almost in the same instant. "You have…on your lower lip."

The breathless quality of her voice twisted his stomach with need. Was he wishful thinking, or did Julia want him? He had to know. He dabbed the right corner of his mouth with the tip of his tongue and waited for her response.

She shook her head, and thick layers of burnished gold tumbled in sexy waves around her face.

Blood pounded in his ears. He leaned toward her in a silent request for her to take care of the offending water droplet. Preferably with her lips.

She reached toward him. That nameless something sweet he'd only ever smelled on her skin teased his nostrils. He nearly gave in to the urge to turn his head and press a kiss to the tender side of her wrist. But he didn't want to cross that invisible line. Not unless he knew.

Her thumb swiped across his lower lip. "Got it," she whispered.

Chapter Eight

Jackson's brilliant hazel eyes locked with hers, holding her captive. With each passing second, the heat swirling through her grew molten, pooling low in her belly. Jackson Tate, the playboy, the rock star, or the guy she never got over. At the moment she. Did. Not. Care. She wanted his mouth on hers. She closed her eyes and leaned forward.

A fire alarm bellowed. Literally.

Julia jumped. Jackson blinked, straightened, and reached in his pocket to pull out his cell phone. He pressed something, silencing the alarm, and brought the cell to his ear. "Hey, buddy, what's up?"

How did he sound so totally normal?

She glanced around and spotted her purse on the floor. When had she dropped it? Didn't matter. She bent, scooping it up, then darted for the back door.

"I don't see a problem except you don't have any overnight gear or clean clothes for tomorrow."

His voice sounded so close. She shot a look over her shoulder and found him at her heels.

His unblinking stare met hers. He gestured with his free hand for her to keep moving. He still planned to walk her home?

She shook her head and shooed him.

"Let me talk to Tommy's mom, Chase."

Taking that as assent, she took off, and the sound

of Jackson's conversation faded.

Adrenaline had her fingers shaking as she shoved the key dangling at her wrist into the back door lock. Lusting after Jackson Tate. She was an idiot for more reasons than she could count.

"Hang on," Jackson said, practically in her ear.

She yelped and spun around.

He stood not two feet from her, his palm over his cell phone receiver, looking cool as a cucumber. "Can I come in?" he mouthed.

Bewildered, she let herself in and left the door ajar. Unsure who had her more vexed, herself or him, she stomped to her small bedroom. She stripped off her jacket and whipped it onto the bed, then unbuckled her ankle straps with violent yanks and tugged off her shoes.

Jackson was a playboy. Jackson had multiple girlfriends. Jackson was her landlord. Jackson was *thee* Jackson Tate. She couldn't be fool enough to think he wanted her.

But if he did and *they* did and his desire died a swift death afterward like what had happened with Chris, she couldn't handle it. This time, she should know better. She wanted to scream.

"Jules?" Jackson called from inside the cottage. "Sorry about that phone call coming in."

No good reply came to mind.

"Julia?"

She hesitated, torn between wanting to ignore him so he'd leave and wanting him *not* to leave.

"I'm going to pilfer your kitchen."

Her kitchen? Pretty much the last thing she'd expected him to say. Curiosity pulled her from her room.

Jackson crouched on the floor, head and shoulders deep in a lower cabinet. Several upper cabinet doors hung ajar.

He slithered out. Eyed her feet. Grinned. "Nice toenail polish. Matches your fingernails."

Aw. He'd noticed her manicure? No. She would not fall for his charm. She fisted her hands at her hips. "What are you doing?"

"Checking to see what you need." He rose and sauntered toward her.

With her wedges off, he stood two heads taller than her. She tilted her head back so she wasn't staring at his chest.

"Yes?" he asked, his lips curving in a grin that threatened to short out all her mental faculties.

"This place doesn't need anything, and if it does, I will get it."

"Not even a fire extinguisher? What if you start a kitchen fire and wind up burning my house down?"

She blinked and opened her mouth to argue, but the truth was accidents happened. "I'll buy one myself." She wasn't sure why she felt the need to dig her heels in.

"Where?"

She scrunched her brows. "Local hardware shop?"

He huffed out a laugh. "Good guess, but it's the landlord's responsibility. Besides, I'm going to get it tomorrow, so you really don't get a say, especially since you still don't have a car." He cocked his head and peered down at her feet. "And I wouldn't want you to ruin your pedicure." His voice had gone husky, and the sexual flames licking at her insides flared to life.

In self-defense she backed away and swept a hand toward the closed french door. "Fine. Knock yourself out."

The playful light in his eyes winked out. He turned and, shutting the cabinets with care, spoke in a low voice. "I'll get out of your hair." He started for the door.

She edged a hip onto one of the high bar stools and tried to ignore the guilt stabbing at her. No use. Just because she fought an inner battle not to fling herself at him was no reason to lash out at him. "Jackson."

His hand gripping the doorknob unfurled. He executed a slow swivel to face her, jammed his hands in his pockets, and eyed the floor at his feet.

She tiptoed toward him. "Thank you. For everything. This place. The ride home. The fire extinguisher." She hoped he heard the smile in her voice and recognized the olive branch.

He didn't looked up, but one corner of his mouth hitched upward. "You're welcome. I want to thank you, too."

"Thank me? For what?"

He raised his magnificent gold-flecked eyes to meet hers, and *boom.* Her breath caught in her throat. Her heart squeezed. Her legs turned to jelly.

She had told her friends her crush on Jackson was *finito*. She had told *herself* the same. Wrong. Way, way wrong. Talk about needing a fire extinguisher. For God's sake, let him say what he needed to say and get the hell out of here before she spontaneously combusted, or worse.

His smile turned rueful. "For putting up with me nosing around while you try to get settled. For agreeing

117

to go with me to the Helping Hands event in a few weeks even though I know you're not a hundred percent sold on the idea. I get that you have a lot on your plate, between your move and your career and your breakup. I don't know what's gotten into me." Abruptly, his expression changed to one of grim determination.

He rocked on his heels. "No. That's not quite true. I just didn't see it coming. Jules, I don't get involved with women like you." He broke off and shook his head, laughed like he couldn't believe what he was about to say.

Then don't say it. Her skin went clammy. She didn't need to hear how unlikely a fit she was for him, especially not with everything Chris had said ringing fresh in her ears. And if he was saying the exact opposite? Well, that had disaster written all over it, too, for a multitude of reasons. She nodded her understanding with vigor, praying he would stop talking.

If Jackson noticed her mounting discomfort, it didn't show. If anything, the high color on his cheeks told her he struggled with embarrassment of his own. "You of all people should know—"

"Oh, Jackson, no, no, no," she blurted, rapid-fire. "I get it. We're *friends*. In fact you've been more than a friend."

"That's what I'm—"

"I…I mean you've gone above and beyond for me since I came home. You've been just great. Nothing's gotten into anybody." *Lie, lie, lie.* She dragged in a breath and prayed he wouldn't bring up the almost kiss in his kitchen. Less than five minutes ago, they'd almost jumped the rails. It had been a near miss. She knew it and he knew it.

Jackson stared at her, an unreadable expression on his face. "Right. Good, then. About that extinguisher. I'll bring one by."

"Great. Thanks. Tomorrow, right? I promise not to start any fires tonight."

"Sure. Tomorrow." A second later, he was outside, crossing the back deck.

She watched him go 'til he was out of sight, unable to peel her eyes off him. The man oozed sex appeal without even trying. Had it been wishful thinking on her part in the kitchen? Had she read him wrong? Maybe she'd been the only one feeling that sexual draw.

But it sure seemed like he'd wanted her, too.

No matter. Better to rip this attraction out at the root, one-sided or two.

****

The sun hadn't yet put in an appearance when she got behind the wheel of her dad's sedan, coffee thermos in hand. Last night, as promised, her parents had delivered the car, right along with dinner—thank goodness, since Julia hadn't yet stocked her fridge.

She parked beside her friend's soft-top convertible, marveling at how Sue managed to beat her there.

When she pushed open the glass door leading into the school administration offices, Sue sat behind her principal's desk, pen in hand, engrossed in paperwork.

"Do you live here now?" Julia asked.

"That's only during the school year." She put down her pen and looked up. The ready grin she wore vanished. "What's wrong?"

119

"Why does everyone ask me that the minute they see me?" Julia complained. "It makes me feel old and tired looking."

"Sorry. And who's everyone? Don't tell me. You spent the night with Jackson and now hate yourself because you figured out what you've been missing all these years." Sue's eyes went dreamy, and she propped her chin in her hands. "The man is seriously hot."

"And a man whore, remember? And besides, it was my mom who commented on my appearance."

Sue grimaced. "I took that thing about Jackson back. Mostly." She glanced at her watch. "We have a half hour. Spill it."

Julia sure as hell wasn't opening the Jackson can of worms—not that she had anything to share besides what her own imagination could conjure.

"Chris emailed me late last night. He wants to talk. Says he and Nicole are history."

Hearing from him had rattled her, mainly because it reminded her of the mess she'd gotten herself into against her own better judgment, which in turn led to thoughts of Jackson and an increasing suspicion her infatuation, or *re*-infatuation, meant she was at it again.

"But you never want to see him again, right?"

Julia sipped the last of her coffee and wandered toward Sue's desk. "Right."

She stared hard at Julia. "Are you sure, Jules? No one's going to judge you if you love the guy and want to give him another chance."

Love. Did she love him? Had she ever? Did she even know the man? "What I want is to forget him." Him and the cutting things he'd said to her at the end.

"Then ignore his emails. He'll give up eventually."

She sat up taller in her chair. "On another note, I have some news that might interest you. It's about Jackson's son, Chase. Looks like an authorized signer okayed his registration."

"Jackson?"

"Nope. Aunt Lisa."

****

Julia made a quick trek to the Handy Pantry after work. The local artisanal market made her father's favorite dessert—apple pie. Her parents had invited her for dinner tonight, and she could hardly wait for one of her mother's home-cooked meals.

Her pulse kicked up when she turned onto the road leading to Jackson's. She passed the circular driveway on her way to the short cutoff to the cottage, and her palms went sweaty on the steering wheel, that fast.

This living situation was turning out to be harder than it looked. Yoga-on-the-deck run-ins and chance meetings whereby she might make a fool of herself drooling over Jackson loomed around every corner. Luckily tonight she had only enough time to change into a comfy dress before heading to her parents' house.

Inside, she strode straight into the kitchen to unload the pie, then hustled toward the bedroom. The sight of a shiny, red fire extinguisher and a vase spilling with purple lilacs and yellow roses in full bloom atop her small dinette stopped her in her tracks. How had she missed the bouquet's sweet fragrance when she'd opened the front door?

An envelope leaned against the vase. She dashed forward and snatched it up, then silently cursed her own shaking hands as she pulled the card from its sleeve. It read *welcome to the neighborhood* and depicted an older man, boosted up by a gray-haired lady, peeking over a picket fence. Chuckling, she flipped open the card. Her breath caught at the sight of the handwritten message.

Jules, enjoy the fire extinguisher but try not to use it too soon. Thanks again for agreeing to be my Helping Hands date. Jacks.

P.S. I hope you like the flowers. The lilacs reminded me of you.

A warm rush of pleasure swamped her before she could talk herself down, and she hugged the card to her chest.

Don't read anything into the flowers.

If anything, she should focus on the yellow roses. Everyone knew yellow roses denoted friendship.

He didn't mention the roses. He mentioned the lilacs.

She shushed her inner commentary but couldn't wipe the smile from her face.

****

"Dinner smells good, Mom." Julia set the apple pie on the kitchen counter before pecking her mother's cheek. She followed her nose to the oven and cracked open the door, releasing a cloud of aromatic steam. "Roast beef? Yum. I haven't had your roast in forever."

"Special request," her mom said and carried a large tossed salad out of the kitchen.

Julia followed her mom to the dining room. Noted the place settings for six. "Are we having"—the doorbell rang—"guests?"

"Honey, can you get that? I've got to drag your dad out of his den. I don't know why he glues himself to the news. It's so depressing." Her mom's words faded as she disappeared down the hall.

Julia threw her hands in the air and headed for the foyer, muttering, "Nobody tells me anything." She swung open the door.

Two freshly showered Tates waited on the stoop.

"Hi, Miss Julia," Chase said, his eyes wide with evident alarm.

"Is everything okay?" Julia asked.

"Far as I know," Jackson answered, an expectant look on his face.

Another car pulled into the driveway. Jackson's aunt Lisa.

The light bulb went on. "You're here for dinner. Come on in."

How bad was it that the prospect of spending the evening with Jackson filled her with giddy delight? Probably pretty bad.

"Yep. Lucky us. I didn't know you were going to be here."

His words might have deflated her excitement if not for the subtle scent of his cologne stealing her good sense. Her tummy shivered with pleasure.

In the foyer Jackson shifted to face her, hands on his narrow, denim-clad hips. "Your mom ran into Aunt Lisa in the grocery this morning and had her call me with the invite right then. Once I heard the magic words, wild horses couldn't keep us away." He clasped his son's shoulder with one hand and gave a squeeze. "Right, bud?"

Chase nodded. His deer-in-the-headlights expression faded slightly when his father's gaze fell on him. Julia guessed the secret he'd asked her to keep had him on edge. She intended to broach the subject with

Lisa but so far hadn't had the chance. Maybe tonight.

"Magic words?" she prodded.

Jackson's hazel eyes twinkled. "Pot roast."

"Ah-ha. So yours was the special request."

His mischievous grin said *when you've got it, you've got it*, and Julia laughed.

"This is a treat, Jules," Lisa said, joining the three of them. She kissed Julia's cheek, then hugged Jackson. "It feels like Thanksgiving, having us all together."

Julia's mom's head appeared from around the corner. "Julia brought pie."

"I love pie," Jackson said. He winked at Julia, then approached her mother, arms open for a hug. "Mrs. Hudson, great to see you."

"Pleasure's all mine. So glad you boys could join us. Now come on back to the living room, and Julia will fetch refreshments."

****

Jackson followed Mrs. Hudson through the house he remembered so well from his high school years when Julia tutored him. He'd loved coming here. The change in atmosphere made him feel like what he thought a kid should. His house, on the other hand, had felt like tiptoeing around a minefield, unless his dad happened to not be home.

And that usually meant worse trouble came later.

"Hold up, Chase." Jackson paused at the formal dining table, set for dinner. He glanced over his shoulder at Julia, bringing up the rear. Her thick, dark-blonde hair was tousled as usual—half up, half down, framing her face and looking sexy as hell. The belted, cotton shirtdress didn't hurt, either. It showed just the right amount of shapely thigh. She had great legs.

124

And hadn't she made it clear yesterday she didn't appreciate his non-friend-like attentions?

She came to a halt and gave him a questioning smile, probably because he was staring like a Neanderthal. "Jackson?"

He had intended to say something, but that tumbled hair shorted out his brain. He looked around, hoping to spark his memory. The table. "I was just telling Chase this was where you performed a minor miracle, teaching me the concepts of algebra so they finally made sense." Jackson laid his hands across the back of a chair.

Chase muttered something unintelligible and scurried after Mrs. Hudson and Aunt Lisa. Jackson frowned after him before switching his attention to Julia.

She remained a good foot away from him, almost like she didn't want to get within touching distance. He couldn't blame her after yesterday. He'd been this close to throwing his good intentions to the wind. To her credit, she'd picked up on it and shut him down with that "friends" speech she loved so much.

And yeah, even now he wanted nothing more than to drag her in for a kiss.

"Scene of the crime," she said softly.

"Did you get the extinguisher?" he asked, because jumping to asking if she'd changed her mind about going out with him felt awkward.

Her lips curved in a shy smile. "I did, thanks." She hesitated, her gaze flicking past him toward the others before she inched closer. "Thank you for the flowers."

"You're welcome." Up close, her sweet-smelling fragrance teased his already heightened senses. Today, at the florist, while picking the flowers for her bouquet, he'd caught the familiar aroma. In truth, he'd bet she didn't have to douse herself in anything to achieve her unique scent. It would emanate from her even scrubbed clean.

He leaned in and drew a breath as inconspicuously as possible. She smelled even better than the florist shop. "I hope you like the combination. I chose the flowers myself." Fishing. But he couldn't seem to help himself when it came to her.

Her eyes widened in surprise and pleasure if he read her right. "I love them."

"I thought I ought to get on your good side so you'd still go with me two weeks from Saturday, in case you forgot." He hesitated a beat. "You are, aren't you? Still going?"

Her cheeks went pink, that fast, but she tossed her hair. "It's a done deal. You're stuck with me."

He bit back a grin. The combination of flustered and sassy looked adorable on her. She was damned adorable, period. She did something to him. He didn't want to like it as much as he did and, in fact, had promised himself he'd keep his distance—at least for a good week. Tonight was not his fault.

Sure, because you had no inkling she'd join her folks for a family dinner.

"What can I bring you to drink, Jackson?" she asked.

"I'm all right at the moment. More hungry than anything."

He'd spoken the simple truth—no hidden message underscored his words. Yet somehow, with their eyes locked, a deeper meaning insinuated itself into the air

126

surrounding them. He could think of no other reason for her blue eyes to go wide as saucers and the tender skin at the base of her throat to tremble with the force of her heartbeat.

Or for his own heartbeat to kick up a notch, for that matter.

Mrs. Hudson chose that moment to remind Julia about her hostess duties.

Julia hustled around him to take drink requests from Lisa and Chase.

Jackson followed her with his gaze as she disappeared into the kitchen. What about her scrambled his brain? The way she didn't try to charm him? Her mane of sexy-as-hell hair he wanted to sink his fingers into? Maybe it was that steaming kiss she'd laid on him out of the blue the other night.

Whatever the reason, he needed to get himself in line, which meant following through on his plan to stay away from her. The idea held less and less appeal.

Maybe he looked at this all wrong. Maybe he should spend *more* time with her. Familiarity bred contempt, right? Or at least boredom. That's usually how it worked for him at any rate. His legs started carrying him toward the kitchen before he'd made a conscious decision to move. "I'll help Julia with the drinks."

"That's my boy," Lisa said.

"And they say chivalry's dead," Julia's mom quipped.

Chase stared at his phone, tapping at the screen. Without looking up, he gave his dad a thumbs-up.

Mr. Hudson alone eyed him with an equal combination of amusement and suspicion. Smart man.

Chapter Nine

Julia leaned back from the dining table, bothered and bemused and hoping the combination wasn't plastered on her face. But really. How was it possible the man made chewing look glamorous and sexy?

Something about him got under her skin, similar to when they were kids, only amplified tenfold now. She wanted the man. Bad.

Life was funny. She'd waited her whole life to feel this dizzying craving for a man. She'd thought it would mean she found her one and only. She knew better now. Men like Chris, like Jackson, couldn't be anyone's one and only.

But why did Jackson alone make her weak in the knees? Even Chris hadn't.

"Who wants coffee?" her mom asked, breaking through her reverie.

"Coffee sounds good, Mrs. Hudson," Jackson replied.

Julia's mom half rose, empty plate in hand.

"No, ma'am." He gestured for her to sit. "You can't cook and do the cleanup. Chase, how 'bout you and I clear the dishes?"

Chase nodded and pushed back from the table.

Julia rose so fast she nearly upended her chair. "That's all right, Jacks. You sit."

He opened his mouth, but she didn't give him a

chance to argue.

"I want to serve the pie, anyhow. But I do need a helper. Chase, you can drop the dishes in the sink and help me with the coffee and dessert."

Chase gathered the dishes from his side of the table, then hurried for the kitchen.

Julia found him standing empty handed near the pocket door dividing the rooms. He seemed poised for flight as if he meant to escape the moment she passed him.

"Why don't you close the door, Chase?" she suggested before offloading her plates into the sink.

The pocket door closed at a snail's pace.

She faced the boy, hands on her hips, and waited him out.

It took all of a five seconds. "Thanks for not telling my dad, Miss Julia. You didn't, did you?"

She shook her head. "But you put me in an awful position. You know that, right?"

He nodded, looking miserable.

"I checked at the school. I know your aunt Lisa signed off on the course you're taking. What I don't know is whether she's aware you haven't told your dad about the class or why you wouldn't."

If he ducked his head any lower, his chin would touch his chest.

"Look, if you don't want to share your story with me, I can respect that. I just need you to understand I'm going to have to tell Jackson—"

Chase's head snapped up, his expression desperate. "No, Miss Julia. You can't."

"Chase, it's wrong for me to knowingly keep information like this from your dad. I don't want to rat you out, but I also don't see why you're so worried. You're not doing anything wrong."

"I know." His shoulders hunched, and he paced the kitchen.

Julia would've laughed at the spectacle of a young person with the world at his fingertips carrying on like a condemned criminal, except Chase was clearly distraught.

"It's just Dad is so set on me *not* having to prove anything. He's always talking about how Grandpa rode him about his grades and sports and everything, and he thinks he's doing me a favor not pushing me the same way, especially in math. But…" He stopped his pacing, and his thin shoulders rose in a helpless shrug.

Julia frowned, trying to make sense of Chase's words. "But you want to succeed in math?"

His eyes lit with hope. "I tried to tell him, but it's like he can't hear me. I don't want to disappoint him, Miss Julia, but I'm tired of being the dumbest one in my math classes." Chase's lower lip trembled, nearly breaking Julia's heart. He shifted his gaze to the toe of his sneaker and spoke in a hushed tone. "Plus there's Alana."

"The little girl who sits beside you in the enrichment course?" she asked gently.

He nodded.

"Does she tease you?" Julia asked. If so, she hadn't seen that coming. Alana was precocious as befitted her age, but she seemed to like Chase.

"No," he muttered. "Billy does. He likes Alana, I think. Last year he made a big deal every time the teacher passed back our math tests, bragging about his As. Calling me out on my Ds…and Fs. Sometimes I just want to sock him."

Julia touched his shoulder lightly. "Not the best idea."

Chase tossed his bangs out of his eyes and grinned up at Julia. "I thought I'd work on my math skills instead." He shrugged. "Plus, Coach says anyone caught fighting is off the football team."

Julia chuckled. "Good to see you have your priorities straight."

He sighed, all seriousness again. "You won't tell Dad?"

How could she now? Then again, how could she not? "Tell you what. I'll start with talking to your aunt Lisa, to see where she stands on all this."

He nodded, but his eyes looked resigned to his fate.

"In the meantime, I hope you'll consider talking to Jackson yourself. Your dad loves you. He'll understand."

"Sure," Chase replied, not sounding at all convinced.

Julia turned back to the counter and opened an upper cabinet where her mom kept the coffee and filters. "I can help, you know, with your math lessons. I used to be a pretty good tutor."

Chase sidled up beside her and watched her scoop the coffee grounds. "That could be cool. Grady told me you tutored Dad."

She smiled and handed him the empty pot, gesturing for him to fill it in the sink. "I did, senior year in high school. Everyone needs help once in a while. Okay it with your dad first, and we can get started."

A knock sounded on the door, then Jackson poked his head in. "You two all right?"

Chase's eyes went round.

"We're good. Come on in," Julia replied.

His canvas shoes barely made a sound on the kitchen tiles. "You two were taking a while. Thought you might need some help."

Julia busied herself, pushing the brew button, gathering plates and forks. She didn't want to meet Jackson's eyes now that she'd agreed to be complicit in Chase's lie. Again.

"Son, you go on out. I'll finish helping Miss Julia."

Chase jettisoned from the room. A heartbeat later, the pocket door whirred softly closed. The spacious kitchen felt suddenly small.

"He's a sweet kid, Jacks. You're a good dad. It shows."

Jackson moved to stand behind her while she sliced the apple pie. He gripped the counter near her hip and peered over her shoulder, watching her work. His body didn't so much as graze hers, but the heat radiating from him told Julia he was standing way too close, for her comfort anyway. Her nerve endings disagreed. A delicious warmth turned her insides to jelly.

"I don't know about that last bit, but he's for sure the best thing that ever happened to me. Pie looks good," he murmured close to her ear.

A flush rode up her neck. Because he stood so close she could smell his cologne? Because of the rough-velvet sound of his voice curling in her ear? Who could say?

His fingertips brushed her cheek as he sifted through her hair and let it fall. "It's as silky as it looks," he said in a hushed voice. "Smells good, too."

Her breath turned choppy, and her hand, holding

the pie cutter, froze mid-air as all rational thought fled.

He reached around her. "Here, let me."

"No, I can—"

He took the slicer.

Her hand, left with nothing to do, fluttered to the counter. She inched to the side to give him room—and save her sanity—and collided with his other arm as it curled loosely around her waist. The warmth of his hand resting just below her ribs burned through the thin material of the dress.

"Didn't mean to come in here and gum up the works, Jules. Pie's a very important food group, don't you know. Only one thing to do, I guess. Only thing I *can* do."

"What's that?" she asked, breathless and more than a little confused.

He finished partitioning the pie, set the utensil on the counter, then stepped back, taking his heat with him.

Before she could chide herself for the disappointment swamping her, he grasped both her shoulders and turned her to face him.

He wore a serious expression—but his eyes gleamed with mischief. "I'm going to buy you a trucker cap so you can hide that wild mane of yours in it and keep me from getting any ideas about playing with it."

She laughed, flattered, flustered, and thoroughly charmed. "You're a scoundrel, you know that?"

He laughed right along with her and stepped back. "Beyond a shadow of a doubt, sweetheart."

Slowly, his words penetrated her Jackson-muddled brain.

When people tell you who they are, Julia Hudson,

believe them. Jackson's casual flirtation, which had her reeling, meant nothing to him beyond harmless fun.

Lucky for her, she could learn. She sent him a jaunty grin. "Or you can keep your paws to yourself, mister."

He barked out another laugh, and she congratulated herself on her fine read of the situation.

"Coffee's almost ready." She beelined for the refrigerator. "I'll get the cream and sugar if you'll grab mugs in the cabinet above the coffee maker."

"Yes, ma'am."

Back in the dining room, Julia kept her expression neutral while she set the pie and whipped cream in the center of the table and laid plates in front of each person. She marveled at her calm. No one but her need ever know of Jackson's superhuman ability to melt her panties off with a brush of his fingers and a few skillfully chosen words.

She'd been an utter fool with Chris. Never again. This was serious progress.

"This one of Hal's pies?" her dad asked, diving in as soon as a slice was in front of him.

"Sure is," Julia answered. Her dad was a big fan of all things baked by Hal from the Handy Pantry.

Her mother sniffed. "My pies taste exactly the same as Hal's."

Lisa, Julia, and her dad chuckled. Her mother's complaint was a long-standing joke.

"Of course, dear," Julia's dad said, then winked at Chase. He forked up a bite and turned to Jackson. "I can recall grabbing up platters of Hal's pastries many a Monday morning to start the work week, back when I went in to the plant regular and your dad was my

134

foreman."

Jackson's fork made an almost imperceptible pause mid-air on the way to his mouth. He popped the bite in his mouth and nodded, chewing, then set the fork beside the half-eaten dessert as if mention of his dad caused him to lose his appetite.

"How is George these days?" Julia's dad asked.

Chase, still digging in to his pie, gazed up at his dad as if he, too, wanted news of his grandfather.

"He's fine. I *hear* he's fine. What do you hear, Aunt Lees?" Jackson asked, lobbing the conversation in her direction. A muscle ticked in his jaw.

"He's hanging in there. He asked about you and Chase when I spoke with him last week, Jackson. He mentioned leaving you a couple messages."

Jackson made no immediate reply, and Julia guessed he would remain mute, based on the fact his face suddenly resembled carved marble. Crackling tension filled the room.

Julia's mom broke the heavy silence. "More coffee anyone?" She stood up.

Jackson's charming smile and relaxed demeanor reappeared like someone flipped a switch. "Thank you kindly, Mrs. Hudson, but Chase and I have to be getting home. Can we help with the clearing?" he asked, pushing back from the table.

"Heavens, no. You go on and get that handsome boy of yours to bed."

Everyone took that as their cue and rose from the table.

She opened her arms to Chase. "Young man, until we meet again."

He hugged her without hesitation. "Bye, Miss

Julia."

Behind Chase, Jackson jammed a hand through his hair and started for the door without a word of goodbye for Julia. What in the world? If she looked up *hot and cold* in an urban dictionary, Jackson's picture would be beside it.

No one else seemed to notice his odd departure. Maybe she was being too sensitive. Either way, she opted not to join her parents in waving everyone off from the front stoop. Not that she didn't have to get going herself. She had an early morning tomorrow if she was going to practice yoga before work. She suspected she'd need it.

But no matter how late it got, Julia refused to leave until she got some answers from her go-to source.

A few minutes later, Julia's hands were immersed in a sink full of hot, sudsy water.

"Honey, you don't have to do that," her mom said, walking briskly into the kitchen.

"Sure I do. Besides, I wanted some girl time."

Julia's mom picked up a dishtowel and plucked a dripping pot out of the dish rack. "I figured we'd catch up more when things settled down. I can't believe how smooth your transition has been so far. A place to stay, a job. Almost as if it was meant to be."

"Yeah, everyone's really come through for me."

"Jackson in particular."

True. She would never in a million years have foreseen that. "Mom, what's the story with Jackson's dad? The air was thick enough to slice after Dad asked about George."

Her mom shook her head in exasperation. "Your father. Always trying to help matters and sticking his foot in it." She leaned down, opening cabinets to put away the large roasting pan. "I don't think you knew, about a year before she died, Marilyn left George."

Julia stared at her mom. "Jackson's mom? She did? Why?"

Her mom raised her brows. "I can't say for certain, but I expect it was years in the coming. George couldn't have been the easiest man to live with."

Julia knew he'd been tough on Jackson. "Yeah, I gathered that much."

"Anyhoo, something must've happened when Jackson and Hannah came to town for a visit, maybe a year into their marriage. Because they cut their trip short, as in left the day after they got here, and that same evening Marilyn packed her things and moved in with Lisa."

"I had no idea."

"Word didn't spread like wildfire for once. People respected Marilyn too much to speculate."

Julia smiled sadly. "She was a wonderful lady. I was so sad when she died. I never saw a man so bleak as George at the funeral." The funeral Jackson had not attended. "They weren't split up then, were they?"

"Nope. As I understood from Lisa, George cleaned up his act. He got counseling, quit drinking, and begged Marilyn to come home." Julia's mom glanced out the kitchen window toward the sliver of moon shining in the night sky. "She did. Then George got sick with the cancer."

Julia put the last dish in the drying rack. She pulled the sink stopper, and the water drained, making a low sucking sound. "I never knew any of this."

"No reason you should. George's cancer went into

remission sometime around Marilyn's death."

"That's good. I'm glad to hear it."

"Yeah, well, the thing is it's back."

"George's cancer?"

"Yes. I expect that's why Jim broached the subject with Jackson. If father and son are ever going to reconcile, it'll have to be soon."

Julia thought of Jackson's brooding demeanor tonight.

"But Jackson isn't over the past. His mother forgave his dad, but he hasn't. It must be a hard thing to live with, all that anger and pain."

"That makes it all the sadder." Because from where Julia stood, a reconciliation was the last thing on Jackson's mind.

****

Half past nine, Julia parked in her designated spot and switched off the engine. No doubt Chase was fast asleep. And Jackson? What did he do at night? Watch TV? Listen to music? Online surf? *Entertain women?*

She slid out from behind the wheel and resisted the urge to slam the door in frustration. But darn it, she needed to stop thinking about Jackson that way. The God-he's-hot-I-want-to-lick-him way. He was a known philanderer and way out of her league.

Her focus should be on her and her life and what she was going to do with the rest of it. She would have to work on that.

Inside, she reached for the light switch, then paused. A flickering light danced on the glass panes of the french door leading out back. She peered outside. A fire burned in the stone pit Jackson had shown her on her first night here. A lone figure lounged in one of the

Adirondack chairs that formed an arc around the pit.

Before she could second guess herself, she set out across the deck. A gust of wind off the mountain set the flames in the pit dancing and reminded her she ought to have brought a sweater. But she couldn't bring herself to turn around.

She hesitated at the steps leading down. Jackson sat with his back to the house, elbows propped on the arms of the chair. He appeared mesmerized by the flames. He hadn't exactly invited her to join him.

"It's warmer closer to the fire, Julia," he called without looking her way.

The night chill seeped through the short cotton dress she wore and turned her exposed toes to ice. The heat of the fire would feel really good about now.

He shifted in his seat and studied her over his shoulder.

The fire behind him made his expression unreadable, but she could imagine his arched brow. She lifted her chin and marched down the stone path to the chair beside his.

"I wondered if you'd come out," Jackson said, his focus once more on the dancing flames.

"I hope you don't mind."

"Why would I mind?"

She decided not to mince words. "I guess because of your mood when you left my parents' house tonight."

He slanted her an affronted look. "My mood?"

"Brooding is the word that comes to mind. Or maybe just flat-out verklempt."

The cheek facing her creased as the corner of his mouth kicked upward.

Tension she hadn't realized she held eked out of her. Jackson, the larger-than-life, self-assured stud, she could handle. Pensive Jackson rattled her.

"I've never been verklempt in my life—not that I actually know what that word means." His eyes narrowed on her, and his smile vanished. "Jules, you're not wearing enough clothes." He extended an arm toward her. "Come over here."

The frigid air had permeated her very bones. But the thought of moving closer to Jackson had all her nerve endings tingling and not from the cold. Good thing her wiser, adult self knew better than to get sucked in by the self-admitted scoundrel.

"I'm okay." She held out her hands toward the fire.

He rolled his eyes. "I can't relax over here knowing you're sitting there freezing." He paused. "But then I get it. You're afraid you can't resist me."

His cocky attitude and, yes, a freezing gust of wind had her out of her chair and at his side in seconds flat. "Where do you want me?" *Oh God.*

His eyes gleamed with devilry, but by some miracle he opted not to comment on her poor choice of words. He grabbed her hand and tugged 'til she was close enough for him to hook an arm around her waist. The next thing she knew, she was on his lap, his arm hugging her into his chest. His body heat burned through her chambray dress, past her skin, melting her bones.

She sighed out her pleasure and let her cheek rest against his broad shoulder. The elusive scent of his aftershave, mixed with smoke from the fire, had her frozen toes curling in her espadrilles.

"Better?"

She nodded and tried to block the mental image of nuzzling the underside of his jaw in search of a direct hit of his cologne.

"Good." His voice, all rough velvet, stirred her already heightened senses.

He shifted so she settled onto him more snuggly. Neither his denim jeans nor her thin dress and silk panties did anything to diminish the hard feel of his muscular thighs beneath her bottom. Sexual awareness screamed through her, along with something more poignant that had her heart squeezing in her chest.

A long minute passed, punctuated by nothing other than the crackling fire and her heart pounding in her ears. She searched desperately for something to break the silence. "The fire's nice. Do you come out here often?"

His shoulders moved in a negligent shrug. "Often enough."

She angled her head back to study him. "When you need to think, maybe?"

Jackson's hazel gaze never shifted from the fire. "What would I be needing to think about?"

His question provided a welcome distraction from her own inappropriate yearning to do something stupid, like weave her fingers into his hair and yank his head down 'til their mouths tangled, and she jumped in with both feet. "My mom told me about your father's illness."

"She did, did she?"

If she hadn't been sitting on his lap, she would've bought the casual tone. But his body tensed up as tight as a bowstring.

She placed a calming hand on his chest. His steady

heartbeat thumped against her palm. "I'm sorry, Jackson."

His eyes narrowed. "You left a boyfriend in New York. What happened there?"

Her mind went blank. "What happened?" she aped.

One corner of his mouth crooked upward, and the hard cast to his eyes softened. "That's what I asked."

A glowing log gave a loud crack, and embers erupted skyward.

Julia chirped and jumped all at once.

Jackson made soothing sounds and wrapped both arms around her, pulling her close. One hand cruised lazily up and down her arm, causing gooseflesh to sprout all over her body and making her want to purr.

"I assume that's why you moved back home," he added helpfully.

His words acted like a bucket of ice dumped on her head. Jackson wanted to rummage through the dismal record of her love life? Oh sure. Maybe she could follow up with a confession that her stupid childhood crush on him had morphed into an even stupider adult crush. Though, in all likelihood, he'd already figured that much out.

"Don't think I didn't notice you turning the tables on me, trying to get me off the subject of your dad." She sounded peevish and didn't care one iota.

Jackson combed a hand through her hair, as if trying to gentle her. "Easy, honey. You want to talk about me and dear old Dad? Fine. I'll spill my guts. But only if you share your story first."

She sat up—as far as she could with both his arms around her. "I don't see how my love life has anything to do with—"

He shook his head, and his arms fell away from her. "Just like when we were kids. You were okay being the helpful one, the girl who had it all together. Then again, you did—unlike some of us," he said, gesturing to himself. He uttered a mirthless laugh. "Some things never change."

His skewed memories left her more than a little bemused. "I had it together, and you didn't? Jackson, you weren't some kid running wild. You were a star player on the football team, the lead singer in *thee* high school band. You had a million friends and your pick of dates on any given night. Whereas I had a solid understanding of mathematics and could count the number of dates I went on before college on one hand. Which one of us had it together?"

"Honey, you intimidated all the guys in town. Too smart, too pretty, too good for every one of us. Grady was the only guy I knew dumb enough to not realize how too good for him you were. *Are* for that matter."

"*That* is ridiculous. This conversation is ridiculous." She wrapped her arms around herself.

"Okay." His stare returned to the diminishing fire, and his jaw flexed. He made no move to resume touching her. In other words, conversation over, good night.

She should thank her lucky stars and take that as her exit cue. Instead she heard herself ask, "You want to know about my boyfriend, Jacks? My *ex*-boyfriend, that is?"

His eyes slanted to hers. "I asked."

"Fine. I'll tell you, then you'll see how together I am. His name's Chris. He's the company's darling, a rising star who moved to the New York branch from

California roughly two years ago. For some strange reason, he took a shine to me." Her face throbbed with the heat of intense embarrassment, and she prayed he couldn't see her insta-flush in the golden firelight.

"I knew it wasn't right, knew he was too California glamorous and socially—" She broke off, searching for the right word. "—invested, I guess."

"I think you mean social climber." One of his arms snaked around her waist. His hand, curving over her hip, seared her skin with delicious warmth that wound through her, pooling in her lower abdomen.

"Maybe. Regardless, I agreed to go with him to a Ryan Moore concert." She chuckled humorlessly, recalling her recent discovery concerning Jackson and the folk singer. "His music's my weakness."

"Really."

She thought he would say something more. When he didn't, she drew a deep breath and forged on.

"To my surprise, we kept seeing each other. The next thing I knew, we were a couple. Eventually he asked me to move in with him. I did. I thought we had a future." She smiled sadly as truth she had no intention of sharing spun through her mind. Prior to Chris, she hadn't met one man she wanted to date on a serious level, much less consider marrying. The only person who'd ever caused her heart to trip over itself was Jackson, and it turned out that hadn't changed. Talk about pathetic.

"So what happened?" he asked in a quiet voice.

"Things started going wrong. He seemed off. *We* seemed off. I started thinking my first impression was right and I'd made a mistake letting him into my life— and then I knew I had." She heaved a sigh. "Turns out he and my assistant had a thing going right under my nose, and I didn't have one clue. Yeah, that sounds like someone who has it all together, doesn't it?"

"How does you dating a sleazeball, then breaking up with him mean you don't have it together?"

She clambered to her feet, somehow evading his grasp when he tried to stop her, and glared down at him. "Isn't it obvious? You have a long successful career under your belt, you've been married, you have a son, and all I have is a job I don't even miss, will probably never have children, and I couldn't keep the one man I let into my bed interested."

The words she spouted in her own personal pity party echoed in her head. Not only had she confessed how undesirable she was, but she'd admitted being a virgin when she met Chris. Now he knew beyond a shadow of doubt how much of a reject she really was. Humiliation burned like acid in her chest.

"Jules, what are you saying?"

He wanted her to say it again? Hell. No. She turned and fled.

Jackson grasped her shoulder in his firm, warm grip before she made it to the deck steps. He moved in close, wrapping an arm around her waist from behind, then spoke into her ear. "Not so fast, sweetheart."

"Jackson, let me go."

He didn't. Instead he urged her around to face him.

The fire had died down, and they stood far enough from the glowing embers that she could not make out his expression. Julia hoped he couldn't make out hers. She couldn't stand for him to see the utter misery surely written on her face.

She ducked her head, and he put his arms around

her, pulling her into his chest. "Honey, you said a mouthful just now."

"And you said nothing at all," she choked.

"You're right. Fair's fair. You wanted to know about my dad, right? You heard he's sick and likely dying. Well, you know what? I don't much care. That sounds awful, right? A man who doesn't give one sh—" He broke off, then said evenly, "Doesn't care for his own flesh and blood."

She knew Jackson and his father had never been close. But he was too upset by the mere mention of his dad to not care as he claimed. People who didn't care about someone didn't bother thinking about them at all, in Julia's experience. Kind of like how Grady never once crossed her mind in all the years since she'd moved to New York, yet she had never forgotten Jackson.

"I'm sure it's complicated for you, but no, I don't think you're awful. I could never think that."

"Never? Yet you held a grudge for thirteen years."

That grudge had bitten her in the behind so many times the last few days it was a wonder she could sit. She dropped her forehead against his chest.

"I guess you know how my dad treated me growing up. But I'll tell you something you don't know, Julia. The reason I can't forgive the man." He stared into the distance, as if seeing into the past.

"Hannah and I had come home on a house-hunting mission and paid a visit to my folks. Dad got sauced. No surprise there. He started in on me for something I can't recall now. I do remember deciding Hannah didn't need to suffer through one of his drunken scenes. We said goodbye to Mom and headed out to the car.

146

But George wouldn't have it. He followed us, screaming at me the whole way about how I was no good, how I didn't deserve Hannah or any decent woman in my life."

She cringed. How could a father speak with such cruelty to his own son?

"Mom came outside, begging him to leave me alone. That's when he really got pissed, and he…" Jackson's voice cracked.

Julia watched him wrestle his emotions into submission. Her fingers itched to smooth his hair, cradle his cheeks, offer any sort of comfort.

He swallowed audibly, then his tortured eyes sought hers. "He cocked back like he meant to hit Mom. I went ballistic, tackled him to the ground, and got more than one good hit in. The truth is I would have pummeled the life out of him if it hadn't been for Hannah and Mom pulling at me. Afterward Mom packed her bags and let us take her to Aunt Lisa's. She finally left him." A bitter smile twisted Jackson's face. "And you know what? That's when he changed. Not when she'd pleaded with him all those years when I was growing up, when she was still young, but then after she'd finally had enough. She stood her ground, Julia, until he got into counseling and rehab. Only then did she go back. Then he got sick, and it killed her."

She frowned in confusion. "What do you mean? Did your dad…did he hurt her? I thought Marilyn died in a car accident involving a drunk driver."

His eyes went glacial. "George got a secondary infection from his chemo and had to be hospitalized. It was on the way home from there she was killed by the damned drunk driver. If it hadn't been for her going to see him, she'd still be alive. Instead she died, and that son of a bitch went into remission."

'Til now hung in the air between them.

Julia didn't know what to say. His dad wasn't to blame for Marylin's death. But saying so now wouldn't help matters. Jackson's hurt and anger ran too deep. So she did the only thing she could. She hugged him hard.

"I'm so sorry, Jacks," she whispered, her cheek against his chest. "For what you've been through, for calling you out and invading your privacy. But…I'm glad you told me. Thank you for trusting me."

His arms around her tightened, and he rested his cheek atop her head. "No big deal. What happens to that old man doesn't affect me one way or another."

She wasn't buying what he was selling, but she opted not to argue for once.

"Besides, the trust went both ways tonight," he said in a soft voice. "Now I know about your idiot ex."

She laughed aloud. After Jackson's revelation, her crappy love life seemed inconsequential—and maybe he'd missed the big reveal about her virgin status. No way to know without bringing it up again, and that she absolutely would not do.

She couldn't handle a repeat of Chris's reaction. When he learned she was a virgin, first had come shock, then humor like he thought she must be joking. Later, he'd used the information as proof something was wrong with her. Maybe it was.

She unwound herself from Jackson. "It's getting late. I better turn in."

"I'll walk you to your door." He skipped up the steps and crossed the deck ahead of her, leaving her no choice but to follow.

Chapter Ten

Jackson let himself inside the dark cottage, conscious of Julia following him. She hovered in the doorway as he clicked on a small table lamp that still left most of the room in deep shadow.

He strode to the hallway. Her signature floral scent was stronger here. He flicked on the light. "Checking for boogeymen," he announced.

"Any there?"

He switched off the light and wandered back to the living area. He leaned a hip on the back edge of the couch. "Nope."

"Ever the gentleman, even though we both knew no one was hiding here."

He snorted under his breath. "Gentleman, huh? Is that why you're leaving a football field between us?"

After a brief hesitation, she approached the couch. When she reached the opposite armrest from him, she halted.

"You're smart to be cautious."

"I…I'm not being cautious. I just thought…" She glanced over her shoulder at the closed door, turned back to face him, and shrugged.

"You didn't invite me in, and you're wondering why I haven't left yet," he said, matter-of-fact. "It's because something you said is sticking in my craw."

She gave him a wary look. "It's late. Maybe we

can rehash my idiocy tomorrow."

"You see? Exactly what I'm talking about. You're no idiot. But you are one stubborn lady. Sorry to put you through it tonight, darlin', but unless I miss my guess, if I want to continue this discussion, it'd better be now, because come morning? The subject will be off-limits."

She groaned and pressed her fingertips to her forehead. "Let's don't and say we did."

He laughed. He did know a thing or two about her. He closed the distance between them, mainly because he couldn't not.

"I don't even remember what I said now."

"You said you couldn't keep your man's interest."

Her mouth gaped in open astonishment. "Gee, thanks. I'd hate it if I somehow blocked those words from my memory."

He grinned. "The point is you've got it all wrong, Jules. Your ex is the idiot. He was lucky you agreed to date him in the first place. He blew it. Now he's begging you to come back."

"Nope."

He crooked a hand under her chin, angling her face upward. "Bull. He's been in touch. Tell me I'm wrong."

She shrugged. "He may have emailed once or twice—"

"And texted you," Jackson interjected. "I saw one of those with my own eyes."

"It's a moot point. I'll never take him back."

He cupped her shoulder and squeezed. "See? *So* not an idiot. You know what he did wasn't your fault, right? Cheaters cheat, babe."

"Sure. I know." Despite her quick assurance,

disbelief flickered in her eyes. She threw a glance at the door, a none-too-subtle hint for him to leave.

Not a chance. Not 'til he made his point. "You don't know. You're owning this, and it's not yours to own."

She gave him a sweet, patently false smile—the kind Chase tried when he wanted to stay up later than he should or have ice cream for breakfast. Jackson stifled a laugh.

"Look, I was annoyed with you, Jacks. I went high drama and exaggerated the situation. It's not that big a deal. My boyfriend cheated, and, yeah, I feel stupid because I had no idea whatsoever, especially since he got where he hardly ever wanted to..." Her eyes bugged as her words dried up.

"Hardly ever wanted to what?"

She clamped her lips together and shook her head in an emphatic no.

"Hold on—the dude had no sex drive?"

She lifted both her hands to her cheeks. "That was what I thought. Until he cheated on me. That's when he told me..." Her hands moved to cover her eyes.

No poker face, whatsoever. He almost felt bad for her.

"Jules, what did he say?"

She dropped her hands to her sides and lifted her chin. "That's not important. What he did speaks for itself."

He articulated each word. "What. Did. He. Say?"

She bit her lower lip. A moment later she spoke in a voice so soft he had to strain to hear. "He said he gave me what I needed but I didn't give the same to him."

"What the hell does that mean?"

She jammed her hands in her hair and stumbled away from him. "You need me to spell it out? I'm missing that certain something. Sex appeal, magnetism, that hot factor, I guess? It's why he went looking elsewhere. He flat-out told me it was just sex with her. He wanted me but didn't *want* me. It's fine. It's just me, I guess. I'm like I've always been. *You* know."

He stalked toward her. "*I* know? You're just you? You're not making any sense."

One fat tear leaked from her eye, and she scrubbed it away.

His insides froze. "Honey, please don't cry."

"I'm not crying." Her loud sniffle belied her words. "Can't we let this go?" She sent him a watery smile.

Jackson glared down at her. She was trying to comfort him now? "Come here," he heard himself growl. He grabbed one of her hands and pulled her into the bedroom, snapping on the hallway light as they passed through.

Enough light spilled into the bedroom he could easily make his way to his destination—the free-standing, full-length mirror in the far corner.

"What on earth—"

"Hush." He positioned her so she stood in front of him, facing the mirror, her back to his chest. Their eyes met in the reflection. He looped an arm around her waist, resting one palm just below her ribcage. Tiny tremors vibrated through her, transmitting themselves loud and clear through his fingertips. Lust slammed through him.

Maybe this wasn't such a good idea.

She drew a shaky breath. "What are we doing, Jackson?"

"My turn to tutor you, darlin'. A little show and tell on the facts of life."

He drew a deep breath, buying himself a moment to quash the feelings running roughshod through him. Anger toward her ex he could handle, no problem. But the perfect storm of tenderness and desire all drawing him into the vortex of this sexy-as-hell, vulnerable woman standing before him rocked him to his core.

But he wasn't a man to back down from a challenge.

"The thing is, honey, I'm beginning to think I was wrong."

"About what?"

"Your ex is an idiot, but maybe you are, too."

She huffed out a laugh, and her nicely rounded rear brushed the part of him clamoring for an invite to this private party.

He shifted backward, then brought his free hand up to smooth his knuckles over her cheek. Her skin was chilled from the outdoor air and dewy as a newborn babe's. "If he really said you were lacking in sex appeal, sweetheart, and I'm having a really hard time accepting that, he's a blind fool. And if you believe him, you have a few screws loose, too. Any red-blooded man and a number of women I can think of would want you."

She grunted in frustration. "I should never have told you." As she spoke, she wriggled against his arm, attempting to bolt.

He tightened his hold, bringing her body into full-on contact with his that had him gritting his teeth. "Can you not?"

She frowned at him in the mirror but stopped

struggling. "Not what?"

He laughed softly. "I'm a man, sugar, with a man's healthy appetite for all things woman."

"So I've heard," she muttered. Uncertainty clouded her eyes, like she wasn't sure if he was saying what he so obviously was.

He grinned despite the war within him. Damn, she was sweet. "Know what I see when I look at you?"

"No," she whispered.

He wanted to show her. *Really* show her. The next best thing would have to suffice. "I see thick, sexy-as-hell hair that always looks like you rolled out of a bed from a recent tumble. I see honey-colored skin that makes me itch to see if it's as smooth and pretty under your clothes as it is here." He skimmed a hand along her thigh, dragging up the hem of her dress to reveal a good bit of flesh.

She gasped, and his erection pulsed to the point of pain. But he wasn't going to think about what he wanted to do with that part of his anatomy. Then she sucked her lower lip between her teeth. He stifled a groan. Sweat trickled down the center of his back, despite the cool night air.

He willed himself to continue and grazed the underside of her jaw with his knuckles. "I see soft, full lips, begging to be kissed, and the prettiest sky-blue eyes that could steal a man's soul. I see a woman's body with curves and hollows in all the right places."

His gaze dropped. "And then there's the shoes." By the time he got to her sexy footwear, his voice had gone hoarse, but dammit, he would finish this.

Julia shook her head as if to clear it and swayed into him. He caught her hips, pulling her close to steady her. Sweet aching torture. Had he ever wanted a woman this bad?

"Shoes?" she prompted, the word a breathless whisper.

Jackson studied her. Eyelids at half-mast. Cheeks flushed. A fine tremor vibrated through her body.

Grim certainty permeated his lust-fogged brain. He wasn't the only one suffering here. The knowledge did not help one iota.

He cleared his throat and tried speaking in a normal tone. "You strut around in those strappy heels, and my mind can't help but imagine you wearing them and"—*nothing else*—"not a lot more."

Her lips parted. God, he wanted to kiss her. To lay her on the bed not two feet away and ravage that mouth. Trouble was it wouldn't end there. And Julia deserved better.

Still he dipped his head to nuzzle her hair as his hands migrated from her hips to splay over her flat belly. "Then there's your scent. You smell so. Damn. Good. Always have. Like lilacs and vanilla. Or cake. Very, very sexy cake."

She covered her face with her hands. Tremors wracked her body. Ah hell, now he'd made her cry?

He caught the soft snort right before she dropped her hands to reveal a brilliant smile. "Cake's sexy? Oh, Jackson, you're so sweet. Beyond sweet. I haven't been here a week, and already you've tried to solve my living situation, my ride, my relationship, or lack thereof." She sobered. "You don't have to fix everything for me. I'm a big girl. I can take care of myself."

She hadn't believed a word he said. Irritated, he

pulled his hands off her to splay them on his hips. "I'm not being sweet."

In the mirror, her lips curved in an angel's smile. Without warning she turned to face him, not stepping back an inch. His heart slammed into his ribs as the urge to grab her and kiss her senseless threatened to overwhelm his good sense.

She cupped his cheeks with warm, slightly damp palms. "Yes, you are," she said in an achingly soft voice.

Warmth flooded his chest, setting off alarm bells in his head. Lust he could handle. But tenderness between them could only mean trouble—for her.

He'd wanted to make her feel good and, yeah, maybe know he'd put a smile on her face. But as a result, he now navigated through treacherous territory.

Because she saw a hero when she looked at him, but the sad reality was he was as bad as they came. He could only cause her more heartache. The best thing would be for him to shut up now and get the hell out of here before either of them got any ideas. *Who are you kidding? You've had ideas since you laid eyes on her.*

He squelched the irritating prick of conscience. "I'm being straight with you, Jules. Your ex is a moron. But I can see talking isn't getting me anywhere." He paused a beat. "I could prove it to you."

Her face went blank. "Prove it how?"

He combed his fingers through her hair. The silken feel of it made him want to fan the golden locks on his pillow and bury his face in the lush waves—while sinking himself into her soft heat. He closed his eyes, hoping to dislodge the image from his brain. It didn't work.

He went on through clenched teeth. "This guy's got your head screwed on backward. Maybe he was trying to control you, maybe he was jealous of you, or maybe he's gay. Don't know, don't care. What matters is you need to hit the reset button."

"Reset button," she said, the way some people said *oh really.*

"Get back in the saddle."

"The…saddle?"

"You need to have yourself a fling."

****

"A fling—to see for myself how desirable I am."

"That pretty much covers it."

Restrained hunger burned in his eyes, stealing her breath. If she read him right—and what else could he mean?—he wanted her.

A terrible yearning filled her, because she wanted him beyond reason. What kind of fool did that make her? Jackson was a playboy, like her ex. But this time around she knew in advance. Plus he was Jackson. Her feelings for him had deep roots. If they did this thing and if he—*when* he—decided he was tired of her or, worse, decided Chris's summation of her was correct, she might never recover.

The risk outweighed the gains. She licked her lips. "That's not my way. I told you—"

"You're choosy about who you let in your bed. I respect that. I didn't say you had to jump into the sack. Just have some fun. Let your hair down a little. Let somebody remind you how desirable you are and always have been."

She chewed over the word *somebody* 'til the last thing he said hit her like a hammer. "*Always*, huh?" She crossed her arms. It was that or wrap them around his neck and plaster herself to him. "Jackson Tate, you're full of it. You didn't know I existed when we were in high school."

His warm palms cupped her shoulders. "And you have this on whose authority?" The softly spoken words threatened to short circuit her brain.

Calling on all her mental faculties, she stayed on point. "Did you ask me to prom? Did you ask me out *ever*? Did you flirt with me or look at me like you did the hot girls?"

"It was complicated. That doesn't mean I didn't find you attractive."

"Complicated. Right."

"I'm telling you the truth."

"Forget it," she said, backing away so his hands fell from her shoulders. "That's ancient history, anyway." She had a clear path out of the room and took it, beelining for the back door. It was past time for him to leave.

His words, buttery soft, stretched out like a hook and caught her before she reached the far edge of the couch. "Maybe I didn't see you like that at first, but…there was something about you. Something special. That hasn't changed."

Goose bumps sprouted all over her body. The fact he could crush her heart into a million pieces seemed less important by the second. She spun slowly to face him.

He'd followed her and now stood a foot away, limned in the light spilling from the hall. "The thing is I knew then what I know now—and trust me, if I forgot for one second…" He shook his head. "That doesn't matter. The point is I wasn't good enough to carry your trash, Jules, and that hasn't changed. I'm still that jerk you left in your dust thirteen years ago."

She rubbed her forehead in confusion. "If that's how you feel, then why all this talk about us having a fling? Because it sure sounds like you're warning me off you."

His eyes widened.

Her stomach nose-dived to her knees as the truth slammed into her—five seconds too late. He wanted her to have a fling—just not with him. Good God, it was high school all over again.

"Hey, Jules, ah…" He scrubbed a hand over the back of his neck.

"Oh, I get it." She forced a laugh. It didn't sound half bad. Almost believable. Time to go for the gold. "You meant with someone else. Um, good idea, I guess? I mean, maybe that would work." She held her breath and waited for his reaction.

His brows arched. "It is? I mean, it is." He rocked back on his heels.

"Have anyone in mind?"

He frowned.

The obviousness of the answer hit her like a brick. "Oh, right. Grady. You want me to go out with—"

"No," he said with vehemence.

"Oka-ay." She drew out the word. More than anything, she wanted Jackson to leave so she could mull over the many ways she'd humiliated herself tonight. Must be some kind of record.

"I mean, Grady, he has a crush on you."

She stared at him.

"It can't be a fling if one of you has real feelings."

She nodded slowly. That made sense, in a twisted sort of way. "Right. Well, Jackson, thanks for the advice and the pep talk." She swung her fist in a rah-rah uppercut. "I'll give it some thought. But, if you don't mind, I'm pretty tired, and tomorrow is a workday."

His eyes narrowed. "Why do I feel like everything I said went in one ear and out the other? I screwed up the message, didn't I?"

She laughed, charmed despite everything, damn him. "No. I heard everything you said, and I appreciate that you care."

He reached for her hands. "I do care, very much."

"I believe you." Her chest ached. He did care. Just not like that, which was best for all concerned. But it still hurt like hell.

Chapter Eleven

Julia glanced at her office wall clock. Three p.m. Quitting time. She could get used to hours like this.

She glanced at her cell phone before tossing it in her purse, hoping she'd somehow missed Lisa's return call. She'd left a message but so far hadn't heard back. It still didn't feel right keeping Jackson in the dark. On the other hand, he had granted Lisa authority to sign off on Chase's comings, goings, field trips, and classes. So technically the school didn't need to notify him. Knowing didn't make her feel better.

She waved at Sue on her way out.

Sue put a hand over the phone she held to her ear and mouthed, "See you at six?"

Julia gave her a thumbs-up and let herself out, enjoying the warmth of the sun on her skin after several hours spent in seventy-two-degree, air-conditioned air. She could drive home—funny how quickly she'd gotten used to calling Jackson's cottage home—clean up, and make it to the Copper Rocket with time to spare. Which meant she still had time to decide how much of last night's Jackson debacle to share with her friends.

She navigated out of the school lot, her mind replaying the post-fire-pit conversation for the fiftieth time. It could have gone much worse. Hadn't she saved herself from total humiliation at the eleventh hour—by pretending to agree his idea for her to have a fling had merit?

She had to give him credit. He got she wasn't a one-night-stand type of girl. To Jackson, that didn't rule out a lighthearted flirtation. If he only knew she had no idea what that even meant. She'd never casually dated in her life. Sure, a few men had piqued her interest enough to see them more than a handful of times. Unfortunately, as their interest in her grew, hers in them stymied.

She didn't want to be alone. She simply wanted… She laughed softly at how *un*-simple what she wanted was. For one thing, she didn't know exactly what she had been holding out for all her adult life. Except— *butterflies*. She wanted someone who filled her with butterflies at the mere thought of him.

Jackson's face, aglow in the light of last night's fire, flashed across her mind, and those recalcitrant butterflies swarmed inside her. She gripped the wheel 'til her knuckles turned white.

Why hadn't Chris, or anyone else for that matter, done it for her the way Jackson did without even trying? Just when she'd concluded she held out for something that didn't exist, Jackson reappeared in her life and threw her whole theory into question. Not that he was the man for her. If anything, he was worse for her than Chris. Not that he claimed to want her. Chris, at least, had done that for a time.

Good-looking, charming Chris, who had women galore vying for his attention, had singled her out. His undeniable interest had both flattered and flummoxed her. They'd had nothing in common other than work, and she'd made it clear she didn't dip her toes in the company pool.

Then he'd walked into the copy room humming her song.

She shook her head. She'd berated herself for a fool, but the truth was she'd have been a fool *not* to go out with him. How could a girl win? Only an idiot wouldn't recognize men like Chris didn't grow on trees. That, combined with the blaring fact she wasn't getting any younger? Little wonder she decided the time had come to put away her pie-in-the-sky dreams.

She'd gone for it. Let her guard down. Let the man into her bed.

Ugh. She cringed, remembering the first time. She didn't think either one of them had enjoyed that. But it had gotten better. Chris had been a good lover. At least she thought he was. *He* certainly thought he was.

"Did you come?"

"I think so."

"You think so? You either did or you didn't. I mean, usually women have multiples with me."

While she did enjoy sex with Chris and did sometimes reach orgasm—she thought—she'd never quite managed that multiples feat. After a while he quit asking.

She navigated the last major curve before the guard gate. Maybe she couldn't experience the fireworks and falling-off-a-cliff feeling she'd read about in novels. Maybe she should've learned to fake it. That was a thing some women did, right?

She slowed to a halt at the gated entrance and flashed a friendly smile. The guard leaned out of the booth to eye her, then waved her on.

Have yourself a fling, Jackson had suggested.

She'd done the conservative thing all her life, and

where had that gotten her? Not married. No children. Never breathlessly in love. Almost engaged to a lying cheat who claimed she was some sort of sexual dud.

Maybe she *should* let someone help get her groove on.

****

The Copper Rocket stood on the outskirts of town and hadn't changed much since Julia and her friends frequented it as high schoolers when they'd come for the live music and people watching. Later, home on college breaks having reached the legal drinking age, they'd come for the same things, plus cheap happy hour.

The old barn and stables turned restaurant bar attracted all sorts, from Honeyville locals to city dwellers from Asheville. Ages ranged from eighteen to eighty.

The place had a definite rustic charm. Scarred wood-plank floors under high-beamed ceilings opened to a large, outdoor, gravel-laid dining section. From there, a sloped lawn lead to a band setup, which stood in front of a canyon drop-off, making for some great acoustics.

Sue, of course, had beaten Callie and Julia to the restaurant and staked out a primo outdoor spot. "I ordered drinks," she said as they approached the table. "And here they come now."

A young waitress set drinks on the round top—white wine for Julia, beer for Callie, and a cocktail for Sue.

They sat and clinked glasses.

"Perfect timing, girls. The band's warming up."

Callie eyed the stage over her shoulder. "These

guys are great. Not as good as Jackson and his crew, mind you, but who is?"

Sipping her ice-cold chardonnay, Julia glanced between her friends. "Who wants to go first?"

Callie raised one hand. "Not much happening in my world, so it may as well be me." She angled her platinum blonde head. "Shop's busy, sales are up, and Frank passed his senior wellness exam with flying colors." She lifted one shiny, turquoise-lacquered pointer finger in the air. "One thing is new. I joined the boxing club that opened recently one block off Main Street."

Sue's look conveyed total shock. "You? Exercise? That's not only new, it's the miracle of the century."

Sue made a good point. Callie hated exercise involving anything more aerobic than walking her dog or dancing. Yet somehow she remained perpetually pixie thin.

Callie shrugged. "It feels more like punching out my frustrations, though I do work up a sweat. It's fun."

"Frustrations? Such as?" Julia asked.

Callie got that deer-in-the-headlights look, and a rosy stain rode up her neck. Interesting.

Julia sent Sue a questioning look.

Sue shrugged.

"There's this new artist in town. I sell his paintings in the shop. Really good stuff."

"And?" Julia prompted. "Is he asking for a higher commission than usual or something?"

"No." Callie smoothed her hair behind her ears unnecessarily. "He wants to paint me."

"Intriguing," Julia murmured.

"I agree. And flattering. What's the problem? Is he

asking you to show up at midnight, naked?" Sue asked with a giggle. She winked at Julia.

Callie's cheeks glowed a hot pink even as she waved a dismissive hand in the air.

"He *does* want to paint you naked," Julia said in awe.

"It's simple. I don't want to be painted. Enough about me. What's up with the two of you?"

Julia and Sue exchanged glances. Clearly there was more to this story, but Callie could be as stubborn as a mule. Until she wanted to share, no one could pry a thing out of her.

"I'll go. I heard from Chris via email again. He threatened to come down here whether I invite him or not so we can hash things out."

"No," her friends chimed in unison.

"That's exactly what I told him. The first time he asked, I didn't reply at all, but in light of his persistence, I wrote back. Short and to the point. Do. Not. Bother. Hopefully that's the end of it."

Sue gave Julia a frank look. "We'd understand if you wanted to at least hear him out."

"We would?" Callie asked. "Stick to your guns, Julia. Next chapter."

"You're preaching to the choir," Julia said. "Your turn, Sue. How's life?"

"I'm sure you'll be shocked to hear I'm busier than a one-legged man in an ass-kicking contest, getting through summer session and preparing for the coming school year. Definitely nothing brewing romantically." She blew air out her cheeks. "To tell the truth, I'm in a rut. I'd like to have some semblance of a relationship in theory, but I don't see where I have the time even if I could meet someone, which I've begun to think is a non-possibility in this town."

"Hey, you don't know everyone who lives here. And besides, people move in and out of town every day. We have a living, breathing example here in our Jules."

Sue nodded, though her expression remained glum. "True."

"Maybe you just need a little action," Callie said with a grin. "That would shake things up."

"No maybe about it." Sue clinked her glass with Callie's just as the band opened with an upbeat cover song that had people flocking toward the makeshift dance floor.

Julia head-bopped to the beat. "Funny you should mention that. Just last night Jackson told me he thought I needed to get my sexy back. I was thinking he may be right."

Sue's eyes bugged as she all but spat out whatever she'd sucked through her straw. "You're just now getting to this? Last night, you said? And we spent the entire day together!"

"You really know how to keep a secret," Callie breathed. "Spill it."

Sue began ticking off her fingers. "As in, where did this landmark conversation take place? What exactly did he say? Then your reply. Verbatim, please."

Julia drew a deep breath. In retrospect, keeping her friends out of her personal life had not done her any good to date. In fact, maybe if she'd discussed her misgivings about her last relationship with them, she'd have sidestepped the humiliation phase.

So she'd tell them the truth—truncated version, in

the interest of privacy.

"After I got home from my parents' last night, I noticed he had a fire burning in his pit."

"After you got *home*," Callie repeated, caramel eyes twinkling.

"Naturally you decided to join him," Sue piped in before sucking on her tiny cocktail straw.

"I never was one to leave well enough alone," Julia admitted.

"No reason for you *not* to join him," Callie declared. "You're a grown woman, no ties, completely free to do as you wish. And Jackson is…*Jackson.* Go on."

Julia smoothed her hair. "We got to talking."

No way could she share Jackson's revelations about his parents. That meant jumping right to their discussion of her failed love affair. "He flat-out asked why Chris and I broke up. I admitted he'd cheated on me with my assistant. Somehow from there, Jackson deduced I might be feeling crappy about myself."

"Go figure." Sue grabbed Julia's hand and gave a little squeeze.

Callie arched her brows. "And you just accepted this show of sympathy."

Julia blinked in confusion. "Why wouldn't I?"

"Because you're you. You're not comfortable making yourself overly vulnerable."

Julia must've made a face because Callie held up her hands, palms out. "Hey, I've been accused of being closed off myself."

A smile tugged at the corners of Julia's lips. "Well, hell. Jackson said much the same as you, Cal. He all but accused me of always having my life together. So I got mad and ran off at the mouth. I told him I didn't have anything together, including not having what it took to hold a man's attention."

"Oh, honey. That's the furthest thing from the truth," Callie insisted.

"That's pretty much how Jacks responded, too. And when I let it slip Chris sort of blamed me for his betrayal, Jackson got all fired up. He came up with several—" She cleared her throat. "—interesting hypotheses concerning Chris's sexual dysfunction."

Callie raised her beer. "Hear, hear, Jacks."

Sue lifted her cocktail, joining her in the toast.

"After that, he shared his bright idea." Julia flashed back to the two of them standing before her mirror, Jackson listing every sexy nuance of hers as he saw it in that husky voice of his. Heat pulsed in her cheeks. She would leave that part out. No question. "He straight-up told me I need to get my sexy back to remind myself how hot I am. I tried to tell him I never had a fling in my life."

"I hardly think he's concerned with your résumé," Callie said. "Sue? Help me out here."

Sue nodded. "Cal's right. He's got enough expertise for the both of you."

The matching gleam in her friends' eyes had her shaking her head. "Before you girls go haring off down the wrong road, allow me to clarify, because *he* certainly did. He said I should definitely have a fling— just not with him."

Sue cocked her head. "He actually said that? I'm shocked."

"Right?" Julia agreed. "It's not something you hear every day."

Callie shook her head sadly. "Sue and I aren't shocked by the fling suggestion."

"You lost me."

Taking a slug of her beer, Callie pointed a finger at Sue.

"We think it's crazy he would push you into the arms of another guy when he so clearly wants you for himself," Sue clarified.

"Bingo," Callie said.

Julia snorted. "For the record, that's what I thought, at first, too. He quickly disabused me of the notion."

As if she hadn't spoken, Callie threw her arms up in a wide V, exclaiming, "Julia and Jackson are finally going to square off."

Julia glanced around quickly. "Keep your voice down. I'm telling you, Jackson doesn't want the job."

Callie chuckled. "Right. Nice try, Jacks."

Sue leaned forward, resting on her forearms. "What about you, Jules? Be honest. If he'd offered himself up last night, would you have accepted?"

She met Sue's eyes, then Callie's. "In a New York minute. Thank God he had his head on straight. I left a disaster behind me in the city. Sue, you all but warned me off Jackson, remember?"

"Yes, but I told you he's seemed different lately. Not quite so *active* if you know what I mean. What do you think, Callie?"

Callie pursed her lips. "I think it's past time Jackson settled down. He deserves someone sweet, beautiful, and smart. Someone with integrity and grit. Someone like our Jules." She leaned back in her chair, taking her beer with her, then froze, the mug inches from her lips. Her amused gaze fixed on something across the room. "Fifty guesses who just walked in, and, oh, looks like he spotted you."

Sue held a hand over her mouth to cover her laughter. "I haven't had this much fun since I don't know when. Julia, why didn't you dump your ex and come home sooner?"

Julia couldn't frame a reply. Not with her mind screaming *Jackson is here?* Giddy anticipation bubbled up inside her before she could nix it. She swiveled in her chair to look behind her.

Jackson and Grady hovered in the space separating the indoor restaurant from the crowded open-air seating area. His eyes locked on to her. She couldn't swear from where she sat, but it looked as if a smile tugged at the corners of his mouth. He lifted his hand in a brief wave.

She returned the gesture.

A moment later he broke eye contact and spoke to Grady. The two of them headed toward the outdoor bar.

She jerked around and faced the table. "See? He's not here looking for me. They headed to the bar. It's Friday night." She hated the disappointment swamping her, but this was just a case of same place, same time.

"That man has it bad," Sue said in a low voice.

"Yep," Callie said with a single nod.

Julia rolled her eyes and took a healthy swallow of wine. "You two are ridiculous. Jackson and I hadn't spoken for years prior to me showing up, literally, on his doorstep a few days ago. He sees me as an old friend with ties to his family who did a few nice things for him when we were kids. And as I already pointed out, he made the friend part amply clear last night."

"We hear you. We just think you're *both* deluded." Sue searched the room. "If you see our waitress, snag her. Another round is in order."

Julia nibbled on her pointer finger, considering. "Did I mention he asked me to be his date for the Helping Hands charity event next weekend? As friends."

Both Callie and Sue stared at Julia, mouths agape.

Callie recovered first. She leaned forward, parting Julia's hair here and there, examining her scalp.

Julia froze. "What is it? Did a bug land on me?"

"No. Just looking for the scar from where your mom dropped you on your head as a child."

Sue, slurping the last of her cocktail, yelped and snatched up her napkin to cover her face. Soundless laughter shook her until tears leaked from her eyes. When her mirth faded to intermittent chuckles, she aimed a playful glare at Callie. "You made my drink go up my nose. That's twice. Warn me next time."

Callie flashed an innocent smile. "Sorry."

The waitress arrived, a starstruck glaze in her eyes Julia recognized all too well. "Who's friends with Jackson Tate?"

Callie and Sue pointed at Julia.

"We all are," Julia said, bemused. "We've all known him for ages."

"Lucky you," the waitress said and set down drinks for each of them. "These are from him."

Callie smirked.

The moment the waitress left, Callie leaned in, motioning for Sue and Julia to follow suit. "I have a plan, and we don't have much time to hash it out."

"A plan for what?" Julia asked.

"To prove both you and Jackson wrong."

****

Jackson had never much minded strangers stopping him as he crossed a room—a good thing, since it happened pretty much every time he went out in public. He'd opted to go into showbiz, after all. His band had several hits, and his songwriting had garnered him even more acclaim. So he got it. People wanted to know him. He just didn't like it much *tonight*.

After the second table of people rose to greet him, Grady zoomed past him, en route to Julia and her friends. Jackson thought he heard a muttered, "See ya, sucker."

Grady. Something about him lately grated on Jackson's nerves. Which was why tonight, when Grady invited Jackson to join him out for a drink, he'd nearly declined. Then Grady mentioned meeting up with Julia and her friends. His assumption that the girls would go out, this being Julia's first weekend in town, had made sense to Jackson.

What hadn't was his own violent opposition to letting Grady crash the party on his own. Especially as he himself had zero claim on Julia.

And up rose another table of folks to flag him down.

Jackson smiled, murmured a few words, then extricated himself. Head down to avoid making eye contact with anyone else, he strode full steam ahead toward the table where he'd spotted the women and arrived to find three half-full glasses, three purses, and otherwise no sign of life.

All three gone plus Grady could only mean one thing. He looked toward the band. Grady, Callie, and

Sue hovered on the edge of the makeshift dance floor. No Julia, though.

She must've made a detour to the ladies' room.

Grinning to himself, Jackson deposited his soda water beside the chardonnay he assumed belonged to Jules, then headed toward the throng of dancers. He'd snag Julia as soon as she rejoined her friends and pull her into the thick of things. It wouldn't be a big statement by any stretch of the imagination. They'd be a couple of old friends dancing, same as Grady, Callie, and Sue. Safe as apple pie.

Several bodies deep on the dance floor, Callie flapped a hand at Jackson in a gesture that was part welcome, part summons.

He gave a quick noncommittal wave, then stood to the side, his eyes loosely trained on the path from the restrooms.

"Hey, you," Callie said from right behind him.

Jackson tried not to let his surprise and, okay, irritation show. He hadn't expected her to leave the dance floor to claim him, and sure as heck didn't want her derailing his plan to tempt Julia into a dance.

"Hey, yourself."

"We want you to join us."

He went blank. He could hardly tell her he preferred to wait.

Callie's eyes gleamed with what Jackson would swear was satisfaction. "I know you're not turning me down, Jacks," she said with a laugh. "But on the off chance you're waiting for"—she lifted her hands to make air quotation marks—"*someone,* she's a little busy right now." She angled her chin toward the small standing bar in the far corner of the patio where a laughing Julia stood conversing—with a man.

Jackson never blushed. Blushing was a chick thing. So he knew damn well the burning in his cheeks had to do with the heat coming off the crowd or a holdover from his tough workout earlier.

"I thought you'd never ask, Cal," he murmured, pasting on his most devilish grin.

"Ooh la la, I do declare, when you smile at me like that, I begin to see what all the fuss is about, Jackson Tate."

Jackson rolled his eyes and followed her onto the dance floor. He put his back to the scene unfolding at the standing bar. Witnessing Julia conversing with some guy held zero appeal. Not that it bothered him.

Within seconds, Callie swished her way around the dance floor, landing him in direct eyeshot of Julia. As he watched, unable not to thanks to Callie, Julia held a glass of wine to her lips and gazed up at a large man he didn't recognize. Dollars to donuts Julia hadn't known the man before tonight either.

The two seemed to be enjoying themselves.

Apparently she had taken his advice to her last night to heart.

Interesting what kind of guy floated her boat. He had the broad shoulders of a linebacker and dwarfed Julia in height, like a grown man beside a little kid. Except he appeared more kid than man to Jackson's mind. He was younger than Jackson, that was for damn sure. No salt and pepper in that full head of hair.

In a series of twists and turns, Callie shifted them on the dance floor again, and there went Jackson's view.

He took her hand, twirled her in a long spin, and

regained his vantage point.

Callie's face split in an ear-to-ear grin. Jackson tried to stop gritting his teeth long enough to return the smile, then the youth leaned one elbow against the wall, effectively caging Julia in.

"What's wrong?" Callie shouted over the thumping music.

"What do you mean?"

"You're scowling."

Jackson started to deny it, then realized *of course* he was. He contemplated asking Callie about leaving her friend to the wolves, or in this case, wolf, then rejected the idea. She wouldn't understand. She'd think he had skin in the game.

A stroke of genius hit him. "I'm hot. Let's grab a drink."

Without waiting for her reply, Jackson darted for the side bar.

He stepped into the path of a harried-looking cocktail waitress and flashed his most charming smile. "Do you mind getting a soda water with a lime for me? And whatever my friend here wants."

The waitress looked confused. "What friend?"

Callie appeared, blowing a platinum lock of hair out of her eyes with overly dramatic flair. "Where's the fire?"

Ignoring the question, he wedged himself into a spot at the bar, right behind Julia.

Chapter Twelve

Julia sipped at her third glass of wine, compliments of Cody, feeling bold and slightly decadent. In fairness to herself, the half-full glass she'd left at the table they vacated in their mad dash to the dance floor would be warm by now. Besides, her foray into the role of femme fatale had caused her mouth to go dry.

The very tall Cody leaned closer, forcing her to tilt her head back to look at his face rather than stare at his impressive chest. And now some joker had squeezed in behind her so she couldn't back up if she wanted to. How had she gotten herself into this?

Callie and Sue, that's how. Callie's grand plan entailed Julia choosing from the three most likely players here, by Callie's estimation. Julia had balked at the idea until Sue said in her most matter-of-fact voice, "That's right, Julia. Don't step out of your comfort zone since, apparently, you'd rather always wonder."

"Wonder what? If one of these guys would be interested? I'm really not concerned one way or the other."

Sue had only smirked. "Not them, my friend. Jacks. You'll always wonder if he *really* wanted you to fall into some other man's arms or if he secretly wanted you for himself."

"How will me talking to another man prove Jackson cares one way or another?"

"That's easy. He'll find a way to derail you. If it was me, I'd want to know."

"It's now or never, Jules." Callie stared over Julia's shoulder. "Grady and Jackson are heading this way."

"I'll do it."

In the end, she'd picked Cody, mainly because the moment she glanced his way, he looked hers. The wide smile he sent her seemed a good omen.

"You sure are a pretty little thing, Julia."

"Thank you, Cody. That's very sweet of you to say."

"Just being honest. Where've you been hiding yourself? I'm sure I've never seen you here before."

"Actually I recently moved back to town from New York."

"New York's loss is my gain. Welcome to Honeyville, honey," he said with a broad smile, holding out his beer 'til she clinked her glass against his bottle. "Do you have a boyfriend, Miss New in Town?"

"Nope."

"I was hoping you'd say that."

Julia forced a smile and took another sip. Why couldn't she relax and enjoy being flirted with by an attractive man? Six foot three, broad and rugged, with eyes only for her. Instead, all she could think about was that she'd read Jackson right. Zero interest.

"Kinda crowded here, don't ya think? Maybe we should take a spin on the dance floor." His gaze slid to the man leaning into her back. He had a definite point.

She shifted her stance and flicked an annoyed glance at the man behind her. A shock of recognition coursed through her even before her brain had time to process the man's height, build, and coloring matched

Jackson's.

Stop it, she chided herself. But couldn't resist casually twisting around, wine glass to her lips, to make absolutely certain it wasn't him. En route her nose caught the briefest hint of spicy cologne. The one a certain someone wore that made her toes curl in her high-heeled sandals, like now.

Jackson's cool-eyed gaze flicked over her, then his hand shot out toward Cody. "Jackson Tate," he said, as if he needed an introduction.

Callie leaned out from where she stood beside, and a little behind, Jackson. She waggled her fingers hello and sent Julia an I-told-you-so grin.

Okay. So maybe her friends had been right about Jackson's interest. Now what? She was so out of her depth. She glanced down at the wine glass she still held. What the heck? She downed the last mouthful and instantly regretted it as she half choked. *Note to self, no chugging the wine.*

"Wow. Jackson Tate in the flesh. Julia, I know you're new in town, but this here is *thee* Jackson Tate. He's locally grown." Cody slid a proprietary arm around Julia's shoulders.

Jackson's flinty gaze fixed on Cody. "We're friends. Very old friends."

The Jackson Julia knew almost always wore a warm, approachable grin when dealing with the public. As a celebrity, it came with the job, didn't it? Right now he more resembled a hardened investigator or a protective older brother or a junkyard dog.

Or a jealous lover?

"Gotcha." As if sensing something off, Cody removed his arm from around her shoulders. "Can I get you and your girlfriend anything?"

"No thanks," Jackson clipped out. "Come here often?" He crossed his arms over his chest and widened his stance, completely walling Callie out of the group.

Callie's glare, aimed at Jackson as she sidestepped, said she hadn't appreciated the move.

The accusatory look Cody gave Julia said he agreed with Cal's assessment.

Guilt washed through her. She and her friends had instigated this, whatever *this* was. Using her eyes, she sent Callie a desperate plea for help.

Callie shrugged.

Super.

Cody cleared his throat. "Often enough. I once saw you perform for a charity event. The boys and I sure enjoyed your show, Mr. Tate."

At the word *mister,* Jackson's eyes narrowed with menace.

Cody's grin turned feral.

This was going downhill fast.

"Thanks, Cody. Glad you and the other kids liked it. But what I really wanted to know was, when's the last time you picked someone up here?"

Julia's mouth fell open. Callie's eyes popped, and she looked ready to explode with laughter.

"Excuse me?" Cody demanded.

Jackson opened his mouth, presumably to repeat his inane question.

Julia jumped in. "Jackson, a word, please?"

Jackson's sullen gaze slid her way and lingered.

In spite of his ludicrous behavior, something warm and delicious swirled low in her belly.

One corner of his mouth hitched up, and his eyes

gleamed with masculine satisfaction, as if he knew he'd melted her insides, just that fast. He nodded once, then gestured for her to lead the way.

"I'll be right back," she muttered, not meeting Cody's or Callie's eyes, and started for the exit.

She thought she heard Callie gasp out between peals of laughter, "Sugar, it's not you. It's them. Lover's spat."

****

Jackson took his time following Julia inside, past all the indoor dining patrons, then out to the front parking lot. No point racing into combat. Besides. He liked the tantalizing scent that trailed in her wake—and the view.

She wore a feminine, loose-fitting blouse tucked into snug jeans and, of course, her requisite heels. Red-striped espadrilles with ankle ties. No matter the three-inch heel height, they didn't slow her down.

He stepped out the front door and looked left in time to see her disappear around the building.

When he rounded the curve, she stood on the grassy curb in the shade, arms crossed, one foot tapping.

He wanted to grab her, press her into the siding, and devour her mouth. Instead he sauntered to within five feet of her, then mimicked her stance. "Yes?"

"You want to tell me what that was?"

He jerked a thumb in the general direction of the bar. "Did you see yourself back there?"

Her eyes widened in momentary shock, then narrowed. "Me? I did nothing wrong. In fact, I did nothing other than what you told me to do last night."

He braced his hands on his hips. "I did no such

thing."

Her mouth fell open in dumbfounded astonishment.

"I made a suggestion, sure, but I never said go hook up with a complete stranger. Instead of being pissed at me, you ought to be rethinking your so-called friends."

She huffed out an exasperated laugh. "Right. Because my friends should have snarled at that poor guy for no apparent reason."

"Poor guy my…" he muttered. "They had plenty of reason."

She slanted him a look. "Enlighten me."

"You have no idea who that guy is. I bet you don't even know his last name."

"Do you know the last name of every person you speak to? We were only talking."

"Right. Talking, all tucked away in the corner while he plied you with alcohol."

"He did no such thing." Her cheeks bloomed with twin splotches of pink. She fisted her hands at her sides as if considering punching him in the mouth.

A sinking certainty in the pit of his stomach told him he would deserve it. He should shut up or, better yet, apologize. Instead he heard himself ask, "How many glasses of wine have you had, Julia?"

She flinched as if he'd struck her. "I'm not drunk. Not *very,* anyway." She dropped her gaze and scowled. "I admit I did have more than my usual share."

Great. He'd insulted her. Her level of inebriation had relevance only because of the likelihood *Cody* meant to take advantage of her—and in point of fact was none of his business. "My concern isn't about how much you drink on a night out with your friends. It's about drinking with a stranger."

"I wasn't planning to go home with him."

"No? It kind of looked like it from where I stood."

She gasped, then, pointer finger out, stalked toward him. "Then *don't*"—chest jab—"*look.*" Chest jab. "Who appointed you my guardian?"

He rubbed at the aggrieved spot where she'd poked him, hard. "Fine. I won't bother next time. I guess I won't worry about how you're planning to get home tonight either, though I know you drove here because I saw your parents' car in the lot, and I also know you wouldn't drive after having had more than a couple. Maybe Cody can run you home."

He'd gone too far, no question. He had no business, no right, nor any reason to accuse her. Not of driving after drinking—something he'd bet money she'd never do—nor of going home with the linebacker—something she'd already denied.

"Ho boy, you have it *all* figured out, don't you?" She paced away from him on the grass.

He noted a slight wobble in her step and would have warned her to take it easy lest she twist an ankle if he didn't think she'd bite his head off.

"Of all the nerve," she said, continuing her tirade. "I don't even know how to respond to your nonsense. I just cannot believe…uh-oh."

Abruptly she bent at the waist, hands propped on her knees, hair hanging down in a blonde waterfall. He thought he heard telltale gulping sounds.

"Jules?" He moved toward her, sidestepping the palm she held out to stave him off. "What's wrong? Are you—"

"Going to be sick? Probably. Go back inside." She

flapped one hand in the direction of the door, somehow looking graceful despite her posture.

"Honey, let me help you." Ignoring her protests, he lifted her hair off her neck with one hand while rubbing her back with the other.

After a minute she straightened only to sway like a limp noodle. He caught her and pulled her into him.

To his surprise, she offered no resistance and instead dropped her hot forehead onto his chest, sighing. "As fun as this has been, think I'll go on home now. Ah hell."

"What is it, baby?"

"I need my phone to call a ride service, which is in my purse, which is inside." She pulled herself upright, shot her nose in the air, and started toward the front of the building with all the aplomb of a runway model.

He hustled to block her path. "Whoa. Where do you think you're going?"

"To get my purse."

"No."

"Excuse me?"

He wrapped an arm around her shoulders and propelled her toward the lot. "You're getting in my car. I'll get your purse and let the girls know I'm taking you home."

"I don't want you to drive me home."

Spoken like a perfect sullen teenager. He didn't know whether to laugh or kiss her. "Babe? I'm not letting you get into a ride share in this condition." To staunch further argument, he asked, "What if you puke in the unsuspecting driver's car? That wouldn't be very nice, and it'd probably earn you a bad review."

She gave him a too-sweet smile. "What if I puke in

yours?"

He chuckled and kept her moving. "I'm sure it would serve me right."

****

Jackson drove home, radio off. He had one eye on the road and the other on Julia. She'd snugged herself into the bucket seat of his car, one slender arm thrown back so the crook of her elbow shielded her eyes. Her chest rose and fell in the steady rhythm of sleep. Small favors.

He scrubbed a hand over his stubble-roughened jaw and took a hard look at how the night had unfolded thanks to him. He'd made an ass of himself, no doubt about it. But there was something else.

He exhaled, long and slow, and resisted the urge to slam his fist against the steering wheel. She'd been having fun, doing—hello—exactly what he'd insisted she should do last night. Then he'd blundered in, stirring up trouble 'til she nearly hurled in the parking lot.

In his defense, he'd had her best interest at heart. Except, yeah, that was a bunch of bull.

"Stop it."

"What was that, honey?" He cupped a hand over her jean-clad knee.

She pulled her arm away from her face to glare at him. Her hair tumbled around her face in messy, golden waves, and her cheeks had regained some color. She looked damn good.

"I can hear you blaming yourself loud and clear."

He forced his gaze back to the road and shifted in the proverbial hot seat. "Not sure what you mean."

When she didn't answer immediately, his gaze

shifted helplessly toward her, and the intensity of her sky-blue eyes stole his breath.

"Jackson." His name on her lips, spoken softly, no recriminations, caused gooseflesh to sprout over his body.

Sometimes it seemed with one look she could divine exactly what he needed. He kind of liked it if he was being honest. The way he liked roller coasters or driving fast on a straightaway or cliff diving. He stifled a snort. He had issues. "Yes?"

"I drank my wine too fast because...well, *because*. That's why I got nauseated, nothing to do with you. Between my little nap just now and your kicking air conditioning, I'm already feeling better. Maybe a little tipsy still." Her mouth curved in a wry smile. "Other than acting like an idiot and appointing yourself my big brother, which, by the way, I don't ever want you to do again, you did nothing wrong."

He flashed her a grin. "You don't want a big brother shadowing your every move?"

"No," came her emphatic reply.

"We'll get back to that in a minute. Right now I have a question. You said you drank your wine too fast *because*." He paused to stretch his neck. It gave an audible crack. "Because you really liked that sumo wrestler?"

She laughed, a soft musical thing that had his own lips curving upward. "Not your business."

His smile died. "So you did like him." He nodded to himself. He ought to feel guilty for ruining her chances with the guy. And he did. He also felt annoyed all over again.

She heaved an exasperated sigh. "For heaven's

sake, if you must know, yes, I liked him, but I didn't *like* him like him." She covered her eyes with the palms of her hands. "I sound ridiculous. No, wait. We sound ridiculous."

His grin returned, and a tightness in his chest he hadn't been aware of loosened. "I admit me swooping in to save you was a bit of overkill—"

"A bit?"

"At least I didn't wreck your budding romance." He shot her another glance. "You really feel better?"

She scrubbed a hand over her forehead. "I'm not light-headed anymore. But my mouth's dry as dirt." She opened and closed it as if in illustration.

"I can take care of that." His words replayed in his head. "That's not what I meant."

Her brows furrowed. "You're losing me."

He cleared his throat. "I meant how about I fix us some dinner? I'm guessing if I get some food in you, it'll counteract the wine."

"Oh."

A long moment passed, and the tightness in his chest returned.

"Don't worry about me. I'm fine."

"Maybe I'm thinking of me. I haven't eaten since lunch, and I hate eating alone, and Chase is out for the night."

Still she hesitated. Out of his peripheral, he watched her worry her plump lower lip between her white teeth.

He got it. He'd acted the fool tonight. Hell, he'd acted crazy around her several times now. She'd probably had it up to *here* with him.

"Sure, you can make me dinner. On one

condition."

No matter the condition, he could've said. But curiosity had him asking, "What's that?"

"I'll tell you later."

The guard booth came into sight. He felt like he'd just won the lottery. "Deal."

****

Julia splashed water on her face, finger combed her hair, applied fresh lipstick, then let herself into the hall. Tantalizing scents, sizzles, and pops emanated from Jackson's kitchen, making her mouth water.

When Jackson began singing along with a ballad playing over his sound system, she froze. She loved the texture of his voice, the special something only he had. Her insides twisted, and her heart filled with a nameless ache that had nothing to do with too much wine.

After a moment, she forced herself to move. She passed the kitchen and slid onto one of the counter stools, relishing the view of Jackson behind the island stove, spatula in hand. He still wore jeans, but he'd traded his pressed button down for a faded T-shirt. He crossed to the fridge and pulled out a wedge of Parmesan cheese. He'd lost the shoes. The man had nice feet. She snorted. No surprise. He didn't have an unattractive bone in his body.

"What? You doubt my cooking abilities?"

Man. Missed. Nothing. "Not at all. In fact something smells very good. What are we having?"

He flashed a cocky smile. "Carbonara. One of my specialties, once upon a time. No promises tonight. It's been a while since I made it."

"Why's that?"

He chuckled. "The clientele. I mainly cook for

188

Chase. He likes Italian, but he prefers red sauce. Lasagna, spaghetti and meatballs."

"What a good dad." As if pulled by an invisible cord, she went to stand beside him. She bent over the steaming pan. Inhaled. Fried onions, pancetta, herbs.

"Carbonara's more of a date-night dish," he murmured.

She straightened, unsure how to respond. Should she reiterate that this wasn't a date? But why bother? Jackson had made it clear he didn't want any part of the fling he recommended.

And yet, if she believed her friends, his actions tonight said he saw her as something more than a friend.

And what about her? What did she want?

As if you don't already know.

"Want to test the linguini?" He dipped a pasta fork into the roiling water and spun out a long noodle. He blew on it, then held it out to her.

Their eyes locked as she sucked the pasta into her mouth.

"Perfectly al dente."

His gaze drifted to her lips. Her stomach shivered with delicious anticipation.

A loud pop sounded from the stove, and a piece of sizzling pancetta jumped out of the pan. Jackson gave her a crooked smile. "I'll plate this up, and we can eat."

He moved around the kitchen, shifting pots to the sink, flicking off lights, then dimming the pendulum lamps hanging over the counter. He set out plates filled with the pasta and Caesar salad he'd whipped up in no time, then rounded the corner toting two tall crystal glasses.

"Sparkling water from my soda stream. Chase's Christmas present to me last year. Save the planet from shipping all those plastic water bottles and all that."

"He's a great kid," she said as Jackson sat beside her.

Jackson picked up his fork and angled his face toward her, flashing her an easy smile that would have had her knees going wobbly if she wasn't already seated. "Bon appetite."

"Thank you. It looks amazing."

"I figured you'd had enough wine tonight, but I'm happy to open a bottle."

She held up a hand and shook her head with a laugh. "You figured right."

She forked up her first bite, tasted, then groaned. "Jackson," she said when she could speak, "no wonder this is a date-night dish."

He laughed aloud. "Okay, I'm pretty sure there's a compliment in that statement, but you'll have to translate."

She scooped more pasta into her mouth and held up a finger for him to wait. After she swallowed, she said, "I mean this is so good you could pretty much talk a woman into doing anything you wanted just by threatening to take her dish away."

His hazel eyes sparkled with mischief. "Oh really?"

"Really," she said and dug in to her food.

For the next few minutes, they ate in companionable silence. Music played in the background, soft and low. To think less than a week ago, she'd been barreling down the freeway, her life in shambles. And now she sat next to her childhood crush, eating a home-cooked, gourmet meal.

Childhood crush? Try again.

Julia set down her fork. Now was as good a time as any.

She opened her mouth to speak just as Jackson swiped her not-quite-empty plate off the counter, derailing her train of thought.

"Um, I'm not finished with that."

"Never said you were."

Laughing, she reached for her plate, but Jackson swung his arm away from her, putting the dish out of her reach.

"Afraid you're going to have to prove what you said a few minutes ago."

If he referred to her date-night comment, the two of them had landed on the same page. But she'd read him wrong before. "How?" she demanded softly.

He slid from the stool, his movements impossibly graceful. He swiped up his own plate with a murmured, "Just in case," then backed into the darkened living area.

She swiveled on the stool to study him, her heart in her throat.

"I'll let you finish your dinner *if...*"

Gathering all her courage, she rose and closed the distance between them. Twining her arms around his muscled neck, she leaned into the hard planes of his body—thigh, groin, belly, chest. "Uh-huh?"

"Julia." He half groaned, lowering his head. His parted lips hovered over hers.

She arched back, pulling her mouth out of reach while pressing her hips more snugly into his, and, *oh yes*, the hot ridge of his erection burned through the fabric of both their jeans. She wanted to purr. "It's time for my one condition."

Chapter Thirteen

He stared at her with dazed, hungry eyes. "Condition? I'm in a bit of a condition, myself. Plus, no free hands."

Her lips curved in a satisfied grin. When she reached for the plates this time, he gave no resistance. In seconds, she deposited them on the counter, then spun back to push at his chest with both hands, forcing him backward 'til his legs hit his couch armrest.

One more playful push and he sprawled on the cushions on his back. Taking her sweet time, her eyes never leaving his, Julia crawled over the armrest.

He reached for her, dragging her up his body to bring their faces level. "Oh yes," he breathed, weaving his fingers through her hair to cup her nape. He lifted his head to claim her mouth with his.

She laid a finger across his lips, stopping him. Everything in her yearned for his kiss, but she had to be sure. "My one condition. You agreed."

He closed his eyes, untwined his fingers from her hair, and flopped back onto the cushions. "Lay it on me, baby. I'll do whatever you ask. Just don't, do not, under any circumstances, get off this couch before I taste your lips."

"You want to kiss me?" She traced one fingertip along his full lower lip.

His eyes cracked open. "That would imply either of

us had a choice. I'm going to kiss you, and you're kissing me right back."

His roughly spoken words emboldened her. "Tonight, when you interrupted my…conversation with Cody. Why did you do that?"

He frowned. Shifted his hips beneath her so his thick erection rolled against her pelvis.

She bit her lip, barely resisting the urge to whimper and press herself onto him.

"I told you why." He reached up to dance his fingertips along her jaw.

She sucked in a breath and forced herself to focus. "I think you left something out, Jackson. I need to hear you say it."

His words came out a hoarse whisper. "Say what, Jules? That I want you? That I hated seeing another man standing close to you because I want to be the one kissing you tonight, last night, hell every night since I laid eyes on you?"

"That's…that pretty well covers it."

He jerked his gaze away from her and scraped a hand across his stubbled jaw. "No, it doesn't. The truth is," he rasped, "I *ache* for you. But I don't want to hurt you, baby, and that's what you'll get with me."

The honest fear in his voice echoed her own worries, and yet everything in her told her he had it all wrong. Time would tell. Maybe he would crush her heart to bits—but one thing she did know. She couldn't turn back now. She cupped his cheeks, drawing his gaze to hers. "You won't hurt me—if we stick to some rules."

"Rules?"

His hands had worked the tail of her blouse out of

her jeans and now cruised over her bare back in slow, sensuous glides. She closed her eyes and shivered with the effort not to groan and writhe in ecstasy. She swallowed hard and went on. "No strings, no promises, no talk about the future and…" A wordless sound of need escaped her as his fingertips skimmed down her spine. "No sex."

He froze.

Oh God. Would he turn her down? "You were the one who said I didn't need to jump into bed with anyone to get my groove on, remember?"

"I remember." His hands resumed their sensual exploration. "Sounds like…a good plan, darlin'."

"It does?" she squeaked.

He laughed, wrapping his arms around her, and she giggled right along with him. Happiness and giddy anticipation bubbled up inside her.

"So we have an agreement?" she asked softly, twining her fingers into the soft hair at his nape.

"Come here," he growled in answer.

Their mouths collided, hot, wet, hungry. In unspoken accord, they shifted to their sides, freeing their hands to roam and caress.

Jackson had Julia's blouse completely untucked from her jeans, and his lightly calloused fingers skimmed over her ribcage one minute, then pulled her into him the next.

The insistence of his mouth, slanting over hers, the low, urgent sounds emanating from his throat, his hands squeezing, exploring, and drawing her close told her he wanted this as much as she did. She'd imagined this moment with Jackson, but the reality of it threatened to shatter her senses. Nothing could have prepared her.

Desire spun through her, pulling at her barriers like a virtual tornado.

She yanked his T-shirt up high on his chest, needing to touch his hard body, feel his heated skin. The sleek muscles of his back flexed under her fingers.

"Yes, baby, touch me," he begged against her lips.

In awe, she traced her fingers over his skin, exploring hard muscles and the carved recesses of his pecs and abdominals. She wanted more. She broke off the kiss and tugged at his shirt, urging his arms up to pull the garment off him.

Stripped to the waist, he was male perfection. Supple muscles, smooth skin, flat belly, trim waist. A fine dusting of hair disappeared into the waistband of his low-hung jeans.

"My turn." He propped himself up on one elbow and unbuttoned her blouse with unhurried, nimble fingers. One-handed he spread the garment open, traced the edges of her bra so gently she trembled.

"You're beautiful, Julia."

His lips found hers again in a kiss so tender it stole her ability to think.

She wove her fingers into his hair and arched into him, sliding her belly against his.

A low growl of pleasure sounded in his throat. In one graceful move he rose up on his knees to roll her on her back, then lowered himself on top of her. The weight of him pressed her into the cushions. Oiled leather mingled with the scents of his cologne and their heated skin.

He gazed down at her. Brought his knuckles to caress her cheek, then smiled at her in wonder. "Who would've thought, one week ago?" He brought his lips to hers and destroyed her with a slow, sensual onslaught of his lips sliding over hers, his tongue teasing hers.

His clever hips melded, shifted, and eased against hers until his erection cradled itself between her legs, its head pressing into her heat. He moved against her with the same seductive rhythm as his kiss, making her want things she shouldn't and bringing her to an edge she ached to topple over.

With a whimper of need she parted her legs, and he sank deeper into her. Desperate wanting pulsed through her. In another moment she'd be begging him to take her.

And that would ruin everything.

Calling on all her strength, she turned her head, breaking off their kiss. "Jackson, I…"

His lips found her throat. "Yes, baby?" He nibbled his way to her collarbone.

"I think…I should get going."

His lips froze. A moment later he dropped his head onto the couch above her shoulder. He lay still and silent except for his choppy breaths.

Unable to resist, she caressed his now-slick back. She might never get the opportunity again. No rules, no promises, no talk of the future. No. Sex. Her rules.

"Jackson?"

He propped himself up on his elbows and gave her a crooked smile. His eyelids hung heavy over slumberous eyes. "Sorry. Just adjusting to the idea of you leaving. Pretty sure I could go on kissing you all night."

She bit her lower lip to keep from admitting that and more.

"Did I stay in the lines?" he asked softly.

She nodded.

He waited a moment, then said, "I'll walk you back."

And because she knew arguing with him would do no good, she only smiled.

She buttoned her shirt while he searched for his T-shirt and pulled it on. They walked to her place in silence.

"That's odd," she said.

"What?"

She shook her head and pulled her wristband key chain from her purse. "I never leave lights on when I go out. Such a waste of electricity."

"You sound like Chase," he said, a smile in his voice, then took her key ring from her to unlock and open the door. He slipped the wristband onto her wrist and stood back for her to enter.

She turned, intending to say good night, and swallowed her words as he sidled past her.

"Bedroom light's on. Sure you didn't leave it?"

"No," she said to his back as he strode toward the room. "I must have forgotten. No other answer. Unless your property has a poltergeist."

"Check the front door. Make sure it's locked."

Rolling her eyes, she did as he instructed. "Locked, just like I left it."

She went to the hallway and looked into her bedroom in time to see him unfolding from a crouch beside her bed, where he appeared to have been checking beneath it.

He faced her, all six foot two of him, in his rumpled tee, hair mussed courtesy of her fingers, and a fresh rush of desire batted at her willpower. She crossed her arms to keep from reaching for him. "Jackson, no one's here. No one could get past your guard gate for starters."

He arched his brows and slid by her on his way to the bathroom. The light flicked on, then back off. "Better safe than sorry."

He passed her again and headed for the kitchen.

When she joined him there, he flashed her a playful grin and closed the distance between them. He fingered the buttons of her blouse. "I don't know, Julia. Maybe I ought to stay. Can't be too careful."

If only he knew how much she wanted him to. Luckily the fear of what would happen afterward had her toeing the line. She spun around and, finger on chin, made a show of eyeing the living room. "Sure. But the couch doesn't quite look long enough for you."

He threw his head back, laughing as he stepped to the back door and let himself out. "All right. I'd ask for a kiss good night, but I'm afraid you really would have to kick me out, then. I don't think I could stop."

Her thoughts exactly. "Thanks for a great night, Jackson. I really enjoyed…" Her face burned. How to even finish that sentence?

"Me, too. G'night." He closed the door with a soft click.

After a moment she locked it. She tried to ignore how empty the cottage felt now that he'd gone, tried to ignore the clamor within her to go after him to finish what they'd started.

In the bathroom she cleaned up for bed, stripping and putting on her robe. All the while recalling the exquisite feel of Jackson on top of her, of his lips on hers, of his hands exploring her body, her hands exploring his. Sweet torture. Satisfying and maddening all at once.

And now what? Would they act like nothing happened between them? Who knew when she'd even see him again. Now that she'd thrown herself at him—because that's basically what she'd done just like a million other women—would his interest evaporate? She might as well prepare herself. That was how the game was played—or so she'd heard. At least she hadn't slept with him.

She carried her dirty clothes into her bedroom, dumped them in the laundry basket, then froze. On a slow pivot she studied her bed as every hair on her body stood on end. She might have forgotten to turn out a light, but she hadn't forgotten to make her bed. She always made her bed.

She stared at the sight of her covers and top sheet pulled back and her pillows in disarray. *Had* someone been in here?

Relief made her almost dizzy as the obvious explanation came to her. When Jackson had searched her room, he'd shifted the covers looking for…for what?

No matter. That made more sense than a stranger breaking into her house and trying out her bed.

Still, she did a quick inventory of her jewelry and found nothing missing—*of course*. Too, her laptop remained where she'd left it on the counter, open. *Open?* Had she left it open?

Of course she had. Evidently thinking about Jackson used up all her brainpower and let her imagination run wild.

She'd have to work on that.

Chapter Fourteen

Julia glanced at her wristwatch. Nine a.m.—a decent hour to return a call on a Saturday morning. She picked up her cell phone and dialed Lisa. At some point last night—likely smack in the middle of Jackson and her making out on his couch—his aunt had returned her call. She'd also received several messages from Sue and Callie.

A helpless smile curved her mouth at the memory of what she and Jackson had been doing while her phone blew up.

"Hello?" came Lisa's cheerful voice.

"Hi, Lisa, it's Julia. Have you got a minute to chat?"

"I do if you'll hang on a sec?" Her voice muffled as she excused herself to Chase. A moment later she said, "I wanted some privacy to discuss what I think you're calling me about."

"Is this a bad time? I don't mean to interrupt your visit."

"No, I'd say your timing is about perfect. Jackson will be here any minute, and we'll surely be in the thick of things then."

"What do you mean?" Julia asked warily.

"What you probably think I mean. Are you calling to discuss the math class Chase enrolled in?"

"I am. I guess he told you I was concerned."

"You could say that."

"I'm not trying to stick my nose in, but I'm in a pickle. I subbed for his math teacher last week, and Chase got that deer-in-the-headlights look and asked me not to mention seeing him to his dad. Once I realized Jackson didn't know Chase was enrolled, period, I suggested Chase talk to him. I mean, it's not like he's doing drugs. We're talking a long-division, decimal-point refresher class. And he's legitimately enrolled since you signed off on it, which Jacks gave you the authority to do. But you do see my conflict, don't you? I feel awful keeping this from Jackson."

"Big time. Especially as I never signed anything," Lisa said dryly.

"What?"

"And, Julia, don't ever think you're overstepping. You're practically family, and besides, I'm glad you got involved. If it weren't for you, Chase might not have come to me. He admitted everything last night: how he forged my signature, how you ended up substituting for his teacher, your suggestion he talk to Jackson, and finally your telling him you intended to speak to me."

"Which nudged him to confess all to you. Oh dear. What a mess."

"It is. And while what he did was wrong, forging my signature, lying by omission to Jackson, I can't entirely blame Chase. He has tried to talk about this, but when Jackson doesn't want to hear something, he simply won't. That boy can be stubborn as a mule."

"I've noticed," Julia murmured.

"I'm sure," Lisa said, a smile in her voice. "When Jackson gets here, we're going to have a family discussion."

"That's great."

"He's not going to be happy. But like you said, we're not dealing with drugs or shoplifting or bullying. We'll work it out. On another note, how are you? How are you settling in? How's my nephew treating you?"

Julia's face bloomed with instant heat as thoughts of how well Jackson treated her last night flickered through her head. "Oh, he's been wonderful, as is the cottage. And obviously you know I got a temporary job with Sue. It's good to be home."

"It's good to have you, honey. Oh, sounds like Jackson's here. Wish us luck," Lisa said. "And thanks for caring. It means a lot to all of us."

Julia wasn't so sure Jackson would agree with the sentiment once he knew she had intel on Chase's subterfuge and didn't say anything to him.

No sooner had she hung up than another call came in. "Hi, Mom."

"Hi, honey. I hate to drop this on you, but you have a visitor." She paused. "Chris showed up at our front door a minute ago."

"You're kidding. I didn't even know he had your address."

"Well, he did. He's sitting in the living room across from your dad who's staring bullets at him. He wanted your address. I said no way, so he asked if you'd meet him at the Hidden Lake Inn where he's staying. I told him I'd call you, but no promises. What should I tell him?"

Julia contemplated briefly, then came to an unwelcome conclusion. "Tell him I'll meet him there shortly."

She didn't rush out the door. First, yoga practice on

the deck to get her head in the right place. Then she washed and dried her hair, applied a little makeup, and put on a cute day dress—not that she spruced up for him. She simply had no intention of showing up wearing no makeup and a bag dress. The man had cheated on her. Let him get a good look at the prize he'd lost.

She phoned his room from the front desk. He answered on the first ring and said he'd be right down.

He looked exactly as she remembered him. Chiseled jaw, clean shaven, and not one blond hair out of place. He wore a fitted button down, showing off gym-built muscles, and tailored, pressed trousers. He was more handsome than a man had a right to be. Certainly the front desk clerk couldn't peel her eyes off him. Some things never changed.

An air of anxiousness replaced his signature confidence, however. If it was a ploy to soften her toward him, it had the desired effect. She almost felt sorry for him.

"Jules, it's great to see you."

"Hi, Chris. Why are you here?"

He frowned, eyed the desk clerk meaningfully, and took her hand to pull her through the lobby's rotating door.

On the sidewalk she yanked her hand free. "Chris, I told you—"

"Can we take a walk? Cooped up on a plane, then this hotel room has me going stir-crazy. The park's right here." He aimed his most charming smile at her. "I came an awful long way, Julia. Besides, I think you'll like what I have to say."

She sighed, glanced at the lake and adjoining park

with its shaded gravel walkways, and knew herself for a sucker. "All right."

They set out toward the lake.

He chuckled. "I wondered if your dad meant to shoot me and bury me in his backyard. What did you tell them?"

She gave him a dry look. "Obviously not much. You're still alive."

His face colored. "I deserve that."

"I know."

His mouth tightened briefly. "Julia, nothing's the same with you gone. Tell me you don't miss me, too."

Not until that moment did it dawn on her. She didn't miss him. Didn't miss the office or New York or his fancy loft apartment or anything about their lives together. And as handsome as he was, her heart didn't flutter at the sight of him. Jackson's name alone sent her pulse racing. What did all that mean? Did she really want to know?

She forced her mind to the present. "Why are you here, Chris, really?"

"I'm here to get my girl back."

She gave him a steady look. "Not gonna happen."

At the lake, the path veered into the park itself. They wandered along a shaded walkway. On either side, people gathered, lying on blankets, picnicking, playing games.

"Julia, I've told you I broke things off with her. I've apologized. What more can I do?"

As if that would fix anything. Yet she couldn't even work up a good temper. Why not? *Because you didn't care about him the way you should have, either.*

They drew near a wooden slatted bench. Chris

touched her arm. "Can we sit?"

She could only nod, as the truth of her feelings hit her. She had some responsibility here.

"Admit it, Julia. We made a good team. Remember all those hours we spent untangling Nathan's books. He's asked when you're coming back. The firm promised to make us both partners when you do."

She frowned, and some of her guilt evaporated. This was his big romantic play? It sounded more like a contract negotiation.

Chris plowed on. "I know I said some hard things at the end, and I regret that."

"You said I drove you to Nicole. That she gave you things I didn't."

"Don't you see? None of that matters to me now. You, our life together, our future at the firm. That's what's important."

Wearing an indulgent smile, he enveloped her hands in his. "You want kids, right? We'll get married, start a family right away. As a partner, you could name your hours, work from home."

She stared at him, dumbstruck. "You can't mean it," she whispered.

****

"There's no shade here," Chase griped, switching the lawn chairs he lugged to his other arm.

"That's what happens when we get here late, bud," Grady quipped.

Jackson said nothing. He simply hefted the duffel he carried loaded with balls, towels, and sunscreen higher on his shoulder and gave Chase a meaningful look. The reason the three of them now tromped past all the taken shady areas on the green owed entirely to their late arrival, which was entirely on Chase.

Chase's shoulders slumped.

Jackson still couldn't wrap his brain around what his son had done. Forging his aunt's signature in order to take a class he didn't need to but *wanted* to? And the kicker? He'd blamed Jackson, and Aunt Lisa had backed him up. It wasn't as if Jackson would have forbidden Chase from taking the damned class.

But where had Chase gotten the idea he had to master anything and everything? Jackson didn't want him to go through life chasing perfection. He knew what that did to a person. He'd tried to let Chase know he didn't care if he aced mathematics as long as he did his work. He wouldn't punish *his* son for having a weak subject.

And what had he gotten for his efforts? Accused of turning a deaf ear to his son. Aunt Lisa had actually lobbied for letting Chase slide on this one.

He wondered what Julia would say when he told her about it. Dropping the bag beside the lounge chairs, he smiled to himself. Already thinking about when he'd see her again. He suspected that would break her rules—if she knew.

He dug out a football from his duffel. "Think fast," he said and chucked the ball to Chase.

Chase caught it one-handed and wound back. "Go long, Uncle Grady," he said and waited as Grady shot across the field toward the lake.

Grady jumped, catching the ball, then twisted to land on his feet. After a brief pause to catch his breath, he started back at a jog, pigskin in hand.

"Did he hurt himself, Dad?" Chase called from the position he'd staked out, evidently wondering, like

Jackson, why Grady was running the ball back rather than tossing it.

He didn't carry himself like he'd landed wrong. Still, he ran straight for Jackson, a serious expression on his face.

"What gives?" Jackson asked.

Grady smiled regretfully. "I hope you weren't blowing smoke with the whole friends thing with Jules." He slapped Jackson on the shoulder.

"What are you talking about?"

He pointed diagonally across the field toward the direction he'd run. "See that bench there? The one in the shade on the other side of the path?"

"Yeah."

"See that couple? That's Julia and her boyfriend in from New York. She'd mentioned he planned to come for a quick, er, visit." He made air quotations around the word *visit*.

An odd sensation hit Jackson square in the chest. It felt like being tackled, hard, and having the breath knocked out of him. "She talked to you about her ex?"

He opened his arms wide in a *come on* gesture. "It's what chicks do. And does that look like an ex situation to you?" He pointed again.

Jackson wanted to smack his hand down. He squinted at the couple but couldn't make out much more than coloring. Her ex—or apparently not ex—boyfriend had flown in to see her, huh? She hadn't thought to mention this last night?

"Are we going to throw or stand here and melt?" Chase demanded.

Jackson forced a smile and gave Grady a devil-may-care wink, then ran full out in the direction Grady had come from.

Grady loosed the ball. It arched high in the air.

He spun himself up, snagged the football with one hand, and landed square on his feet. He smacked the ball twice, wound back, and sent it flying toward Chase.

Then he made a slow pivot to face the bench across the path.

Julia, wearing a summer dress and her requisite high-wedged sandals, sat knee to knee with a man who could have his picture in the dictionary beside *Malibu*. Thick, dark-blond hair, tanned skin, designer sunglasses. He thought back to how Julia had described her so-called ex. *A rising star who moved to the New York branch from California.*

For Christ's sake, he'd suggested she needed a fling to bolster her ego after her ex did a number on her, then volunteered for the job. He felt like a fool and more than a little used.

Last night had blown his mind. Julia's lips sliding against his, her little shivers of pleasure, her fingers kneading his skin like she couldn't contain her ecstasy. He couldn't reconcile that woman with the one on the bench meeting her lover. It didn't make sense. Grady must have gotten it wrong.

He'd go say hello. Introduce himself, friendly like. Get a feel for things, up close. He took a half step toward them and froze mid-stride when Mr. Malibu angled in for a kiss.

He jerked around and trotted toward Grady and Chase, a queasy feeling roiling his guts. He was some kind of idiot. He'd wrestled with warning her off him, only relaxing when she uttered the magic words *no strings.*

He'd read the situation all wrong.

Scowling, Chase met Jackson beside their piled things. "Now what, Dad?"

"I decided you're right. It's too sunny here. Let's move."

Grady slung a couple chairs across his back. "Your dad's not having the best day."

Jackson jammed the football in his bag and zipped it shut, not meeting Grady's eyes. "Nothing bothering me but the heat," he muttered and set off to get as far away from Julia as possible.

****

"So I've been thinking about what we discussed this morning," Jackson began.

He and Chase sat at the dinner table eating the fried chicken, coleslaw, and baked beans they'd picked up from the grocery on the way home from the park. From the drive home 'til now, neither had much to say. Jackson, for his part, had a lot of nothing good on his mind. He figured his son waited to see where he would land concerning his punishment.

"Okay," Chase said and set his fork down beside his plate.

"I wondered what you think I should do."

Chase blinked. "What do you mean?"

"I mean, you forged your aunt's signature, which is a very big deal."

He lowered his eyes. "I know."

"On the other hand, Aunt Lisa seems to think that resulted from a breakdown in communication. Primarily due to me. Is that what you think?"

"I don't know about all that," he said, sounding wary.

Jackson waited.

"I thought if I asked to register, you'd tell me what you always do."

"Which is?"

Chase deepened his voice, purportedly mimicking Jackson. "I told you, Son, you don't have to worry about getting ripped off the football team for getting a C in math. Your best is good enough for me."

The smile curving his lips at his son's impersonation vanished as Chase continued speaking.

"I want to get it, Dad. I want to understand. It's not about you or what Grandpa did when you were a kid. I just need a little help. It's not wrong to ask for help, is it?"

He felt like he'd been punched. His aunt, as usual, had it right. He had heard what he wanted to hear, what made sense to him. He hadn't listened to his son.

"No, Son, it's not. Everyone needs a little help sometimes."

"It's important to me, Dad."

"Okay."

"Plus, there's this girl."

Finally something he could understand. Jackson grinned. He stopped when he caught his son's glare. "Sorry." He cleared his throat. "Tell me about her."

Chase somehow managed to look down his nose at him. "Her name's Alana. She's in my math class. She's smart. I like her. That's it."

Jackson drummed his fingers on the table and nodded. "Anything else you want to tell me?"

"Nope."

"Let's wrap this up, then. There's the what and the why. The why we've dealt with. As to the what, you

211

forged your aunt's signature and lied to both of us. Due to the extenuating circumstances, you're getting off easy. You're going to write a letter of apology to principal Lightbody."

Chase groaned his dismay.

Jackson went on. "You'll tell her what you did, tell her you confessed to your aunt and me, and tell her she can expect a call from me to discuss any consequences she might wish to dole out. In addition, I think we need to find you a tutor."

Chase's eyes lit with excitement. Over a tutor. His kid never ceased to amaze him.

"I would have said we could ask Miss Julia, but—"

Chase's nodded exuberantly. "Miss Julia already offered to tutor me."

Jackson concentrated on decimating the chicken thigh on his plate. "She did?"

Chase smiled and snatched a chicken wing from the platter. "She said after I cleared it with you, she'd be happy to help."

"That's great," Jackson said, trying not to grit his teeth. "While you clean up the dishes, I'll go have a chat with Miss Julia." *If she's home. And alone.*

****

Julia lay in a heap on her bed where she'd wallowed since returning from the Hidden Lake Inn. She knew she should get up and stop feeling sorry for herself. But today's revelations concerning her relationship with Chris, specifically her part in its demise, had knocked the breath out of her. Then there was the whole Jackson thing, which shouldn't be a *thing* at all, based on their agreed-upon rules.

For hours she'd listened for a knock on her back

door, the door Jackson favored since she'd moved in, minus that first night. She hadn't meant to. She'd meant to be thankful he hadn't come by. No Jackson meant no temptation to venture down another dead-end road.

She'd have to work on the thankful part. Add it to the list.

She sniffed. At least she'd stopped crying.

A sharp *rat-a-tat* sounded on her front door. Her head jerked up off her pillow. Her mom must have decided to check on her. Little wonder. She really owed her more of an explanation than her quick call to say, "Everything's fine. He's going back to New York tonight. I'll call you later."

She dragged herself off the bed, snagged the large pair of black sunglasses off her dresser, slid them on, and trudged to the door. She opened it in time to see Jackson's back as he stepped onto the trellis-covered walk leading from his front door to hers.

He must've heard her, because he threw a look over his shoulder. He froze when he saw her, an odd, grim expression on his face. Certainly not the light and flirty one he'd worn last night. Her heart, already bruised from her emotional roller coaster of a day, squeezed in her chest.

She'd anticipated a potential do-over at best or a friendly brush off at worst. But not this. He looked downright cold. She was suddenly very glad she'd had the forethought to don her sunglasses.

Jackson strode toward her. He wore heather-gray sweatpants with the waist rolled down and a brilliant, white V-neck T-shirt that, though not tight, accentuated the broadness of his shoulders and his hard, flat stomach.

When he got close, the fresh scent of his shampoo and aftershave assaulted her senses. Recently showered and shaven. Her legs turned wobbly.

She tried for a casual tone. "Hi, Jackson. Sorry, I didn't expect you to knock on the front door."

He cocked his head, and a flicker of warmth lit his eyes, disappearing as quickly as it came.

"I mean, you usually come to the back." *Like last night. After you kissed me senseless.*

"I didn't want to disturb you. In case you had a"— he scratched his nose—"*guest.*"

Her turn to cock her head. Had she imagined his odd emphasis on the word *guest*? "No, no one here but me. And even if I do have people here, you're always welcome to—" She broke off with a vague wave aimed at the back door. "Want to come in?"

He lowered his eyes and gave a curt nod.

Maybe he'd had a worse day than she had—or maybe she should accept the obvious. She went inside and perched on the couch, leaving him to see himself in.

He closed the door, then stood with his back to it, arms behind him, studying her. A muscle ticked in his jaw.

"Are you all right?" she asked, at the same moment he asked, "Is it bright in here?"

She cleared her throat and adjusted her glasses, assuring their secure fit, and opted not to answer.

"I'm fine," he said. "Why wouldn't I be?"

"Right. You wanted to talk?" She lifted her chin a notch. No reason for her to feel bad just because Jackson regretted their kiss fest and clearly never wanted it to happen again.

If this was how he intended to make his point, never again was fine with her.

Moving with a slow predator's gait, he joined her on the couch. He sat as far from her as possible.

She forced a sunny smile.

"Nice dress. Go somewhere special today?"

Her smile faltered. She glanced down at herself. She'd picked the pale-blue halter dress because it made her feel pretty. She'd wanted Chris to eat his heart out, a little at least. He had. It hadn't made her feel better. "Thank you. Not particularly, no."

Jackson blew out a breath. "You lost the stacked sandals, I see."

"Sandals?" She looked down at her bare feet and wiggled her toes. How would he know she'd worn heels today?

"Never seen you in flats, is all," he said, reading her mind.

"Oh." She shrugged.

He leaned forward, resting his elbows on his knees. His gaze narrowed on her face as if trying see her eyes through her shades. "I had a talk with Chase and my aunt this morning."

"Oh?" she squeaked. An altercation about the secret she'd helped Chase keep would be a perfect punctuation to her day.

"Evidently Chase got it in his head he wanted to take a summer enrichment course, math of all things, and instead of discussing it with either me or at the very least his aunt, he…" Jackson gave a grunt of frustration. "Julia?"

"Yes?"

"Can you please take off those glasses? I can't

have a conversation like this."

Her hand went to her face and hovered there. "Oh. I don't think—"

He frowned, slid closer, and reached for her glasses with both hands. With infinite care, he removed them from her face.

For a moment, they simply stared at each other, her with her red-rimmed, puffy eyes, him with his magnificent, gold-flecked, hazel eyes with their ridiculous, thick fringe of black, curling lashes. Not. Fair.

"Satisfied?" An edge of defiance sharpened her tone.

"Sweetheart, what's going on?" he asked in a lightning-swift change of demeanor.

She steeled her heart. She didn't need his pity. Anything but that. "Allergies," she lied. "You were saying?"

His brows furrowed. "I was saying Chase forged my aunt's signature to get into a math class."

She nodded and tried to forget the fact she looked like a hag while he sat there utterly gorgeous. Tried to forget melting in his arms last night when, based on his frosty attitude, he had a serious case of buyer's remorse. What had she expected? At least she hadn't slept with him.

"Are you listening to me, Julia?"

She bit her lip. "I'm sorry. I may have tuned out."

The look he gave her confused and disturbed her. It said *she* had hurt *him*.

On reflex she laid her hand on his knee. "Jackson, I'm sorry. Please repeat what you said."

He didn't. Instead he stared at her hand.

Embarrassed heat bloomed over her body. "S-sorry," she said again and jerked her hand back.

Jackson caught her hand mid-air and held it. His palm was warm and slightly damp. He lifted his gaze to hers. Molten gold and green blazed in his eyes, like a volcano erupting into a roiling sea.

She sucked in a breath.

"Chase said you offered to tutor him."

"He did?" Her voice pitched high as Jackson's cold, almost sullen attitude finally made sense. He resented her for not disclosing Chase's lie to him. She couldn't blame him. Though she would have foreseen a more direct reproach from him, she needed to remember people dealt with things in their own ways.

"He did," he replied in a flat voice. "I told him I'd ask you but not to get his heart set because I'm not sure you have time, what with all your extracurricular activities."

"Of course I have time. Of course I'll tutor him." She replayed his words. Extracurricular activities?

He glanced away. A muscle rapid-fire ticked in his jaw.

"Jackson, I'm sorry. I really am. I knew I should tell you, but I wanted to give Chase a chance first. I did feel conflicted, but I didn't think it would be right for me to, you understand, jump in before he spoke to you, and, too, I thought Lisa had signed and—"

"Julia," he clipped out. He released her hand and dragged both of his through his hair. "I saw you today. With your boyfriend or fiancé or whatever he is. In the park? Not that there's anything wrong there. Nope, you set the rules. No strings. I just wondered, between your out-of-town guest and who knows what else you have going, if you'd have five minutes to do a little tutoring."

A pregnant silence passed.

"You were at the park?"

His cold mask disappeared. A ruddy stain darkened his cheeks. "Forget I said anything. It's not my business. So I can tell Chase you'll tutor him?"

"Jackson. What do you think you saw today?"

His gaze drifted to her lips. "I saw a—" He laughed under his breath. "—not-unattractive man sitting beside you on a bench at Hidden Lake Park. I even contemplated coming to say hi. Then I saw him kiss you."

Chapter Fifteen

Jackson knew he dug a deeper hole for himself with every word out of his mouth. Still, the words spilled out. "I gotta hand it to you, Julia. The men line up for you. Not that I blame them."

"Jackson."

The softness of her tone tore at his insides. He rose. "I'll tell Chase to come see you in the school office on Monday. Or if you'd rather—"

"Please sit down."

Embarrassment, humiliation, some combination of the two, slammed through him. How many times now since she returned had he acted the fool? He'd lost count. "I shouldn't have said anything. Your business is—"

"Please don't make me beg you."

He dropped onto the sofa like a lead balloon. He felt like a kid about to get a well-deserved talking to.

"You didn't see me kissing anyone."

He frowned at her in exasperation. He might be a fool, but he was no idiot.

"The man you saw with me was my ex, down from New York."

"Your ex. Yes, I know. Grady told me he was planning to come for a—" He cleared his throat. "— visit."

"Grady told you?" She looked genuinely

perplexed.

"He spotted you first," Jackson muttered. The pit of his stomach burned like he'd swallowed a glowing coal. "So the two of you are, what? Reconciling?"

She shook her head.

"He's visiting, though?" *Visit* had taken on a whole new meaning. If he never heard that word again, it would be too soon.

"He showed up at my parents' house this morning unannounced. He asked me to meet him. I agreed." She crossed one leg over the other and twined graceful, manicured fingers over her knee.

The move revealed a hint of thigh and a mouth-watering expanse of smooth skin. His gaze drifted down over toned calves and pretty feet topped off with glossy, red toenail polish. He fisted his hands to keep from touching her.

"He wanted to talk about getting back together. You already know where I stand on that."

She unfolded her legs and rose from the couch. Her signature scent wafted over him as she rounded the coffee table, pacing.

She looked like she'd rolled in bed for the last hour. Disheveled hair that hadn't had the benefit of a brush framed a face absent of makeup. Crying and not allergies, he'd bet, had shot the whites of her sky-blue eyes with red. Wrinkles marred the fabric of that pretty dress. And he couldn't take his eyes off her. Worse, the urge to pull her into his arms gripped him hard. He needed to get the hell out of here.

But she needed to talk, which was rare for her. So he'd sit and listen.

She wrung her hands as she spoke. "He said we

made a good team and how the firm would make us both partners if I came back, as if that would tempt me after what he did." She stopped pacing long enough to stare into Jackson's eyes, as if willing him to understand. "Jackson, he said if I came back, we could get married, start a family." Her eyes welled with tears.

Because he couldn't not, he went to her and pulled her close. "Sweetheart."

When her small hands flattened against his chest, he thought she meant to push him away. Instead she fisted her hands in his shirt and tilted her head back to gaze up at him. "I didn't care. Not because of what he'd done wrong, not because he seems to see me more as a business asset than a lover, but because he and I, we were never right. I blamed him for what went wrong, and what he did *was* wrong. But maybe, in the end, it *was* me that caused him to cheat."

He shook his head. "No. He had a choice. No one made him stay with you. I still say he's a fool."

She grinned and dropped her forehead against his chest. "I should have trusted my instincts from the start. Today he offered me everything I thought I wanted on a silver platter, and I had to tell him no, even knowing the opportunity to have all those things may never come again. You don't know what it's like being a woman."

He laughed softly, and the tension plaguing him since seeing her with Chris eased. "You're dead on there."

She tilted her head back, and the corners of her lips curled up a fraction.

"I can see how that would be hard, though. Saying no to a sure thing to wait for the right thing."

Her grin faded. "Jackson, I don't know what you

think you saw today. Yes, he did try to kiss me. It almost felt like a contract negotiation and he wanted to seal the deal. But I pushed him away. And, to clarify, he is *not* staying for an extended visit."

He smiled down at her, smoothing a hand over her hair.

"Do you believe me?" She relaxed her grip on his shirt, and one hand did a slow glide up his chest to cup his nape. As her hand traveled, his body reacted. The thin sweatpants he wore made the evidence of that reaction all too obvious to both of them.

"Of course I do, and I'm sorry for..." His words drifted off. He had to get out of here. She'd needed someone to listen, and he had. But now his body was off to the races like it had a mind of its own. He tried not to notice the delicious coolness of her fingers against his hot skin. The softness of her breasts resting against his chest. The more he tried to block the sensations, the more mind-numbing hunger clawed at his insides.

"Sorry for what?" she asked. Her other hand finger crawled up to the V of his T-shirt.

He didn't know. He couldn't think. "That he...that you..."

Her fingertips danced featherlight over the hollow between his collarbones. She gazed up at him, wide-eyed, a hint of a smile playing at her lips. She knew. Knew how the press of her body and her clever little fingers and her sweet scent had his insides twisted up so tight with desire he wanted to howl.

"Baby, can I kiss you?" he asked, his voice hoarse.

She didn't reply immediately. Instead she rose on tiptoes, sliding her body up his to bring her lips inches from his. "Yes, please."

A shudder of need coursed through him. He hoisted her up, one arm wrapped around her waist, as she hooked an arm around his neck and encircled his hips with her bare legs.

He swallowed the whimper that sounded in her mouth, lips locked over hers. Male satisfaction roared through him. She wanted him as desperately as he wanted her.

He moved with her in his arms, knocking into furniture, the entranceway to the hall, her bedroom doorframe, until finally he tumbled with her onto the bed.

He lay on top of her, her arms encircling him and her legs parted around his hips. He feasted on her mouth, wove his hands into that thick mane of gold hair, and reveled in the feel of her softness beneath him.

He fought the urge to grind his hips against hers, to press his erection into her heat—a major feat as her dress rode up 'til only the thin cotton of his briefs and sweats, plus the scrap of lace she wore separated the tip of his cock from her sweetness.

Beneath him she cooed, wriggled, and arched, driving him out of his ever-loving mind.

She moaned her displeasure as he tore his mouth from hers to ease his body toward the foot of the bed. It was that or humiliate himself completely by losing it, something he had never done, even as a teen.

Plus there were parts of her he needed to taste. His lips trailed down her neck, to the hollow at her throat. His hands stole behind her to untie the bow of her halter.

When he had the two halves apart, he paused. He

looked down at the loosened material covering her breasts, drew one hand over a mound to trace the swell, to toy with her hardened nipple through the fabric. He inched half of her halter to the side, uncovering one graceful collarbone and an expanse of pale flesh, then hesitated. New territory. More risk.

"All right?" he asked, his voice husky.

She brought a hand to her face, nibbled her fingertips, nodded.

Propping himself up on an elbow, he folded the material down and took in the sight of her perfect, round breasts, sized to fit in the palms of his hands, crowned with sweet pink nipples. He traced a finger down her breastbone. Both nipples puckered, and a fine layer of gooseflesh sprouted over her tender skin.

His hand seemed dark and clumsy next to her pristine flesh. The first flicker of doubt assailed him. This was Julia. Smart, funny, classy, and definitely too good for the likes of him.

But. He lowered his head and sucked one nipple between his lips. She tasted like she smelled.

She crooned and twisted her body in a sensuous glide, rustling the bedding. Her hands found their way to his hair, pulling, sifting, and scratching his scalp while his mouth feasted and his hands explored.

His erection throbbed with desperate insistence, and he was helpless against the urgent demands of his body to realign their mouths and hips. A hoarse groan tore from his lungs when the tip of his erection once again nestled into the apex of her thighs. His hips swiveled into hers. Once. Twice. Three times. A shudder wracked his body as a tidal wave of desire crashed through him, and he tore himself off her.

Everything in him ached to sink into her welcoming flesh, and just the semblance of the act had him ready to explode.

His chest heaved with the effort of breathing. He rested one palm on her bare thigh and squeezed. "Babe," was all he could say.

She rolled onto her side, trapping his hand between her damp, warm thighs. She traced a hand over his torso. "That was quite a kiss."

A wry smile curved his mouth, and his eyes cut in her direction. "I need a cold shower to go home and not clue my son in to exactly what we've been doing over here."

She bit her lip. She seemed on the verge of saying something.

Jackson held his breath and prayed to hear her utter one small sentiment that would solve his problem in a great, big, amazing way.

She twisted away and rolled off the bed, grasping the ties of her halter to refasten them around her neck.

Disappointment curled in his belly, though he knew it was for the best. He got up and padded into the bathroom. He turned the faucet on full blast to splash cold water on his face, then finger combed his hair. He called to mind images of trucks and baseball and anything he could think of that wasn't the sexy-as-hell woman in the next room.

When he felt he could maintain a level of composure, he wandered into the living room. Julia stood in the kitchen, downing a glass of water.

"I filled a glass for you," she said and set it on the counter between them.

He slammed the entire contents, then set down the

empty glass with a click. "Well," he said.

"Well," she agreed.

"Guess I better get back. I'm—" He huffed out a laugh. "—glad I came by. It was enlightening. And, by the way, I really, really like kissing you."

She smiled into her glass.

"I'm pretty sure it's gonna happen again. Just thinking out loud. Wishful thinking out loud. Is that all right?"

A pretty color of pink flooded her cheeks. "Yes."

"Okay, then." He walked to the back door, opened it, and turned to smile at her over his shoulder. "You're right. I do tend to use this door. I'll see you soon?"

"Yes," she said again.

"And I'll tell Chase you'll tutor him?"

"Please do," she said.

Jackson started to shut the door behind him, then stuck his head back inside. "Why don't you come for Sunday night dinner as a kind of thank you for helping? You and Chase can work out the details for his tutoring."

"Oh. Okay. That'd be nice."

He let himself out and crossed the deck. He had come in like a bull in a china shop, making an ass of himself. Again. But in the end, things had turned out okay. More than okay. Except for the fact he wanted to go back and finish what they'd started.

The trucks and baseballs hadn't stuck.

He lowered himself onto the stoop of his back door and tried the old counting-to-a-hundred trick. At fifty, footsteps sounded on the deck coming from Julia's. He turned toward the sound, a ready smile curving his lips.

His smile faded when he spotted Grady's loping

stride eating up the distance. "Hey, bro, I was heading to Jules' place when I saw you leaving."

"Oh yeah? Did we talk about dinner today, and I forgot?" Jackson got to his feet, giving silent thanks Grady hadn't arrived to witness his full-on state of arousal. Now he merely idled along at a simmer.

"Nah. I came by to see how you were holding up, after the Julia thing, but I see I didn't need to worry. You worked it out amongst yourselves like good kids."

Jackson scratched his head. "Not sure what you're talking about. There wasn't anything to work out." Nope, the problem had been all his.

Grady pursed his lips and shifted his eyes in the direction of the cottage. "Today I got the feeling you thought there was something going between the two of you. Call me a mother hen. I thought I'd scope things out with her. You know, stop by to shoot the breeze, see what's what with Chris, pass on the intel to you. Then I see you coming out of her place."

Annoyance pricked him on several fronts.

One, *Chris*. Grady knew her ex's name. Clearly she'd talked about him with Grady. It shouldn't bother him. It did.

Two, Grady should mind his business and quit digging for details about the relationship between Julia and him. Not that they had one. As for baring the particulars of their recent interactions? No way in hell.

"Don't go rooting around in her private life, Grady, not on my behalf. I mean it."

Grady's tone went defensive. "What Julia shares with me is up to her. I came by as friend because it looked like you needed one. When you dropped me off today, you reminded me of when we were kids and your dad had knocked you around some."

A beat of silence passed. "Where the hell did that come from?" he finally asked.

"From you looking like a whipped puppy. Maybe I overstated a bit."

"Maybe you picked up on tension between me and Chase. I was deciding what to do about that school thing he pulled."

Grady nodded. "Guess I read you wrong. I just don't want to see either of my friends get hurt." He threw a glance in the direction of the cottage. "So. Does she have a house guest?" He waggled his brows.

"Nope. Want to come in?" Without waiting for a reply, he went inside, and Grady followed.

Chase darted into the loft area above, cell phone in his hand. "What did she say, Dad? Hi, Uncle Grady."

"Hey, bud," Grady called.

"She agreed to tutor you, just like you said she would."

"Yes," Chase exclaimed, pumping his fist. He brought the phone to his ear and dashed out of view.

Jackson thought he heard "Alana" in his son's conversation. He grinned and turned to Grady. "There's some fried chicken left if you're hungry."

"If the offer comes with a beer, I'm all over it."

They started for the kitchen.

"That's cool she's going to tutor Chase. Like father like son. You could have told me that's why you went over there. What a relief."

Jackson looked a question at Grady and ducked into the fridge.

"She's not your type, and I'm certain you're not hers."

He pulled out the box of chicken and a beer, then set them on the counter in front of Grady. "Oh really?"

"You know what I mean. You and Julia run with different crowds, frequent different establishments."

"Different crowds? Grady, we know all the same people. We're from the same town." He grabbed a napkin out of the pantry, then reached for a plate.

Grady dug through the chicken, Goldilocks searching for just the right piece. "Yeah, but she's not likely to hang out in a pool hall or a sports bar."

Jackson set the plate and napkin in front of Grady who nodded his thanks, chewing a mouthful of chicken.

"I don't hang out in those places either."

"Forget I said anything."

He narrowed his eyes. He was starting to get irritated.

Grady wiped his mouth. "I'm just saying Julia's not like the girls you've dated. Monica?"

"I never dated Monica." That was something else entirely and, as it turned out, a mistake. "Thanks for letting her know where I was the other day, by the way."

Grady chuckled. "She pulled the information out of me."

"Uh-huh."

"What about Valerie?"

"Valerie Rowland?"

"One and the same."

"What about her?"

"You dated her. That fish only swims with the fat cats if you know what I mean."

Jackson crossed his arms over his chest, definitely irritated now. Valerie was the mother of one of Chase's schoolmates. She'd married an older man who happened to have a substantial financial portfolio. Maybe she'd married for love, maybe for money. Jackson didn't know and didn't particularly care. He knew her through the boys' get-togethers at each other's homes, carpooling, and sporting events.

A year and a half or so ago, when her husband left her for her so-called best friend, she'd turned to Jackson as a shoulder to cry on. When she made moves on him, Jackson had tried to gently dissuade her. She wasn't unattractive, but Jackson saw her as friend material only. He neither wanted to add to her problems nor complicate his own life or that of his son's. However, she wasn't one to take no for an answer and had insisted she only wanted friendship with benefits. He did enjoy his no-strings benefits. Exclusively no-strings.

It had been a short-lived affair, with Jackson extricating himself the moment he saw the inevitable shift from lighthearted rebound sex to a longing for something more. "Again, not a dating situation. And how did you know about her? We kept that very much on the down low."

Grady frowned and pulled out a drumstick. "I don't remember. I could swear it was you."

"Nope."

He shrugged. "People talk. The point is she's as different from Julia as night is from day. And I could come up with a million examples just like her."

Jackson snorted. He didn't know about that. Grady had one thing right, though. Julia wasn't like the women here or anywhere else for that matter. She was special. Always had been. A stab of guilt pricked him.

A friends-with-bennies situation seemed beneath her, even without the sex.

"I get it," he snapped, although now he couldn't say for certain who had him more annoyed, Grady or himself. "She's too good for me. Tell me something I don't already know."

"Jeez, you are in a foul mood today. That's not what I meant and not what I said."

"I was in a perfectly fine mood before you got here," he muttered.

Grady rose from the stool, tossing his napkin on the plate of bones. "I'm outta here. I want to knock on Julia's door before it gets too late."

Jackson bit back a reproach not to bother her. He couldn't think of a good reason Grady shouldn't say hi, other than his own nonexistent claim on her. He settled for warning Grady off grilling her again.

"Who's playing mama hen now?"

****

Sunday evening at six thirty p.m., Julia crossed the deck. Her stomach fluttered with nerves. She'd spent the entire day with anticipatory excitement zinging through her, knowing she'd see Jackson tonight. Would the thought, sight, sound, and smell of him always make her as giddy as a schoolgirl?

Always? How long do you expect this spice of life to continue?

Jackson swung open the back door as she approached. Seeing him halted her in her steps before her brain kicked in to remind her feet to keep moving. He looked good enough to eat.

Damp hair brushed the collar of an untucked, dark-blue, patterned button down, sleeves rolled to his elbows. Well-worn jeans. No shoes. Tan feet.

He flashed his superstar smile and beckoned her in. She could swear her heart beat a staccato as she passed him.

The house smelled like fried butter and garlic. "Someone has been cooking up a storm in here. What's for dinner?" she asked and followed her nose toward the kitchen.

Chase stood in front of the island stove, pan-frying what looked like potato wedges. He flashed her a sunny smile. "Hi, Miss Julia. Dad and I made chicken piccata from scratch, and I'm finishing up some potatoes now."

"You helped cook? I'm impressed."

"Have a seat." Jackson pulled out a stool for her. "Can I get you a glass of wine?"

She pulled her sheer maxi skirt out of the way and sat. "If you're having one."

"I will now. White or red?"

"White," she decided.

He went into the kitchen and pulled a bottle of wine from the refrigerator, then set about opening it.

"Dad says you really don't mind tutoring me," Chase said, poking the potatoes with a wooden spatula. "I don't know how it works. I've never had a tutor before."

"Nothing too complicated. You'll bring your lessons, your book, and whatever tools you have, calculator, etcetera, when we meet, and we'll go from there. I'll need to figure out where your strengths and weaknesses are, and then we'll work on bridging the gaps between them."

"Sounds about right," Jackson said.

"Where will we meet? School?" He grimaced.

She chuckled. "Where would you like to meet? At my place? Here?"

Jackson poured two glasses of wine and set one in front of her.

She smiled her thanks and turned her attention back to Chase. "My place probably works the best. We won't interrupt anything your dad may have going on that way."

Chase snickered. "Interrupt Dad?"

"What's that supposed to mean? You trying to say I'm boring?" Jackson asked in mock offense.

Chase rolled his eyes. "No, Dad. I'm not saying you don't do anything while you're home. You work. You write. You hang out with me. But you never have anyone over. At least not when I'm here." He eyed the pan. "These taters look good if I do say so myself."

"Good job, Son." Jackson snapped off the burner. "Why don't you put water on the table for all of us?"

The moment Chase disappeared from the room with the filled glasses, Jackson moved toward Julia. He swiveled her chair and stood in front of her, hard thighs pressed into her knees. One whiff of his spicy aftershave had her insides tightening. He sifted his fingers through her hair. "You look very pretty, Miss Hudson."

"Thank you, Mr. Tate," she murmured.

"Can I steal a kiss from the teacher?"

Without waiting for an answer, he cupped her nape and pressed a warm, soft kiss on her lips. Afterward, his face hovered inches from hers, his gaze fixed on her mouth. Delicious warmth pooled low in her belly. She curled her hands over the edge of her seat to keep from reaching for him.

"Hold that thought," he whispered, sliding one fingertip along her jaw. A moment later he moved to the oven, and Chase reentered the kitchen.

Jackson cracked the oven door to peek inside. Aromatic steam worthy of a gourmet restaurant filled the kitchen. "Dinner's ready. Chase, take Julia into the dining room while I dish things up. Julia, honey, can you grab my wine?"

Honey.

Stop it.

Chase led her to the nook where Julia and Jackson had eaten that first night. Tall candles surrounded by a ring of fresh flowers burned in the center of the table.

"I feel special," Julia said as she slid into her seat.

"You should," Chase said without guile. "I wasn't joking about Dad not having people over often. I can't remember us ever having a lady dinner guest other than Aunt Lisa, and she's family."

Julia blinked. "Never?"

"Nope. Dad said tonight's dinner was a thank you for tutoring me." He grinned at Julia and lowered his voice. "Personally I think Dad thinks you're cute. But don't tell him I said that."

With a soft laugh, Julia mimed locking her mouth and tossing the key over her shoulder. Delight bubbled up inside of her at Chase's words. Not good. She *must* not allow any self-delusion that she and Jackson were an item, although clearly their flirtation had not yet run its course.

But it would. All good things came to an end, right? If she kept her head, and not sleeping with him would insure that, she'd end up with some fantastic memories and no harm done. One glaring problem had presented itself, however. She wanted Jackson. Desire for him that no kisses could assuage burned inside her. She'd never experienced anything like it.

But she could manage, she assured herself. She had to. With an effort, she refocused her thoughts.

"Chase, I'm really proud of you for talking things through with your father. I figured he'd be okay with you taking a math class once he understood it was what you wanted."

Chase's eyes cut toward the kitchen. "Grandpa gave my dad a hard time when he was my age. Aunt Lisa says it left a mark." He sounded wise beyond his years, until he added, "Whatever that means."

Julia made no remark. She wondered exactly how much Chase knew about Jackson's troubled relationship with his father and how he felt about his grandfather as a result. Families were complicated.

Jackson appeared, somehow balancing three loaded plates.

"Your talents never fail to amaze me," she told him, and he sent her a playful wink.

Under the table, Chase gave her leg a little kick.

She glanced at him. His face gave nothing away.

****

Julia insisted on doing kitchen duty following the delicious meal Jackson and Chase had prepared for her. Jackson agreed so long as he and Chase cleared the table and put away leftovers. Comfortable chatter underscored the whole post-dinner orchestration, as if the three of them had done this sort of thing a million times.

"Eight twenty, Chase," Jackson announced, eyeing his wristwatch. "Time to get ready for bed."

Julia set the last pan into the drying rack and released the sink stopper. Sudsy water swirled down the drain, making a low growl as she dried her hands on a kitchen towel. "That's my cue. Thanks for a wonderful meal. Oh, and, Chase, I'll let you in on a little secret. I would've tutored you without the food bribe."

"Now she tells us," Jackson quipped. "Say good night, Chase."

Chase murmured a cheerful farewell and headed upstairs.

Jackson leaned against the counter, arms crossed over his chest. "Why don't you stay and finish your wine?"

She looked at the two empty wine glasses, washed and drying on the rack. "I think I already did that."

Jackson grabbed one of the stemmed glasses between two fingers and set it upright on the counter. He retrieved the bottle of wine from the refrigerator and overfilled the glass.

She laughed softly. "I hope that's for both of us."

"Of course," he said, scooping it up. "Follow me."

He flicked lights off and led her into the living room where a few strategically placed lamps burned, bathing the space in a romantic glow.

"Make yourself comfortable."

He set the wine glass on the coffee table in front of the couch and padded over to the music area, as she thought of it, where a drum set, an electric guitar and bass, and a microphone stand all waited, stage ready. He moved behind the instruments and picked up an acoustic guitar.

He returned to sit beside her. Cradling the instrument in his lap, he strummed random cords as if warming up his fingers. He lowered his gaze to his guitar, and his silky hair fell over one brow, gleaming in the lamplight.

Tender longing swamped her, overwhelming her senses and scaring the hell out of her with its intensity. If this was what a lighthearted flirtation felt like, she was the Easter Bunny.

She drew a calming breath and silently chided herself for overreacting. Jackson's music affected the whole world. He stirred her senses? Welcome to the club.

He hasn't played anything yet.

She scooped the wine glass off the table and sipped, willing her inner critic to shut the hell up.

His gold-flecked eyes lifted, locking on hers. "Any requests?"

"You choose."

A slow smile curved his lips. "How about a new one I've been working on?"

"I'd love that." She kicked off her slide sandals, bent her knees, and tucked her feet under her skirt.

The haunting melody mesmerized her. He either hadn't written the lyrics or chose not to sing them, but an occasional hum in his rough-velvet voice accompanied the music, acting like a finger down her spine.

Far too soon, he slapped a hand across the strings and grinned at her. "Just something I've been kicking around. I'm still toying with the lyrics."

"It's beautiful, Jackson. Thank you for sharing it with me."

He tossed his head once to clear the hair from his eyes, setting the guitar aside, then slid across the leather couch, bringing his hip in contact with her bent knees. He laid an arm along the back of the couch and fingered the ends of her hair. "You going to share your wine?"

His nearness sapped her ability to speak. She held out the glass to him.

He took it, sipped while eyeing the empty loft area above the living room.

"Did Grady catch you at home yesterday? He came by here after I left your place." He set the glass down with a click.

"He mentioned that. Yes, he stopped by. I wasn't expecting him." A part of her hadn't wanted to open the door, but good manners prevailed.

"Good visit?" Jackson asked.

She shrugged. "He wanted to say hi and see how I'm settling in." He'd also put her on the spot.

"What?" Jackson asked, eyes narrowing.

"What, what?"

"You made a face."

"I did?"

He nodded once, and his expression turned wary. "Let me guess. He advised you to keep your distance from me."

"No. You didn't come up." Not precisely.

Grady had followed *hello, how are you* with *how would you like to go to the Helping Hands charity event with me?*

When she refused, citing the honest excuse she already had a date, he hadn't asked with whom. Instead he'd issued friendly, unsolicited advice. Something along the lines of hoping she was playing it smart, not involving herself with another smooth talker. *Another*, he'd said, which gave her the distinct impression someone had blabbed.

"You didn't talk to him about my situation, did you?" she asked cautiously.

"What situation?"

"My breakup."

"With *Chris*?" he asked, his snarky emphasis on the name making her laugh. "Why would I? It seemed like you already had, anyway."

"Me? Talk to Grady? About Chris?"

He held his hands out in a conciliatory gesture. "I thought that's what he said. He did have the guy's name when we, er, spotted the two of you in the park."

She flushed at the reminder.

"But Grady has been known to embellish."

Had he embellished in the restaurant when he called Jackson a womanizer in so many words? Sue hadn't seemed to think so.

Little feet pounded above. Chase appeared in the loft, dressed in his pajamas.

"Dad, I'm going to bed." He grinned down at Julia. "Good night, Miss Julia."

"Good night, Chase. See you tomorrow, five thirty for our first study session. My place."

He grinned and nodded.

"Did you brush your teeth?" Jackson called.

"Yep."

"Okay. I'll be up in a minute." He looked at Julia as Chase disappeared down the hall. "Nightly prayers."

A helpless smile curved her lips. Could the man please stop being so darned irresistible? "I should go."

Jackson's eyes locked with hers. "Not yet. Let me tuck Chase in and—"

"You'll walk me back," she said with a resigned

laugh.

She sipped the wine while she waited and contemplated the moment Jackson played his guitar for her. Raw and violent emotion had surged through her, like a lightning-strike fire gone out of control. But she *had* reined herself in.

So she enjoyed Jackson's company and cared for him as a person. Did that have to spell disaster for her? They didn't call it friends with benefits for no reason. The friend part—that intimated caring, right?

She'd entered into this with her eyes wide open, totally unlike her last fiasco. Chris had started out as Mr. Wrong, only she'd tried to convince herself otherwise. Big mistake. Wanting a man to morph into Mr. Right in the hopes of eventual marriage and family did not work.

This time was different. What she and Jackson were doing had nothing to do with forever. *And yet,* whispered a little voice inside her. Jackson tugged on her heart strings in a way no one, not Chris or anyone else besides, ever had.

If she wanted to be truly safe, she would run.

But the things she felt in his arms, she liked. A lot.

"You ready?" Jackson stood beside the couch, hand outstretched.

She slipped her fingers into his warm grip. "As I'm ever going to be."

Chapter Sixteen

"I can smell the wood burning, you're thinking so hard," Jackson said. "Do you want to tell me about it?"

"Not sure what you mean. Nothing to tell." She wasn't lying. She had put her inner conflict to rest.

The night smelled of blooming jasmine and fresh mountain air. Cicadas chirped, and fireflies winked in and out of view.

"It's a nice night. Lots of stars out and an amazing moon," Jackson said. "Care to walk off some of that dinner?"

"I'd love to."

He scooped her hand into his. "There's a trail across from the access road, a little down the street. I had it cleared for Chase and me when we moved in."

"Of course you did," she said with a rueful shake of her head.

"Meaning?" He led her down the trellis-covered path toward his front yard.

"Meaning you think of everything, Jackson Tate."

He snorted. "Yeah right." They approached the short access road. "Am I walking too fast? I'd twist an ankle if I wore those heels. Nice shoes, by the way."

"Thank you. Your pace is perfect, as is your illustration of my point."

"Hmm," he said, leading her across the street. "That's just good manners." The smile he shot her flashed white in the moonlight. "But feel free to name some of my other thoughtful deeds."

She laughed. "I don't know. I wouldn't want you to get a big head."

He walked them toward a solid-looking hedge where one section actually jogged out to conceal the mouth of the trail.

They entered and strolled along a graveled, winding nature walk, lined with faux-rock lights—solar, she guessed—and a wire fence with tree limbs serving as posts. Aromatic, blooming vines of different varieties crawled up the wires, giving the path a whimsical feel. She had no doubt Jackson had dreamt up the design. He could do romance and private like nobody else.

"It's really lovely. How long is the trail?"

"It's two miles, give or take, ending at the top of a ravine. Killer view. Where it's situated on the mountain makes it impossible to get to by any means other than on foot, so it's remained pristine. Sometimes I go up there to write or to think. One of these days you'll have to trade in your heels for running shoes, and I'll show you."

"Running? No, thank you."

He faux punched her shoulder. "Come on, you can do it. It's a gradual incline, and on the way back, it's downhill."

"We'll see."

"Trust me. The view's totally worth it."

She told herself not to overthink the talk about future plans.

Ahead and to the right, a white, domed structure reminiscent of the Greeks glowed in the moonlight.

"What's this? A folly? Did you really have one built here in the middle of a North Carolina trail?"

"Isn't that the point of a folly? A building where no building should be?"

Delighted, Julia pulled her hand free of his. She jogged to the dome and up the short flight of steps into the open-air structure. She traced a hand along one of its cool polished rails, then leaned back against a night-chilled column. "I love it."

"I'm glad." Jackson climbed the steps with languid grace. He dropped onto a curved stone bench across from her.

"Ready to tackle teaching math to another generation of Tates starting tomorrow? Seriously, if it's too much, you don't need to feel obligated."

"It's not obligation, Jackson. I want to do it. I'm so proud of Chase, wanting to learn, willing to put in the time. He's really a great kid. I'm happy I got the chance to meet him."

"Me, too, Jules. Lately I'm glad about a lot of things." His voice went buttery soft.

A light breeze whispered through the trees, riffling the small hairs on her bare arms. Once again, she'd forgotten a sweater. She wrapped her arms around herself.

He held out an arm. "Come here."

Wordlessly, she pushed off the column and moved toward him.

He hooked her waist, pulled her onto his lap, and gathered her close. "Best if you use me for a cushion. This bench is solid marble. It'll freeze your...er...bones."

"Very considerate." Closing her eyes, Julia leaned

her head against his shoulder and gave herself over to the pleasure of Jackson's arms around her, the feel of his hard thighs under hers.

He rubbed a hand over her thigh, and delicious warmth permeated the sheer material of her skirt.

"I want to tell you something."

She tilted her head back to look at him. In the moonlit night she could make out the square line of his jaw and his full mouth. She waited. When he didn't speak for a full minute, she straightened away from him. "Jackson, you're scaring me. What's wrong?"

He gave an airy chuckle. "Nothing's *wrong*. I'm trying to figure out how to frame this. I'm not so good with words."

"Says the songwriter who happened to write the best song of all time," she murmured. She twined her arms around his neck to comb her fingers through his thick hair.

"Oh really? What song would that be?"

"I'll make a deal with you. Use your words to tell me what's on your mind, and I'll tell you which song."

"You're a crafty one."

She gave a throaty laugh. Happiness and a dizzying compulsion to press into him, to erase any remaining distance between their bodies, thrummed through her.

"The thing is, having you around…there's no one I'd rather have spend time with my son, for one thing." He broke off. "That feels really good." He articulated each word in a rough voice, turning his head back and forth, dragging her fingers through his hair like a kitten demanding petting.

"Good, because I like playing with your hair," she admitted in a low voice. "I'm glad you trust me to help

Chase."

"I told you I'd bungle it up. That's not it. I mean, yes, trust's part of it. But what I'm trying to say is I like you. I like spending time with you. I'd forgotten how much. Then again, it has been thirteen years."

She moaned and covered her face with one hand. "Not that again."

He laughed and pulled her hand to his lips, then pressed her palm high on his chest. "Okay. I'll stop beating that particular drum. For tonight."

She doodled her fingers over his collarbone. "It's funny. I don't remember you liking me all that much when we were kids."

"How do you remember it?"

"*I* liked *you*. You were sweet to me, and I hadn't expected you to be. You were so popular. So...in demand. Yet you always took time to ask about my week and then seemed to really listen." She shrugged.

"Yeah. Sounds like I couldn't stand you," he said dryly.

She swatted his shoulder, then leaned into him, nestling her face against his neck.

"I asked you questions because I liked the sound of your voice. I liked how your cheeks turned pink the longer you spoke." His warm, slightly calloused palm cruised up and down her arm in a languid caress. "I liked how you seemed to really want to help me, never asking anything in return, except that I do my homework."

She huffed out a laugh. "I don't remember that."

"No?" he asked, a smile evident in his voice. "You did, believe me." After a beat of silence, he said, "You were like an exotic species to me. I didn't know anyone

245

like you, and I still don't. When you're around, everything feels…" He made a sound of frustration in his throat. "You bring something to my life."

Her heart constricted and expanded as a jumble of words and emotions collided in her head, robbing her of coherent speech. "Jackson," she finally breathed.

"It's your turn. What's the song?"

" 'Falling.' I only found out recently you wrote it. I never knew."

"Ah yes. Written a very long time ago." He took his hand from where it rested on her thigh and crooked his finger under her chin. "You said earlier I think of everything," he said, his voice a low rumble. "Can you guess what I'm thinking now?"

Anticipation heated her veins. "Why don't you tell me?"

"Why don't I show you?"

His head dipped, painstakingly slow.

Her hand fisted in his shirt as she waited, lips slightly parted, for his kiss.

After an eternity, his mouth slanted over hers, soft, slow, tender. So tender.

A mew of need sounded in her throat. An answering shiver vibrated through his body.

He pulled his lips from hers and pressed his forehead into hers. This close she could see his unblinking stare, feel his breath stir the fine hairs at her temples.

He opened his mouth to speak, then snapped it shut as a car alarm sounded, shrill and insistent. He sat bolt upright. "Is that your car?" He put his hands on her hips and urged her to a standing position, then rose himself.

"I've never actually heard it. It has to be, though,

right? Yours are all locked in the garage."

"Come on. Probably a possum or raccoon jostled it. But it'll wake Chase."

They hurried up the path, across the road, down the trellis-covered walk. The closer they got to the parked sedan, the louder the alarm bellowed.

Outside her cottage, the motion detector light illuminated the front door area and the parked car.

"Key?" Jackson demanded, palm out.

She slipped the key-chain bracelet off her wrist and handed it to him.

He unlocked the front door, allowing her to enter ahead of him. She retrieved her car key, pressed the lock button, and the shrill alarm abruptly ceased.

In mutual unspoken agreement, they inspected the car. It sat silent in its parking space, doors closed, locks engaged, and nothing apparently amiss.

Jackson leaned in to peer at the hood and windshield.

The breeze off the mountain picked up, and she inched closer to him. "What are you looking for?"

"Varmint prints."

"Good call. See any?"

He straightened. "Nope."

"Weird. I'll have to ask my parents if the alarm goes off at random times."

He nodded. "Probably just a fluke." But his eyebrows furrowed, and he glanced around as if searching for a predator. "Let's get you inside, then I need to check on Chase."

She waved him along. "Go on. I'm fine."

He gave her a look.

"Okay, okay," she said, gesturing him inside.

He switched on a living room lamp, then checked out the cottage in swift order.

She trailed after him. "I don't know why you feel the need to do this. I don't even know why I lock the door. It's just us out here."

He shook his head and headed for the back door. "You don't know that, Jules. I hate to scare you, but I do draw my share of crazies. The minute you leave your place unsecured, you'll walk in to find some stalker sitting on your couch."

"Are you saying you think a stalker person set off the alarm?" She joined him at the back door.

He turned to face her, hand on the doorknob, lips twisted in a crooked grin. "We've never had an incident here, and no, I don't think there's anyone lurking in the cypress trees." He dropped a kiss on her nose. "But humor me. Take precautions, just in case."

She thought of the time she'd left the light on in the house and Jackson turned down her sheets checking for an invader. She considered asking about that now, but really, would he remember? She'd succeed only in looking paranoid.

"Gotta go check on the kid. Good night, Jules. Get some rest." He brushed a hand down her arm, then stepped outside.

"Good night, Jackson. Thanks for a lovely night. I enjoyed dinner and spending time with you and Chase and…everything else."

He flashed her a grin. "Lock up behind me."

She obliged, then watched through the door pane as he disappeared into the night.

****

Chase shoved his math book, notebook, and pencil

inside his backpack, then zipped it closed. "Dad was right, Miss Julia. You do make numbers make sense, at least while you're explaining them."

"You're a quick study, Chase. We'll get you up to speed in no time."

"Really?" He nodded, as if to himself. "Maybe."

"Definitely."

"When's our next study session? Tomorrow I have football practice after school. But I'd like another session this week if that's okay. I have a test Friday. I want to ace it."

Julia smiled, charmed by his enthusiasm. "How about Wednesday night? That way if you feel you need more help, there's always Thursday."

"That would be great." He stood up and slung his backpack over his shoulder. "I'm sure glad we decided to study here. Dad's in the house rehearsing for his show Saturday."

"Distracting?" Julia asked. She pictured Jackson in his living room, jamming out on his guitar.

"Loud," Chase said with a grin. "Are you sure you won't come over for dinner?" He had extended the invitation when he arrived.

Julia shook her head. "No, but thanks, and tell your dad thanks."

She waved him off, and he disappeared out the back door.

The truth was she had Jackson on the brain. The idea of seeing him so soon after last night tempted her worse than driving past the *hot donuts now* sign without stopping, which was precisely why she'd had to say no—to prove to herself she could and that she wasn't confusing this fling thing with the *real* thing.

Stripping out of her clothes, she made her way to the bathroom and a hot shower to rid herself of work grime and sweat from the thirty-minute yoga practice she'd indulged in prior to Chase's arrival.

Twenty minutes later, shampooed and shaved and wearing a short silk kimono and nothing else, she studied the contents of her refrigerator and bopped to the beat of the music pouring out of her portable speaker—Jackson Tate radio. Just because she liked his music. Nothing to do with not being able to get the man out of her head or fantasizing about kissing him.

"Slim pickings," she muttered to herself, pulling out wilted arugula, an overripe avocado, tomatoes, and Pecorino Romano cheese. A grocery run after work tomorrow was definitely in order.

A rap sounded on her back door. Her first thought was Jackson. But it could also be Chase if he'd forgotten anything.

She peeled back the sheer panels and peeked through the door pane. Jackson stood, bathed in the golden light of the waning sun, all six-foot-two hot man of him. He looked relaxed and patient in his usual head-cocked-back, cool-guy stance only the truly self-assured could pull off. He wore a short-sleeved, black T-shirt with a band insignia printed across the front and a pair of jeans torn across both knees and worn in all the right places.

Meanwhile she had on a robe.

She unlocked the door.

****

Julia opened the back door a crack and squeezed her face into the opening. Her hair looked damp, as if she'd recently showered. She had it twisted up in a bun of sorts that hung askew. Her cheeks glowed a vibrant pink. The whites of her eyes shone bright alongside those sky-blue irises. She wore not a stitch of makeup. She looked like a little bit of heaven.

"Hiya," she said.

"Hi."

Her blue gaze shifted as if looking to see if anyone accompanied him.

"Just me," he said and spread his arms wide. The bag of food he'd brought dangled from one wrist. "Can I come in for a sec?"

She bit her lower lip. "Sure."

She disappeared from sight, and the door hinge creaked as the opening widened.

Inside, music emanated from a speaker sitting atop the granite counter. Ryan Moore belted out one of the songs Jackson had written for him. The cottage smelled of coconut shampoo and flowers, otherwise known as Julia, freshly showered.

She stood in the middle of the kitchen wearing a pale-blue and pink, floral, kimono-style robe, tied at the waist. It hit mid-thigh and appeared to ride higher at the hips. His mouth went dry, and his brain shorted out.

Julia pulled at the lapels of her robe and tightened her sash. The thin material, silk if he had to guess, hugged the outline of her breasts the more she tried to conceal herself. The splash of color he'd noticed on her cheeks now covered her entire face.

In fairness, his own face felt hot. He'd laugh at the pair of them if he could force air from his lungs.

"You caught me just out of the shower. I can... I'll get dressed."

She darted around the counter and would have

zoomed past him if he hadn't captured her wrist.

"No need." He cleared his throat and forced his eyes to focus on the bag he held. "I came to drop off dinner for you."

He clenched his jaw against the tantalizing Julia scents floating around him. He was too aware she stood in touching distance. Helpless to resist, his gaze slid back to her, drinking in the sight of her smooth, toned legs and bare feet.

She shifted and fidgeted with the hem of her robe. "I told Chase you didn't need to feed me."

His brain needed a reboot. With an effort of will, he headed into the kitchen. "I know what you said."

Groceries of the vegetable variety were laid out on the granite counter.

"Is this dinner?" He gestured to the array.

Unfortunately, or fortunately depending on his perspective, she joined him in the kitchen. "Yes."

With serious effort, he stayed on point. "Honey, you can't live on rabbit food."

Her soft laugh curled into his ear. "I haven't had time to shop. It's fine for tonight."

He reached in his bag and pulled out a half loaf of bakery-wrapped french bread and a glass container he'd loaded with Julia's dinner. "Coq au vin and scalloped potatoes au gratin. Real food. You can add the rabbit food as a side dish."

She pried the lid open, inhaling the savory aroma that wafted out. "Oh, yum. Did you cook this?"

Jackson spread his arms wide and watched as her loose bun tumbled free of its knot to unfurl down her back. "What can I say? When I'm practicing songs for an event or writing, working in the kitchen whipping up gourmet dishes helps keep the creative juices flowing."

She turned a wide-eyed stare on him. "Really?"

He kept a serious face for a full second before hooting with laughter. "No. I ordered from Chez Vincent on First Street and had it delivered to the guard gate before I picked up Chase earlier."

"You brat. I bought it hook, line, and sinker." She wound her hair into a thick twist over her shoulder. The front of her robe splayed slightly, revealing the rounded tops of her breasts and an intriguing glimpse of cleavage. "Seriously, though. Thank you. But I don't want you to feel obligated to feed me every time I tutor Chase."

He leaned back on the counter and crossed his arms over his chest. He yanked his gaze to the ceiling where it stayed for half a second. "Maybe I like feeding you. Did you ever think of that?"

"I'll admit what you brought is a lot more appetizing than what I had lined up. Especially the bread." She ripped off a piece of the crusty baguette and popped it in her mouth, grinning at him as she chewed.

An odd warmth filled his chest, then spread, heating his extremities 'til his palms went damp.

With a jaunty toss of her head, she crossed the kitchen and opened an upper cabinet. He watched, unblinking, as she reached for a dinner plate, and her short robe got much shorter. He could swear she had nothing on underneath. He swiped at the fine sheen of perspiration dampening his forehead.

Julia crossed back to set the dish beside the glassware, then gestured for him to move so she could open the silverware drawer. "Chase said you were rehearsing for this weekend's event while he and I studied. Is it because you're doing new songs this weekend, or is that standard operating procedure? You did mention writing when you tried to take credit for preparing the food." She narrowed her eyes at him in mock reproach.

"Yes, and yes. I always rehearse before I perform. I don't want to get up in front of people and realize I've forgotten half the words to my songs," he said with a playful grimace. "But I am writing the last few days. That's something unexpected, in a good way. The inspiration to write hasn't hit me for—" He blew air out his cheeks. "—too long."

She leaned a hip against the counter, facing him. "That's wonderful, Jackson."

Their eyes met and held. He really wanted to kiss her. "Maybe tomorrow after you get home you could come by, and I'll play one of my new ones for you. If you're not busy."

"I'd love to."

He nodded. "Great. I'll get out of your hair then and let you eat in peace."

It took all the willpower he had, but he left.

Or meant to.

He made it three steps across the deck. Stopped. Jammed a hand in his hair. "Don't do this," he muttered to himself. Then he turned around.

Before he could raise a fist to knock, the door opened. Without breaking stride, he went inside. He shoved the door closed with one hand as his other arm reached for her, encircling her waist and raking her into him.

Their lips collided in a voracious kiss. Julia twined

her arms around his neck, dragging him closer, whimpering with need. Her urgent keen slammed through him, sending a jolt of pure, unadulterated lust straight to his rigid cock.

Primal satisfaction roared through him as she hooked one sinewy leg over his jean-clad hip, pressing herself into him with a desperation that matched his own.

He spun with her in his arms, raising her so her hips aligned with his, then held her against the wall with the weight of his body. She was soft and warm and inviting as hell.

Her hands reached for the hem of his T-shirt, tugged upward, dove underneath. Cool fingers grazed his back, skimmed lower to squeeze his ass through his jeans and cocoon him snugly into her heat.

Slowly, the frenzied abandon of their kiss gave way to a molten-hot, devastatingly erotic, mutual exploration of lips, tongues, and salty skin. The air between them resonated with gasps and quiet pleas. As if it had a will of its own, Jackson's free hand cruised over her silk-covered hip, bunching the fabric 'til he could push it aside to caress the warm, smooth flesh beneath. As he'd suspected, she wore nothing under her robe. His hand cupped her bottom, squeezing and riding the curve down, inch by slow inch, 'til he reached her apex. The slick, feverish flesh hidden there stole his breath. Pure gold. In awe he traced her opening, drinking in her soft cries. Shivers coursed through her, fueling the lust spiraling through his veins. He needed more.

With a growl, he tore his mouth from hers and slowly lowered her to her feet.

Panting softly, she stared at him through passion-dazed eyes.

He reached for the sash at her waist, his eyes begging the silent question. At her slight nod, he tugged. Her robe gaped open to reveal her beautiful, gloriously naked body.

Hands trembling, he reached out, widening the edges of her robe. "Can I…?" he began, already lowering his head to take one hardened, rosy nipple into his mouth.

Tremors vibrated through her as his lips toyed and tugged, as his hands roamed, cupping her other breast, cruising down her soft, flat belly to find that sweet, hot flesh between her legs. *Like melted, dripping honey.* He slid one finger between her silky, slick lips while his tongue taunted and teased and pulled at her nipple.

Sounds of desperation thrummed in her throat. He understood. His own body's demands threatened to overwhelm him, then his name poured from her lips on a long croon, and it almost undid him.

He became aware of Julia tugging at his shoulders, urging him upright.

The rules.

He straightened, gasping for breath, head spinning with the force of his desire. "It's okay, baby," he whispered. He cupped her cheeks with shaking hands, reining in his passion with brutal effort. His mouth sought hers, gentling her, telling her he could—would—follow her lead, no matter how it cost him.

When her hands found the waistband of his jeans, his breath froze in his lungs. She tugged, unbuttoned, unzipped, and finally hooked her fingers on his briefs to push them down. Cool air surrounded his freed erection, then one smooth hand encircled him while her other hand brushed, featherlight, over the tip of his cock. His turn to whimper and tremble. He flattened both palms on the wall beside her head and fought the clamoring demands of his body to lift her by her hips, lower her onto him, and pump himself into her 'til they were both spent.

But. Her rules.

Calling on every ounce of will he possessed, he reached between them to pull her hands away from him.

Her wordless sound of loss and frustration echoed everything he felt.

"Shh." He scooped her like a doll into his arms and stumbled to the first armchair he came to. He lowered into it, holding her tight across his chest.

"Jackson?" she asked, sounding achingly innocent and unsure. She wriggled on his lap, twisting to wrap her arms around his neck. His erection, once again safely ensconced in his briefs, throbbed against the exquisite friction.

"Baby, wait. I can't think when you move like that," he choked.

Though she stilled in his arms, the tremors vibrating through her threatened to unman him.

"I want you. So. Bad. But…you set the rules, and I agreed. If we break those rules now, with no discussion…" He huffed in frustration. "The point is I want you to be sure. I *need* you to be sure." *Please be sure.*

"But I—" She broke off.

Everything in him tensed. She'd been about to say she *was* sure. He knew it. But she stayed silent. Because, the truth was, she wasn't.

He cursed himself inwardly. He shouldn't have said a damned word.

But this was Julia. If they did, and if afterward she regretted it, what then? He couldn't risk it.

She shifted, pressing away from him.

Something like terror gripped him, and his arms tightened around her. "You don't have to decide now," he rasped. "We have time, all the time in the world. You can think about it. Can you do that for me, baby? I don't want anything to happen you don't want. But know this—I want you in my bed."

She ducked her face into his shoulder and nodded, then spoke so softly he had trouble making out the words. "Thank you, Jackson. And you're right. We should…shouldn't—" She swallowed. "It should be a decision, not an accident."

An accident? *Ouch.* He leaned her back in his arms and pulled her robe closed, then retied her sash. His hands shook, and his cock twitched like a teenage virgin's. If he wasn't teetering on the edge of control, he'd laugh at himself.

She watched his efforts, an unreadable expression on her face.

"Jules, trust me when I say you, in this sexy, little robe, nothing underneath? Enough to make a grown man cry."

Her laugh sounded forced and more than a little like a sob.

If she wanted him half as bad as he wanted her, he understood.

The song playing on Julia's portable speaker penetrated the fog of lust clouding his head. "Falling." Her favorite. He kissed the top of her head and rose,

Julia tucked into his arms. He carried her to the kitchen and set her gently on her feet.

He grabbed the glass bakeware, popped it in the microwave, and hit start.

"I can do that," she protested, sounding almost normal, as if they hadn't avoided crossing into uncharted territory by a hair's breadth. It helped.

"Just making sure you eat, sweetheart." He sighed. "I better get back." He searched her eyes. "See you tomorrow?"

She nodded.

He left before she could change her mind.

****

Approaching the microwave on shaky legs, Julia withdrew the dinner Jackson brought her, not because she felt any desire to eat, but to halt the occasional ding the machine made since finishing its heating cycle.

She couldn't wrap her mind around what just happened. One minute she'd verged on throwing her carefully erected safeguard out the window with gleeful abandon, and the next Jackson Tate pulled a rip cord, and everything came to a crashing halt.

He'd done the right thing. Of course he had. She snorted. So much for Jackson, the debauched womanizer. He'd left everything up to her. She got to decide if their so-called fling remained on the same terms or not.

She pulled the lid off the coq au vin. Fragrant steam plumed out to reveal slow-roasted chicken in a rich brown sauce and decadent scallops au gratin. Her stomach growled.

Abandoning the plate she'd taken out, she grabbed up the fork beside it and rounded the kitchen counter.

She propped one hip onto a stool and forked out a bite. The tender, flavorful chicken all but melted in her mouth.

Jackson. He'd brought her dinner after she expressly told him no. Why? She mulled it over for a moment, forked up another bite, then reached a simple yet profound conclusion. He cared. He brought her food because he cared.

And? her inner analyst prodded.

In a blink, the truth dawned. *Several* truths. One, he'd wanted to see her as badly as she wanted to see him.

And two? He'd called a halt to their mad make-out scene, not because he wanted to, but because he cared. He didn't want her blaming him should, afterward, she develop a case of buyer's remorse.

She scooped another bite, chewed slowly, and allowed her mind to linger over the moment his hands had found their way beneath her robe. With every squeeze, every gentle exploration of those clever fingers, desperate desire like she'd never known—to be touched, tasted, filled—had bloomed within her like a flower opening for the sun. A low whimper sounded in her throat. She still wanted him so much her insides ached.

She'd planned her course, set her rules, all to protect her heart from the pain she'd suffer if she got in too deep.

But she hadn't understood. Not really. How could she have? No man had ever made her feel the way Jackson did. Now she knew the truth. She stood to suffer a worse consequence if she kept playing things safe. What Jackson made her feel might never come again with another man. Based on her past, she could bet it wouldn't.

If she passed on this opportunity, she would regret it the rest of her life. She owed it to herself as a woman to take the next step with Jackson, no matter what came afterward.

Jackson had left the decision up to her. Well, she'd made it. Now what? How would she broach the subject? And when? She had no experience with these kinds of things.

Tomorrow, her insides whispered, *when he plays his music for you. What could be more intimate?*

Her fork scraped the inside of the container and came up dry. She'd eaten the entire contents. Apparently she had been hungry.

Humming a little, "Falling," of course, she went to clean up her mess. She had a few calls to make, then she needed to get a good night's sleep.

Tomorrow would be a big day.

Chapter Seventeen

The front doorbell chimed. *Huh*. Jackson checked his watch and headed to the foyer. Quarter to five. *Could* be Julia if she'd come in a hurry from work. He wouldn't mind that one bit, but somehow he knew she'd arrive via the back door. The saying *back-door guests are best* flashed in his mind, and a grin split his face.

He looked out the peephole, hand on the doorknob, then jerked back, his heart jackhammering in his chest. A split second later he cursed himself for a fool. Whoever he thought he saw, it was not Sheila's ghost. He looked out again and saw Grady's goofy mug, grinning ear to ear.

He pulled open the door, prepared to tell his oldest friend to get lost, then shifted gears when he caught sight of the woman standing arm in arm with him.

"Hey, Grady and…Bethany? Is that you?"

The woman stood the same height as her sister had at five foot seven, and looked pretty much as he would have expected Sheila to look now, had she lived. Heart-shaped face, wide-set green eyes, long, wavy auburn hair.

She smiled coolly. "Hi, Jackson."

Bethany Malone, Sheila's younger sister who he hadn't seen in a million years.

"Wow, this is a surprise. Come on in."

He led them to the living area where he'd been getting things together for Julia's visit. He'd moved pillows around the couch, twice. He'd tossed a soft chenille throw over an armrest and bought lilac-scented candles, currently burning on the coffee table. He'd dragged an ottoman to the music area for her to sit near him while he played the guitar. He'd even propped open the back door.

He'd anticipated her arrival all day with the excitement of a child waking on Christmas morning. Nervous that what he most wanted to find under the tree wouldn't be there. Hopeful it would.

Then his past showed up at the front door. His gut burned like he'd swallowed a lump of live coal.

He dragged a hand through his hair and offered Grady and Bethany a seat on the couch.

"Smells nice in here," Grady said, eyeing the candles. "Big plans tonight?" He sounded a little too innocent.

"Not really. Rehearsing 'til Chase gets home. What brings you by?" He really ought to offer them a drink of some sort, but then they'd stick around for sure. With any luck, Grady's visit had a purpose. Something short-lived.

"Rehearsal's why we came by." He clapped his hands and rubbed his palms together, then turned to Bethany. "Do I know my man Jacks or what? I said let's surprise him, listen to some good tunes, catch up on old times."

So much for a short-lived visit, and Jackson couldn't think of anything he'd rather not do than take a walk down memory lane with Bethany. Resigned, he asked, "Can I get you two something to drink?"

"No need to wait on us, Jacks. I can make myself at home. Speaking of which, Bethany needs to visit your little girls' room."

Jackson showed her the way to the restroom and then rejoined Grady. "She's a blast from the past," he said in a low voice.

Grady leaned in and spoke in a conspiratorial whisper. "She called me, out of the blue. Said she heard you were the entertainment for this weekend's charity deal, and it made her think of me." He shrugged. "After she dropped several hints, I finally asked her to go with me, especially since the girl I intended to take already had a date."

Jackson waited for Grady to elaborate. When he didn't, it dawned on him Grady had asked Julia and been turned down. So much for stopping by to check on Jackson the other day.

He gave Grady a frank look. "All's well that ends well."

"Damn straight. I've got a date with a hot younger woman. Speaking of, you want to join us for dinner tonight when you finish here? We can hang out 'til you're ready to go."

Jackson imagined spending the evening with Bethany, and pressure with the force of a mini volcano erupted just behind his eyeballs. She had been a mess after Sheila's fatal jump, grilling Jackson relentlessly—between wrenching sobs—for clues as to why her sister had done it. His answers could never satisfy her. Because he didn't know why.

Then he'd discovered the truth. *He'd* happened to Sheila. He just hadn't known until it was too late.

"Sorry, man. Can't."

Grady eyed the candles on the coffee table again, scratching the side of his nose. "I see." A second later his expression lightened. "Here she is, looking gorgeous as the day we met her. Remember, Jacks? That summer, hanging at the springs? Up strolled Bethany and Sheila, all long legs and attitudes."

"Sure I do," Jackson said lightly, but he shot a warning look at Grady. This couldn't be an easy topic for her.

He guessed Bethany read something in his expression when she said, "I like talking about her. To remember her *before*."

"Of course." He hoped he sounded believable. He supposed it would be different for her than him since she wasn't the reason her sister had taken her own life. More than anything, Jackson wanted them to leave. "Mind if I get back to rehearsing? I've only got so much time before Chase gets home."

"Go for it," Grady said.

He checked his wristwatch as he headed for his guitar. Five after five. This was not what he'd had in mind for the evening. He'd thought about Julia all day. About kissing her and about whether she'd utter the words he longed to hear. *Take me to bed, Jackson.*

Now he just wanted her here. She made him feel good, clean, like he didn't sully everything he touched. But that was the thing. He did.

****

Julia took her time freshening up, though a part of her had wanted to dash over to Jackson's the second she arrived home from work.

Instead, she'd opted for a shower, shaving her legs, freshening her makeup. Feeling just a little decadent, she slipped on a gorgeous designer lace bra and panty set she'd saved for a special occasion, then mulled over the question of what else to wear. She decided on a boatneck, tan linen romper, paired with nude-colored flip-flops stacked for height.

Her palms went clammy as she crossed the deck. She'd imagined broaching the subject of their new and improved fling with Jackson countless times throughout the day. None of the scenarios she'd envisioned felt right. She would have to let the evening play out and take it from there. She knew where she stood and thought she knew where Jackson stood, and those were the most important pieces to this puzzle.

The back door to his house stood open, and unmistakable strains of live guitar spilled out. A few more steps and she stopped in her tracks. More than music, she heard voices, conversation. Since she knew Chase had ball practice, Jackson had guests.

She snorted and strode ahead. She'd geared herself up all day for the talk they would have, and it turned out she needn't have bothered.

"Hello?" she called and entered the large living room that made up the back half of Jackson's home.

Jackson sat in the music area, his guitar across his chest. Two other people huddled together on an ottoman near him, Grady and an auburn-haired woman whom Julia didn't recognize. When the woman glanced in her direction, however, a distant memory pinged, one she couldn't quite place.

"Hi, stranger," Jackson said in that rich velvet voice that turned her insides to mush.

He set his guitar on its stand and rose. His mouth curved in a charmingly uncertain smile as he crossed to

her.

Grady and the woman followed suit. "Look what the cat dragged in. I figured we'd see you today."

Jackson lingered over his hug. Heat poured off him, like he'd just come in from baking in the sun. "Glad you came by." His rough voice curled into her ear, and she felt it all the way to her toes.

Grady reached past him to squeeze her shoulder in greeting. Addressing the woman at his side, he said, "Bethany, this is Julia, the friend I mentioned who recently moved back to town."

She gave Julia an appraising look and a tight smile. "Hi."

Bethany. The name didn't ring any bells. She definitely reminded Julia of someone, but exactly who remained just out of reach.

"Bethany went to school with Jackson and me, in the class after ours." To Bethany, he added, "Jackson's dad worked for Julia's. She went to Our Lady of the Blue Ridge." The way he said it implied a haughtiness about having gone there Julia didn't feel. "Got herself a job there now, too."

"A temporary one," she clarified. "It's nice to meet you."

"Grady mentioned that you lucked into Jackson offering you a place to stay here."

"Luck? Talked her into it, more like," Jackson said, rubbing the back of his neck.

"My move couldn't have gone any smoother thanks to him," Julia murmured. She looked at him. "Everything all right, Jackson?" She barely resisted the urge to touch him.

"Fine," he said, lowering his hand. "Great."

His tight expression told her he lied through his teeth.

"Grady, can you fix the ladies drinks? I need to get to it."

"Nothing I'd rather do than service two beautiful ladies." He winked at Julia. "You can pawn your distractions of the female variety off on me any time, Jacks."

Jackson's steady gaze met Julia's. "Join me when you're set."

She wanted to go with him now, but Grady wrapped one arm around Bethany and the other around her and propelled them toward the kitchen.

"Glad you came by, Julia," he said like he owned the place. "Saves me the trouble of bringing Bethany by to meet you. She's my date for Saturday night. We can all hang together, you and your date, me and mine. The more the merrier, right?"

Julia smiled, noncommittal. Okay, so did he know she and Jackson were going together or simply suspect? Either way, she had no intention of doubling with Grady. She would have to make that clear to Jackson. Grady had been nothing but warm and welcoming to her since she came home. Yet his persistence in seeking her out made her increasingly uncomfortable.

Still, the fact he'd asked Bethany out was a step in the right direction.

"Are you from around here, Bethany?" she asked.

"More or less. The boys and I go way back." The proprietary note in her voice hung in the air.

Across the room, Jackson strummed his guitar, the same haunting melody from the other night. A new song, he'd said. A tingle of anticipation zinged through

her.

"Jackson, Bethany, and I are old friends from school. Since we're going to see Jacks perform this weekend, I thought why not do one better and bring her by to see him in his natural habitat? I figured we'd catch him rehearsing." He pulled out three frosty mugs from the freezer and set them on the counter. "Not surprised you showed up, either." He slid Julia a knowing look.

Heat rode up her cheeks. "He invited me last night."

"Oh," he said drawing the word out. "Last night."

For some reason his tone put her on the defensive, though whether on behalf of herself or Jackson, she couldn't say. "After I tutored Chase, he mentioned working on something new and said he might play it for me if I came by. How could I resist?"

"Resist Jackson Tate? You couldn't. No woman alive could. That man's a lady-killer." He chuckled, pulling three bottles of beer from the refrigerator. He filled one mug and handed it to Bethany. "Beer, Jules?"

"Sparkling water, I think."

"Party pooper," he said, softening it with a playful hip bump that rocked her sideways.

Across the room, Jackson strummed his guitar in fits and starts. She strained her ears for lyrics and heard none.

Glancing over, she saw him nose-deep in a notebook. He set it aside and played a few more chords. Shaking his head as if he waged an internal argument, he picked up the notebook again and scrawled something on the pages.

What had Grady called her? A distraction of the

female variety? He had it partly right. They were all disturbing Jackson's concentration.

"I'll probably just stay a short time," she said, thinking aloud.

Grady shrugged. "We're sticking around. The three of us have dinner plans. Lots to catch up on. Weekends at the springs, bonfire parties, all that good stuff."

"Sounds nice," she said, hoping she didn't sound as disappointed as she felt. She'd built up tonight in her head. Meanwhile Jackson had clearly only intended for her to stop by. She didn't fault him for her wrong assumption. She'd misunderstood, plain and simple.

Grady popped the tab on another beer and poured it into a mug for himself. "You could tag along. I'm sure Jacks wouldn't mind."

If the sharp look Bethany shot Grady hadn't been enough to dissuade her, the idea of crashing the three's party would have on its own. *Tagging along* when Jackson hadn't thought to invite her seemed pathetic. Clingy. She didn't own him and didn't want him to think she had other ideas.

Their talk could wait. And if it couldn't, it didn't need to happen at all. "Thanks for thinking of me, but no. You all have fun."

"Always," Grady said with a wink. He handed her a glass of sparkling water, then called, "Hey, Jacks, bring you a beer?"

Jackson scrubbed a hand over his face. "Sure."

Drinks in hand, Bethany and Julia made their way into the living room while Grady poured the beer. Bethany went straight for the ottoman where she and Grady had been sitting when she arrived. With nowhere else to go, Julia veered toward the couch.

Jackson followed her progress with his eyes, an unreadable expression on his face.

He had told her he always rehearsed before a show. Grady reiterated as much. Yet since she arrived, he hadn't sung a word or played a complete song. That settled it.

She took a long swallow of her drink then set her glass on a coaster beside two softly burning candles. She dug in her purse and pulled out her cell phone to feign reading the screen. "Oh dear," she said to no one in particular.

Jackson set his guitar across his lap, and, though she didn't look up, she felt his gaze on her.

"I have to make a call. I'll see you all later?" She rose and started for the back door. "Nice meeting you, Bethany. Have fun tonight." She waggled her fingers and disappeared out the door.

****

Jackson sat dumbstruck for a good five seconds. Then he turned to Grady. "What the hell just happened?"

Grady gave him a blank look. "I don't follow."

"I mean, why did Julia leave?"

His arched brows told Jackson he'd lost a few brain cells. "She needed to make a call? She had somewhere better to be? She heard the ice cream truck? How should I know, man? I was sitting right here."

Jackson nodded and pinched the bridge of his nose. "Right. Sorry."

"No worries, brah. How about we slam these beers and go grab a bite? It'll clear your head, and you can get back to work afterward, fresh."

He grabbed the ice-cold beer Grady had brought

him and took a long drink. Probably better for Julia that she left. She must've sensed something off in him. "Thanks, but no. I'll walk you out."

****

Jackson played the new song start to finish. He smiled to himself for the first time since Grady showed up with Bethany and his day unraveled. It was a good song. Maybe one of the best he'd written.

An insistent pounding at his front door ripped his burgeoning mood out at the root. Gritting his teeth, he set his guitar in its stand and stalked toward the door.

Damn it, Grady. He knew he needed to work. He might mean well, but Jackson had already told him—twice—he had no interest in joining them for dinner.

He yanked open the door, and his harsh words evaporated along with all coherent thought.

Julia stood on the stoop, hair up in a ponytail, dressed in her yoga gear and sneakers.

"Hi," he said.

"Hi."

"I didn't think I'd see you again tonight." He paused. Frowned. "What are you doing out here? Yoga on the front lawn?"

She gave a little laugh. "No. I was about to explore the trail. Then I saw Grady and Bethany drive away and… Can I come in?"

"Of course." He stepped back to allow her inside and led her to the living room.

"It smells good in here," she said. "I didn't have a chance to say so earlier. Like fresh flowers."

"It's the candles. I thought you might like them." He shrugged, slightly embarrassed by the admission.

She gave him an uncertain smile. "Am I

interrupting? I don't want to keep you from rehearsing."

He reached out to tuck a loose strand of hair behind her ear, then lightly tugged her ponytail, just needing to touch her. "No. I told you I wanted you here. Is everything okay? You kind of ran out of here earlier."

She nodded and bit her lower lip. "I thought Grady, Bethany, and I being here had thrown you off your game, and, too"—she gestured vaguely—"your dinner plans."

"Dinner plans? Chase isn't due home for an hour at least."

She scratched her head. "Can we sit down, Jackson?"

"Of course." He took her hand and pulled her toward the couch.

The leather gave a creak of protest as they sat.

Jackson leaned back, stretching his arms across the tops of the cushions. "What's on your mind?"

She took a deep breath as if gearing up for something. "You *were* off earlier. But not because you had guests."

He scraped his knuckles across his jaw. "I'm not sure where you're going. I was concerned when you hightailed it out of here. That's for damn sure. Did Grady say something to offend you? I'll talk to him."

She shook her head. "No, he didn't." Her eyes opened wide as if she suddenly remembered something. "Except I do not want to double date with Grady Saturday."

He shook his head, trying to make sense of what she said. "Who said anything about that?"

She slanted a suspicious glance at him. "Grady. I

got the feeling he knew you were my date for Saturday when he suggested we go as a foursome. I certainly didn't tell him."

Ouch. "You embarrassed about going with me?"

She frowned at him, confusion clouding her eyes. "What? No. Why would you ever think that? I didn't tell Grady we were going together because I felt like it might hurt his feelings to know that I preferred…" Her lips compressed, and her face went beet red.

A slow smile spread over his face. "Go on."

She sniffed and examined her nails. "All I'm saying is I don't want to go with him and Bethany Saturday."

Still grinning, he picked up one of her hands to play with her fingers. "Don't worry. I won't set up any double dates with the competition."

She snorted and made a half-hearted attempt to pull her hand free.

He brought it to his lips and pressed a kiss to her palm. "He asked you to go with him when he stopped by your place the other night," he stated rather than asked.

She gave a one-shouldered shrug.

"He can be a dog with a bone. Lucky for you, Bethany looked him up. Apparently she hinted about wanting a date to the charity event long enough that he asked her."

She pinned his gaze with an unblinking stare. "Yeah, about Bethany. I know who she is."

His stomach hollowed out in an instant.

"I was heading to the trailhead when I saw them drive past. It suddenly came to me, why she looked so familiar. She's Sheila's younger sister, isn't she?"

He broke eye contact. "Yes. So?"

"So I think seeing her upset you. It dredged up memories you didn't want to revisit."

He lifted his gaze to hers. How did she do that? How did she see right through him when she hadn't been part of his life for years? He released her hand to trace his fingertips down her cheek.

A satisfying shiver rippled through her.

"I feel better now."

She searched his eyes. "Because she's gone?"

"Because you're here."

"Oh."

"I thought about you all day."

She twined her fingers in her lap. "Me, too."

He wanted to ask about last night's discussion, if she'd come to any decision. But he held back, fearing he might not like the answer. "I finished the song I've been working on. Want to hear it? You'll be the first."

Her blue eyes sparkled with excitement. "Really?"

He chuckled as she all but pushed him off the couch. He retrieved his guitar, slung the strap over his shoulder, and played the ballad that had poured out of him over the last few days. The song told of a man chained by his past, freed by love.

When he finished, he stood quiet for a few seconds, absorbing the haunting feel of the music. Then he sighed in satisfaction and replaced the guitar in its stand. "What do you think?"

Julia gave a loud sniff.

He trotted over to her. "Honey? Are you crying?"

She swiped at her damp eyes. "No."

He lowered to the couch and pulled her, unresisting, into his arms. "Not exactly the reaction I hoped for." He pressed a kiss to the top of her head and rubbed circles over her back. God, she felt good.

She nestled into him. "It was just so beautiful. Jackson?"

"Uh-huh?"

She spoke in barely a whisper. "I want to change our rules."

He stopped breathing for half a second, then he shifted her out of his arms and rose, pulling her up with him. "Come on."

****

"Where are we going?"

He bent to blow out the candles. "My room. I don't think you've ever seen it. Now's as good a time as any for a tour," he said, a smile evident in his voice.

She drew a shuddering breath and followed him up the stairs.

At the landing, they walked in the direction she'd seen Chase go from the loft.

"Chase's room. Bit of a disaster," he said, jerking a thumb toward it.

Julia glanced inside as they passed. The large room was dark, window shades drawn, but she caught red and black decor, a sports poster on the wall, and a few random piles littering the floor.

At the end of the hall, they took a sharp right and started down another hall.

"Guest room one and two." He aimed a finger at each room in turn. "Adjoining guest bath between."

He didn't pause for her to look inside.

"Nice tour," she teased, breathless with anticipation.

They paused at a double doorway where one of the

doors stood open. Turning to face her, he tugged her with him as he backed into what was obviously his bedroom.

It smelled like him. A hint of his spicy aftershave. His shampoo. Fresh laundry.

Her eyes drank in the space as she circled, her arms linked behind her back. It was huge. Her entire cottage could fit inside these walls. Too, it suited him. Dark hardwood floors and taupe-colored walls. A massive, four-post bed flanked by two nightstands took up one wall. A matching chest of drawers stood in the corner, and a dresser and an armoire took up another wall.

A stone-mantel fireplace divided the sleeping area from a lounging, reading area, equipped with a sofa and two armchairs, as well as a well-stocked, built-in bookcase. She skimmed several worn book spines. History books, crime novels, autobiographies filled the shelves.

"Have you read any of these?" she asked, buying time to settle her nerves.

"All of them."

She strolled to an oversized archway, through which gleamed a massive, floor-to-ceiling, marble-tiled bathroom and the master closet.

"Julia."

She jumped a little. Jackson, silent moving as always, stood directly behind her.

He gripped her shoulders and, with gentle pressure, turned her to face him. "We don't have to do this. I don't want anything to happen you don't—"

She held two fingers against his lips. "Shh."

She reached up and pulled the elastic band from her hair, then shook her head. Bending, she untied her sneakers, kicked them off, then peeled off her socks, feeling decidedly unsexy.

When she reached for the hem of her shirt, he took her hands. "Uh-uh. That's my job." He pulled her toward the bed.

He wrapped strong hands around her hips and lifted her to a perch on the edge of the mattress. One hot palm cupped her nape, then he dipped his head.

Jackson's mouth slanted over hers in a tender, sensual assault that turned her bones to melted wax. She reached for him, twining her arms around his neck. Like a wildfire out of control, their kiss grew deeper, hotter, hungrier until all at once he straightened, locking eyes with her. "You're sure? Because, if you're not, we need to stop now."

"I'm sure."

He closed his eyes briefly. "Thank God. When you left today, my mind went in a million directions." He rubbed his hands up and down her arms. "I wanted to chase after you. I almost did, then I thought maybe you'd decided to call things off." His mouth took hers in a searing kiss, then he murmured against her lips, "I thought I'd go crazy today, wanting you."

"I felt the same way," she admitted softly.

"Good." He reached for the hem of her tank, tugged it up and over her head, then dropped it on the floor.

Jackson fingered the lacy edges of her bra, and gooseflesh sprouted over her chest and arms. The appreciative gleam in his eyes made her very glad she'd opted not to switch her expensive bra and panties for a more practical set when she'd changed into exercise clothes.

"Now yours," she said, shimmying his T-shirt upward.

"Yes, ma'am." He yanked it over his head and off in one move.

Confronted with the unmitigated beauty of him, she stared in awe. Because she couldn't not, she traced the carved muscles of his chest and abdomen. Beneath her fingers, his flesh quivered and twitched. Mouth watering for more, she pressed kisses along his collarbone and dipped her tongue into the hollow at the base of his throat, reveling in the warm, slightly salty taste of his skin.

He made a sound that was half growl, half groan and tangled his hands in her hair. Cupping the crown of her head, he tilted her face upward then bent to take her mouth with his. Her fingers kneaded into his skin as drumbeats of desire thrummed through her.

"Your turn again," he murmured and curled his fingers under the waistband of her leggings. In seconds, the garment landed on top of the other discards.

He studied her half-naked body through heavy-lidded eyes. "Mm. I thought you had fine taste in shoes." He drew his fingertips up her thighs, over the curve of her hip, to the base of her rib cage. "Did you pick these panties out for me, Julia?"

Shivering with delight, she parted her lips and drew in a choppy breath. She could barely breathe, let alone speak. She managed a jerky nod.

A lazy smile tugged up one corner of his mouth as his fingertips trailed over her stomach, down the front of her panties, between her legs. Reversing course, he traced up her torso, over the curve of her breast. He lingered there, toying with one hardened nipple.

Slowly, he dipped his head. His soft hair tickled her skin as his mouth found her other nipple through the lace. His lips tugged, his tongue lolled, his teeth grazed. She closed her eyes as waves of unbearable pleasure rolled through her.

She swayed toward him, hands seeking the waistband of his jeans. Breathless, she forced out, "Yours," and undid the metal button.

After she made a few unsuccessful swipes at his zipper, he huffed out a laugh and pushed her hands away. He unzipped his jeans, pushed them past his hips, and kicked out of them. She had only a moment to stare in wonder at the very large bulge straining against his black briefs before he wrapped her in his arms, recaptured her mouth, and tumbled her backward onto the bed.

His warm, slightly calloused hands glided over her body as if he wanted to touch her everywhere at once.

Her hands traveled over him just as greedily. When she reached between them to trace the hot ridge of his erection, he tore his mouth from hers and turned his face into the pillow, whimpering with need.

Emboldened, she squeezed him gently through his briefs.

He groaned and pulled her hands away, raising them up over her head. He rained kisses across her cheek and nibbled down her neck. "Too good. Feels too damned good," he murmured between kisses. "Let me show you."

He released her hands and, in a blink, rid her of her panties.

The sound of their labored breaths filled the room as his fevered gaze coursed over her body, bare from the waist down. His playful expression had vanished, leaving raw hunger in its place.

His palm glided down her belly, then lower, finding the seam between her legs. Breath hissed between his teeth. "So hot. Relax for me, baby. Can you do that?"

She nodded, only realizing she'd tightened her thighs together as he urged them apart. A flicker of panic seized her as Chris's words echoed in her head. Always asking. Always disappointed. What if, despite her incredible yearning, she couldn't?

Then, with gentle pressure, his fingers parted her, and she forgot all her fears. She forgot everything but Jackson, his touch, his urgent whispers against her lips. His fingers danced over her sensitive flesh, teasing, circling, fast, then slow, retreating, then back again 'til, trembling with violent need, she arched into his hand in a wordless demand for more.

Jackson gave a low growl of satisfaction and continued his delicious torture.

He stroked her, faster now, his touch so light she wanted to scream. His lips to her ear, he uttered hoarse pleas, coaxing her desire to a fevered pitch. Higher and higher she climbed until finally, gasping and shuddering, glorious, sparkling sensation cascaded through her like a million shooting stars.

Afterward, she lay boneless and bemused. "So that's what all the hubbub is about," she murmured, then giggled.

Jackson propped himself up on one elbow to gaze down at her.

Their eyes met. She read tenderness—and abject desire in his face. Amazingly, an answering hunger filled her, even having just experienced the most stunning climax of her life.

She sat up, reached for the waistband of his briefs, and pulled them off. Then she straddled his hips, pressing her sex to his.

He shuddered violently. "Wait," he choked and craned his head toward the nightstand. He dug in the top drawer one-handed and yanked out a small packet.

Unwilling to wait one moment longer, Julia snatched the condom from his fingers. She tore it open and rolled it onto his hot shaft.

Jackson hissed and bucked. His lips parted on a silent gasp when, finally, she guided him inside her.

Oh God. He felt so good.

Jackson's lips parted on a silent gasp. His unblinking eyes went wide and fixed on hers.

She threw her head back and, inch by slow inch, rose, easing him out of her, then just as slowly sank, filling herself with him. Once. Twice. When she began her third ascent, he whimpered her name. He grasped her hips and increased the tempo of their lovemaking until, with a groan that sounded like a combination of pleasure and pain, he flipped her onto her back to piston into her.

Julia arched to meet him, lost in a conflagration of sensation and emotion. She wanted more, needed more—of Jackson. Only Jackson. It had only ever been him. She wrapped her legs around him and rose up, inviting his long, deep thrusts.

Sweat covered his back. He closed his eyes, his face a tight, rapturous mask. Hips pumping, he kissed her, murmuring rapid, nonsensical words against her lips, 'til on a hoarse cry, he convulsed above her.

Another cataclysmic release crashed through her.

After he'd wrung every last bit of pleasure from her, he collapsed, wrapped her in his arms, and rolled with her onto his back.

Smiling—she couldn't not—she pressed her cheek to his chest and listened to the solid thump of his heart.

He combed his fingers through her hair with unhurried strokes. "Worth the wait," he murmured, and she dragged herself up on her elbows to look a question at him.

One corner of his mouth curved up. "That was worth the thirteen-year wait."

Chapter Eighteen

Wednesday evening Julia pulled in to her parking space, switched off the ignition, and glanced at her watch. Eight p.m. Late for her, and the dark skies made it seem even later. A summer storm had rolled in during the grocery run she'd put off too long.

She wondered if Jackson noticed her absence, then silently cursed herself for the thought. Again. She couldn't start thinking their fling meant she'd see him regularly. That wasn't how flings worked. At least not as far as she knew.

Too bad her newly awakened inner sex fiend couldn't grasp the concept. She would have to work on that.

She pressed the trunk-open button and hustled out of the car, eyeing the roiling black clouds above. Of course Jackson would know about Chase coming by the office to ask if she'd mind tutoring him at school. He'd explained his classmate, Alana, wanted in on the session.

His young friend hadn't really needed the help. Still, seeing the children together and witnessing Alana's kind efforts to aid Chase's progress warmed Julia's heart. As a bonus, staying on campus kept Julia away from home—and temptation.

She scooped up her groceries and closed the trunk.

A gust of wind, thick with moisture, caught her

hair and whipped it in front of her face. Thunder rumbled as she hurriedly looped all the bags onto her arms.

She made it inside as the first splats of rain fell. A gust of wind slammed the door closed behind her. Lightning flashed, thunder boomed, and the skies opened.

With a sigh of relief that she'd made it in before the deluge, she unloaded her bags on the kitchen counter.

The windows lit up briefly like the sun at high noon. A split second later came deafening cracks as if the cottage itself had been struck, and then the house went dark and quiet as a tomb.

Smiling to herself in spite of the electrical outage, she opened the under-sink cabinet and pulled out a giant flashlight, courtesy of her landlord.

He really did think of everything.

As quickly as she could, she shoved her perishables into the refrigerator, then shined the beam before her feet and moved to the bedroom. A shower would have been nice, but not during this storm. She could at least get out of her work clothes.

Minutes later she tugged a spaghetti-strapped sundress over her head. Pounding on her back door sounded as it fell into place.

She hurried out and flung open the door to find Jackson beneath a large black umbrella. Her nose said he'd recently showered and shaved. A lightning flash showed he wore casual drawstring pants and a plain white T-shirt and looked unreasonably magnificent.

"Come in before you get electrocuted," she said, breathless for more reasons than she could count.

He closed the umbrella and propped it under the eave. Inside, he kicked off his canvas shoes. "As I suspected, your power's out."

"Yours isn't?"

"Yes and no. We're plugged into a generator in the garage."

"Oh, fancy. Lucky for me, my landlord made sure I have a working flashlight."

"Which, by the way, doubles as a club in a pinch." He pulled a delicious-smelling candle and lighter from a bag she hadn't seen him bring in. A moment later, the cottage glowed with flickering light, and the scent of warm vanilla filled the air. "Emergency house calls like these generally command a hefty fee. I'm pretty sure you know what that means."

Before she could comment, he swept her into his arms and covered her lips with his.

She wrapped her arms around his neck, trying to drag him closer, to feel his hard body, tight against hers.

He walked her backward 'til her legs met the couch, then hooked a knee over the armrest and tumbled with her onto the cool leather.

The room filled with the small urgent sounds of kissing and creaking leather, of rustling clothes and desperate murmurs.

Jackson bunched her skirt in his fist to bare her legs and panties. He slid a hand under the elastic band of her silk undies to cup her bottom and press her into his hips.

Julia wriggled against his very hot, very hard erection. The simmering arousal plaguing her all day now boiled over into feverish need. She reached between them, untied his pants, and shoved them to below his hips. Then she freed his pulsing shaft from his briefs and guided him to her core. She rubbed him against her through the thin scrap of silk separating them. "Please, Jackson," she begged.

"Holy God," he murmured low and fumbled a hand in a scrunched-up pocket of his pants. He brought the foil packet to his mouth, tore it open with his teeth. In seconds, he'd sheathed himself in the condom, pulled the crotch of her panties aside, and thrust into her.

Again and again he sank himself inside her, kissing her all the while, sometimes tracing his fingers over her cheek in tender supplication, other times cradling her head to anchor it in place as his mouth and body plundered hers. "Wait," he breathed and tugged at the waistband of her panties.

She shimmied out of them and wrapped her legs around his hips, part invitation, part demand.

"Oh yes," he whispered and plunged into her.

She shoved his shirt out of the way, smoothing her hands over his sweat-dampened back, arching upward to pull him deeper, until the dizzying frisson of desire inside her broke, and she could only sob his name and hold on for dear life.

As if her release sparked his own, Jackson gave a hoarse, exultant cry, torso writhing as he spent himself inside her.

Afterward they lay in each other's arms, Jackson still inside her. Their heavy breathing slowly returned to normal.

Rain spattered against the windowpanes, across the roof, and trees whispered and howled as gusty winds tore at them.

"Payment in full for the house call?" she teased.

He shifted on the couch, easing himself out of her, and sank into the seam of cushions, Julia in his arms. He smoothed her dress down to cover her hips and thighs. "For starters," came his laconic reply. After a moment, he asked in a hushed voice, "Baby, do you know how incredible you are?"

She shook her head, at a loss for what to say.

"I still don't get it. How that—" He broke off to clear his throat. "—guy could have tried to convince you otherwise."

Julia gave a one-shoulder shrug. She didn't much care about that. Not anymore. She doodled one finger over the skin at the base of his neck. "Maybe we just weren't each other's cup of tea."

"Yesterday you said *so that's what all the fuss was about* or something to that effect. Later, I wondered."

She froze. Maybe if she didn't reply, he'd let the subject drop. At least he couldn't see the hot flush covering her cheeks with her head tucked into his shoulder.

"Julia, was that your first orgasm yesterday?"

She squeezed her eyes closed. "All I can say is I never felt anything like that with Chris."

A beat of silence passed. He smoothed a hand over her hair. "And what about anyone else?"

She fisted her hand into his shirt and wished she could disappear.

"Julia?"

She shook her head.

"Was he your first?"

"Yes."

"I see." He didn't sound pleased.

"Yeah. Pretty weird, I know."

"Weird? That's not the phrase I'd use. More like *travesty*. I'd kind of like to knock him on his too-cool ass." He sifted his fingers through her hair. "You waited for someone special. For the man you thought deserved you," he said, his voice going rough. "And he didn't."

She swung her legs over the side of the couch and sat up. "That's not exactly right. Yes, I waited for that, for a very long time. But I finally had to accept the facts. That magical connection doesn't exist. Chris was me trying to get real." She slid her gaze toward him.

He stared back, unblinking. More than anything, she wished she knew what he was thinking. In the long shadows, she couldn't read his expression.

"I wish…" He sat up. Jammed a hand through his hair.

She waited, barely breathing.

He leaned his elbows onto his thighs and twined his hands between his knees. "I don't know if it exists or not. Hannah and I married because, you know—" His chuckle held no mirth. "I knocked her up."

People had speculated. The timing made sense.

"We were young, but we loved each other, so we went for it. I thought we were happy. I guess you never know."

You never know? Hadn't he and Hannah been happy?

He turned his head to look at her. "I know I'm glad you're here and that you didn't fall for his comeback lines."

"Me, too," she said, her heart in her throat as, inside, she lectured herself not to read too much into his

289

words.

The power returned with a whoosh of refrigerator sound and glowing over-the-counter pendulums.

Jackson's eyes crinkled at the corners. His gaze never shifted from her face. "Anyone ever tell you you're a knockout, Julia Hudson?"

She rolled her eyes, but warmth filled her to her toes.

"Hair a crazy mess…"

Her hand shot up to pat her head. "Thanks to you," she argued. It did feel as if she hadn't brushed it in a week.

"Cheeks pink from my stubble." He rubbed a thumb gently over the abrasion, then leaned in to brush his lips over hers. "I'll let you in on a little secret."

"What's that?"

"The power outage just gave me an excuse. Been desperate all day to get my hands on you again. Does that break any of our covenants?"

She shook her head, eyeing him somberly. "Not in light of how well it turned out."

After a beat of silence, he roared with laughter, which drew helpless laughter from her. When they both breathed normally again, he unfolded from the couch and righted his clothing. "I better get going. It sounds like the rain is dying down again, and I need to make sure Chase is getting ready for bed, not to mention shut off that generator."

"Right."

"Probably won't see each other tomorrow," he said.

She didn't like the dismay she felt at his words. Not one little bit. She hoped it didn't show on her face.

"Oh?"

"I'm picking a friend up from the airport in Asheville. It'll put me home late."

"Oh? Who's that?"

He bent to slip his shoes on his feet. "Old friend in town for the Helping Hands event."

A woman friend? She shoved aside her inappropriate suspicion at his vague answer. He didn't owe her a thing. No answers, no fidelity.

"Good to know."

"Friday? Do you have plans?"

"Dinner with the girls."

He crooked a finger under her chin. "Guess that means I'll have to wait 'til Saturday. Don't go getting into any trouble without me if you know what I mean."

"Who me?" she asked, putting on her best innocent expression.

He snorted and stepped outside.

"Thanks again for the house call," she said softly.

He winked at her. "Anytime. Just remember, hefty fee."

****

Julia eyed herself in the full-length mirror and nodded with approval. The never-worn cocktail dress and shoe ensemble she'd purchased for the weekend in the Hamptons with Chris was coming in handy.

The sleeveless black dress stopped an inch above her knees and hugged in at her waist. The demure neckline skimmed her collarbones, but—she shifted around to scrutinize her backside—aside from a thin strap reaching shoulder to shoulder, a low scoop left her bare from her nape to just below her waist. No way to wear a bra with this little number, but Julia wasn't the bustiest of women, and the designer dress did have cups built in for modesty's sake.

Glancing at her shoes made her smile. Suede stiletto booties that let her shiny, red toenail polish peek through and elongated her legs. Based on previous comments Jackson had made, she thought he would approve.

Two days had passed since that mad, passionate interlude on her couch. Make that two days, twenty hours, and—she glanced at her dressy wristwatch—fifty-five minutes, putting her at nearly six p.m. Finally.

She applied red lipstick before dropping it into her tiny black purse.

A knock sounded on her front door, setting off a horde of butterflies in her stomach.

She opened the door to find Jackson waiting on the stoop looking unreasonably handsome in a jet-black suit tailored to perfection. The crisp white of his collared shirt made a nice contrast with the healthy bronze of his skin. A light breeze drifted into the house, carrying a hint of his spicy aftershave.

Her insides shivered. Her senses were reeling, and the evening hadn't even begun.

"Hi," she forced out.

Jackson's gaze traveled the length of her, starting at the top of her head, winding down to her toes. He shook his head. "You take my breath away."

A rush of warmth filled her. "Thank you."

He quirked a grin. "I'd sure like to kiss you hello, but I don't know how that color lipstick would look on me, and truthfully?"

"Yes?"

"I'm not sure we'd make the party."

She chuckled. "I suppose a kiss on the cheek will have to do."

He bent and brushed his lips over her cheek, lingering there. "For now," he breathed in her ear.

****

Jackson checked them in at a reception table situated at the entrance of Dave's Steak House. The smiling women manning the table aimed openly speculative looks at Julia. They handed him bidding numbers for the live and silent auctions, plus two empty wine glasses etched with the words Helping Hands and a mountain scape.

"Let's get these filled," Jackson suggested, then put his hand to the small of her back to lead her through velvet divider curtains and into the venue.

He did that a lot. Touched her to guide her. Every time shot a thrill of excitement through her. Tonight, the skin-on-skin contact made her insides quiver.

"Posh," Julia murmured as she and Jackson approached one of the free-standing bars.

"They did a nice job decorating the place."

The high-ceilinged crystal chandeliers sparkled on a dim setting, and flameless candle centerpieces flickered atop high, round tops lining the room's perimeter. Long tables covered with black tablecloths and silent-auction offerings ran the length of the room's center. Already a large crowd of guests, drinks in hand, scrutinized the items up for bid.

Jackson cocked an eyebrow at her. "Chardonnay?"

"Please."

He set the wine glasses on the bar and ordered.

The bartender filled the glasses, and Jackson dropped a five-dollar bill in the tip jar.

Glasses in hand, they surveyed the room.

"If you want to eat before your set, we'd better get to the food tables. Since we got here, at least thirty people have come in, and it doesn't look like the influx is abating." She glanced toward the door. "There's Grady and Bethany coming in now, and..." She let her words die. If she wasn't mistaken, that was Monica, the one she'd seen plastered to Jackson on Main Street, scanning the room.

Putting a hand to the small of her back, he murmured, "Good idea on the food. I heard the best stuff's in the back."

She set a brisk pace. More than wishing to avoid Monica or Grady, she didn't want Bethany's presence to upset Jackson. Nothing could shake her inner conviction that he had not recovered from Sheila's death so many years ago.

"You move pretty good for someone wearing stilettos. I guess you're hungry?" His eyes gleamed with amusement.

Before she could answer, a silver-haired dynamo darted into their paths.

"Hi, you two," Lisa Tate said with an exuberant smile. "Doesn't the place look great?"

Jackson leaned down and kissed his aunt's cheek. "Sure does, and so do you." He straightened. "Aunt Lisa's on the Helping Hands board, and this fundraiser's her baby. She oversees everything from the auction items to the venue to the entertainment." He punctuated his last words with a wink directed at his aunt.

Lisa swatted Jackson's shoulder, though she beamed with obvious pleasure. "He's exaggerating. But

I have been busier than a long-tailed cat in a room full of rockers these last few days."

"Your hard work has certainly paid off," Julia said.

Lisa gave her an appreciative once-over. "Thank you, sweetie, and might I say you look *hot?* Jackson, you better keep an eye on your date. Some eligible bachelor's liable to steal her out from under your nose during your set. Maybe she'll even bid on one."

"Bid on one?" Julia asked, glancing between Lisa and Jackson.

Ignoring her question, Jackson draped an arm over her shoulders. "Don't you worry, Aunt Lees. My eyes are wide open."

Lisa gave a gratified smile, then her gaze shifted across the room. "Janelle is waving me down, which means a certain celebrity has arrived." That chiding look came back to her face. "*He* agreed to be auctioned unlike someone I know."

Jackson gazed longingly toward the food table.

"Every year we auction off an evening out with handsome, eligible, distinguished bachelors," Lisa told Julia. "Last year we got our local news anchors to do it. You can't believe how high the bidding goes."

"You didn't want to be auctioned, Jackson?" Julia teased. She could only imagine the bidding frenzy over a date with him. Her heart thumped hard in her chest as the realization hit home. *She* was on a date with him, no bidding required. *She* was having a fling with him.

And getting in way, way over my head. Resisting the urge to frown, she squelched the thought.

"Maybe next year," he muttered.

"That's what you said last year." Lisa wagged a finger at him and disappeared through the crowd.

"I wonder who the celebrity is," Julia murmured, following Lisa with her eyes.

Jackson hooked a warm finger under her chin and guided her gaze in his direction. "Never you mind. Where were we?"

Lost in his swirling gold-flecked eyes, she couldn't immediately formulate an answer. "Running to the food table?" she finally managed.

"I am hungry." His gaze locked on her mouth. "You?"

She couldn't answer. She could barely breathe.

He lowered his head infinitesimally.

"Jackson?" A woman's voice shattered the moment.

Julia thought she heard Jackson utter a low curse, but he spoke in a neutral tone. "Monica, good to see you."

The buxom blonde was decked out in a body-hugging, red-sequined mini dress and platform ruby pumps. She had suntanned legs for days and looked fantastic, like sunshine Barbie come to life. It was enough to take the wind out of a girl's sails.

Monica's lips pinched into a tight smile. "Who's your friend?"

Jackson hesitated as if he didn't want to answer.

Julia extended her hand. "Julia Hudson."

"Julia, this is Monica. Monica, Julia is an old friend."

"Yes. I heard she's staying at your place. In that cute, little garden apartment that's a stone's throw from your door. Convenient."

A muscle ticked in Jackson's jaw. "Where'd you hear that?"

Monica blinked at his sharp tone. "Around."

"Right. If you don't mind, Julia and I want to grab a bite and a moment alone before my set."

Monica looked taken aback, then she went full-on fan. "I can't wait to hear you play, Jacks. I'll be right up front."

"Great."

Without a backward glance, he turned away and led Julia toward the food table.

****

"You seem very serious about your food selection," Jackson murmured. Accepting a plate of steak tips and sweet potato soufflé, Julia pasted a strained smile on her face that he wasn't buying for a minute. She'd changed after the run-in with Monica. He wanted to tell her she had nothing to worry about on that front, or any for that matter, but he had no idea how to broach the subject. She had set the rules of engagement. *No relationship discussions* was one of them.

He understood. He habitually steered the conversation away from the R word in friends-with-bennies situations. But this was different. He simply wanted to make Julia understand…*understand what?*

"Let's grab that table there." He gestured with his small plate.

She started toward the dark corner table. "It's gotten really crowded," she said neutrally. She slid around the table to face the room.

He moved in beside her so the heat of their bodies mingled. He picked up his wine and took a healthy swallow. "It's a popular event."

She nodded and moved the food around her plate

with her plastic fork.

He scooped up a bite, drew it halfway to his mouth, then set it across his plate. "What's going on in that pretty head of yours, sweetheart?"

Her brows puckered. "I don't know what you mean."

He took a breath and crossed the invisible line. "If it's meeting Monica, don't let her bother you. There's nothing between us, Jules. There's..." He blew out a breath. "There's nobody you need—"

She shushed him, holding two fingers over his mouth. He read terror in her eyes for lack of a better word. Wow. He'd never been on this side of it.

"You don't owe me an explanation."

He huffed out a laugh. "I know I don't. But I'm telling you all the same. You have to know women approach me all the time, honey. It comes with the package." He thought of Hannah, of how insecure she'd gotten at the end. Nothing he'd said or did changed it.

Abruptly, her expression softened. She smiled at him. Open, accepting, real. "Jackson, it's okay. You didn't do anything wrong. Contrary to what you seem to think, you never do as far as I can tell. Maybe I did let her get to me. I mean she's gorgeous. Plus there was that scene on the sidewalk." She shook her head and gave an embarrassed laugh. "That's on me."

Something in him shifted, like a key fitting into its lock, and it. Felt. So. Good. He couldn't help himself. He kissed her. A lingering slant of his lips over hers. Everything in him wanted to deepen the kiss.

Calling on all his willpower, he drew back, then took a long, steadying breath.

He took some satisfaction from Julia's dazed

expression. At least he wasn't alone in this madness.

"By the way, sweetheart, you're the prettiest woman in this room. Nobody holds a candle to you."

She laughed, sounding delighted and utterly unconvinced. "Oh, Jackson."

An answering smile curved his lips. He loved the woman's laugh. He'd liked it when they were teenagers, too. Soft, authentic, guileless.

She forked up a bite of food and said, "Tell me more about your aunt roping defenseless men into going on dates for charity."

He sliced into his medium-rare steak. He cared a lot too much about what this woman thought of him, but he couldn't stop himself blurting, "I did donate myself, you know, maybe not as an escort, but my set. And I also give a week at one of my properties every year. Usually the condo I own in Colorado. So I do contribute. Just not the date thing."

She set her fork down. "I don't blame you for not agreeing to be auctioned off. My God, imagine the stampede if you d—" She halted so abruptly Jackson thought she might have a piece of food lodged in her throat. Then he saw the stain crawling up her neck and cheeks.

A slow, satisfied smile spread over his face. "A stampede, huh? What about you? Would you bid on me, Julia?"

She gave him a haughty look, tossing her head. "Why would I do that? I got a date with you for free."

He erupted with laughter.

Beside him, her shoulders shook with silent mirth.

"Guess I walked into that one," he finally said.

"Guess you did," she agreed, eyes twinkling.

He scooped up the last of the sweet potato soufflé on her plate.

"Hey," she protested.

"You can get more," he said with a grin, then glanced at his watch. "We need to head over to the silent-auction tables if I'm going to get a chance to bid before my set."

"Lead the way."

Chapter Nineteen

Jackson wove through the crowd, his pace relaxed, his warm hand clasping hers. Open stares and murmurs followed them. By the time they reached the queue to view the silent-auction items, a layer of perspiration dampened her brow. How in the world did he deal with the constant scrutiny?

She forced her mind off the onlookers to study the auction items, one by one. Sporting-event tickets, spa days, dinners for two. All the while, Jackson's hand lingered on the small of her back. His fingers danced over her skin in a light caress, simultaneously delighting and torturing her as arousal screamed through her to finally coil low in her belly.

Focus on the auction items.

Three-month gym memberships, week-long luxury cruises, costume jewelry.

He gestured to an auction for a year of monthly flower delivery. "What do you think?"

She blinked. "I suppose I could bid. But a year? I'm not sure where I'll be in a month, much less a full year."

Her words hung in the air between them like a beacon. She wished she could take them back. She didn't want to think about leaving the cozy bubble of unreality that made up her life these days. Especially not tonight.

He gave an indeterminate grunt, picked up the pen, and jotted down his name and a bid.

Oh. He'd asked what she thought in a more general sense.

"Or you could bid," she muttered.

They moved on.

"This one I donated," he murmured in her ear.

One week at a chalet in Copper Mountain Ski Resort.

"Very generous, Mr. Tate," she said, sending him a little smile.

The background music quieted suddenly, and Lisa's voice came over a loudspeaker. "Welcome to the Seventh Annual Helping Hands Fundraiser."

They looked toward the stage where a beaming Lisa stood, microphone in hand. "The silent auction closes in another few hours, so bid your little hearts out now as you know all the proceeds go right back into our community. In Honeyville, we take care of our own." She paused while applause rippled through the crowd. "Tonight, we're in for a special treat. Our very own Jackson Tate performs for us in a few short minutes."

Whistles and cheers reverberated through the room. He smiled and waved in general acknowledgment.

When the din quieted, Lisa continued. "Last year we introduced our *date with a bachelor*. If you all recall, the ladies bid up a storm—all in the name of charity, right, ladies?"

Raucous, feminine laughter greeted Lisa's question.

"Tonight our newest tradition continues. We'll be auctioning off none other than…" She paused dramatically. "Singer Ryan Moore. Ladies, get your checkbooks ready."

Julia gasped, shifting to face Jackson as excited murmurs filled the room. Music once again played over the speakers. "Did you know?"

One corner of his mouth curved upward. "Remember the friend I picked up from the airport Thursday night?"

"Wow. You can keep a secret."

Ryan Moore was here. Ryan Moore who sang her favorite song—"Falling."

"You have an interesting look on your face," he said. "Kind of like a cat eyeing a bowl of cream."

"I do?"

"You do." His eyes narrowed. "You're not planning on bidding on Moore, are you? Because if you want to meet him, I can arrange it."

She laughed. If she didn't know better, she'd say Jackson was jealous. He was teasing her, of course. Still, she couldn't resist asking, "How would that benefit Helping Hands, though?"

He gave another of those indeterminate grunts.

She giggled and started to tell him she wouldn't bid on the singer. She had no interest. *Because only Jackson will do.* Her amusement faded as the truth hit home.

Jackson glanced at his watch. "Time to go. I'll come find you as soon as I wrap up my set. Any special request?"

"Can I ask for two?"

He gave her an indulgent smile. "I can guess one. 'Falling?' "

"Of course."

"What's the other? I have some pull with the

singer. I may be able to arrange it."

She laughed softly. "Your new one."

"I'll see what I can do." He ran his hand down her arm.

A moment later, she stared after him as he wove through the crowd, making his way to the stage, her traitorous heart in her throat.

****

"I forgot how hot Jackson is." Sue half shouted into Julia's ear in order to be heard over the speakers.

They'd found a great spot to catch the show. Sue had scoped it out early, of course. Not too far from the stage, but well clear of the throng of dancers crowding beneath Jackson—which included Monica.

As for Sue's comment, Julia couldn't agree more. Jackson looked good enough to eat, seated on the stool in front of the mic, one leg bent with the guitar braced on his thighs, the other leg stretched out, thick hair tumbling over one brow.

And that voice. Butter wouldn't melt in his mouth.

Still, Julia didn't answer for fear something in her tone might show how totally under his spell she was. She pasted on a bright smile, threw a thumbs-up in Sue's general direction, and swayed to the music.

"Oh my gosh, you slept with him. You little vixen, why didn't you tell us?"

She stopped swaying. "It's that obvious?"

Sue grinned. "Only to those of us who know and love you. Wait 'til Callie finds out, wherever she is. Have you seen her?"

Julia shook her head.

Jackson's song blended into another hit, drawing their focus back to the stage.

His performance tonight gave her goose bumps. An acoustic set, every song reeked of intimacy. By the end of his show, every woman in this room would be in love with Jackson if they weren't already.

And you should know.

Julia shushed the unbidden thought as her gaze fell on the lady in red dancing solo, front and center. The shapely blonde knew how to move, and she only had eyes for Jackson. But it wasn't Monica he'd asked to come with him tonight.

Earlier, she could swear he'd been about to tell her he wasn't seeing anyone but her. She hadn't paused to think about why. She'd simply known she had to stop him. Now the reason for her fear came to her loud and clear. She didn't want to start thinking of them as a real couple. Because giving him up would hurt so much more if this was actually real.

"Hi, girls." Grady's voice sliced through the music like nails on a chalkboard. He squeezed in between Sue and Julia, draping one arm over each of their shoulders. He kicked a hip into Julia's, flashing her a grin.

"Hey there," she said. A quick scan told her Bethany was nowhere in sight.

On stage, Jackson introduced his next song to a fresh round of whistles and applause.

"Man, I love this one," Grady said, "and as my date is visiting the ladies' room, looks like I'm in need of a dance partner." He shifted to face her, grabbing her arms and reeling her out for a spin before she knew what hit her.

From her new vantage point, she caught sight of a couple dancing, one of whom appeared to be Callie.

"What, or should I ask who, are you looking at?

The man of the hour is on stage."

Grady's voice had an edge. First time she'd ever caught one. How hard must it be, having Jackson as his BFF? Empathy softened her reply. "I thought I saw Callie on the dance floor, but it's too crowded and dark to be sure."

Grady let go of her hands and slung an arm around her shoulders. Leaning close, he said, "I saw Callie earlier—arguing with the new artist in town. Maybe they kissed and made up."

The Irish artist she'd mentioned a few times, no doubt. But arguing? She would ask Callie about it if she ever found her.

Abruptly the smooth sounds of Jackson's guitar morphed into a jarring, fast-paced strumming—like the scene from Burt Reynolds' *Deliverance* on crack, then the music winked out altogether.

"I think Jackson is looking at you, Julia," Sue said with an elbow to her rib.

His gaze did appear aimed straight at her. But with the lights shining on him, could he really see into the shadowed crowd? Unlikely.

He stood up and, holding his guitar to one side, took a short bow. "Thank you, everybody. You've been an awesome crowd."

"One more song," shouted a man from the crowd.

"We love you, Jackson," someone of the female persuasion called.

Jackson quirked a half grin. "I love you all, too. There's really nothing better than playing for your homies." Once again he appeared to stare at Julia. "*Almost* nothing."

Laughter, cat calls, and applause filled the room.

Jackson patted his free hand in the air, quieting the crowd. "Don't disappear just yet, folks. There's a surprise for the ladies to whet their appetite for one of tonight's main events." He paused dramatically. "Please welcome one of my oldest friends, a musician whose singing abilities make angels weep, and whose looks—" He broke off to roll his eyes heavenward and shook his head in dismay. The audience ate up his antics, laughing, clapping, and whistling. "Let's just say he makes the rest of us men look like trolls. Ladies and gentlemen, the one, the only, Ryan Moore."

Riotous applause filled the room. From the curtained backdrop, Moore appeared. He sauntered on stage in black trousers, a crisp, white button down with the sleeves rolled up, his suit jacket hooked on one finger and slung over his shoulder. The dark-haired man looked like he'd just flown in from the Caribbean. Tan skin and the gleaming, white smile he bestowed on the crowd *worked*, to put it mildly.

Contrary to what Jackson had said, however, one man in the room far outshone the folk singer. But who could compare to Jackson Tate? Still, seeing the two side by side was enough to make a woman swoon.

Jackson waved to the audience and made his exit, inspiring another explosive round of applause.

Moore didn't wait for the din to die down. He reached behind the sound board for his guitar and jumped straight into one of his hit songs. Not Julia's favorite. Come to think of it, Jackson hadn't played it. He had played his new song to the crowd's delight. She'd assumed he planned to do "Falling" last. Maybe he'd run out of time.

"Jules, you still owe me a dance," Grady said, arms

open wide.

"I hate to leave Sue. And Jackson—" *Will be looking for me*, she meant to say.

But Grady interrupted her with a chuckle. "Sue's not going anywhere, and Jackson? Honey, I don't mean to burst your bubble, but right about now he'll be schmoozing with all the hot mamas out to get a piece of him. You gotta know that, right?"

She looked to Sue who stared at Ryan Moore as if in a trance. Turning back to Grady, she opened her mouth to tell him…what? That Jackson wasn't like that? But what if he was?

"Sorry, bud, this dance is taken."

Jackson.

He grasped her hand and twirled her around. In one fluid move Julia found herself wrapped in Jackson's arms, her face pressed into his shoulder. His shirt was warm and slightly damp from exertion. God, even his perspiration smelled good. With effort, she stifled a face-splitting grin. Nobody but her needed to know the world could stop spinning and she would die a happy girl.

He led her in a smooth arc across the crowded floor toward a more spartanly populated corner.

"You were incredible, Jackson. You're lucky if half the women here don't follow you home."

He smiled into her eyes. "Oh really?"

"I think you know very well how your performances affect women."

"And how many times have you seen me perform?"

At least eight times, but who was counting? She feigned a considering frown. "I can't recall."

His snort told her he didn't buy it. "I'm glad you enjoyed the show."

"I never wanted it to end. Except...then we wouldn't be here." In the darkened corner, she prayed he couldn't see the hot blush staining her cheeks. She always did that to herself, blurted out exactly what she thought.

"Now that would be a crying shame."

Moore's first song ended, and he addressed the crowd. "Folks, I've got a special request for this next one—one of my first gold records, and I owe it all to the lyricist—thanks, Jackson."

Julia gazed up at him, her heart filled to bursting. "You remembered."

"Baby, you doubted me?"

Ryan started singing "Falling," and Julia melted into Jackson's embrace. Cradled in his arms, dancing to her song, which *he* had written? It couldn't possibly get better than this.

Except it could and did when his hand at the small of her back began drawing slow circles. Every trace of his fingertips sent hot spirals of desire spinning through her 'til her insides bubbled like volcanic lava. She bit her lip to keep from moaning—or panting. Any moment she expected to burst into flames. She wanted to beg him to stop, except the torture felt too good.

The song ended. Their feet stilled. Jackson gazed down at her, eyes a roiling mixture of sea foam and the hot, burnished gold of sunset. "I think it's time we get out of here, don't you?"

"Yes," she answered on an exhale.

He took her hand and pulled her through the crowd like it was his life's mission to clear the building. Along the way, people tried to congratulate him on his show, but he was having none of it. He smiled, barked out thanks, and kept right on moving. Until the moment Julia crashed into his back within throwing distance of the exit.

Before she could ask what in the world happened, a male voice, rough with age, reached her ears.

"Hello, Jackson. I came to see your show." The man's words held an edge, as if he expected Jackson to either blast him or flat-out ignore him. That alone gave Julia a pretty good idea of the speaker's identity.

With her hand still gripped in his, she stepped to Jackson's side to see a man thin to the point of frail, who had lost quite a bit of hair and more than an inch of height, but who she would recognize anywhere. George Tate, Jackson's father.

Jackson's grip tightened in time to the rapidly ticking muscle in his jaw. "George, sorry you missed it."

"I didn't. I—"

Jackson went right on speaking. "Say hello to Julia. You remember her, don't you, George? Your old boss's daughter? The one you never missed a chance to tell me was out of my league?"

She flinched.

Looking both wary and determined, George met her eyes. "Hello, Julia. Lisa told me you moved back to town. It's good to see you."

"Hello, Mr. Tate." She bit her lip. Her instinct was to ask how he'd been, but Jackson's obvious distress had attracted a growing number of interested onlookers, and she didn't see this as an appropriate moment for small talk.

"We were just leaving. Bar's that way." Jackson jerked a thumb over his shoulder and beelined for the door, Julia in tow.

He released her once the door closed behind them and scrubbed his hands over his face. Shaking his head as if to clear it, he strode toward where he'd parked earlier. He gave no indication he remembered dragging her outside with him.

Uncertain what to do, she trailed after him. She reached the corner of the building and peered across the lot.

He stood facing her direction, as if waiting for her, hands clenched at his sides. "I thought maybe you weren't coming."

"I wasn't sure you wanted me to."

He didn't answer in words. He simply held out his hand. She didn't hesitate. More than anything she wanted to wrap her arms around him. She settled for twining her fingers with his.

Seconds later, holding the passenger door for her, he gave a humorless laugh as she slid into the bucket seat. "Do I know how to wreck a good time or what?" He shut the door before she could reply.

Jackson exited the lot without once looking her way. That and his rigid jaw told her he didn't want to discuss the run-in with his dad.

Well, too bad. "Kind of a shock, seeing your father like that, I guess."

He slid her a quelling look, then returned his attention to the road. His hands flexed on the steering wheel 'til the leather creaked in protest.

She reached across the console to comb her fingers through his hair. "Talk to me," she whispered.

He took one hand off the wheel to capture her hand and pull it to his mouth. He pressed his lips to her palm. "I already told you how it is."

"Do you think, maybe, he's trying to make amends?"

Without a word, he reached down, flicked on the stereo.

She took a deep breath and clicked it off. "At least tell me about what you said back there." She swallowed. "About me."

He tapped his fingers on the steering wheel and snorted softly. "You never miss a thing. You always tune in to"—he lifted a hand off the wheel to pinch his thumb and forefinger together—"the absolute heart of the matter, no matter how minuscule."

She folded her hands in her lap and waited as seconds, then minutes ticked by. She had accepted he intended to tell her nothing when his words pierced the silence.

"He was always a mean son of a bitch. I'm not sure if you remember or if you even knew. Always on me about"—he shook his head—"everything. Anything. If I got a B in a class, it should have been an A. If I got a C on a test, it was because I was either lazy or stupid."

"Jackson, I don't understand. Marilyn. How could she stand it?"

"She said he wasn't always that way. She said he went to war and came back changed and addicted to the drink. And to be fair, when he wasn't liquored up, he could be all right with me, more so with her. Only I did my best to stay away from him. It's just, when he was drunk, he wouldn't let me get away. It was like he needed someone to take it out on."

Tears filled Julia's eyes, and she hastily scrubbed them away. She didn't want Jackson to change his focus to her and her feelings like he always did.

"Growing up, one thing Dad always made sure I knew. He said I should never forget I was my father's son. He didn't deserve Mom, and I didn't deserve a woman worth a damn either. He said I'd wreck their lives just like he wrecked Mom's. He damn sure didn't want me around you. He made that very clear."

"Jackson, that is…that is plain horse manure. *Shit*. Horseshit."

For a moment, a real smile split Jackson's face, and his shoulders shook with laughter. Then he sobered. He reached over and squeezed her knee. "No, babe, he was right."

She bit her tongue as he slowed his sports car to a purring roll at the guard gate, exchanged waves with the on-duty guard. The moment he stepped on the gas, she turned to him. "How can you think that? You're one of the best men I know."

"No," he said hoarsely. "I'm not. I've seen what happens when women get involved with me. So have you. Look at Sheila."

And there it was. She'd already picked up on his guilt, even if she hadn't worked it all out 'til now. It had stared her right in the face.

"What Sheila did had nothing to do with you."

He spoke through gritted teeth. "It had everything to do with me."

"How? Did you push her over the balcony?"

"You know I didn't. But I made her unhappy."

"How?"

He banged a hand on the steering wheel. "I don't

want to talk about this."

"How? Did you abuse her? Mistreat her?" She might not have spent any time with him over the last decade, but she saw him now. And she saw no signs that he had an abusive streak.

"No. But sometimes you can't tell." He shook his head. "Then Hannah…"

His wife? "What about her?"

"She died, too," he whispered.

They rounded a curve, and for a brief moment, his mansion of a house came into view, looming silent and dark against the moonlit sky.

"You're not making sense."

"I don't want anything to happen to you," he hissed.

She combed her fingers through his hair. "Hannah's car accident wasn't your fault. And nothing is going to happen to me. Especially not while I'm with you."

Funny, she'd been the one living in fear. Fear of Jackson rejecting her, fear of not being good enough. But now, looking at fear from the outside, she saw what a waste of emotion it was.

They reached his house, and he turned onto the circular drive. The garage door opened. He pulled in to his parking slot and switched off the ignition.

"Chase is spending the night out, right?" she asked, studying him in the glow of the car's interior light.

He ignored the question. "Come on. I'll walk you home."

He'd decided to shut her out. Whether to take his pain and punishment like a man or because he thought he didn't deserve someone like her—which was ludicrous—she couldn't say. But she was having none of it.

"No."

He turned to look at her. She read hardheaded stubbornness in his expression.

"Excuse me?" he asked in a menacingly soft voice she did not buy for one moment.

She climbed out of the car, strode to the door leading into the house, and waited. She held her breath until he twisted the mudroom doorknob and gestured for her to precede him inside. One hurdle cleared.

She moved on sure feet through the darkness, not pausing until she reached the granite bar between the kitchen and living room. There she dropped her handbag and turned to wait. She expected to see the outline of his shape moving in her direction. Instead he stood not one foot away from her.

Her mouth quirked into a helpless smile. He moved as gracefully and silently as a cat, and he took her breath away.

Then he closed the remaining distance between them.

He wrapped a strong arm around her waist, lifted her off her feet, and in several ground-eating strides fell with her onto the leather couch. His scent, his heat, the aura of chaotic emotions engulfing him had her stomach doing flips and the area between her legs thrumming with molten need.

Jackson's face hovered over hers. One of his hands came up to cup her cheek and smooth her hair back from her face. His palm was rough and feverish against her skin. She couldn't make out his expression, but she could feel his searing gaze. Could feel the force of his desire—for her.

Seconds ticked by, punctuated by his labored breathing and the drumbeat pounding of his heart against her ribs. Still he made no move to kiss her, as if he wrestled some invisible inner demon.

She wanted to beg him, but the words lodged in her throat. She resorted to nonverbal communication. Wrapping her hands around his damp neck, she tugged.

He resisted.

"Jackson," she pleaded, helpless to stop herself.

Slowly, his head dipped toward hers.

Too slowly. She could stand it no longer. She arched up to press her lips to his, and the air hissed from his lungs. He pulled back, dropped down to brush his mouth over hers, retreated again. Then something between a groan and a whimper sounded in his throat, and his mouth crashed into hers.

Tremors coursed through him like the aftershocks of an earthquake. His arms tightened around her, and he broke off the kiss to press his forehead to hers. "I need you, Julia. This, what you make me feel. I know who I am, know I'm the last sort of man you should get mixed up with—"

"Jackson." She'd already told him what she thought of his crazy notion and had gotten nowhere. The time for talking had long passed. "Shut up and kiss me."

He huffed out a short laugh. "Yes, ma'am." His breath fanned over her parted lips as he angled his head, this way and that, then finally, *finally*, sealed his mouth over hers.

Jackson's kiss was everything a kiss should be. His soft, full lips molded to hers. His tongue tasted and teased until her entire body burned with dizzying need. A moan of pleasure escaped her, and in the next instant he rolled onto his side, pulling her bodily with him. The demand of his lips turned desperate.

She matched him kiss for kiss, hot, wet, tongues tangling. This was what she needed, too, she told him, in a language as old as time. He tasted like moonlight and stormy seas and sex, and she didn't think she could ever get enough of him. She hooked a leg over his hip, trying to draw him closer, to feel his body against every part of hers.

His hands slid over her naked back. "You, in this dress. I didn't stand a chance."

She wriggled her hips, inching herself higher, positioning him lower, untucking his shirt from his trousers so her hands could slide over his torso. His skin was damp with sweat, and his muscles, bunching under her touch, turned the blood in her veins to fire.

"My turn." Jackson grabbed a fistful of her skirt and tugged the stretchy material to her waist, not stopping 'til her lace-covered bottom met the cool leather of the couch.

And then he rolled atop her, hips aligned with hers. She spread her legs, a silent invitation for him to fill her most intimate places. He ground into her, and neither his trousers nor her thin silk panties offered much of a barrier against the head of his erection pulsing into her soft, aching flesh. The delicious friction twisted her in knots, left her wet, quivering, and. So. Close. And still too many damn clothes between them.

"I need to feel you," he said, echoing her thoughts.

His fingers skimmed up the back of one thigh to slip beneath the edge of her panties. He traced over the curve of her bottom, and a shudder coursed through her.

"Your skin's so soft, like satin," he whispered against her lips. His kiss turned molten. Utterly seductive. His fingers grazed unhurriedly over her hip, up the front of her thigh, then nestled between her legs. He traced back and forth over the tiny scrap of material covering her, and she moaned in desperate pleasure, as her climax hovered just out of reach.

He slipped one finger under the silk and, with a gentle touch, parted her. He murmured low, urgent words between kisses as he teased her most sensitive flesh, bringing her to the brink of orgasm again and again.

"Please," she all but sobbed and reached for the zipper of his trousers.

He moved her hands away, frustrating her efforts. He grabbed the hem of her dress where the material bunched at her waist and peeled it off her.

"Mmm," he said, rubbing his palms over her bare legs. "So soft." Then he reached for her panties.

She hinged up, pushing his hands aside this time, and unfastened the fabric-covered buttons of his shirt, then went to work on his trousers. "Take these off," she demanded in a husky voice she barely recognized as her own. "Everything."

She rose as he rose and stripped off her panties. Her eyes had adjusted to the darkness, and the moonlight pouring in through the bank of windows illuminated him. She drank in the sight of his body, the hard lines of his shoulders and chest, his slim hips, and muscular legs. The long shadow of his arousal. Male perfection.

She bent to unfasten her heels.

"Not this time, babe." He gripped her shoulders and eased her to a standing position. His teeth flashed white as he scooped her off the ground.

She wrapped her legs around his hips and twined her arms around his neck. Her lips and teeth found his stubble-covered jaw and worked their way to the soft lobe of his ear. "*Please.*"

He groaned and, as if she weighed nothing, headed to the stairs. He mounted them, two at a time. He strode through the upper hall, pausing to press her back into the wall as he feasted on her mouth, and his fingers slid into her heat. He swallowed her cries and mercilessly teased her, bringing her closer and backing off again until finally his clever ministrations tumbled her over the edge of euphoria. Hanging on to him for dear life, she kicked, shuddered, and cried out with the unyielding ecstasy of her release.

With a wicked laugh, he continued into his bedroom and set her on the bed. He moved to his nightstand, yanked open the drawer, and found a condom.

Julia rose and moved to the foot of the bed. She wrapped one arm around a bedpost, propped one knee on the mattress, and waited, open and ready for him.

He came to her, grasped her hips, and plunged into her. His growl of male satisfaction sent shockwaves of arousal through her.

She grasped his nape, drawing his mouth to hers as he plundered her body. She held nothing of herself back, and he took all she had to offer, driving into her with relentless, powerful thrusts until she came apart, head thrown back, screaming his name. As her legs gave out, he caught her close, and his own exultant roar ripped from his lungs as he found his own shuddering release inside her.

Slowly, Julia sank onto the edge of his bed, her entire body shivering from the aftershocks of their lovemaking.

Breathing hard, Jackson grinned at her and crouched to remove her shoes. Afterward, he snugged an arm around her waist and tugged her up the mattress toward the pillows.

"That was…" Each word aligned with a heavy exhalation. "Amazing."

She curled into him, smiling into his chest. She couldn't agree more.

Chapter Twenty

Jackson poured himself a cup of Joe, added a large dollop of cream, and, sipping, padded over to his guitar. With pen and notebook in reach, he sat down.

Glancing at the ceiling, he allowed himself a small smile. Soon enough Sleeping Beauty would awaken and find her way downstairs. But not too soon, he hoped. She needed her rest. He'd kept her up half the night.

Just thinking about what they'd spent hours doing had a certain part of his anatomy urging him to go up and wake her properly. Chuckling, he reached for his guitar instead and strummed the melody he'd woken to find playing in his head.

He hadn't written since God knew when. All of a sudden, he couldn't stop the outpouring. He'd have to be a fool not to recognize why, or rather *who* had come into his world and unlocked his chains.

She'd freed something inside him. It felt way too good to believe the lie he'd clung to like a toddler gripping his mother's apron. This thing between them was no simple fling between friends, at least not on his part, and it never had been. *Fool.* He'd known better than to start anything with Julia. He simply hadn't been equipped to will away his need for her. He had no road map. He'd never come across anything like this. Like *her.*

His craving for her, for how she made him feel,

overpowered his good sense. And now that he'd tasted her, been inside her—he gritted his teeth against the wave of lust rolling over him at the memory—he didn't see how he could ever let her go. But he would. He had to. For her sake.

He covered his eyes with one hand and made a promise to himself. He would wait. An opportunity would inevitably arise, something that would let her feel it was her call to end things, and he'd seize it. Hell, maybe she would end things. The mere thought filled him with dread.

With grim determination, he grabbed up his notebook and scratched out poignant words torn from his own heart.

"Hi," came a soft voice from the hallway. She peeked around the dark corner at the base of the stairs.

He hurt at the sight of her, like an invisible hand had reached inside his chest and squeezed. He set his guitar on its stand. "Hi, yourself. Come here."

She crossed toward him, wearing last night's sexy black dress, carrying her stilettos, hair cascading around her shoulders in a mass of tumbled waves that would make what they'd done in his room obvious to a blind man.

She sent him a shy smile, almost as if she didn't know what to expect after last night.

When she got in reach, he snagged an arm around her waist and pulled her onto his lap. He pressed his face into her hair and breathed deep. She still smelled like heaven.

"I put some fruit out and brewed coffee. Want some?"

She nodded. "Like you wouldn't believe. Some sex

maniac kept me up all night."

"That's funny. The same thing happened to me." He pressed a kiss to her forehead and urged her up.

They headed to the kitchen, her hand in his. He just needed to touch her.

"You were working?" she asked.

He nodded. "Messing around."

"How long have you been up? You could've woken me."

"Nah. Then I would have missed seeing you come down in last night's dress, looking like a true sex kitten." One side of his mouth crooked up as he filled her mug.

She took a moment to doctor her coffee. "When's Chase due home?"

"I'll pick him up in a bit, take him to the park for our usual Sunday gig, him, me, and Grady." He eyed her as she drank and heard himself asking her to join Chase and him for pizza and a movie tonight before he knew what was coming out of his mouth.

She gave him a level look. "Are you sure? I mean, is Chase okay with it? I don't want to intrude."

He rubbed a hand down her arm and grinned with pure satisfaction when she shivered and her gaze drifted to his mouth.

"That kid's crazy about you. And what's the big deal? We're old friends, and you're new friends." He wrapped his arms around her. "You can pick the movie."

She laughed into his T-shirt, then slipped her cool hands underneath the cotton. "Any movie?"

He swallowed and forced himself to concentrate. "Chase gets veto rights. Fair?"

She nodded and pressed her lips to the underside of his jaw. "When did you say you have to leave?"

"We have some time," he said and proceeded to make very good use of it.

****

Julia gave Chase three movies from which to choose. He picked *Iron Man.*

She hadn't been sure how the evening would unfold. Would Chase sense things between his dad and her had changed? Would he resent her interloping on family night? As for Jackson, how would he act now? Had anything, in fact, changed?

When she crossed the deck at half past six that evening, Chase greeted her at the back door with a bright smile and giant hug, allaying her fears immediately.

Jackson stood behind Chase in the kitchen, serving up the pizza. His gaze met hers, and he winked as if to say, "See?"

They mowed on pizza and chicken wings in what Jackson called the media room. It boasted a giant-screened television claiming most of one wall, booming surround-sound speakers, and plush, leather electric reclining seats with cup holders and individual retractable tables. Better than most movie theaters, she decided.

She glanced beside her at Chase, then past him to Jackson and hid a smile behind a large bite of pizza. Eating with the two of them, relaxing over a movie, comfortable as a family, she wanted to burst with contentment.

On the cusp of that admission came a tidal wave of fear threatening to swell over her internal levies. This couldn't last. This wasn't real.

Just breathe. She'd already jumped, both feet, into the deep end. No sense second guessing whether she could swim now.

During one of the robot fight scenes, Chase turned to Jackson, a slice of pizza dangling in his hand. "Hey, Dad, can you take me and a friend to the Honey festival Friday night?"

"That's right, Honey fest is this weekend. Sure I'll take you, if I get to hang around. Who's the friend?"

Chase stared at the television. "Alana."

Jackson nodded slowly. "I've heard her name a few times now. Good friend?"

"She's all right." Not taking his eyes off the screen, he added, "Miss Julia, you should come, too. You can keep Dad out of my hair."

Jackson laughed aloud. "You do know I'm sitting right here?" He reached behind his son and squeezed Julia's shoulder. "What do you say? Be my partner in crime?"

Chase grinned at Julia, like a kid with a secret.

She blinked, and his expression vanished, making her wonder if her mind played tricks on her. "I suppose, for Chase's sake. I wouldn't want you to cramp his style."

When the credits started rolling, Julia announced her departure. "I have an early morning and"—she glanced briefly at Jackson—"I didn't sleep much last night."

Jackson stretched and refrained from looking at her. "Oh, that's a shame. I wonder why?"

Chase hopped up and stacked pizza boxes and the dirty plates.

"Thanks, Son. Leave everything on the kitchen counter and go get cleaned up for bed."

"Okay, Dad. Good night, Miss Julia," Chase said, eyes intent on his pizza-box tower.

Julia half rose after he left, and Jackson held up one finger for her to wait. He unfolded from his recliner and moved to crouch in front of her. He slid his hands under her skirt and up her thighs.

Her breath hitched. "Jackson," she whispered, warningly.

"Shh. I needed a little fix, that's all." He grasped her by her hips and pulled her to the edge of the seat, lining them up from pelvis to breastbone.

He slanted his mouth over hers, and she bit back a moan.

After he turned her bones to jelly, he sighed and helped her to a standing position. "C'mon. I'll walk you back."

She knew better than to argue.

At her door, he kissed her breathless again.

"Not fair, Jacks," she said with a shaky laugh. "You're leaving me in a fine state."

A wicked smile spread over his face. He traced his fingertips along her jaw. "Just making sure you dream about me. I for one don't anticipate getting any sleep, knowing you're here, a few steps away."

He brushed a tender kiss over her lips, and her chest filled with an all-too-familiar ache.

A husky laugh escaped him, and he pressed his forehead to hers. "I'm beginning to wonder if you're some kind of witch, Miss Hudson," he said in a hushed voice.

"Why's that?"

His face went serious. "Because I can't stop thinking about you for five minutes even when we're in the same room. Tonight I could hardly concentrate on the damn movie."

She wanted to respond in a teasing tone, but the intensity in his eyes stole her words.

After a moment, he cracked a smile, straightened away from her, and slapped his palm on the siding. "Inside with you, babe."

She stepped into the cottage, started to close the door, then blurted, "If you wanted to sneak over later—"

His teeth gleamed white in the glow of the outdoor light. He leaned in and pressed a kiss to her lips before she finished speaking. "I accept. See you in two hours."

Inside, she shut the door and leaned into it. She drew a deep breath and said in an awed and tremulous voice, "I'm in love with him." A nervous laugh escaped her. "Talking to myself and in love with Jackson Tate. I really have lost my marbles."

But she couldn't wipe the smile off her face.

****

Jackson finished shaving and checked his work in the mirror. Satisfied he could kiss Julia without scouring her cheeks, he patted on some aftershave. A steady thump of bass down the hall told him Chase was still getting spruced for the festival to his usual backdrop of music.

He pulled on jeans, a casual button down, slip-on canvas loafers, then eyed his watch. He was early. He rolled his eyes at himself. Imagine that.

Since their pizza-movie night—capped off by his late-night visit—he'd had dinner with Jules once this week after talking her into letting him deliver it at the end one of Chase's tutoring sessions. His secret weapon had been showing up with a mouthwatering lasagna.

They'd also had a picnic lunch at the school after he scheduled an afternoon meeting with Chase's math teacher. If his son wanted his support, he needed intel from the source. Seeing Julia afterward was his reward.

Besides the impromptu meals, they'd arranged several clandestine rendezvous at his place or hers, always after hours, during which they made out, made love, teased, and screwed each other's brains out, and not necessarily in that order.

He couldn't get enough of her. It thrilled, bewildered, perplexed, and scared the hell out of him. And now he could add guilt to the mix. Because he'd never felt this way about any woman, not even Hannah.

He had loved Hannah. The charismatic older-woman-about-campus at three years his senior had intrigued him with her self-assurance and wit. He'd wanted her, pursued her, and won her over. He hadn't considered marriage one way or the other until Chase happened. Making things official before his son came into to the world seemed right, and he'd never regretted it.

He'd tried to be a good husband and father. Unfortunately, his best efforts with Hannah had not measured up.

He pushed the depressing thought from his mind and strode from his room. He rapped his knuckles on the doorframe of Chase's bedroom.

A jean-clad Chase stood beside his bed, staring at a pile of discarded shirts he'd evidently tried and rejected. Jackson hid a grin. He looked forward to meeting this Alana who had his son so intent on impressing her.

"Yeah, Dad?" Chase looked up, brows furrowed.

"Heading over to Julia's. Text me when you're ready, and we'll meet you in the garage."

Chase rubbed his chin in a considering manner.

Jackson crossed his arms over his chest. "Something on your mind, Son?"

"I was wondering. Would you consider this kind of like a double date?"

Jackson wandered into the room. He had not seen this coming. "Well, I…" He went blank, unsure what to say.

"You haven't dated much. I mean, since Mom. You never really said why."

Why did it suddenly seem Jackson and Chase's roles had reversed? "A lot of reasons."

Chase nodded. He plucked at the shirts piled on his bed. "Am I one of them?"

"Of course, buddy. Because you're the most important person in the world to me. I can't bring any old broad around."

They both laughed.

"In all seriousness, meeting someone hasn't been a priority."

"Even now?"

Jackson shrugged. "What are you getting at, Chase?"

"Just that, if it *is* a double date, and if you *do* want to see Miss Julia, you know, *more*, I wouldn't mind."

He swallowed hard against a sudden lump in his throat and riffled his son's hair. "Thanks."

"Hey," Chase groused.

Jackson lifted his hands in a placating gesture. He started for the door, then paused, hand on the doorjamb. "One thing."

"Yeah?"

"Seems like I missed the discussion about *you* dating."

Chase's face registered *oops.*

Jackson huffed out an amused breath. "If your dating life includes dragging your dad along, I've got no concerns for the moment. Something more and we need to talk, fair?"

"Fair."

"About Julia. You like her?"

Chase grinned, though whether due to talking about Julia or the subject change, who could say? "Yeah, Dad, I do. She's really great."

"I like her, too. Text me when you head down."

****

With her finger hovering over the send button on her computer, Julia reread her reply email in which she agreed to a phone conference with her old boss. She'd politely declined his first two requests to discuss a quote-unquote career opportunity. But in his last email, Shawn, senior partner at the firm, flat-out asked her to give him a few minutes of her time.

He'd been a good boss and had deserved better than her walking out with no notice.

She hit send.

Jackson walked through the open back door. "Hi. You look very festive."

He strode toward her and grasped the back of the stool where she sat, spinning her to face him. His gaze cruised lazily over her pale-yellow, linen sundress, down her legs, crossed at the ankles, and landed at her butter-colored, stacked espadrilles. His eyes flicked up to meet hers, one brow arched.

"They're amazingly comfortable," she insisted.

"And I'm sure you can run in them." He gave a throaty chuckle.

She lifted her chin a notch. "If someone gives me a good enough reason."

He slid a finger down her nose. "We can work on that when we get home."

Home. Jackson's casual use of the word set off a cacophony of emotions within her. Heady warmth and yearning, hope and desperate fear.

"Hey, now," he said, his face registering concern. "What's going on in that pretty head of yours?"

She bit her lower lip. The man never missed a thing. She could hardly give voice to the thoughts roiling in her head. Per her rules, they didn't discuss the future, much less the status of their so-called fling.

That worked for her. She'd grown convinced those rules of hers were the difference between keeping this raft afloat and watching it smash into the rocks.

He frowned and flicked his gaze over her computer screen. "Is it your ex?"

"No." But she grasped the avenue he offered like a lifeline. "I've received several emails from the firm I left, from my ex-boss."

"Really? Why?"

She slid off the stool. "I get the impression he wants to offer me the job back. Or something to that effect."

"Huh."

Julia slung on her soft leather crossbody. "I told

him I'd hear him out." She held her breath, waiting for Jackson's reaction.

His eyes met hers. Then a fire alarm bellowed, which she now knew signified Chase's ring and text tone. He pulled his cell out of his back pocket and studied the screen. "Chase is ready. I told him we'd meet him in the garage."

****

They separated from Chase and Alana after agreeing to meet up before the band came on.

At Jackson's suggestion, they proceeded directly to the mead wine tent. Inside, festive bubble lights hung from the support cables, illuminating the crush of people in a warm, happy glow. Julia's quick scan of the crowd revealed Callie and Sue, Grady and Bethany, though the two didn't appear to be together, and even the very pregnant Jane with, she guessed, her husband.

The other seventy or so attendees, though strangers to her, seemed anything but to Jackson. The moment she and Jackson had their plastic cups filled with the sweet, honeyed wine Honeyville was famous for, people crawled over each other, clamoring for his attention. No sooner had he finished talking with one group than another pulled him their way.

Like now. He caught her eye and mouthed, "I'm sorry."

She waved him off with a contented smile just as Sue and Callie materialized in front of her.

"When you said our Friday night girls' outing had to move to Saturday because of your *festival date*," Callie said, stressing the last two words, "we decided you had a great idea. You look fabulous by the way, girlfriend."

Sue nodded. "You do."

"Thanks." Julia eyed her dress. "You don't think it's too much for a fair?"

Callie leaned in. "Forget the dress. I mean you're glowing."

Her cheeks pulsed with heat. She slid Sue an accusatory glare. "You told her."

Sue looked at her like she had two heads. "Of course I did."

Julia chuckled, nodding her understanding. "I planned to spill the beans tomorrow night."

"The fling is going well, I take it? You're welcome." Callie gave a short bow.

Julia refused to discuss her love life in the middle of the crowded tent. "Who was Mr. Tall, Dark, and Handsome that Sue and I saw you dancing with last weekend?"

Callie shrugged. "Just Irish."

"Irish?" Julia prompted.

She waved a dismissive hand. "The painter who recently moved to town? I could swear I mentioned him. Not that anything's going on there."

"I call bologna," Sue said.

"I'm not looking for a relationship. Neither is he."

"A fling, then?" Sue asked.

"Not even that. It's a long story."

They waited for Callie to go on. When she didn't, Sue rolled her eyes and held up her empty plastic cup. "I need another one."

Callie's broad smile said she was all too happy to let the subject drop. "Can we get you one, Jules?"

"No, thanks. I just got this one. You guys go on. I think Jackson is heading this way."

Or not. He sent her a regretful look as he got stopped by yet another friend, fan, or acquaintance.

She contented herself with sipping her honeyed wine, and Jane waddled up.

They exchanged hellos, and Jane asked how she was getting along at the school.

"I have to admit I'm enjoying the change from my typical public accounting work. Still busy, but less pressure, and you gotta love those banker's hours."

Jane nodded. "Good to know."

"Why do I get the feeling you're asking out of more than mere curiosity?"

Jane rubbed her ginormous belly. "David and I have talked about making my leave more permanent. Before I decide, I wanted to know if I'd be leaving Sue high and dry. Any chance you might consider staying on?"

Julia pursed her lips. "I'll have to give it some thought. I don't want to commit and then, in a few months' time, tell Sue I'm taking a CPA position somewhere else."

Gloom descended over her like a wet blanket. She couldn't imagine leaving now. Her family, her friends, *Jackson*.

"At least you're not out the gate with no," Jane said with a grin. "Now if you'll excuse me, my bladder seems to have shrunk since this kid inside me grew to the size of a baby elephant."

Jane no sooner left than Jackson appeared at her side. He aimed his superstar smile at her, and her heart tried to beat right out of her chest.

Leaning down, he whispered in her ear, "Did I mention how stunningly gorgeous you are? Every man here wishes he was me tonight."

She laughed aloud.

He frowned as if perplexed by her reaction.

She gave him an indulgent look. "Thank you for the compliment, Jackson. But of course every man here wants to be you. What sane man wouldn't? You're…" She searched her mind for some description he could understand, other than the *Jackson Tate* she found perfectly descriptive. "You're practically perfect," she settled for saying.

A teasing light shone in his eyes. "Know what I think?"

She shook her head, a helpless smile curving her lips.

"I think you have it bad, Julia Hudson."

Her smile froze, and a cold sweat broke out all over her body. She knew he'd meant the words as a joke, but they hit a lot too close to the truth.

He went on, his eyes locked with hers. "Because no one, *no one* in her right mind would confuse me with Mr. Perfect."

Oh God, she had given herself away. How she really felt about him. A queasy feeling rolled over her, and she glanced around the tent, looking for the closest exit.

The humorous glint in his eyes faded. Concern took its place.

"I need to find a restroom. Will you excuse me?"

"Julia—"

She didn't stay to hear what he said next. Blind panic drove her past a blur of faces. Outside, she sucked in air and all but ran along the sidewalk, heedless of the direction, until she came to a relatively pedestrian-free area. She stumbled toward an empty bench and sank onto it with shaky legs.

She drew several deep breaths, but instead of finding the calm she sought, reality smacked her in the face. She'd arrived with Jackson and his son. She'd rejoin them soon, eventually leave with them. If only for Chase's sake, she didn't have the luxury of indulging in a fit of hysterics simply because Jackson had likely realized the truth—that she'd fallen head over heels in love with him.

She huffed out a mirthless laugh. *Fallen* in love? Had she ever *not* loved him? The miracle was that it took him this long to see. She didn't know how to play games. She'd worn her heart on her sleeve from the start.

"Julia? That *is* you. I thought so. It's Bethany. We met at Jackson's. Are you all right?"

Julia glanced up at the tall, auburn-haired woman approaching. Having a heart-to-heart with the virtual stranger was the last thing she wanted right now. She drew herself up and put on her best game face. "Hi, Bethany. I'm fine. I"—she glanced down at her wedges—"needed to give my feet a rest."

"Mind if I join you?" Bethany didn't wait for an answer. She sat and gave Julia a level look. "I remember you, you know."

"Oh?"

"My sister pointed you out once, at a party. She didn't like you. She always said you were after her boyfriend, Jackson."

Julia bit her lip. "I did have a crush on him, but so did every girl. It wasn't like he knew anyone besides Sheila existed."

Bethany nodded, and her mouth curved in a grim smile. "True. But Sheila always said he treated you differently than the other girls. He talked about you like you were"—she tossed her head—"superior to everyone else. It would irritate anyone."

Julia blinked, unsure how to respond.

"The night of prom, her senior year, when Jackson left her to take you home, she blew a gasket. To tell you the truth, I'd half forgotten, but Grady reminded me. He knew all Sheila's secrets." A sad look came over Bethany's face. "Unlike me. I thought she was happy. She had graduated, she had snagged the most popular boy in town, then she up and…did what she did."

"I'm so sorry, Bethany. I can't even imagine."

She nodded. "Few people can." After a brief pause, she went on. "Once I learned how miserable she was—I dug it out of Grady bit by bit—I figured out she must have told Jackson, her boyfriend, if she shared all that with his best friend. But he never admitted a thing to me.

"Thank goodness for Grady. No wonder she leaned on him. I got a little crush on him at the time. Knight and shining armor and all that. But Jackson? Town hero? What a joke."

Julia struggled to find words. She didn't want to pick at Bethany's old wounds, but she couldn't stand by while she maligned Jackson for her sister's mental health issues. "If you think Jackson didn't suffer, if you think he didn't blame himself, you're wrong on both counts. But you have to know it wasn't Jackson's fault, Bethany. He was only a boy."

Bethany's chin lifted a notch. "Yes, I understand that now. But he still should have told me the truth. I guess that's why I agreed to go out with Grady when he called me out of the blue. I wanted to look Jackson in the eye and let him know he and his secrets hadn't fooled anyone." She gave an embarrassed laugh. "Well, that and the little crush I had on Grady."

Things weren't adding up. She distinctly recalled Jackson telling her Bethany called Grady out of the blue and not the reverse. He'd have gotten that intel from Grady. Which of them lied? On the other hand, did it matter? The poor girl was clearly distraught.

"When I got to Jackson's house and Grady reminded me who you were, I got mad all over again." Bethany studied her hands, folded in her lap. "Then I got sad. And for what? Even my longed-for date was a letdown. Grady spent the whole night acting like I wasn't there."

She shot Julia a wry look. "He seemed very interested in your whereabouts, though. It drove home how my sister must have felt all those years ago. But then I decided any guy who's going to treat me like that isn't worth getting upset over. I wish my sister had figured that out."

"I agree with you there."

She twisted a finger in her auburn hair and sighed. "When I saw you sitting here, I knew I had to warn you to be careful. Jackson may seem nice, but he has a way of tearing a girl down. That's what he did to my sister, and she never saw it happening 'til it was too late."

Julia frowned. "Hold on a minute. I can't speak to what happened between them. But Jackson is one of the kindest, most selfless people I know."

Bethany gave her a pitying look. "If you don't believe me, ask Grady. He knows everything. He told me Jackson's wife defended him the same way you do until she discovered a few key truths about her perfect husband, and look what happened there. I'd hate you to be number three."

Julia had heard enough. She rose, smoothing her skirts while she reined in her anger. "I appreciate your concern, Bethany, and I truly am sorry about your sister. But regardless of what you've heard, Jackson is a good man. I would stake my life on it."

Chapter Twenty-One

Jackson spotted Julia making her way back toward the tent. Wherever she'd hared off to was sure as hell nowhere near the ladies' room where he'd waylaid a woman, demanding she go in and ask after Julia. The woman had looked at him like he was a madman. As she hurried away, he'd overheard her muttering something about celebrities losing their marbles due to too much fame.

He'd contemplated correcting her. His own particular brand of insanity owed more to one sexy-as-hell woman who'd crawled right under his skin and set up camp. Instead, he'd backtracked, doing his best to ignore the gnawing suspicion hollowing out his insides that he and his big mouth had blown it, and Julia had left.

Now that he'd found her, he couldn't decide if he was more irritated or relieved.

Okay, relieved won. Still he stopped in his tracks, waiting her out. Hands on his hips, he stared while replaying their conversation in his head for the fiftieth time. He knew what he'd said had put that look of terror on her face, but he didn't know *why*. And why was crucial.

She sent him a tentative smile. Some of the heat eked out of him.

Biting her lip, she closed the last few feet between

them. "Sorry about that."

"Still need to use the restroom? Because it's back there," he said more gruffly than he intended, jerking a thumb over his shoulder. "After waiting outside for ten minutes, I finally asked someone to check on you."

Her eyes went as wide as saucers. "Oh no."

Staring into her bottomless blue eyes, he felt his annoyance evaporate. What's more, with Julia in touching distance, the hilarity of the moment hit home. He snorted. "I made an utter ass of myself."

She moved into him then, butting her face into his chest and fisting her hands in his shirt. "I freaked out. I'm sorry."

His guts twisted with fear and a bittersweet emotion he didn't care to analyze. He should ask what set her off. But he couldn't form the words. Because she might answer. And every one of the answers he could imagine her giving scared the living hell out of him.

He wrapped his arms around her and breathed in her familiar, heady scent, lilacs and something sweet, like passing an ice cream stand on a summer evening. "No. I'm the one who's sorry. I know I said something...wrong." The coward's way out, but still the truth.

She straightened away from him and gave him a smile equal parts consternation and compassion. She raised one damp palm to cup his cheek. "You did nothing wrong. It was me. All me."

With ruthless control he stifled the shudder threatening to roll through him. "Do you know how badly I want to kiss you right now?"

Her smile turned coy. "Maybe."

He threw his head back and hooted with laughter. Relieved beyond measure, he shifted them around, then slung one arm across her shoulders. "Time to go find Chase and stake out a place to watch the band."

"Um, Jackson?"

He angled his head to look down at her. "Yes?"

"I really do need to use the restroom now."

He laughed until he couldn't draw breath. When his amusement died to a simmer, he drew her to a halt and, heedless of onlookers, kissed her.

****

They found Chase and Alana with Grady, and if memory served, Grady's father. The four waited at the railing surrounding the concert greens.

Julia watched as Grady and Jackson exchanged one-armed hugs and slaps on the back.

Her thoughts turned to the things Bethany had said earlier. Her claim that both Sheila and Hannah, Jackson's wife, confided in Grady who then shared those confidences with her seemed wrong on so many levels. First, that they'd gone to Grady when she herself would never consider leaning on him, and next that he revealed their intimate secrets to Bethany and God knew who else.

And what about Jackson? Did he know about Grady's involvement in his personal business? Did he approve?

It was certainly an odd dynamic. One she would never consider entering into herself.

Mr. Toller extended a hand to Jackson. "Always good to see you, son. And who do we have here? This couldn't be little Julia Hudson?"

Jackson smiled down at her. "Sure is. Julia, you

remember Ed Toller, Grady's dad?"

"Of course. How are you, Mr. Toller?"

He barked out a laugh. "Who's that? Call me Ed. Grady told me you'd moved back. Glad to see you're keeping good company." The older man grinned at Jackson.

Chase sidled up and tugged on Jackson's sleeve. "Dad, should we go in? It's starting to get crowded."

They filed through the gate and found a patch of lawn large enough to accommodate all of them.

"I ran into your dad recently at the hardware store on Main. He wasn't looking too hot," Ed said to Jackson.

Julia held her breath, wondering how Jackson would react.

"Aunt Lisa mentioned his treatments had gotten rough for him lately."

So far, so good.

Chase, who had appeared deep in conversation with Alana, suddenly joined in the men's discussion. "We haven't seen Grandpa in a long time, Dad."

Jackson's questioning gaze fell on his son.

"Well?" Chase asked.

A ruddy stain covered Jackson's face. "Well what?"

"Can we go see him?"

Jackson cleared his throat. He looked to Julia, a helpless expression on his face.

She gave him an encouraging smile.

"Sure, Son. We'll talk about it later."

Chase hugged his dad and went back to Alana.

Jackson looked bemused, as if he didn't know what just happened.

Ed slapped a hand on his shoulder. "You're a good man, Jackson. It's not always easy doing the right thing, but you usually do just that."

A warm burst of pride spread though Julia. She couldn't have said it better herself.

Jackson gave a noncommittal grunt.

Ed went on, laughing under his breath. "You're a good influence on Grady, too. Lord knows where he'd be if it wasn't for you."

Julia pretended not to hear Ed's statement, congratulating herself on her decision when Grady's head jerked in his father's direction. He didn't look terribly upset by what his dad said, more like amused meets offended, but still. *Fathers and sons,* she thought. *Complicated.*

"Thanks but I think you're giving me too much credit. If he still runs on the wild side sometimes, it's because he hasn't found the woman who can tame him. He needs to get himself a wife."

Ed arched a brow and murmured something in Jackson's ear. Jackson drew back to regard Grady's father with a look of incredulity.

Julia hadn't caught Ed's words. Something to do with Grady following in Jackson's wake? She shook off her curiosity, a little chagrined. Whatever he said hadn't been meant for her ears.

A ripple of applause spread through the crowd and gained momentum. On stage the band members had taken their positions.

"Good evening, Honeyville," the man at center stage holding the mic said. He wore a large cowboy hat, a wide smile, and a guitar slung over his shoulder. "Are you ready to rock?"

The crowd responded with shouts of *hell yes*, claps, and whistles, and the band jumped into a fast-paced country song that had everyone head-bopping or outright dancing to the beat.

She slid a glance toward Jackson. He moved with the music, all grace and crazy sex appeal. The usual. She sighed inwardly. She could watch him for hours. How sad was that?

As if he felt her scrutiny, his gaze shifted in her direction. The moment their eyes met, his mouth quirked into a knowing grin, and he winked.

Yelling over the music, Ed asked if anyone needed anything from concessions. Grady asked for a beer, and Chase jumped up and down, excited over the prospect of popcorn and soft drinks.

"Okay, but you go with Mr. Toller and come right back here," Jackson said. "Julia?"

She shook her head. "All good."

Ed, Chase, and Alana disappeared into the crowd.

Once the opening song finished, the band thanked folks for the warm reception. Then the stage lights turned to the onlookers.

"We heard tell we have none other than Jackson Tate in the house tonight."

People standing nearby shouted and pointed at Jackson. The spotlights honed in on him.

"Let's see if we can talk him into coming up for a song. What do you folks think?"

The crowd went wild, jumping, clapping, whistling, chanting Jackson's name, until, with an embarrassed laugh and an apologetic look at Julia, he allowed himself to be corralled toward the stage.

Grady moved next to Julia, laughing. "Man, oh

man, that guy never gets a break. Somebody always want a piece a'him." He grinned at Julia. "Can you blame them? The guy is good."

She nodded and returned the grin, inwardly wary.

"I wanted to say you two really fit together. You make him happy, Jules. Happier than I've seen him in years. I can't even resent him for getting the girl I had my sights set on."

Julia's face went hot. "Grady, Jackson and I—"

He brought his hands up and made air quotation marks as he finished her sentence, "Are friends. Yeah, yeah, you keep telling yourself that, kid."

She breathed a sigh of relief when Chase, Alana, and Ed made it back, drinks and snacks in hand. Though Grady's comments seemed refreshingly sincere and well intentioned, she didn't need the reminder she and Jackson's fling had morphed into something well beyond the safety of the rules meant to guard her heart.

****

The coffee maker sputtered at the end of its brew cycle, then beeped. Jackson set his guitar in its stand and padded across the cool hardwood floor to the kitchen. He filled a large ceramic mug with steaming coffee, added a dollop of cream, and leaned against the counter, sipping.

Something had changed last night. It started when he made the idiotic statement to Jules about her *having it bad*, which he'd meant as a joke. But Julia had taken the teasing like he threatened to shoot her dog.

Later, everything had seemed okay again. The night had rolled on smoothly with Julia appearing to enjoy herself, as if her earlier disappearing act hadn't happened. After the festival, they'd dropped Alana at home, and he'd put Chase to bed. Then he'd gone to her place, as nervous as he could ever remember being. After her unexpected behavior at the festival, he'd wondered if she'd leave him standing at her back door.

She hadn't. Far from it. She'd met him wearing nothing but that sexy kimono, pulled him into the unlit cottage, and led him straight to her bed.

He closed his eyes and basked in the memories. Him, reaching for the tie to her robe. Her, brushing his hands away, then taking her time stripping his clothes off. Her fingers had caressed as they bared his skin, her lips followed her hands to press kisses over every part of his anatomy 'til he literally shook with the need to touch her, taste her, fill her. 'Til he half begged. Still she denied him, squeezing every ounce of his control from him.

When finally he sank himself into her, he intended to return the favor of her slow torture with long, languid strokes. But he gazed into those blue, blue eyes of hers and lost the battle with himself. An overwhelming need to possess her took him like a riptide, consumed him like a raging fire, burning him from the inside out. His own hoarse groans had erupted from him as he made love to her like he would erase the trace of anyone else from her, body and soul, marking her as his and his alone.

She took his breath away, stole his self-control. He couldn't quench his thirst for her, couldn't slake his hunger. Even now he wanted nothing more than to go to her, slip into her bed, and make mad, passionate love to her.

Who had it bad?

He set his mug on the counter and dropped his

head in his hands. He needed to get a grip. This couldn't last. Even if it could, he couldn't risk inflicting his own personal brand of misery on Julia. Could he?

He wasn't such a fool he couldn't name the ache in his heart, the soul yearning he felt at the sight of her. He loved her.

He'd loved one other woman in his life and had set out to make her happy with everything he had. He moved them home to slow down their lifestyle when the big city got too much for her. He quit touring to calm mounting insecurities concerning his fidelity, the source of which he couldn't fathom. He'd never cheated on Hannah regardless of the ample opportunities his career brought him. He worked hard to dispel her doubts.

He thought he got through to her. Thought they were good.

Then the new album came out, and he scheduled that damn tour—*her* idea. She pushed him 'til he agreed. Then she got behind the wheel, all smiles, and ran herself off the cliff.

He'd done his best, and it hadn't been good enough. Maybe she'd tried to tell him what she needed, and he hadn't heard. Like Chase and that damned math class. Jesus. He couldn't let it happen again.

"What's a'matter, Dad?" Chase asked.

Jackson hadn't heard him come down the stairs.

He studied his son. Hair mussed from sleep, cheek creased from his sheets, decked out in his dragon-covered pajamas—and far too young to carry the burdens of his dad.

Time to shake off his dour thoughts. "Nothing's wrong, pal. Hungry? Want me to whip up some eggs for you?"

Chase yawned and nodded.

Jackson got to work on breakfast. "What's on our agenda for today? Should we hit the trail?"

Chase climbed up on a stool. "I texted Grandad to see if we could go see him later. He said yes."

Jackson froze, egg in hand. "Probably something we should have discussed."

"We did, Dad. Last week and the week before that and then last night when you said okay. Are you backing out?"

Jackson's gaze slid to Chase who stared at him, a belligerent expression on his face.

"Aunt Lisa says he's pretty sick. I asked her if he was going to die soon. She said he might. Don't you want to see him, Dad? If it was you, I would see you."

In rapid succession, Jackson cracked four eggs into the hot pan and watched the whites bubble in the hot butter. *No sense lecturing myself on listening, then doing the exact opposite.* Besides, maybe Julia was right, and it was past time to allow the old man to make amends. "We'll go see him for a while."

He'd give his father a shot. If he screwed up with Chase, however, he would not get another chance.

****

Julia sat at her counter, sipping water, thinking about her conversation with her ex-boss. Thinking about her life here. Thinking about Jackson.

She had decisions to make. Her mind told her one thing, her heart another.

A knock sounded at her back door. She smiled and moved to open it.

Jackson came in wearing baggy khaki shorts, a

well-loved T-shirt, and leather flip-flops. He looked as beautiful as ever, but his eyes seemed to carry the weight of the world.

"What's wrong?"

He ran a hand through his hair. "Nothing's wrong. You've been practicing yoga?"

She grinned and glanced down at her white, scoop-necked tank, tied off at the hip, and purple capri leggings. "What gave me away?"

He tugged on the tie. "Chase is heading to a friend's tonight for a sleepover. Want to come over? I'll fix us dinner and let you take advantage of me."

She sent him a regretful frown. "Can't. It's girls' night."

"Oh." He stared at her for a minute, then blurted, "We went to see my father earlier."

"You did? Today? How did it go?"

He swallowed. "It went okay. He showed Chase a bunch of pictures of Mom and me. I didn't know he'd kept them, of me anyway."

She took his hand and rubbed her thumb over the back of his knuckles. "I'm proud of you, Jackson."

He shrugged, his cheeks going ruddy. "I wanted to tell you. Hell, if I could've brought you along for moral support—" He broke off with a chuckle that sounded more than a little self-conscious. "You know, since we talked about my family…"

She spoke gently. "How do you feel?"

He considered a moment. "Surprisingly okay. Lighter, maybe? I don't know." He grinned. "I'm overdramatizing things."

She shook her head. "There's a lot of history to sort through. But letting go of anger and resentment has to feel good after all this time, even well deserved."

"You always know what to say."

Warmth spread through her at his softly spoken praise. "Thank you, Jackson, but you're giving me too much credit. What you did, going to see him, allowing him to see Chase, it took courage. I'm proud of you, and I'm glad you wanted to share it with me. I have something to tell you as well." Her heart hammered in her chest so hard she wondered if he could see it. "Can you sit down a minute?"

He scooped his fingers around her hand and dragged her to the couch. Plopping down next to the armrest, he pulled her onto his lap, then snugged her up against him.

Reveling in the feel of his arms around her, she nestled her face into his stubble-roughened neck.

"You smell good," they said in unison, then both chuckled.

"You smell better," he added, one-upping her. "What's on your mind?"

Wanting to see his face, she leaned back slightly. "I didn't mention it last night, but Jane told me—"

"Jane? The pregnant bookkeeper you replaced?"

She nodded. "Temporarily replaced. She asked me if I might be interested in taking over permanently."

Jackson's teeth flashed white. "That's great news, isn't it? I mean, do you like the work?"

"I like aspects of it, like being home again, working with Sue. I'm not sure if I want to make it my lifelong career, and the pay is"—she grimaced to indicate *not great*—"but it could work. The cost of living here is nothing compared to New York, despite the outrageous rent my landlord charges."

Jackson smiled and combed his fingers though her hair.

"I also spoke with my ex-boss."

His hand fell away. "Already?"

"Yup. Apparently," she said dryly, "Chris and Nicole are fired. They messed up big time with one of the firm's largest clients. Evidently he bargained to keep his position by promising to bring me back." She snorted.

"I'm sorry, Jules."

"Why? Because Chris's marriage proposal was nothing but a ploy to get his job back? Don't be. It only reinforces the wisdom of my decision."

"You doubted that?" he asked in a low voice.

"That's not what I meant."

He nodded slowly. "Okay. So the big guns used the direct approach to get you back. What did they offer?"

"To make me full partner. They want to fly me to New York to make the formal proposal." She concentrated on taking even breaths. He hadn't shown much of a reaction.

"I see. When do you plan to go?"

Her stomach dropped, and for a horrific moment she thought she might be ill. She had no idea what she'd expected, but it wasn't this. No discussion. No argument. No plea to stay.

She rose and headed for the kitchen. Anything to avoid looking at him, to keep him from reading the misery on her face. "I'll have to talk about what works best for Sue, as far as traveling and—" She swallowed to force the hard lump forming in her throat down. "—and finding a replacement for the replacement." She laughed breezily, or so she hoped. "A lot of moving parts to work out."

Jackson didn't say a word. The leather couch creaked. A moment later, he wandered into view. Going by his expression, they could've discussed the weather.

"I better get back to the house. I'm not sure when Chase wants to go to his friend's, and you probably want to get spruced up for your girls' night out."

Julia could only nod.

"Tomorrow Chase, Grady, and I will do our usual park thing. Later, I promised to drive Ryan to the Asheville airport. He's got a night flight."

Julia waited for him to go on.

"I'm not sure when I'll be back. Could be late."

"Okay."

"Okay, then. Have fun tonight." He let himself out.

Julia stood there a long moment, too stunned to cry. He'd accepted her leaving North Carolina without question. *She* hadn't even gotten that far. Then the final death knell. He left without kissing her goodbye. Jackson had officially ended their fling.

Chapter Twenty-Two

Sunday morning dawned muggy and overcast. After one look out the window, Julia tromped back to bed and buried herself under the covers. It was a good day to wallow.

She'd lain awake last night, hoping to hear Jackson's knock or a message alert asking her to come over. She'd heard neither. So much for her friends' insistence about Jackson's feelings for her.

She had shared all the salient points with them. How her ex-boss had offered her partner. How Jackson had accepted her leaving without a blink. How she'd fallen in love with Jackson. How he did not return the sentiment.

The girls had argued the latter point with vehemence.

"The man practically trips over his tongue when you're in his sights," Sue insisted. "He's as smitten as I've ever known a man to be."

Callie echoed Sue. "He has his issues, don't get me wrong, but he's completely gonzo over you."

"You didn't see him today when I told him about the firm's offer."

"Maybe he's trying to be unselfish. You need to ask him what he wants, directly," Sue suggested.

"I agree with Sue. Then, if he doesn't know what a prize he has in you, kick him to the curb." Callie had lifted her chin a notch. "Call his bluff. Whatever happens, Jules, you're going to be fine. It's really all up to you. Decide what you want and go for it."

What *did* she want?

Duh, Jackson. But he didn't want her, and knowing hurt like hell.

But she didn't regret her decision to open herself to him. In fact, she could thank him for making one thing amply clear—she was no sexual dud. She wasn't broken. Just, apparently, a one-man woman.

She flung back the covers. "To hell with wallowing." Step one, yoga practice. Then she'd see about the rest of her life.

****

Julia scrolled down the list on her computer screen, then grabbed her pen and made another set of notations. Phone number, location, price.

A knock sounded at her front door.

Steeling her heart, she slid off the stool. It wouldn't be Jackson. He didn't use the front door, and he'd told her plainly he'd be en route to Asheville right about now.

Grady stood on the front stoop. Based on their last conversation, he wasn't here to ask her out. But she would sure love it if the man quit showing up unannounced.

"Hi, Grady, what's up?"

"Hey, lady, just dropping by to say hi since I'm in the neighborhood. I brought dinner for Chase, and the kid's not home. I guess Jackson took him along and neglected to mention."

She stepped back, gesturing for him to enter.

He eyed the yoga clothes she still wore from this

morning's practice. "What are you up to this gorgeous Sunday besides working out and looking hot?"

The quip about the weather was pure sarcasm. Outside, the day had gone from muggy to downright dismal. Wind gusted in the trees, and intermittent rain showers soaked the ground.

"I'm doing some research."

"Oh yeah? What kind?"

She didn't feel inclined to tell him, but she couldn't think of a good reason not to. "I'm looking for a rental."

He wandered into the living area and leaned on the back of the couch. "Oh." His expression turned thoughtful. "Jackson told me about you moving back to New York. It's really a bummer about you two. Ah, well."

His words hit her like a punch. Jackson had wasted no time putting the word out about her leaving. Had he also told Grady how he ended their fling?

Pride overrode her aching heart. She lifted her chin. "Actually, I haven't decided whether I'll take the offer, Grady."

He frowned. "No? I could have sworn Jackson said—" He abruptly broke off and glanced down. He reached into the front pocket of his khakis and slid out his cell phone. He thumbed the screen, then dropped it back into his pocket.

"Can I fix you some tea? I was about to make a cup for myself."

"Thanks, Julia. Tea sounds great." He kicked his legs over the back of the couch and sank into the cushions. "So no New York but still moving? I'm sure it stinks to give up this sweet deal, but it will be less awkward for you both, considering."

Jackson *had* shared intimate details about the two of them with Grady. She could hardly believe it. Then again, Sheila and Hannah and God knew who else had all happily confided in Grady. Why not Jackson, too?

Not me. She refused to be yet another of Jackson's exes crying on Grady's shoulder. "I'm not sure what you're getting at. I simply don't want to take advantage of Jackson's generosity."

"Uh-huh."

Gritting her teeth, she filled the teapot and set it on the stove. On the counter, her phone buzzed. She snapped on the burner, then reached for her phone.

Chase had sent her a message? She opened the screen and read. Her skin went cold. "Oh no." She tapped out a speedy reply.

Grady unfolded from the couch. "Something wrong?"

She turned off the stove and hustled around the counter, skirting Grady as she answered. "Chase needs help."

He followed her to her bedroom, hovering in the doorway. "What kind of help? Why didn't he text me?"

"I'm guessing it's because he didn't know you were here. He took his bike up the trail across the street and got into trouble." As she spoke, she grabbed her long-neglected running shoes, a pair of socks, and a baseball cap.

"Jesus. What kind of trouble? I'll go with you. We can take my car."

Outside the rain picked up, and she fought a wave of panic. "He slipped over the edge trying to catch his bike," she said, tying her laces. "I'm guessing the ground's eroding because of all the rain."

She slapped on her cap and moved toward the door, looking at Grady. "Maybe I should call emergency services."

"Hell no. We'll have him up in no time. I know the spot. There's a ledge beneath the drop-off. It's not that dangerous. It's just tricky getting back up."

She bit her lip as her heart squeezed, imagining Chase on the side of the mountain, wet, cold, and afraid. "I'm so glad you're here. I don't know if I'd manage pulling him up myself. But we can't take your car. There's no way to get it onto the trail."

He snapped his fingers. "That's right. Give me a sec to change into running shoes. I keep a pair in the trunk."

"I'm no runner," she said with an apologetic grimace. "But I'll do my best."

"Don't worry. We'll get there in time. You know what? My backpack's in the trunk, too. I'll get a plastic baggie and put our phones inside in the pack to keep them dry. I can take care of that if you want to grab a towel we can use to dry the poor kid off."

"Thank you, Grady," she said, grateful for his steady nerve.

Less than a minute later, they headed out.

Grady opened his passenger side car door and tossed his keys inside. "We've got a good hour at least before it gets dark." With a flick of his wrist, he closed the car door. "We'll have Chase safe and sound before Jackson gets back. He'll never even know he was missing."

****

Jackson hit the dial button on his steering wheel.

The phone went directly to Chase's voicemail. No doubt about it, the kid was getting a talking to when Jackson got home.

Yesterday at the park Chase had pleaded to stay home while Jackson drove Ryan to Asheville's airport. Grady had jumped on the band wagon, insisting Jackson stop acting like a scared grandmother, even promising to deliver dinner if that made him more comfortable. Jackson had finally caved.

He nearly changed his mind again this morning. Only learning Ryan wanted to leave early to meet a friend at the airport, putting Jackson back in Honeyville before dark, had swayed him to leave things as they were, with Chase staying home unsupervised.

Tapping his fingers on the steering wheel, he told himself the situation merited a call to Julia to ask her to check on him. Julia, who'd gone out last night. Julia, who hadn't phoned or stopped by afterward. Julia, who had become as vital to him as air.

Julia, who he had to let go. Why couldn't he wrap his brain around it?

When she dropped the bomb about New York, he'd wanted to howl. Sheer willpower alone allowed him to remain calm and treat her leaving as a matter of course.

He hadn't had a moment's peace since. His mind spun out a million arguments for her staying. Fear of opening his mouth and blowing this perfect opportunity to get her safely away from him had kept him from reaching out last night. But he'd lain awake, hoping she'd contact him. She hadn't.

Palms sweating, he scrolled to her number on the dash screen and hit dial.

It rang four times, then went to voicemail. Great.

He gripped the wheel and stepped on the gas.

****

Julia and Grady jogged in tandem, heads down against the rain. A half mile in, the rain let up. She slowed and motioned for Grady to do the same.

"Can I get my phone while it's not pouring? I want to see if Chase has messaged me."

"Good thinking." He pulled off the pack, unzipped the pouch, then dug for the baggie. "This canvas pack is soaked through. Good thing we put the electronics inside a…uh-oh."

"Uh-oh?"

He grimaced. "I must have been on auto pilot. I didn't put your phone in the baggie."

She swiped water from her face and blinked at him.

"No worries. I'll call him." He tapped on his phone screen through the plastic, then held his phone to his ear.

She heard ring tones, then the sound of Chase's voicemail picking up.

He ended the call, dropping the baggie in the pack. "We should keep moving."

They set off again. Julia huffed and puffed, even though, she was sure, Grady set a pace he thought she could handle. The exertion hardly seemed to faze him, soaked khakis and polo notwithstanding.

"Jackson is probably beside himself," she managed between pants.

"Why would he be?"

"I'm sure Chase put a call or text in to him."

"I don't know. Ryan's flight is a ways off. Chase knows Jackson won't be home for hours. He wouldn't want to worry him."

Julia sure would have. But maybe boys handled situations like these differently. "I still don't understand why he messed around at the trailhead, alone, in the rain. It doesn't seem like Chase."

"You strolled into the picture after how many years? What makes you think you know the first thing about what Chase would or would not do, or what makes Jackson tic for that matter?"

She slanted a glance at Grady.

He wore a grin, but for the briefest moment, she saw something else mirrored in his eyes. A hardness, there and gone. A chill ran down her spine that had nothing to do with her soaked clothing.

At a fresh onslaught of sheeting rain, she lowered her head so her hat took the brunt and chided herself for making more of his odd statement than necessary. Maybe he meant exactly what he said and nothing more, curt though he was.

Still. They were alone in a highly secluded place, no one around for miles. If he went nuts on her... *No.* She had enough to worry about without allowing her imagination to take her down a rabbit hole.

"What's our plan when we get there?" she asked.

"Let's see what the kid's gotten himself into. I know how to handle situations like these, trust me. Well versed."

****

Jackson navigated the winding road. Almost home.

The guard confirmed Grady's arrival about an hour ago, which made sense. What didn't was Grady not answering his phone. He'd rung him, Julia, and Chase repeatedly and hadn't received one return call. He was beyond frustrated, not to mention terrified. If something

happened to Chase because he'd left him home alone…
It didn't bear thinking.

His tires skidded onto the short road leading to the
house. He pressed the garage door opener, pulling onto
the circular drive. In seconds, he was out of his truck
and inside the house.

"Chase!"

"Dad?" Chase's voice came from the living room.
"I'm starving. Did you bring dinner?"

In stunned silence, Jackson stalked into the living
room.

"Hi, Dad." His son sprawled on the leather couch,
TV remote in hand. One look at Jackson and he sat
upright. "What?"

"I've been calling you. What do you mean you're
hungry? Where's Grady?"

"Heck if I know. I…uh…kind of lost my phone.
The only place I can think where it might be is Uncle
Grady's car. I was going to ask him when he came with
dinner, only he never showed."

Jackson tapped his fingers on his hip. Maybe he'd
come here, and Chase hadn't answered the door? But
Grady had a key. First things first. "You're sure your
phone's not here?"

"I've looked everywhere."

He shook his head as relief turned his bones to
jelly. "Buddy, I've been worried out of my mind."

Chase rolled his eyes. "Dad. C'mon."

"I'll show you come on," he muttered with a grin
and pulled out his phone. He opened his find-my-phone
app linking their phones, installed in case Chase ever
disappeared. Or, less dramatically, in the event one of
them lost his phone. Like now.

"Hmm. It doesn't appear to be far from here. Did you leave it outside?"

"I haven't been out. It rained all day, Dad. Can we order some food? I'm starving."

"Two seconds." Jackson held his phone in front of him. He followed the blinking dot out the back door straight to Julia's.

This was getting weird. Julia might have reason to ignore him, but she wouldn't ignore messages about Chase. He rounded the cottage. Her car sat in its parking spot with Grady's right beside it. The two of them home yet neither answering their phones or returning his calls?

He stalked to her door and gave three solid raps.

No answer.

After a moment's hesitation, he tried the knob. Locked.

He dialed her number, pressing his eye, then his ear to the door's stained glass center. Inside he heard a faint, brief, repeating refrain of one of his songs. He grinned. Her ring tone was one of his songs? He sobered when her voicemail picked up. Now what?

Her car was here. Her phone was here.

He ran home and rummaged in the kitchen drawer 'til he found the spare key.

"Dad, what's going on?"

"Stay here, Chase."

He pounded across the deck, unlocked the back door, and let himself inside. "Julia?" he called.

No answer. *Think, Tate.* Chase's phone. The app indicated it was here. He called it. It went straight to voicemail.

Half crazed, he searched the cottage for a phone, a

person, a clue, and found nothing.

Damn it, think. He drew a steadying breath and gave the space a closer look. Julia's laptop sat open on the counter; a notepad with neatly penned columns lay beside it. He touched the mousepad, and her computer screen lit up. Glancing between the notepad and the screen, he frowned. She'd been researching available local rentals?

He raked a hand through his hair. He would deal with this later—after he figured out where the hell she had disappeared to without her phone and car, found Chase's phone, and, oh yeah, figured out how Grady fit into things.

Start from the beginning, Tate. He pulled out his phone, dialed Julia's number again. Once again, a refrain of one of his songs sounded, coming from Julia's living area. He moved to the couch. Pressed dial again. Music came from *inside* the couch? He slid his hands beneath the back cushions, feeling his way—and touched a hard, flat object. Make that two.

He unearthed Chase's and Julia's phones. Dumfounded, he stared at them for a timeless moment, then pressed the home button on Chase's phone. The screen notifications revealed several missed calls from Jackson—no surprise there—one from Grady, and a text from Julia.

He tapped Julia's message. It read —*I'll be there as soon as I can. Hang on!*—

He scrolled up the text thread to Chase's preceding message.

—*Help! I'm at the trailhead. I slid over the edge behind the guardrail trying to grab my bike, and now I can't make it back up without the ground melting under my feet.—*

This. Made. No. Sense.

Taking both phones, he sprinted home.

Chase sprang up from the couch the moment Jackson crossed the threshold. "You found it. Where was it?"

Jackson didn't have time for a discussion. "Did you take your bike up the trail today?"

"What? No. Why would—"

"Did you play a prank on Miss Julia, asking her for help up there?"

Now Chase looked offended. "No. Dad, where are you going?"

Jackson charged past him to the stairs and ran up to his room. His mind whirled, sorting the disjointed facts as he stripped out of his rain-soaked linen shirt, trousers, and loafers, exchanging them for running pants, a poly gym shirt, and running shoes. The text for help had come from Chase's phone. But Chase hadn't had his phone. If Chase left his phone in Grady's car, and Grady came to deliver dinner and said phone…had Grady sent the misleading text to Julia? But why?

Jackson tied off his shoelaces with vicious yanks, as impotent fury turned his blood to ice. He vaulted down the stairs, pausing at the garage doorway to yell to Chase. "I can't explain right now, but lock the doors behind me and don't let anyone inside until I get back. Not even Grady. Then call the police. Tell them there's an emergency at the trailhead."

Chase appeared in the hallway. He stared at Jackson, wide eyed. "Is Miss Julia okay?"

"She's…she's fine," he answered hoarsely and prayed to God he spoke the truth.

In the garage, he glanced between his motorcycle and his road bike. The motorcycle would be faster but noisy and would announce his arrival to whoever happened to be there. An image of Grady sprang to mind.

Was he crazy, thinking his oldest friend had orchestrated this whole mess? He had to know Jackson would see his car at Julia's.

But then Jackson wasn't supposed to be back for hours yet. Grady hadn't known about Ryan's change of plans. He yanked his road bike off its storage hooks and muscled it outside.

****

They jogged along a sharp curve in the trail, and the guardrail marking the trailhead finally came into view. Julia yelled for Chase. Her voice echoed in the canyon like a lonely wolf's howl. No reply came. The silent doubts assailing her over the last mile went into hyperdrive.

Too many things didn't add up. The gravel path, muddy with all the rain, showed Grady's and her footprints as far back as she could see. But no groove from Chase's bike wheels marred the surface.

Then there was the timing. Grady just happened to show up as Chase messaged her, in the nick of time to offer his assistance?

But what she couldn't dismiss was the gaping hole in his story. The reason he'd given for being there in the first place. Then again, maybe she had misunderstood him.

You're being paranoid, Julia. Focus on what's important—saving Chase.

No more than thirty feet separated them from the

railing—and the gorge beneath. Acid burned in her belly, and fear tightened her throat no matter how hard she tried to talk herself out of it, making it hard to breathe.

She could just ask. A reasonable explanation would wash away all her suspicions. Before she could second-guess herself, she stuttered to a halt. Eyeing his broad back as he jogged on, she broached the question plaguing her. "Grady, didn't you say you brought dinner for Chase?"

"Sure did." He slowed to a stop and turned to face her, polite curiosity in his eyes.

"The thing is, there wasn't any food in your car."

He looked amused. "I intended to order a pizza and watch the game with Chase. Got a problem with that?"

"But you said you'd *brought* dinner." His words had not reassured her. Far from it. A sickening dread filled her, flooding her system with adrenaline. Tremors shook her from head to toe. She put her hands on her thighs, hinging forward to suck in deep, calming breaths.

"We can discuss this later since you're so concerned. But first, Chase, remember?" He jerked a thumb over his shoulder.

From her stooped position, she met Grady's cool stare. Too cool. Everything in her warned her not to move one step closer to that drop-off. "You go ahead."

His eyes narrowed.

And she knew. She straightened and tried to hold steady though her legs shook like unhardened Jell-O. "Why did you bring me out here, Grady?"

He spread his arms wide and shuffled backward. "Are you nuts? Chase is hanging on for dear life, right over the edge there."

She wrapped her arms around her shivering body. "No. Chase isn't here."

He reached the guardrail, craned his head to peer down the gorge, then, grimacing, slid his gaze to her—and abruptly burst out laughing. "Day-um. You are good. A little late, but good. Maybe you are as smart as Jackson's always bragging on you about." He peeled off his backpack. "I'll hand it to you. The others never had a clue."

Two miles separated them from the private road. She could never outrun him. She had to keep him talking until she could figure a way out of this. "What others?"

****

Branches scraped at Jackson's arms as he maneuvered around the jogged hedges that marked the trail's entrance. He braked hard, studying the ground. Two sets of footprints. One large, obviously male, the other Julia sized.

He took off as the coldness inside him gave way to white-hot rage. Grady had lured Julia out here. Nothing else made sense.

But why? To make one last pass at her? Jackson wished he could believe that. But his gut told him there had to be more to this story.

Grady had acted strange since Julia's return. Jackson had been so immersed in her himself he hadn't paid much attention. Smart woman that she was, Julia had and had wanted nothing to do with Grady. Maybe he harbored some holdover obsession with her from their high school days. Maybe he just didn't like taking no for an answer.

He just needed to get to them. To Julia. To see those eyes see him. To grab her in his arms and never let her go.

Chapter Twenty-Three

"*What others*, she asks." Grady spoke through gritted teeth and rummaged inside his pack. "Let me ask you a question, Julia. What would you do if you had a thorn in your side for as long as you could remember, always swooping in to take what should have been yours, not good enough to wipe your shoes on, yet always coming out on top?"

Evidently having located whatever he sought in the bag, he tossed the pack aside. Loaded plastic grocery bag in hand, he sauntered toward her, calm, cool, collected.

Instinct drove her backward. "You mean Jackson."

He paused mid-stride to clap mockingly. "Give the woman a prize. I mean, come on. This kid from the wrong side of the tracks with his loser father ends up with a never-ending herd of girls trailing after him, all because he can sing passably and lucked out during tryouts to beat me for the best spots on the teams?

"I was always better. Athletically *and* scholastically. But he had the devil's own luck. He sucked in math, but you fixed that for him. And what did my dad say? *Look at Jackson. He wants something, and he works hard for it. You should be more like Jackson, Grady. Practice more if you want the better field positions, Grady.*"

Righteous anger swelled inside her, dulling some

of the fear. "Jackson does work hard for what he wants. *Everyone* should be more like him. Hell, *I* want to be more like him."

His eyes burned with manic rage. "Shut your filthy mouth!" he shouted, spittle flying. "You're all the same. I told Sheila to dump him, pointed out every time he brought up Little Miss Perfect—you. But he flashed that smile, and she forgot all about it. That last night, at the beach party, Jackson and his band were on the deck about to go on. I went to her room and offered to show her how a real man treats his woman. She laughed— right in my face. I couldn't have that."

Bile rose in her throat. He couldn't mean what it sounded like he meant.

He shrugged, nonchalant. "In the end, Sheila did me a favor. Her death leveled Jackson. I had him half convinced to take a job working for me and put school on indefinite hold. He nearly quit the band. Too bad my dad butted in with the big pep talk about not giving up on his dreams."

His jaw hardened. "Next thing I know, he's in school, his band takes off, he knocks up Hannah, gets hitched, and ends up on top again. Successful, *rich*, a kid, a wife. And my dad says *maybe I should have been tougher on you, and you would have made something of yourself, too.*"

As Grady vented his fury, Julia shifted backward, putting much-needed distance between them. She scanned the surrounding brush for an escape route. She had to get away from him. He wasn't the creepy guy she took him for since moving home. He was a deranged murderer.

"Hannah was a tough nut to crack. She loved that

son of hers, and Jackson as usual could do no wrong. But then I told her about Jackson screwing around with groupies on tour." He smirked. "I made her drag it out of me, since betraying Jacks, my BFF, didn't come easy." His smirk turned into a snarl. "Bitch promised to keep her mouth shut. But eventually she went to Jackson and let him convince her it was all bullshit."

Grady laughed, sounding unhinged. "She didn't think I figured it out—that she'd confronted him, that he'd denied everything. But I wasn't born yesterday. When she asked to meet me, I was ready. I picked the perfect spot. Mountain lookout, way up high." His mouth split in a horrific grin. "Jackson's going back on tour with my blessing, she said, and stay out of our lives or else. She actually threatened to tell him I spread the lies about him. But I came prepared. A little of this"—he gestured to the bag he held, and his face took on a look of mock pity—"and she plunged down the mountain in her hot little sports car. Oops, Jackson wrecked another life."

"And you stepped in to help him pick up the pieces, like always, right? You're sick, Grady. You need help."

His eyes went hard. "He needed to learn that he doesn't deserve happiness. That he destroys the people he cares for."

"But he didn't hurt those women. *You* did."

"Their choice. If they'd gone away, they'd have lived. Jackson sure got it. Look at Monica and Valerie and every other woman since Hannah. If they try to get too close, he ejects them from his life. He *learned.*

" 'Til you. I knew right away he wouldn't be able to resist you. He never could. But for once I had the upper hand, because you hated him. I could almost taste it, getting you in my bed and shoving it under his nose. But you screwed that up. You caved for his charm. You should've chosen the better man, Julia," he said, wagging his finger at her.

"I tried to save you—I really did. I told Jacks about Chris visiting after I read his emails on your laptop. Seeing the two of you at the park? That was pure luck."

She had been steadily retreating. But his words froze her in her tracks. "My laptop? You were in my house?"

He snorted. "You didn't have a clue. You really aren't that bright, are you? Remember the time your car alarm went off when you were playing kissy face with Jackson on this very trail?"

Grady's long legs ate up the distance she'd put between them as he withdrew a bottle and cloth from the bag. "I'd hoped Bethany might remind him what happens to women dumb enough to get involved with him. Plus, once she knew who you were, I figured she'd let him have it out of loyalty to her sister. Dumb bitch didn't say a word."

She eyed the bottle in his hand and knew she had to keep him talking. "You lied to her about Jackson. You told her he made her sister so miserable she killed herself. How do you live with yourself?"

"Just fine. And I'll be even better when I get rid of you. This time, maybe Jackson snaps. If not, there's always Chase."

"What does that mean?" But she knew. He meant to turn his sick sights on Chase. She would not let that happen, no matter what. She took a bracing breath and planted her feet.

"I'm done talking." He opened the bottle and doused the cloth with its contents, shaking his head regretfully. "It seems Jackson's pushing another woman to off herself. Poor Julia, couldn't take being another in a long list of discards."

Grady tossed the bottle aside and charged.

Julia charged right back.

They crashed together midair and went down hard, Julia flat on her back with Grady half on top of her. The force of her landing knocked the wind from her lungs. Grady scrambled off her as she fought to breathe, gulping for air like a fish out of water.

From the corner of her eye, she spotted the poisoned cloth on the ground. He'd lost it in the scuffle and now crab-crawled toward it. She pushed to her feet just as he clutched it in his fist. In seconds he'd be up, coming at her again. She wouldn't get a better chance. This was no longer about her survival. She had to think of Chase.

Raising her knee, she leapt, all her weight aimed at his groin.

His blood curdling scream told her she'd hit the mark.

She bounded off him and ran full out for the road. She had miles to cover. If he reached her, it was all over.

Was he up? Was he already closing in? She couldn't spare a moment to look back to see. All she knew for sure was that her lungs burned like fire, and her eyes had started playing tricks, probably from oxygen deprivation. Because it looked like someone careened toward her at breakneck speed.

Then the apparition screamed her name. *Jackson.*

He soared toward her on his bike like a dark avenging angel. When he came within ten feet, he leapt off his still-moving bike and dove for her, scooping her into his arms.

She clung to him, and her gasps turned to sobs. He'd come. He'd come for her.

He held her, murmuring words of comfort, pouring his heat into her soaked and shivering body.

She wanted to stay in his arms forever. But she needed to warn him. She choked out the words. "J-Jackson, I have to tell you."

He released her to gently cup her face, swiping his thumbs over her cheeks. "Sweetheart. Are you hurt?"

The tenderness in his voice heralded another flood of tears. Unable to speak coherently, she settled for shaking her head.

Looking grim and decidedly unconvinced, he patted her down. "Why are you covered in gravel and mud, baby? Where's Grady?"

"He's...back... there," she managed. Hugging Jackson fiercely, she pressed her face into his chest. Like a dam broke, the words flowed from her lips. "Jackson, he's deranged. We have to go *now*. We have to call the police. He told me he killed them. He pushed Sheila over that railing, I think, and then sent Hannah's car over the cliff. He drugged her and brought the same drug to use on me, too. Jackson, no," she said when he ripped himself out of her arms.

He started in Grady's direction. "Your phone is in the bag. Go home," he growled.

"No, Jackson. He's obsessed with you, crazy with jealousy. Please."

But he was already sprinting away from her toward

the trailhead.

****

Jackson saw red. He'd heard the saying many times. Now he understood as full-on, deadly rage consumed him. Grady, his lifelong friend, had set out to decimate his life and had nearly succeeded. He had killed Sheila and Hannah, all because they had the misfortune to care about Jackson.

Julia. My God, he'd almost lost her, too. *Why, Grady?* Nothing about this made sense, and yet, for the first time, all the pieces of the puzzle congealed into gruesome focus. Fury and betrayal and a terrible sense of his own ineptitude slammed through him, driving him harder.

He rounded the final switchback of the trail and saw Grady running toward him. No doubt he'd been coming after Julia, the bastard. The moment he spotted Jackson barreling toward him, he turned and sprinted back toward the guardrail.

Jackson closed the distance between them with brutal physical effort, but Grady reached the railing, catapulting himself over it to stand behind it, hands gripping the metal.

Jackson jammed to a halt mere yards from him. He'd been so close. His hands shook with the need to tear Grady limb from limb, but he had to be smart. With Grady standing on the edge of the drop-off, tackling him would tumble one or both of them to their deaths. And he wasn't letting either one of them off that easy.

"Grady," Jackson ground out, "get over here and face me like a man."

He held one hand up, palm out, and shifted his feet. Rocks skittered down the ravine behind him. "Whoa,

Jacks. I don't know what she told you, man, but you gotta listen to me. Julia's seriously unhinged. She lured me out here with some bullshit story about Chase."

Breath hissed through his clenched teeth, but his words, when he spoke, betrayed nothing of the storm raging within him. "Why don't we talk about it over here, away from the drop-off?"

Grady ignored his suggestion. "She must've stolen Chase's phone, because she showed me a text on hers from him asking for help. Then we got here and—"

Jackson fisted his hands. "Stop. Talking. I know what you did. What I don't know is why. Sheila, Hannah, and now Julia?"

Grady glanced down into the gorge, one hand palm out toward Jackson, staving him off.

Jackson inched forward. When he got close enough, he would grab Grady and pull him over the railing to solid ground. Then all bets were off.

Behind him, he heard bike wheels pushing through the wet gravel. "Julia, go to the house. Please, babe."

"I'm not leaving you. Did you tell him the police are coming?" Julia asked, her voice shrill.

Unmistakable hate burned in Grady's eyes when he looked at her. "I knew you would cause trouble." He shifted his focus to Jackson. "Don't you see, Jacks? I did it all for you. Sheila was a tramp, holding you back. And Hannah? She wanted to wreck your career. This one? She thinks you're trash. She's leaving you for her big shot in New York. You said so yourself."

Jackson had slowly, steadily moved ahead and now stood in arm's reach of the railing. He regarded Grady as if seeing him for the first time. Wild desperation glittered in his eyes, as if he still thought he could somehow manipulate the situation and come out on top. And why not? He'd done it time and time again. All the senseless loss perpetrated by this man washed over him. Sheila, who had died so young. Hannah, snuffed out in her prime, leaving their son motherless. And Jackson hadn't suspected a thing.

Julia had brought the truth to light. Julia, the one Grady hadn't taken from him.

No, he'd almost managed that feat on his own. The truth hit him with the force of an anvil.

"You're not worth the effort, Grady. The police can deal with you."

He turned to face Julia.

She stood beside his bike, covered with grit. She'd lost her cap, and her hair was wet and matted to her head. She had red-rimmed eyes, tear-stained cheeks, and wore not a stitch of makeup, and she was the most beautiful thing he'd ever seen. A sweet yearning filled him, taking up all the space in his chest, and for once he didn't fight it. He needed this woman like air. He opened his arms to her.

Her eyes overflowed with abject tenderness, then, in an instant, went wide with horror. "Jackson, look out!"

He half turned as Grady flew over the railing, catching him in a bear hug.

"You won't turn your back on me, you bastard!"

Time seemed to slow as Julia's scream rent the air and Grady heaved them over the railing.

Then everything moved at the speed of light. Jerked off his feet and hurtling backward, Jackson jammed his elbow into Grady's ribcage with as much strength as he could harness. It broke the smaller man's hold, but both continued careening over the cliff.

"Nooo!" Grady cried, hands flung out in a vain attempt to grasp anything to stop his fall.

With everything he had, Jackson kicked down while swinging his arms overhead. His heels dug into the muddy narrow ledge beneath the guardrail, and his fists grabbed craggy earth, stone, anything he could grasp to stop his fall.

Somehow he hung there, upside down. Clinging with every ounce of strength he had, he watched Grady topple like a rag doll to the rocky stream below.

He became aware of Julia's weight, anchoring him into the earth. She'd slithered beneath the railing and wrapped her hands around his calves.

"Julia, no. You'll go over, too," he begged, his heart in his throat. "Please, if you care for me at all, get back and wait for help."

Other than heaving heart-wrenching sobs that tore at his insides, she made no reply. She tugged at him until he gave up trying to stop her. Straining his arms and legs, he dragged himself uphill. With their combined efforts, he gained enough ground to risk hooking an ankle around the railing. He jackknifed up, grasping the metal, then crawled through to safety where he promptly collapsed onto his back.

Julia piled on top of him, holding him like she thought he might disappear.

Exhausted, he managed a small smile.

Sirens sounded in the distance.

****

Hours later, he and Julia stood on his front stoop, watching the departing police cars until their taillights turned into tiny red dots.

Back inside, the house was quiet. Chase had gone with Aunt Lisa for the night despite his noisy protests. Jackson hadn't wanted him to hear the details of Grady's heinous crimes and violent death. Time enough to explain when he'd given some thought to how.

Julia plucked at her grime-covered clothes and eyed the door.

Ah, hell no. One corner of his mouth crooked upward. "You really need a shower." He took her hand and led her upstairs. They showered in his marble walk-in.

Innocent soaping led to lingering caresses which led to Jackson's mouth kissing every bruise, every scrape as if he could erase the last several hours of her life.

With the water sluicing over them, he crouched in front of her. His lips and tongue slid over her slick flesh as a desperation to taste her, to assure himself she was here and whole and his, took him over.

His fingers danced over her belly and hips, then cruised lower, urging her legs apart. His lips followed his fingers, exploring her most intimate places until she clawed at the marbled walls, gasping his name.

He straightened, pressing her back into the wall and hooking her legs over his hips to bury himself inside her in one powerful thrust. Her exquisite heat wrapped around him, tightening with every thrust. She was his. *His.* Unquenchable primal need drove him faster, deeper, claiming her with his body, uncaring of his own hoarse cries of exultation and love echoing off the walls.

Love. He loved her, desperately. The sheer magnitude of his feelings for her overwhelmed his senses, shattering every wall within him and triggering the most intense climax of his life. As violent shudders wracked him, Julia's release crashed through her. Her feminine heat, squeezing and pulsing, milked every last ounce of pleasure from him until they trembled in each other's arms, held upright by nothing more than the solid marble walls and sheer will.

****

He dried her gently with a fluffy white towel, pausing periodically to kiss her lips so sweetly her insides shivered. Afterward he scooped her into his arms and carried her to his bed.

Cocooned in his arms, she didn't remember falling asleep, only waking, however many hours later, in the dark, alone.

She lifted her head from the pillow and, bleary-eyed, spotted Jackson's naked body silhouetted in front of the window where he stood gazing out at the mountains.

"Hi," she whispered in a sleep-scratchy voice. She propped herself onto her elbows. "Can't sleep?"

"Something's weighing on my mind." He padded back to the bed, slid under the sheets, and wrapped her in his arms. "I didn't mean to wake you."

"You didn't." She pressed her face into his warm, stubble-covered neck. "I just missed my human blanket."

His shoulders shook with silent laughter.

She finger doodled the hollow at his throat. "Do you want to talk about what's on your mind?"

"I think I do need—we do need—to talk."

She drew a bracing breath and reminded herself the man she loved lived and breathed, despite Grady's attempt to plunge both of them to their deaths. Whatever Jackson had to say, she could handle it. Last night he'd made love to her like his life depended on it, but that had been on the cusp of harrowing revelations. It didn't erase how he'd left things between them the day before.

"I saw your list in the cottage. When I went looking for you."

Her mind went blank. She leaned back to study him. In the darkness, his expression was unreadable. "I'm not sure what you're getting at."

He traced his fingers over her cheek and spoke in a whisper. "It looked to me like you want to live somewhere else. Somewhere else, here, not in New York."

She bit her lip. "And?"

He huffed out a laugh. "Julia, did you decide against New York?"

She sniffed. "I'm surprised you're asking. You seemed ready to ship me off without so much as a blink when I mentioned it."

He sighed, leaned toward his nightstand, and snapped on the lamp. Then he crooked a finger under her chin, tilting her face up. "I told myself I had to let you go, and the perfect opportunity presented itself. Only, now I can't."

She stared into his hazel eyes and forced out the hated words. "Jackson, I won't let you do this out of guilt."

His brows furrowed. "Excuse me?"

She drew a shaky breath. "You don't have to make amends for what Grady did. I'm a big girl. I can handle it."

"Babe, I have no idea what you mean."

She gave him a frank stare, trying to ignore how enticing he looked, bare-chested, hair mussed from sleep, five-o'clock shadow darkening his cheeks. "Yesterday you couldn't have made it more clear you wanted to end our fling."

His lips parted. "Why would you say that? The last we spoke, I invited you to my house for dinner, and you said no. How is that me ending our relationship?"

Relationship, not fling.

Stop it.

She ducked her head. "You left without kissing me goodbye. Then you never texted or called or came by once I got home last night."

He must think her ridiculously needy. Which, in truth, she was when it came to him.

"Did you kiss me goodbye? Did you knock on my door?" he asked softly.

"No, but…" She hesitated, then said in barely a whisper, "You never leave without kissing me goodbye."

"You're right."

Her heart seized in her chest. She'd known. But it still hurt to hear him admit it. She nodded and swallowed over the hard lump forming in her throat.

"I didn't kiss you goodbye because I couldn't get out of there fast enough."

She sat up, searching the room for her clothes. On second thought, she might have to borrow his robe to go to her cottage.

Jackson continued. "I couldn't let you see how—" He broke off and blew air out his cheeks. "How the thought of you leaving tore me up inside. I promised myself I'd let you go so I wouldn't destroy your life, like Sheila's or Hannah's—"

He had her undivided attention at *tore me up.* "But Grady—" she began.

Jackson held one finger over her lips, shaking his head. "Let me finish, baby. Please?"

She nodded once. Hope filled her chest like a hot-air balloon.

"I didn't sleep a wink that night. I couldn't stop thinking about losing you, about how empty my life would be without you. My mind came up with a thousand reasons you should stay, even as I cursed myself for being a selfish idiot." He looked to the ceiling and smiled as if the words coming from his mouth surprised even him. "I almost stopped by before I left to get Ryan, but I was afraid I'd wind up begging you to stay. And I was determined to let you go."

He pulled her hand to his lips to press a kiss on her palm. "Before I reached Asheville, I was out of my mind missing you. I hadn't figured out what to do about it, but one thing became glaringly clear." His eyes locked on hers. "I love you, Julia."

She gasped, and her eyes stung. "You do?"

One corner of his mouth crooked upward. "I do." He looked at her expectantly, cheeks going ruddy. "This is when you say I love you, too, Jackson. That is, if you do. God help me if you don't, because I don't think I can be without—"

"I love you, Jackson, so much," she interrupted, then laughed wonderingly. "I think I always have."

He flashed his glamorous smile and swiped at a tear rolling down her cheek. "You know it tears me up when you cry."

She wafted a hand in the air. "Happy tears."

He chuckled briefly, then his face turned somber. "When I figured out Grady lured you to the trailhead, my mind conjured all kinds of scenarios. I've never been so afraid in my life. Julia, I didn't know I could love anyone this much. It scares the hell out of me, and I imagine it's only going to get worse."

She smiled at him, her heart full to bursting. "You make it sound like a life sentence or a terminal illness."

He laughed. "I don't know how to do this or what to say. I've never felt this way."

She cocked her head. "Not even Hannah? I would understand."

He gave her a level look. "I did love her. But it was different. We were kids. I wasn't thinking of spending my life with her, then she got pregnant. Marriage seemed like the next step, and I was happy with her." He grimaced. "All this time, I thought she'd killed herself because of how lonely she was with me. Grady…he helped paint that picture. Now I don't know what to believe."

"There's a lot for you to rethink, Jacks. Grady did a lot of damage."

He nodded. "I need you to know this—what I feel for you is different than anything I've ever known. You're—" He broke off to sift his fingers through her hair. "I can't breathe without you. You make good days great and little, insignificant moments special. I'll never get enough of you and—"

She silenced him with her lips pressed to his. But really. She couldn't *not* kiss him.

A long time later, they lay on his bed, twined in each other's arms.

"Tell me about New York, sweetheart. Do you have your heart set on going? Because we can work it out. I can get a place there—"

"Nope. I declined the firm's offer. This is home. I'm not going anywhere."

"Then what about this house-hunting stuff?" he murmured into her hair.

"It seemed like a smart move."

"Anywhere that's not here, you'll be too far away. Say you'll stay, babydoll. For me?"

She smiled and nuzzled the underside of his stubble-rough jaw. "Hmm. Convince me."

"It comes with perks, courtesy of the landlord."

She lifted her head to arch a brow at him. "Such as?"

He arched a brow right back. "Free and unlimited house calls to take care of any *needs* you might have, day or night." A lazy smile spread over his face.

Julia snuggled into him, hiding a smile of her own. "I don't know. You may have to sweeten the deal."

"Name your demands."

"I have two."

"Go on."

"Carbonara made to order."

"Done. What else?"

She propped herself up on his chest to smile into his eyes. "You'll play my song whenever I need a fix."

"Day or night, baby."

She rolled onto her side, and he pulled her into his body.

"When you put it like that, I'd have to be a fool to say no."

Epilogue

Chase voted for November. They had so much to be thankful for, so why not have a Thanksgiving wedding, he'd said.

Jackson pressed for December, saying all he wanted for Christmas was to sleep with Julia every night and wake up with her every morning. Plus, he insisted, he always woke with new lyrics in his head after a night spent with her in his bed. And that could only happen on the regular once Julia Hudson became Julia Tate.

With love shining in her eyes, she reminded both of them that Jackson had been clear that he wanted to do it up right—the dress, the flowers, a small but inclusive number of guests, and a rockin' reception—and that meant she needed time to plan.

They finally settled on June. The weather would be perfect for an outdoor ceremony. Besides, the following month she'd turn thirty, and she'd be darned if she'd let that mile marker hit before she married the man of her dreams.

So it was, that late morning on the twelfth of June, Jackson and Julia became husband and wife. The sun shone bright in clear blue skies as Julia, dressed in a designer gown of white silk, led by her beaming father, crossed the petal-strewn deck of Jackson's—and now her—home. Everyone said she'd never looked more beautiful. Certainly Jackson's eyes grew damp when he turned to see her walking toward the lilac-covered altar where he awaited her.

Ryan Moore and Chase stood as his groomsmen, while Callie and Sue, co-maids of honor, made up the rest of the wedding party.

When it came time for the vows, Jackson surprised Julia by pulling out a handwritten note. The paper trembled visibly as he read the words. He spoke of loving her forever, of knowing even when they were kids how special she was, and though he didn't deserve her then or now and didn't understand how he got so lucky as to win her heart, he would spend his whole life trying to not let her regret marrying him.

After the guests' laughter and tears abated, Julia surprised Jackson right back. She had also written her vows.

She read through a haze of happy tears. She'd loved him from the moment she laid eyes on him at sixteen. A little time spent together and she'd fallen even more deeply in love. Only as book smart as she'd always been, she hadn't recognized the feeling for what it was. Not even after spending her whole adult life looking for someone who made her feel half the way Jackson had just by walking into the room.

And then Aunt Lisa pulled a fast one, dragging her straight to Jackson's house on that fateful morning when she'd first arrived home, and the rest was history. She'd never stop being grateful to her.

The pastor announced that Jackson could kiss his bride, and the celebration began.

Jackson had hired a local band for the reception, but when the deejay announced it was time for their first dance as husband and wife, Ryan took the mic to sing their song, "Falling."

"You think of everything, Jackson Tate," Julia said.

"Let's hope you always think so, Mrs. Tate."

Six weeks later, the doorbells jangled overhead as Julia stepped inside Frank's Fair Trade Cafe to meet Sue and Callie.

She headed back to the cafe section of Callie's eclectic shop. Frank lounged regally in a strategically advantageous spot that allowed him to oversee the coffee shop while also keeping an eye on the front door. Tongue lolling, he appeared to give Julia a head bob of welcome.

"Hi to you, too, pal," Julia said, scratching the dog's soft ears. "Hi, guys."

Sue sat at the bar, enjoying what looked like a steaming cup of tea, and Callie stood behind the counter, sipping an iced coffee.

"Well, well, well, if it isn't Mrs. Tate, back from her month-long honeymoon," Sue said with a happy grin.

"You're glowing," Callie said. "Sit down and tell us all about Colorado." She paused. "Maybe don't tell us *all* about it."

"Just the juicy sex parts," Sue said.

"Duh," Callie agreed.

"Ha ha," Julia said and slid onto a swivel stool. "Where to begin? Colorado was incredible. We hiked most days and caught some incredible vistas. There were festivals going on in town two of the weekends, one for country-music lovers, another an arts and crafts deal. We rode the gondola up the mountain for dinner a few times, and we rented inner tubes and floated down the river one day. Chase really enjoyed that."

"Ho hum," Sue said, feigning a yawn.

Julia put her finger to her cheek and pretended to consider. "There was also a lot of amazing sex."

"Now we're talking," Callie said. "Can I fix you a latte, Jules?" she asked, already starting the milk frother.

"Um. Maybe a decaf?"

"Decaf? Are you crazy? What's the point of coffee without caffeine? Unless…oh my God." Callie stared at Julia, steamer forgotten.

"Wait." Sue sat up tall on her stool. "Are we talking baby?"

Julia put her palms to her cheeks and nodded, tears filling her eyes. "Yep. Aside from that one time in the shower, we were so careful—up until the wedding night. And then"—she dragged her shoulders to her ears in a shrug—"we decided to go *au naturel*. We figured, why not? We're married now, and we knew we wanted to have more children, especially after Chase requested a younger brother or sister." She grinned. "We thought it might take a while, with me turning thirty. Who knew Jackson had such good little swimmers?"

Sue bounced off her stool to wrap her arms around Julia. "I'm so excited. Callie, we're going to be aunts."

Callie darted around the counter to make it a group hug. "Sorry, Jules, your decaf will have to wait."

The front doorbell chimed.

Frank got up, moved around in a circle, and lay back down.

A moment later, Jackson appeared. He took in the

scene in a blink. "I take it you gave them the news?"

Nodding, Julia sent her husband of a month and two weeks a watery smile.

He shook his head. "What am I going to do with you, Mrs. Tate?"

"Happy tears." She swiped at her eyes. "Um, not that I'm not always glad to see you, but what are you doing here?"

He huffed out a laugh. "I was on my way to see Mr. Toller. I promised I'd come by to say hi when we got back to town, and…I missed my wife."

Callie and Sue both made dramatic gagging sounds, but Julia only gazed at Jackson. "Have I told you how much I love you today?"

He grinned like a kid. "All right, then. I'll see you in a few hours. Text me when you're ready to go home."

The doorbell jangled as he went out. Two seconds later, it jangled again.

"For crying out loud," Sue said, brows raised. "Talk about separation anxiety."

Abruptly Frank got to his feet, a doggy-style smile on his face, and trotted to the door, tail held high.

Callie's face went oddly stiff.

A distinctly male voice greeted Frank. Baritone, with a very attractive Irish lilt unless Julia missed her mark.

Callie's chin came up, and her gaze fixed on something—or someone—in the front of the store. "I'll be right back," she said and marched away, back stiff.

Julia turned questioning eyes on Sue.

"There's been a few—" Sue cleared her throat, and her eyes lit with intrigue. "—developments since you left."

"Oh my gosh. What did I miss? Tell me everything."

"It's about Irish…"

A word about the author...

Kimberly Keyes is the multi-published author of steamy contemporaries and sensual Victorian-era historicals (hello, the women's fashions during that time are a romance writer's dream). Her books and works-in-progress have won awards in contests held by romance writers groups across the country. One contest judge wrote, "Super pacing, characterization, conflict, building tension. Are you sure 100 is the maximum score?"

Reviews really make her day. Please leave one at your favorite vendor.

~*~

Find out more about Kimberly online at:
http://www.kimberlykeyes.net
https://www.facebook.com/kimberly.keyes.romance
https://www.bookbub.com/profile/kimberly-keyes